Praise for *The Nature of Witches*

"*The Nature of Witches* is unlike anything I've read before. With its wholly original take on witches, thought-provoking commentary on climate change, and a swoony romance I would die for, Griffin has crafted a magnificent debut that will have readers on the edge of their seats. To put it simply—I'm obsessed with this book!"

—Adalyn Grace, *New York Times* bestselling author of *Belladonna*

"The forces of nature and magic blend perfectly in this masterfully told story. *The Nature of Witches* is one of the most well-developed magical worlds I've read in a long time. I couldn't love this book more."

—Shea Ernshaw, *New York Times* bestselling author of *The Wicked Deep* and *Winterwood*

"*The Nature of Witches* is a timely, thoughtful tale of the responsibilities we have to our planet and to one another. Griffin's well-developed world building and complex main character make for a read that will resonate deeply."

—C. L. Herman, co-author of *All of Us Villains*

"A bright, fresh read from a glowing new voice, *The Nature of Witches* is both timely and stirring. Griffin's emotional writing that cuts to the heart will make her a new YA favorite."

—Adrienne Young, *New York Times* bestselling author of *Fable*

Praise for *Wild Is the Witch*

"A strikingly tender enemies-to-lovers romance told in the cozy love language of warm fires, s'mores, and small acts of kindness, juxtaposed with wild magic and a treacherous hunt through the ethereal woods of the Pacific Northwest. I devoured every word of this rich and emotive novel."

—Julia Ember, author of *Ruinsong* and The Seafarer's Kiss duology

"Griffin is a masterful storyteller that uses all five senses to draw the reader into a rich emotional landscape. Using the Pacific Northwest as a backdrop, Griffin never forgets to remind you of the magic of nature as Iris and Pike figure out the truth about each other. *Wild Is the Witch* is magical, romantic, atmospheric, and beautifully written. All things we are learning are the hallmarks of Griffin's work."

—Kristin Dwyer, author of *Some Mistakes Were Made*

"A contemporary fantasy brimming with tremendous empathy for the natural world and all its creatures. The moody Pacific Northwest is the perfect setting for this book, a romantic adventure mixed with some of the cleverest magic I've read in a long time. Iris, Pike, and MacGuffin the owl stole my heart. I loved getting lost in the woods with them."

—Rachel Lynn Solomon, *New York Times* bestselling author of *Today Tonight Tomorrow*

Praise for *Bring Me Your Midnight*

"Prepare to be bewitched. Achingly beautiful, devastatingly romantic, and deliciously atmospheric, *Bring Me Your Midnight* casts a powerful spell. Readers who pick up this book will feel the sea spray of the ocean, the heart-pounding romance, and the impossible choices that Tana must make."

—Stephanie Garber, #1 *New York Times* bestselling author of *Once Upon a Broken Heart*

"Darkly enchanting and lush, *Bring Me Your Midnight*—with its forbidden romance and gorgeous atmosphere—is sure to cast a spell on you."

—Kerri Maniscalco, #1 *New York Times* bestselling author of *Kingdom of the Wicked*

"Griffin's best work yet! *Bring Me Your Midnight* is a beautiful exploration of first love, the familial ties that bind us, and trusting your own heart's desires. Steeped in Griffin's signature lush atmosphere and a deeply romantic tone, this dazzling fantasy is bound to be a new favorite."

—Adalyn Grace, *New York Times* bestselling author of *Belladonna*

"With its deeply romantic prose, swoony hero, and original magic, *Bring Me Your Midnight* will sweep readers off their feet from the first page. I could have stayed lost in this beautiful and moonlit world forever."

—Isabel Ibañez, author of *What the River Knows*

"Mesmerizingly atmospheric, achingly tender, and fiercely passionate, *Bring Me Your Midnight* holds the depths of an ocean within its spellbinding pages. Griffin weaves enchantment with lyrical prose that is at once intimate and bold, vulnerable and sweet, in a magical, romantic masterpiece."

—Amélie Wen Zhao, author of the Blood Heir trilogy

"Both tender and fierce, *Bring Me Your Midnight* is a deftly woven tale of friendship, secrets, incandescent spells, and a forbidden romance that smolders on the page. I was utterly captivated by the magic of Rachel Griffin's prose. This is a story I will return to again and again."

—Rebecca Ross, international bestselling author of *Divine Rivals*

ALSO BY RACHEL GRIFFIN

The Nature of Witches
Wild Is the Witch
Bring Me Your Midnight

THE SUN AND THE STARMAKER

THE SUN AND THE STARMAKER

RACHEL GRIFFIN

Copyright © 2026 by Rachel Griffin
Cover and internal design © 2026 by Sourcebooks
Cover design by Hannah DiPietro/Sourcebooks
Cover art by Viv Tanner
Cover images © Chorna_black/Shutterstock, Peter van Haastrecht / 500px/
Getty Images, Jan von nebenan/Shutterstock, graphic Stockses/Shutterstock
Endsheet images © Jan von nebenan/Shutterstock, Peter van Haastrecht/500px/
Getty Images, Line work and Photography/Shutterstock
Internal design by Tara Jaggers/Sourcebooks
Internal images © Anya Filipeva/Getty Images, Kirill Veretennikov/Getty Images

Sourcebooks and the colophon are registered trademarks of Sourcebooks.

All rights reserved. No part of this book may be reproduced in any form or by any electronic or mechanical means, including information storage and retrieval systems—except in the case of brief quotations embodied in critical articles or reviews—without permission in writing from its publisher, Sourcebooks.

No part of this book may be used or reproduced in any manner for the purpose of training artificial intelligence technologies or systems.

The characters and events portrayed in this book are fictitious or are used fictitiously. Any similarity to real persons, living or dead, is purely coincidental and not intended by the author.

Published by Sourcebooks Fire, an imprint of Sourcebooks
1935 Brookdale RD, Naperville, IL 60563-2773
(630) 961-3900
sourcebooks.com

Cataloging-in-Publication Data is on file with the Library of Congress.

ISBN 978 1 464 27250 9

The authorized representative in the EEA is Dorling Kindersley
Verlag GmbH. Arnulfstr. 124, 80636 Munich, Germany

Manufactured in the UK by Clays and distributed by
Dorling Kindersley Limited, London
001-355722-Feb/26
10 9 8 7 6 5 4 3 2 1

For Mom,
who taught me at a very young age
that the best evenings are the ones
spent with a book. ♥

Contents

——··✧··——

PROLOGUE: Star-Crossed	1
ONE: Grave Circumstances	9
TWO: The Hand of a Stranger	21
THREE: An Improbability	29
FOUR: Liar	42
FIVE: Falling Stars	52
SIX: Poor Assumptions	58
SEVEN: Rest	71
EIGHT: A Classic Instance of Fleeing	83
NINE: A Very Peculiar Door	95
TEN: An Amusing Plight	105
ELEVEN: In Contract Only	123
TWELVE: Snow Angel	137
THIRTEEN: The Honor of Your Presence	150

FOURTEEN: A Decent Husband	163
FIFTEEN: Clarity	174
SIXTEEN: Very Old Wine	182
SEVENTEEN: Melting Snow	196
EIGHTEEN: Ruins	209
NINETEEN: Unfortunate Longings	219
TWENTY: Vivid Imagination	233
TWENTY-ONE: Seven White Wolves	240
TWENTY-TWO: Denial	252
TWENTY-THREE: The Heart Seldom Yields	261
TWENTY-FOUR: Reflections	269
TWENTY-FIVE: Dying Star	280
TWENTY-SIX: Tragic Symmetry	290
TWENTY-SEVEN: Beginning and End	303
TWENTY-EIGHT: Waking Up Slow	311
TWENTY-NINE: A Midnight Wedding	321
THIRTY: Illusion	330
THIRTY-ONE: The Endless After	341
THIRTY-TWO: Darkness	351
THIRTY-THREE: A Discovery	355
THIRTY-FOUR: Eternally Yours	366
THIRTY-FIVE: Even a God Can Forget	376
THIRTY-SIX: Standing at the Top of the World	385
THIRTY-SEVEN: Asleep in a Haze of Lavender	396
THIRTY-EIGHT: The Most Brilliant Thing	398
THIRTY-NINE: She Lives	410
EPILOGUE: Double Star	415

AUTHOR'S NOTE: The Author and the Brain Injury   419
ACKNOWLEDGMENTS   423
ABOUT THE AUTHOR   427

Prologue

Star-Crossed

Deep in the mountains of the Lost Range, in a small village on the tallest peak, a young girl was listening to a bedtime story. It was a story she had heard many times before, and yet when her parents tucked her in and she pulled her blankets close, it was always the tale of the Sun and the Starmaker that Aurora Finch wished to hear.

"There once was a village so far north that most considered it the top of the world," her mother began, brushing a piece of long brown hair from Aurora's face. "Or rather, they surely would have, had they known of its existence. But as very few did, the village was rarely considered at all.

"The Sun had always held a fondness for it, though. Nestled in the snow-covered mountains, the small village was the northernmost point her light could still reach year-round, and she thought it an intriguing curiosity that it was so far removed from the rest of the world.

"One day, the ground beneath the village began to shake, and the Sun watched in dismay as the plates of the Earth moved past each other. The gently sloped mountain that held the village cracked and broke, and steep rocky peaks rose up, taller than anyone had ever seen. So violent was the quake that the Sun could hear the terrible groaning of the Earth from her perch in the sky, a powerful, frightening sound that lasted longer than it took to read a child a bedtime story." Aurora's mother paused, winking at her. "As the mountain rose higher, so did the village, moving up and up and up until finally, the shaking stopped.

"The Sun tried to find the village, but a great cloud of dust hung in the air, blocking her view. Impatience ate away at her as she waited for the sky to clear, anxious to learn the fate of the small village at the top of the world.

"Days passed, then weeks, and finally, the dust settled.

"The Sun searched frantically for the village, surveying vast swaths of land, but she could not find it, not even a trace. Then, impossibly, she heard it.

"At first, she did not believe the sounds were real, sure she was making them up to ease her sorrow. But what had started as indistinct noise soon clarified into undeniable cries. The Sun tried to follow them, but still she could not find the source, and she realized with utter heartbreak that the movement of the Earth had shifted the village beyond her reach, surrounding it in jagged peaks that she could not rise above.

THE SUN AND THE STARMAKER

"The village had survived, but it was now shadowed in eternal darkness."

Aurora's favorite part of the story was approaching, and she turned to her sister, smiling in anticipation, but Elsie was already fast asleep. Aurora couldn't believe her sister could sleep through so thrilling a tale, and she turned back to her mother, eager for her to continue.

"As hard as she tried, the Sun could not rise high enough to see the village, could not find her way over the severe peaks, and so she did the only thing she could do: she made herself human so she could go see the village for herself. And perhaps so she could say goodbye, for she knew it could not survive without her light.

"Her time was limited, of course, as the rest of the world needed her, but she knew she would be unable to let go of the village until she saw it one final time.

"When the Sun arrived on the mountain, she was wholly unprepared for what she found. The absence of light had created a colder cold than the village had ever known, and a deadly frost had begun to form. Plants and animals, dwellings and humans were covered in a frozen white film as if they were statues made of cloudy ice. The Sun was horrified, and she went from person to animal to plant, trying to save whatever she could. Whoever she could.

"It was then that she met a man who was doing the same, and he offered her his assistance.

"He taught her the burial rituals of the mountain and cried for each and every lost life, and she cried with him, a deeply human experience that moved her to her very core. They saved lives as well. The Sun was able to heal using the warmth within her, and slowly, the cries ebbed as more and more of the village recovered.

"The days were long and the work endless, but the Sun enjoyed the man's company, and the man enjoyed hers. He answered the Sun's questions about the villagers, such as how they spent their time at night when the Sun was on the other side of the world, and he taught her what it meant to share a meal and share a kiss and share a bed. And as they shared those things, they fell deeply in love.

"Finite time was particularly cruel when one found oneself in love."

Aurora's mother paused, looking behind her at Papa, absolute adoration in her eyes. They shared a moment that eight-year-old Aurora could not understand, and she tugged at her mother's sleeve, impatient for the story to continue.

"Okay, okay," her mother said, laughing. "The Sun had come to the village to say goodbye, but what she had found—resilience and beauty and love—were things she could not let perish. And so she spent her remaining time with her lover crafting a plan that would save not only him but his entire village.

"It was hasty and preposterous to be sure, a plan she wasn't even certain was possible, but there is nothing quite like a woman desperate with love.

"When her time was up, the Sun took the man to the glacier at the edge of the village and created a lamppost using the magic within her. It rose up before them, a shimmering gold that glowed even in darkness, tall and sturdy and lasting. The lantern at the top of the post contained a glimmering hook that could hold only one thing: sunlight.

"'Are you ready?' the Sun asked, heartbreak straining her beautiful voice.

"'I am not ready to live without you,' the man replied, his eyes rimmed in red. 'But I will do what I must to save my home, and every moment of every day, I will love you.'

"The Sun slowly reached out her hands. The man took them, and she held on tight.

"'I thought I saw the world before, but I was wrong.' She paused. 'I see it now.' She was the Sun, illuminating everything, but for the first time in her very long existence, someone had cast their light on her, and she shone brighter for it.

"'I owe my life—and my home—to you. Thank you.' The man's voice cracked, and the Sun nodded because she did not trust herself to speak.

"The Sun kissed him, gentle and slow, and when a tear fell down her cheek and touched her lips, she pulled away and closed her eyes. She whispered incantations that stirred the power within her, heat and light tangling around each other, held together with magic. The Sun knew she was taking a risk, that they both were—she could very well incinerate him if she made the slightest error—but they had agreed that this was his best chance at living.

"The Sun met the gaze of her lover once more. She paused for a single beat of her heart, committing every line of his face to memory: the angle of his jaw and the curve of his lips and the crinkle of his eyes. She thought he was the most beautiful thing she'd ever seen. Then, all at once, she sent her magic into him, flooding his bloodstream with her light, forming an unbreakable connection between them. He did not cry out when the heat found him. Instead he kept his eyes on the Sun, whispering his own sort of spell, one of devotion and sacrifice and a love that could span the whole universe.

"The Sun felt the enchantment take hold, and the man who had once been mortal now held her heart within him. His life stretched out before him, year after year after year, his body no longer aging. The mountain was his responsibility now. He would call to the Sun every morning, pull her light into the village, and though they could not be together, they would feel each other's presence.

"The Sun held on to him as tightly as she could, even once the spell was done. She held on because the thought of letting go was unbearable. She knew that one day, many years hence, she would lose him entirely; true immortality could not exist in a human, not even one with her magic, and after he had lived a very long life, his body would be given to the mountain to fight the Frost. Then she would choose someone new to call her light each day. She had promised the man that his home would survive even in his absence, and it was a promise she would keep.

"They held each other for several breaths, and before the Sun ascended back into the sky, she kissed the man one last time as tears of gold fell down her face. Leaving him was the hardest thing she had ever done, but she would feel him in the mornings, pulling her light toward him, and that would be enough. It would have to be.

"The Sun wept as she was pulled away from him, clinging to his hands as she returned to the heavens, his fingers finally free of hers. She reached toward him, frantic for one more touch, but there was too great a distance between them, and she was met only with the frigid air. As she was dragged through the vast emptiness, she kept her eyes on his until he was no longer a man but rather a distant point of light in an otherwise dark void.

"The villagers came to call him Starmaker, but he thought of himself simply as hers.

"And so it was.

"He was hers, and though an astronomical amount of space had come between them, she was his." Aurora's mother smiled. "The end."

There were tears in Aurora's eyes, and she blinked them away, reminding herself to breathe. She loved the lore of the mountain, and yet it knocked the breath straight out of her every time she heard it. Her parents took turns kissing her on the forehead, and then they quietly slipped down from the loft, not giving a second thought to the unsettled look on their daughter's face.

Bedtime stories were harmless, after all. Nothing like, say, a sharp rock or an open flame, both clear threats to a young child. But cuts could close and burns could heal, and if they were minor enough, they could be entirely forgotten in a few days' time.

Not a story, though.

A story could weave its way into one's mind, growing roots

so vast and wide it could infiltrate one's entire being, making it impossible to weed out. A simple story could turn into a great fear or a lifelong dream or a deep wound.

It could turn into anything, really.

Perhaps, then, a bedtime story was not so harmless after all, and one ought to be mindful of the stories one told.

The end, Aurora's mother had said, but it wasn't the end for Aurora. In fact, it was much more like a beginning.

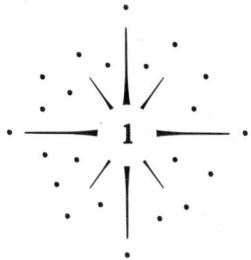

Grave Circumstances

Three days before her wedding, Aurora Finch rose early to visit the grave of a man she'd never met. She slipped out of the small stone cottage while the rest of her family slept, a dying fire in the hearth providing the only light. She found her thick wool cloak on its hook, put on her gloves, and silently pushed through the door.

The biting cold hit her instantly, stinging her skin, and she pulled her hood up over her head. The Starmaker had yet to pull in the light for the day, and Aurora held a small lantern that illuminated the space in front of her. Her boots crunched through the snow, and she tugged her cloak tighter around her as she made her way to the outskirts of the village.

Aurora quickened her steps, hoping to be far away by the time her family woke, not wanting them to know where she was going.

Especially her sister. Elsie had been touched by the Frost a fortnight ago, and though she wasn't getting worse, she wasn't healing as she should. Aurora had assured Elsie that there was nothing to worry about and that she would soon recover, but there was an awful feeling in the pit of her stomach warning her that Elsie's condition was dire.

Aurora had known the Frost was a threat since she was old enough to read. Perhaps even longer. Their home was closest to the peaks, tucked right against the face of the mountain, and not even the Starmaker could angle the light enough to reach them. There was sufficient magic in the land for them to survive, but the absence of sunlight meant that the Frost was a constant threat, and it had come for Elsie first.

Every night since, Aurora had dreamt of the way her sister had screamed. Every night since, Aurora had woken in a cold sweat she could feel deep in her bones. She wanted to postpone her wedding until Elsie was well, but Elsie wouldn't hear of it. And though Mama would never say it, Aurora knew she was depending upon the glare line that would form between their home and Farren's as soon as the wedding took place. They all were.

The lines were a gift from the Sun, a magical connection between the two homes a couple came from as well as their new home together. They magnified the magic in the land, and every couple received one as a wedding present. And because of the location of their home, Aurora's family was truly dependent upon the glare.

Living in total darkness did have its advantages, though. They had the most land of any family on the mountain, and over time, they had learned to tend it well. Aurora had been fascinated by mirrors since she was a girl, and she'd realized at an early age that if she set up enough mirrors to reflect sunlight onto their land, they could put their fields to use. They could grow certain crops and even sell the surplus at the market.

Aurora had collected mirrors ever since, large and small, rusted and cracked; it didn't matter what they looked like so long as they could reflect what they saw. The Finches' closest neighbors were in the path of the light, and they let Aurora's family lease a sliver of their land for their mirrors. Over time, Aurora had put more than one hundred to use, all reflecting precious light onto her otherwise shadowed land.

Her family would never be able to afford a plot even half the size of their current one if it was touched by sunlight, and even if they could, Mama would never agree to leave their home. It was the house she had shared with Papa before he died, and she refused to live anywhere else. Aurora's mirrors had taken the day-to-day uncertainty out of living in darkness and tending to soil that was unreliable at best, but still, it was not the same as working light-filled land.

Growing up in the shadow of the peaks had never bothered Aurora, not until the Frost had found Elsie. Aurora had bought all kinds of herbs and tinctures at the market, but nothing had made much of a difference. The doctor had said that only time would reveal the extent of the damage, but Aurora was entirely unwilling to leave the fate of her sister to time.

And so she walked through the darkness to the grave.

Finally, the dim lights of the village came into view. Candles with orange flames outlined the rooflines of shops and flickered in the streetlamps, all of them perpetually lit due to the magic in the land. The fireflies were out in droves, taking advantage of the hours before the Starmaker lit the mountain, and there was a soft haze in the air that morning that made Reverie look as if it was glowing. Aurora smiled to herself. She loved this mountain and this village wholeheartedly.

Reverie stood in total isolation, the village cradled in a valley tucked into the highest peak. There was no way on or off the mountain, but Aurora had heard stories of the outside world, of villages and towns that did not need a Starmaker, towns where the Sun was not out of reach. But even if there were a way out of Reverie, Aurora would never take it.

There was no other place in the world as magical as Reverie, no other place that survived solely because the Sun had decided it should. Reverie had lost many people, animals, and dwellings to the Frost, which had almost decimated the village entirely, leaving nothing but cracked white ruins. But then the Sun had fallen in love, changing the fate of the mountain town. Now, with three Starmakers buried and another pulling the light each day, the Frost was only a threat on the darkest parts of the mountain.

The Sun had given up her greatest love so that his home would not perish, and Aurora thought it a painfully romantic story, one that twisted her insides with grief whenever she thought of it.

Aurora followed the perimeter of the village until she reached the grave site. It was enormous, a white stone monument of a man reaching up toward the heavens, golden flecks inlaid in the stone that seemed to shimmer even in the darkness. It was remarkable, as if the statue itself was filled with magic, and Aurora swallowed hard.

The very first Starmaker.

The statue was much taller than Aurora, and she had to crane her neck to see the top of it. It somehow looked just as romantic in the darkness as it did in the light, surrounded by fresh flowers and dozens of candles, letters, and even a few gold silks draped at its base. Aurora had been here many times before—it was common for the villagers to give thanks to the Starmakers, who protected their home—but she usually came with her siblings at their mother's insistence, fidgeting while Mama laid flowers or herbs at the grave. Today was the first time Aurora had ever visited alone.

The Starmakers were not gods, and yet many people prayed to them as if they were. Aurora had never been one of those, but Elsie's condition had changed that.

She was glad she was the only one here. Aurora loved the lore of the Starmakers, but she didn't know how to pray to one. It probably didn't matter, though; Aurora didn't have much hope that this would heal her sister, but she had tried everything else, and living without Elsie was not something she could accept.

Aurora cleared her throat. "Please heal my sister," she said, ignoring her self-consciousness. "Elsie Finch. She was touched by the Frost a fortnight ago, and she is not improving." Aurora reached into her cloak and pulled out a bundle of daisies, Elsie's favorite flower. She laid them at the base of the statue, swallowing hard. "Please," she whispered. "I'll give anything."

After several moments, Aurora looked down and ran her fingers over the crystal plaque in front of the statue.

>Here lies the first Starmaker,
>who loved the Sun and was loved in return.
>Thank you for the light.

The Starmakers were never known by their given names. Mama had told Aurora it was because the original Starmaker didn't want his lineage to be seen as more special than anyone else's, but Papa had always said that when you loved someone the way the Starmaker loved the Sun, you wanted that love to be your legacy. He always smiled when he said it, because he had loved Mama that way.

Aurora wasn't sure how long she had stood in front of the grave site, begging for healing for her sister, before she heard the market come to life behind her. The village had been built just south of the statue, as the burial sites of the Starmakers were some of the most magical places in all of Reverie. The only area that held more magic was the castle, but it was far up the face of the mountain, away from the rest of the town.

"Aurora?" a voice said behind her, and she whipped around to see Aspen.

"Brother," she said, pressing her palm to her chest, trying to steady her heart. "You startled me."

"That was not my intent." He placed his own bouquet of daisies at the base of the grave, and Aurora had to fight against the sting in her eyes. "I'm surprised to see you here."

"Yes, well," Aurora said, her voice quiet. "I came for Elsie."

"As did I."

Aurora nodded. Aspen was the most religious in their family and had always held a deep respect for the burial sites. He took a step back and looked up at the statue, his face full of reverence. Without speaking, he reached out and took Aurora's hand, and they stood that way for several breaths before finally turning away from the grave.

"Please don't tell Elsie I was here," Aurora said. "I don't want her to know how worried I am."

"It will be our secret," Aspen assured her. He looked at her with understanding, his blue eyes soft and kind, and Aurora gave him a small smile.

"Thank you."

"I was thinking I would stop by the market and bring back cider and biscuits for everyone. Join me; that way you won't need to come up with an excuse for where you were." He winked at her and started toward the village.

"I would like that." Aurora took one more look at the statue before catching up with her brother. It was rare that they visited the market for anything other than necessities, and bringing back Elsie's favorite treat would be a wonderful surprise. At sixteen, she was the youngest in the family, and though she was not even two years Aurora's junior, they all enjoyed doting on her.

Elsie had borne the brunt of their father's death, young enough to still be following their mother's every movement, old enough to know she was being neglected. Their mother had been wrecked by grief, and it had taken many years for her to claw her way out. Aurora had stepped in as best she could, raising Elsie and trying to shower her with as much love and warmth as the rest of them had received. Aspen and their eldest brother, Evander, had taken over their father's duties, and the four of them had kept things going despite their mother's grief. They'd had to.

Aurora didn't harbor resentment or anger toward her mother, but Evander did, and now that he was married, he only visited when Mama was out. She never said anything about it, but Aurora knew their mother had noticed, knew that it broke her heart. Aurora would no sooner judge Evander for his anger than she would her mother for her grief, and she had decided long ago that she would never subject herself to the same kind of vulnerability that Mama had.

It was early, and the normal bustle of the market had yet to begin. Small stone buildings lined the perimeter of the village, covered in ivy and moss, housing shops that sold books and ice cream, medicines and wool. The market sat in the center, dozens of stalls with offerings ranging from tapestries to meats, and while most were not yet open, several merchants were setting up their tables for the day. Towering evergreens surrounded the village, and each morning they bent over the storefronts and swept the ground clean, clearing the snow from the cobblestones. Reverie was full of oddities, and no one really knew where magic would turn up.

Aurora and Aspen found the Sparrows' line. On most days, theirs was the first stall to open. Their pastries and hot drinks were the best in the village, and there were already several people waiting. Large lanterns surrounded the vendors, radiating heat, and though the market was outdoors, it was never too cold.

"Aurora, Aspen!" Mrs. Sparrow said when they reached the table. "How is your sister?"

"Still recovering," Aspen said with a warmth Aurora would not have been able to muster. "We thought bringing back some cider and biscuits might help her along. Four, please."

"Indeed it will!" Mrs. Sparrow said, turning to gather their order. She smiled as she handed over a large carrier and a small basket. "I threw in some extras," she whispered.

Aurora and Aspen paid, thanked her, and began their walk back home. Just as they were leaving the village, the first rays of the sun appeared between the peaks, and Aurora watched as Reverie was flooded with light. She closed her eyes and felt the warmth on her skin, and even though she was preoccupied with thoughts of her sister, she felt hopeful, too. Perhaps Elsie would be fine and Aurora's worry was unfounded.

"How are you feeling about the wedding?" Aspen asked as they walked back.

"Truthfully, I would like to postpone it," Aurora said, trying not to sound as indifferent as she felt. "What good is a wedding when the people I most care for can't celebrate?"

"We will all be celebrating," Aspen said. He stopped walking and turned to look at his sister. "You must continue to live,

Aurora; no one—not Elsie or me or anyone else—wants you to put your life on hold just as it is getting started." Aspen squeezed her hand and held her gaze. "Let Elsie see all of what life may hold for her. Make her desperate to experience it for herself." Aspen's voice shook as he spoke, his eyes turning red, and Aurora realized then that he was as worried for Elsie as she was.

Aspen cleared his throat, and they began walking once more, but a mixture of fear and disquiet churned in her stomach. Aurora wasn't sure that her life would inspire Elsie in the way Aspen hoped. It was wholly unremarkable. Ordinary. The kind of life she had always wanted, but seeing it through the filter of Aspen's words made an inexplicable sadness spread through her.

Aurora shoved the thought from her mind and looped her arm through Aspen's, trying to cheer herself. The walk back went quickly in the light, and by the time they reached their home tucked in the darkness, everyone was awake. The fire was crackling in the hearth, and their mother was boiling water for tea.

"There you are," she said, looking up from the stove. "Where have you been?"

"We went to the market for a surprise," Aspen said, setting down the cider and biscuits.

Elsie was sitting on the floor by the fire, covered in blankets. She closed her eyes and inhaled deeply. "I can smell that from here," she said, smiling. "I hope you did not do this just for me."

"On the contrary," Aspen said, giving Elsie a mischievous look. "I did this entirely for myself and just happen to be in a sharing mood."

THE SUN AND THE STARMAKER

Aurora watched the two of them, how easy they were with each other, how normal. Even with Elsie's illness and Aurora's upcoming wedding, there was a calmness in the cottage that warmed Aurora to her core. It made her feel guilty for visiting the Starmaker's grave, guilty for not being able to summon the optimism that Elsie had for herself.

Elsie and Aspen sat down at the wooden table, faded and stained from many years of use, and Aurora set out plates and mugs before joining them.

"Is something troubling you, sister?" Elsie asked, pouring herself some cider.

Aurora looked to her brother before focusing on Elsie. She forced the tension from her face and smiled. "Only that Aspen is eating the biscuits so quickly that I fear there won't be any left for the rest of us."

"Then I better start eating," Mama said with a laugh, hurrying over to the table.

Aurora could feel Elsie's eyes on her, but she looked down at her plate and hoped her expression didn't give away the unbearable worry she was carrying.

The Frost had been easy to ignore before now because it was an ever-present threat. They had all learned to live with it, and as the years had passed and Aurora's collection of mirrors had grown, there had been very few casualties among their crops, and the threat had somehow lessened in Aurora's mind. Then Elsie had been infected, and Aurora's world had shattered in a matter of moments.

The Frost had found Elsie's ankle, turning the skin on her leg an awful shade of white. Cracks had formed along her calf as if she were turning to stone. Sometimes she was not herself, irritable and confused and angry in a way she had never been before. While all of that had subsided and Elsie's demeanor was back to normal, her skin remained a dull alabaster, and she still slept for the better part of each day.

Aurora hated herself for thinking it, but she was terrified of what another loss might do to her mother, terrified she would disappear into her grief and never return.

She blinked, forcing herself out of her thoughts.

The four of them sat around the table, talking and laughing as they always had, but the dread in Aurora's gut continued to build. She repeated her prayer from earlier in her mind over and over until it became a kind of meditation.

Please. I'll give anything.

And though she scorned herself for it, she knew she would visit the grave site again tomorrow, and every day after until Elsie was better.

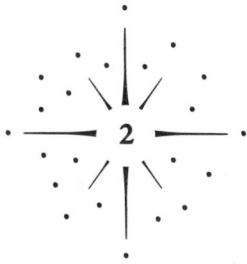

The Hand of a Stranger

It was a fine day for a wedding.

The Starmaker had yet to pull sunlight across the village, but Aurora's cottage was already bustling with activity. Mama was in the kitchen baking, and Aspen was outside, preparing the sled for the journey into Reverie. Aurora tried to busy herself, but the space was small, and she felt more in the way than anything else.

"Aurora, come here, darling," Mama said, pulling her into the kitchen. She picked up an iron pot from the corner and removed the cloth that covered the top. The sharp scent of fresh bread filled the room, and Aurora breathed in deeply.

"It's perfect, Mama," she said.

Her mother took a knife and sliced off the end, then put it on a plate for Aurora with dollops of butter and strawberry jam. Her mother's jam was the best in the village, and she always saved the year's first jar for Aurora. "Go enjoy this with your sister," she said with a glint in her eye. "But don't tell your brother, or there won't be any left for the wedding."

Aurora climbed the wooden ladder to the loft, careful not to drop the plate. Elsie was still in bed, and even with the heat from the stove rising up to where she slept, her quilt was pulled all the way up to her chin. Aurora had visited the first Starmaker's grave three times now, but it had not helped, just as she knew it wouldn't. She tried not to be resentful, but she was, her body tense and fraught with bitterness.

Perhaps she had been hoping more than she'd allowed herself to believe.

"I brought you something," Aurora said, causing her sister to stir. Elsie rubbed her eyes and propped herself up on her elbows, her face breaking into a smile when she saw the bread.

"It smells divine. If only all these treats you bring me were effective antidotes to the Frost." She said it casually, as if it were a silly joke, but it was the first time Aurora had ever heard her acknowledge that she wasn't healing. Aurora watched her carefully, but Elsie just smiled and sat all the way up, changing the subject before Aurora could speak. "I can't believe you're getting married today."

Aurora crawled onto the bed and tore off a piece of bread, dragging it through the butter and jam before handing it to Elsie. "It certainly snuck up on me."

"You are excited, though, aren't you?"

"I am," Aurora said, leaning into her sister. "I had hoped that Farren's father might let me write something before the ceremony, but he wanted to wait. I'm very eager to start." Farren's family owned and distributed *Eternal Reverie*, the village's only newspaper, and Aurora loved the idea of contributing to the stories of the mountain, but she'd been forced to summon a patience she did not possess.

"I meant, are you excited to marry Farren?" Elsie said, eyeing her sister.

Aurora looked down, unsure why her thoughts had immediately gone to the paper. "Well, yes, of course. But I doubt I'll much care for living apart from you."

"An hour walk is far too long, but I wager I could get it down to half that if I use the sled."

"That would be much more tolerable," Aurora agreed. "How are you feeling today, sister?"

"I had a good night. Perhaps I'm getting better."

Aurora suspected Elsie was saying that for her benefit so she wouldn't worry on the day of her wedding. Aurora cared far more about her sister than she did about the wedding, though, and she would happily trade the big celebration for an intimate ceremony. She had never enjoyed being the center of attention, but the families had insisted on something grand.

When not a single crumb of bread remained, Aurora tucked her sister back into bed. "Get some rest; you will need your energy later."

Elsie nodded, her eyelids getting heavy before Aurora had even stood.

"She's not getting better," Aurora said to her mother when she was back downstairs, keeping her voice low even though she suspected Elsie was already asleep.

"We're doing everything we can," her mother replied, taking Aurora's hand in hers and squeezing tight.

"It isn't enough."

Her mother paused and looked at her, a slow dread building in Aurora's stomach. "Today is for celebration and merriment, not for worry. Save your troubles for another day, my darling."

Aurora wanted to argue, but then her mother's eyes brightened. "I made you something," she said, walking over to the basket by the hearth and pulling out a bundle of hand-stitched ribbons. Aurora had seen Mama working on them late at night, and she couldn't help but smile.

"That's enough ribbon to wrap around the entire mountain."

"And then some," Mama said, running her fingers through the fabric. "When it's time to get ready, you can pick your favorites for your hair and bouquet, and I'll use the rest for decorations."

"They're beautiful." Aurora pulled her mother into a hug, holding her tight. "Thank you." It meant so much to her that her mother was here for this, truly here. There had been times after Papa died that were so bad, Aurora hadn't been able to imagine that her mother would make it to the other side. Grief had left its mark on her, of course—it was still present in the lines of her face and the curve of her spine, in the far-off look she often had at night—but she had fought her way out of the depths of it, and Aurora never took that for granted.

"I'm sure you could use some time to yourself before the festivities begin, and I need more winterberry for the tables. Would you grab me a basketful, and then you can get washed up and ready for your big day?"

"Of course, Mama," she said. Aurora was always happy to walk through the woods, and her mother was right: she would appreciate some quiet before the wedding. She grabbed her bow and arrow in case any game was out and pushed her way into the cold.

First she stopped at her mirrors, brushing the snowfall from them and making sure they were reflecting as much light as possible. Aurora loved looking at them and was proud of the solution she'd found for their land; she would miss tending to them every day, but Elsie had assured her several times that she would take good care of them. Aurora had always hoped her collection would one day allow them to grow their own tomatoes—they had been Papa's favorite—and she was sad to move before that happened. Perhaps one day, though, they would grow under Elsie's care.

When Aurora was done cleaning her mirrors, she made her way to the forest. It was quiet and still. The snow had a way of absorbing the sound, and one could mistake Reverie for an unwelcoming place, though that was far from the truth. Many people preferred to be indoors, where sounds carried and echoed, bouncing off walls and filling spaces. Aurora would miss all the sounds that filled her family's cottage, though she was sure there would be much to appreciate in her new home with Farren.

Aurora held her basket close and stepped carefully through

the snow so as not to disturb any wildlife. It was rare for her family to have fresh meat—animals seldom wandered as far from the light as her cottage, and hunting took more time than she could usually spare, but since she was out anyway, she wanted to be ready.

Aurora picked winterberry sprigs as she went, filling her woven basket. The berries were coated in a sparkling layer of ice, the bright red color standing out against the white landscape. She looked at her basket, and a wave of contentment coursed through her as she pictured the boughs surrounding her mother's baked goods. She knew how happy Mama was about the wedding, and that was enough for her.

At first, Aurora had thought of Farren only as a good, solid match that made sense for her family. Being able to write for *Eternal Reverie* was a dream she could hardly believe was coming true, and Farren's home was so close to the village square that it was bathed in light, which meant the glare line would be strong, brimming with magic.

As Aurora got to know Farren, though, she realized it was more than just a solid match. The happiness she felt when she was with him was proof that she could have both a match that was good for her family, and a match that held genuine affection. The first time Farren had kissed her by the light of the moon, a stolen, sweet brush of the lips that had lasted for just one beat of her heart, Aurora was convinced it was love.

Not an epic love bound to end in tragedy like that of the Sun or her parents, but a quiet, lasting love that felt safe.

THE SUN AND THE STARMAKER

Aurora kept walking, swinging her basket that was near to overflowing with winterberry boughs. She was about to return home and get ready for the celebration, take a bath and let Mama tie ribbons in her hair, when she caught a movement in the corner of her eye. She quietly removed her gloves and pulled an arrow from her leather satchel, placing it on her bowstring. Her heart began to race as she pictured returning home with a rabbit or quail, something special to celebrate the day, and she steadied her hands as she carefully took a step forward, surveying the land.

Aurora squinted against the light reflecting off the forest floor, the glittering earth that seemed to dance in the rays of the sun. A pile of snow dropped from a nearby tree, crashing to the ground, startling both Aurora and the animal she hunted. She still hadn't found the source of the movement, but as soon as the snow fell, an enormous white stag dashed out of the woods behind her and started running.

Aurora was so surprised that she didn't have time to shoot. The stag turned its head to look at her as it ran past, its eyes locking with hers, and suddenly it came to a halt. It was breathing heavily, clouds of vapor rising into the air from its nostrils, and Aurora took a step back. The animal was beautiful, the most beautiful she'd ever seen, and she hesitated as it watched her.

It didn't seem right to kill such a gorgeous creature, not when her family could survive without it. But then she thought of the way the meat would feed her family for months on end, even if they used some for the wedding. What a gift it would be before starting the next chapter of her life. It would ease the burden on her mother and be a rare delight for her siblings.

Aurora slowly raised her bow, taking a deep breath.

A shiver crawled down her spine. The stag still wasn't running, and Aurora counted one, two, three seconds, part of her begging the animal to move. But it waited too long, and as it kept its eyes on hers, Aurora tugged back on her bowstring.

She released her arrow along with her breath. It was a perfect shot, and Aurora closed her eyes, not wanting to watch the animal fall. But when she didn't hear anything, not a wail or a cry from the stag, she slowly opened her eyes.

The stag stood unharmed, Aurora's arrow stuck in the snow beside it. She blinked, her heart slamming against her chest, surveying the woods for anything that could have thrown her arrow off course. But there was nothing, no wind or trees it could have brushed against; it was a clear path. She pulled another arrow from her satchel with shaking fingers.

Perhaps her nerves were causing her to lose focus, and she centered herself once more.

Keeping her eyes on the stag, Aurora pulled the bowstring back and exhaled, but when she tried to release the arrow, nothing happened. Everything stayed exactly where it was, her bow and her arrow and the stag.

She looked at her weapon, checking her form.

And there, holding the back of her arrow, was a hand that did not belong to her.

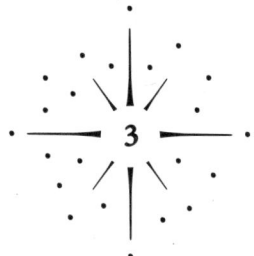

An Improbability

Aurora couldn't move, frozen in place by the cold and the hand and her fear. A stern, harsh voice said, "Don't."

The stag moved its gaze from Aurora to whoever stood behind her, then took off at a run. Aurora wanted to do the same, but she forced herself to confront the stranger who had stopped her arrow.

Slowly she turned, gasping when she saw the figure who stood before her.

The man was tall, with striking gold eyes the color of her mother's wedding band. His hair was straight and gleaming and fell down his back in a cascade of liquid pearl that seemed to sparkle in the light like the snow. He was pale, and while his jaw was set in a severe line, Aurora couldn't help but notice that his lips were the same soft red as her winterberries. He wore a stark white cloak that blended in with the world around him, and though he looked young, no more than twenty, he had an authority about him that made him seem much older.

She had never before seen him, of that she was sure, and for the span of a breath she thought she might die to see him again—he *overwhelmed* her.

Then Aurora cleared her throat and stood up taller, finding her senses. "You owe me an apology," she said.

The man appraised her. "Do I?"

"Yes," Aurora said. "You cost me food for my family for the better part of a year."

"It is forbidden to hunt snow stags. Are you unaware of the laws, or do you simply not care for them?"

Aurora looked away. The truth was that she had forgotten. She had never happened upon a snow stag before, and the hope of providing so well had eclipsed the law in her mind.

"I forgot," she said, wincing at how ridiculous it sounded.

"Well, the price for forgetfulness is not nearly as high as the price for a kill, but I'll be taking these to help you remember in the future." The man reached around Aurora for the remainder of her arrows, pulling them out of her satchel.

Anger rose in Aurora's chest, and for a moment she couldn't speak, stunned that he would steal from her.

"Those are mine," she said, reaching for the arrows.

The man took a step back, and Aurora lunged toward him, grabbing for them. Instead of grasping the arrows, though, her hand closed around his wrist, and an intense heat moved through her. In an instant, the veins in her hand began to glow, an impossible golden hue that spread beneath her skin.

Aurora jumped back, and the gold faded.

The man watched her intently, staring at her hand before his gaze slowly moved up to her face. His eyes widened just slightly as he studied her, and Aurora could have sworn that a small smile passed over his lips, but it was gone almost as soon as she saw it.

He sighed, soft and slow. "I've been waiting a long while for you."

The words broke something open inside of her, fear cascading through her body.

Run.

Aurora clung to her basket and took off, her lungs burning from the cold. Her boots sank deep into the snow, slowing her down, and she fought to move faster. One of her gloves slipped from her cloak and onto the ground, but Aurora dared not stop. She looked behind her to see if she was being followed, but the woods were as empty and quiet as they had been before the stranger's arrival, her own steps and breaths the only sounds she could hear. When she turned to face forward again, she almost ran headfirst into the large white stag, the man standing coolly beside it.

Aurora stumbled backward, her body shaking. Murder was not something that happened in Reverie, and yet Aurora wondered if that was about to change.

The man took two steps forward and stopped in front of her with an annoyed look on his face. "Don't move," he said, and something about the severity of his voice made her obey. He reached out and took her wrist, and once again her veins began to glow golden.

"Who are you?" she asked, pulling her hand free.

"Isn't it obvious?"

Aurora took in his glimmering hair and impossible gold eyes, his stark white cloak and the air of *something more* about him, something that wasn't quite natural. He was painfully handsome, and even though they were standing in the middle of a snow-covered forest on a mountain crawling with deadly Frost, he was warm, like the stones of the hearth in her cottage.

He was a man, yet he wasn't a man at all.

Understanding slammed into her, and Aurora covered her mouth, slowly shaking her head. "You're the Starmaker."

She could hardly believe the words that fell from her lips, and she almost thought he would laugh at her outlandish guess. But he did not laugh. Instead, he bowed, a movement so small it was almost imperceptible. Aurora knew people who had seen him before on the rare occasions when he'd had to address magic that had gone awry in the village, but it was a well-known fact that the Starmaker kept to himself.

"But it is common knowledge that you hardly ever show your face."

"It is also common knowledge that snow stags are not to be hunted, yet here we are."

Aurora's cheeks flamed because she knew she should never have considered shooting the stag. The animal was far too beautiful, far too special to kill, and she was glad her arrow had fallen short of its heart.

"I'm sorry," she said, but she kept her head high instead of cowering like she wanted. "I'm glad that I missed."

The Starmaker did not reply. An uncomfortable warmth rose within her, and Aurora wondered if it was the Starmaker's doing or her own body's reaction to him.

"What did you do to my arm?" she asked, remembering the way it had shone gold like his eyes. The way it had flooded with heat. "What did you do to me?"

"What is your name?" the Starmaker asked instead, studying Aurora with an intensity that made her heart race. She dropped her gaze to the ground.

"Aurora Finch."

"Aurora Finch," the Starmaker repeated, as if considering whether he liked the way it felt on his tongue. "There is sunlight in your blood." He said the words softly, almost with disbelief, and it made a shiver run down Aurora's spine.

"Did you do that to me?" she asked.

Just then, the snow stag huffed, reminding Aurora that she, too, was ready to go home. If the Starmaker wanted to harm her, he would have done so already, and she was no longer interested in standing in the cold with fear in her gut. Still, the Starmaker was revered, and Aurora didn't want to offend him, especially now that he knew her family name.

"I did not," the Starmaker said, a hint of surprise still present in his voice.

"Then I presume I am safe and can continue on with my day? I truly am sorry for threatening your stag—I assure you it won't happen again." Aurora wasn't clear on the etiquette when leaving a Starmaker, so she bowed slightly before turning on her heel to go, clutching the basket of winterberries to her side.

Aurora made it only three steps before the Starmaker was in front of her again, blocking her path. "Do you not know the stories of our mountain?"

"Of course I do," Aurora said, unsure why he would ask such a thing. Her mother had been telling her the stories of Reverie since she was a young girl. Aurora always lay as still as possible as Mama sat on the side of her bed, telling her tales of the Starmaker and his magic, of enchanted lands and epic loves. She knew them all and held them close to her heart because they made her ache with devastation and gratitude to be alive.

"Then you ought to know that the sunlight in your blood means that you possess magic."

Aurora took a step forward but lost her footing, almost falling into the snow, and the Starmaker reached out to steady her. Again, her veins shone gold.

"That's impossible," Aurora said.

"Improbable," the Starmaker countered. "Not impossible."

"Are you playing a trick on me?" It was all Aurora could think of to say, wondering if this was perhaps an elaborate joke concocted by her brothers to mark the day of her wedding.

"Do I look like the kind of person who"—the Starmaker paused, and his lips turned down in disgust—"plays tricks?"

"No," Aurora admitted. "You do not."

"If you're done running through all the ways in which this isn't possible, I would much appreciate if you could skip to the acceptance part so that we may get on with things." Impatience laced his tone, and he ran his hand down his stag's neck with an irritated sigh.

"Get on with things? What does that mean?"

"For someone who claims to know the mountain's history, you are quite obtuse."

"Then why don't you speak with clarity and tell me what it is you want?" Aurora made sure her lack of patience was as evident to him as his was to her. "And do it quickly, because there is somewhere I need to be."

"There is magic in your blood." He looked at her expectantly, and when Aurora showed no sign of understanding, he spoke again. "You are to be the next Starmaker."

He paused, his ridiculous claim hanging in the space between them, and frowned when Aurora began to laugh.

"I am no more a Starmaker than you are a villager."

The Starmaker looked down at his immaculate cloak, and Aurora could have sworn she saw the smallest hint of self-consciousness cloud his features. But it vanished as quickly as it had arrived.

"I will teach you," the Starmaker said. "That is my role now."

"You will teach me nothing," Aurora said, panic rising inside her. "Respectfully, I must go."

"The moment you touched me, your magic awakened. If you do not use it, it will kill you."

"Then I suppose I will die," Aurora said, lifting her chin and squaring her shoulders. She grabbed her skirts and turned away, walking as quickly as she could. Relief flooded her as the woods fell silent again. The Starmaker was not following her, nor was his stag, and she breathed out for what felt like the first time since encountering him.

Aurora tried not to dwell on his words. A Starmaker was only born every several hundred years—there was no way she could be the next one. Still, hearing she was going to die was decidedly unsettling, and she quickened her pace, trying to ignore the dread that had woken in her gut.

The snow crunched beneath her boots as she hurried home, and though she was still a bit disquieted by the encounter, she had relaxed considerably by the time she crossed the tree line and stepped onto the path that led to her cottage. Her face was cold, and the basket shook in her hands. She hoped her long absence hadn't made her family worry.

Aurora walked around to the front of the house but stopped abruptly when she saw a large snow deer. She couldn't make sense of it, and she ran to the door and shoved her way inside, slamming right into the back of the Starmaker.

He slowly turned and looked down at her, scowling.

"We must work on your entrance," he said, not a hint of amusement in his voice.

"And you must work on your manners. What are you doing in my home, unannounced, on the day of my wedding?" Aurora glared at him, then stepped around him and handed the basket of winterberry boughs to her mother.

"Aurora," her mother scolded, her face flushed with embarrassment. "That is no way to speak to the Starmaker."

"I have come to inform your family of the magic in your blood." The Starmaker said it with a certainty that made Aurora's heart skip, fear and adrenaline and nerves colliding in her chest.

"That is not your place," Aurora said, unable to keep the anger from her tone. "And certainly not on the day I marry."

A look passed between the Starmaker and her mother, and Aurora wished she knew what it meant.

"Is it true?" Aspen asked, his voice quiet with unease. It was the same tone he had used at the first Starmaker's grave, and Aurora realized it wasn't unease at all; it was reverence. Her gut revolted, and she inhaled slow and deep so she wouldn't become ill. "Did you see the sunlight in your blood, as he claims?"

Aurora looked around the room, to her brother and mother and Elsie, who sat frozen at the table, her tea all but forgotten. It was as if they were holding a collective breath, waiting for her to say it wasn't true. And she wanted to, she wanted to so badly, but she did not make a habit of lying to her family, and she wasn't about to start now. "I did," she said, hoping the Starmaker recognized the hostility in her voice.

Aurora heard Aspen's exhale and her sister's sharp intake of breath. Her mother looked at her with an expression so soft it made her chest ache. "Darling, you must know that this changes everything." Her mother walked toward her, gently putting her hands on either side of Aurora's face. "The Starmaker says you will die if you do not use your magic. You are walking a different path now, and we cannot pretend otherwise. You must move to the castle and learn your new role."

The words made Aurora tremble, the weight of them, the awe. They felt impossibly heavy, and she wished she could go back to before she'd left the house this morning, tell Mama that they had enough winterberries. Anything to keep her from going into the woods.

"It changes nothing. I don't want any of this, and I refuse to move to a castle with a man I do not know to learn magic I did not ask for. Now, if you'll excuse me, I'd like to ready myself for Farren."

"I am not speaking in riddles when I say you will die," the Starmaker said, his words tense, as if he was trying to demonstrate a patience he did not have. "It is a fact, but I can help you. I will teach you to use your magic."

Aurora stared at him. She didn't want to die—she knew that much. But were her options truly limited to dying or upending her entire life? There had to be another way. She began to move about the room, acutely aware of all the eyes that followed her.

"Surely you can teach me something small that I can do in my own home, just enough to keep me safe?" She hated how desperate her words sounded, the way they felt like giving in.

"That is not a possibility. There is nothing *small* to teach you; you must learn to pull in the light. That is what your magic is for."

"Darling, you must go with him," Mama said, her voice shaking. "I will not lose you."

The words clouded Aurora's mind with memories of the days and months following Papa's death, the way Mama could no longer care for Aurora or her siblings, could no longer sell produce at the market or tend to their land. It terrified her, the possibility of losing her mother again.

"You won't," Aurora whispered.

"I apologize for the blunt delivery, but she will if you do not come with me; it is the nature of the magic inside you. It demands to be used." The Starmaker paused, running a hand through his hair. He looked exasperated, as if he couldn't believe it was *this* difficult for Aurora to turn her back on the life she had worked so hard to build.

"Why should I believe a word you say?" Aurora asked, seething.

"You shouldn't; you do not know me. But you saw the light in your blood, saw the gold beneath your skin. Your body is not deceiving you."

Aurora paused. He was right: she'd seen the gold flowing through her veins. She'd felt the heat of it.

It was then that Aurora's eyes met Elsie's, and suddenly, she knew what she needed to do. It crashed down on her all at once as she remembered the prayer she had spoken every morning for the past three days. Aurora closed her eyes and inhaled deeply.

Please. I'll give anything.

On her exhale, Aurora opened her eyes and leveled the Starmaker with a glare. "I will move to the castle and learn your magic on two conditions. If you do not agree to them both, I must insist that you leave so that I may proceed with my day." Aurora looked at Elsie one more time before turning back to the

Starmaker. "The first is that you heal my sister. She was touched by the Frost and has not yet recovered."

"Aurora," Elsie said, pushing back from the table, a staunch objection in her voice. But she was too late; Aurora's mind was made up.

"And the second?" the Starmaker asked.

"My wedding to Farren Glenn would have produced a glare line that we are reliant upon." Aurora took a deep breath, willing her voice not to shake. "If I am to give that up, I insist that it be replaced." A glare line to the castle could heal their land, could provide protection from the Frost. Aurora despised the situation she was in, but as it seemed she could not change it, she would at least use it to benefit her family.

"You are not suggesting we marry," the Starmaker said with disgust, his eyes narrowing.

"It is not a suggestion," Aurora replied, keeping her tone even. "Unless there is some other way to produce a glare line?"

"You know very well there is not," he said through gritted teeth.

"Those are my conditions. You may take them or take your leave. The choice is yours."

The Starmaker appeared to be having a rather heated debate with himself, but by the fifth beat of Aurora's heart, his expression had neutralized. "Done," he said, offering her his hand. Aurora shook it, sealing their agreement, and she heard her mother gasp when her skin began to glow with the light of the Sun. "I will be back tomorrow before dawn. Be ready."

And with that, the Starmaker left the small cottage, nobody saying a word, the pounding of the stag's hooves as it ran away echoing Aurora's racing heart.

It was done.

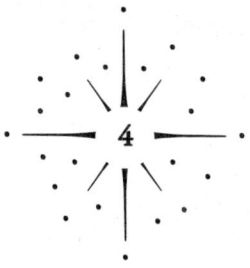

Liar

Elsie rushed to Aurora, taking both of her hands, her eyes filled with tears.

"You don't have to do this," she said, and Aurora was struck by how fiercely she spoke the words. How firmly she believed them. Elsie was so strong, so brave, and Aurora knew she would make the same choice over and over if it meant giving her sister back her life.

Aurora closed her eyes and squeezed Elsie's hands. She wondered if this was an elaborate answer to her dire prayer or if she had carried magic in her veins long before visiting the grave site. She wasn't sure, and she doubted she would ever truly know, but never in her wildest thoughts had she considered that her plea would lead to this: marrying a man who wasn't Farren. It had been Aurora's idea to marry the Starmaker, and it was only right that he compensate her family for what they stood to lose, but the reality of it was devastating, sitting heavy in her gut.

Aurora knew she could have fought for Farren, asked that he move to the castle with her, but if she was truly to be the next Starmaker, she did not wish to involve him. She wanted Farren to have the life he had always spoken of, running *Eternal Reverie* and watching his sisters grow up and one day having children of his own. Sequestering him in a castle far from his friends and his family and his business was unthinkable, and she wouldn't hear of it.

As difficult as it was to accept, Aurora's time with Farren had been nothing more than a shooting star in the clear black night of her life, a magical moment that had come and gone too quickly. The ache in her chest returned, and she let go of Elsie's hand, pressing her palm to her sternum.

"I do," Aurora said, looking at her sister. "It is a small price to pay for your life. For our livelihood." There were many people who married for reasons other than love, and securing a glare line to the castle seemed a very good reason indeed. Aurora suddenly felt a deep gratitude for Farren and his safe love; she couldn't imagine going through this if they'd had something more akin to the love between her parents. Because the truth was that Aurora could live without Farren, but she couldn't live without Elsie.

Aspen walked over to join them, grabbing Elsie's hand, then Aurora's. "You are the Starmaker Rising," he said, disbelief lacing his tone. "You have the Sun's favor, an honor the rest of us could never dream of."

"An honor I do not want," Aurora said, but even as she spoke, she held tightly to Aspen's hand.

Mama walked over then, and Aspen and Elsie parted to let her into the circle. "You have lit up this home from the moment you entered our world. What an incredible gift to be able to illuminate all of Reverie." She took a deep breath, and her eyes filled with tears. "Your father would be so proud."

It wasn't something Aurora wanted to hear, that Papa would be proud of the very thing ruining the life she had planned for herself. To her, this was a terrible, loathsome thing that had nothing to do with who she was or what her talents were. It was nothing to be proud of.

Aurora didn't say that, though. Instead, she held on to her family because she was afraid she would break if she didn't. They stood together for a long time, and while she could feel that her mother meant what she had said, Aurora could also feel the sadness in the room. The uncertainty. Her family didn't want to let her go just as much as she didn't want to leave, and that gave her the strength to finally step back and do what she needed to do.

"I have to see Farren," Aurora said, moving toward the door.

"I can inform his family," Aspen said.

"No. If I am to give up our life together to marry a stranger and try to learn a magic I'm not convinced I have, I must be the one to tell him."

Aspen nodded. "Of course. I was only trying to help carry the load."

"I know." Aurora hugged her brother, then walked to the

hook on the wall for her cloak before realizing she was still wearing it. She tightened it and hurried outside, letting the door slam shut behind her.

It was only then that she allowed the sob that had been building in her throat to break free, and tears ran down her cheeks and froze on her skin, tiny rivers of ice that would soon disappear, just like her life with Farren. They had picked out a small house on the outskirts of the village, and Farren had promised that their very first piece of furniture would be a desk where Aurora could fulfill her dream of writing for *Eternal Reverie*. She would tend to their home and bake her Mama's bread, distribute the paper in the mornings and write by candlelight in the evenings. It was more than she had ever hoped for, and it was being ripped away before she got to experience the joy of it.

The cold had never bothered Aurora, nor had the darkness—she found both to be immeasurably comforting, and there was a stillness that blanketed her home that never seemed to find those that were touched by the Sun. She had come to think of the light as a treat, like the Sparrows' biscuits or game for supper; she didn't need it, but she enjoyed it when it was available. But now, as she stepped out of the darkness and crossed into the sunlight, she paused. She did not close her eyes and soak in the warmth, nor did she marvel in the lore of her mountain. That day, the stories felt more like fairy tales with all of the curses and none of the happy endings.

Aurora continued on until Farren's home came into view. His younger sisters were in the yard playing, building an enormous snowman and yelling with glee. She loved Farren's sisters and would mourn their absence in her life. She was giving up so much, all because the Starmaker had seen something shine within her. But what if a life with him dimmed her to nothing, snuffed her out completely? What then?

She shook her head; there was nothing for it. Elsie had said she didn't have to do it, but of course she did. Aurora loved her sister for saying it, for acting as if Aurora had a choice, but there was no choice, not when there was so much at stake.

"Aurora!" Kitty yelled when she saw her, running through the snow to greet her. It came up to her knees and spilled into her boots, but the young girl kept running. Aurora couldn't help but laugh, and she hoped her smile hid her fear and her anger, her sadness and resentment. Kitty launched herself into her arms, and Aurora caught her and swung her around.

"You're even taller than the last time I saw you," she said.

"Papa says it's all the berries I've been sneaking," Kitty said, laughing, still out of breath from her run.

"The whole point of sneaking is not getting caught." Aurora gave Kitty a conspiratorial glance, and Kitty smiled broadly as if it was all part of an elaborate plan that was working perfectly. Then she took Aurora's hand and pulled her closer to the house.

Farren's other sister dashed into the house and loudly announced, "Aurora's here, Aurora's here!" before rushing back out and crashing into Aurora's legs, hugging her tightly.

"Hello to you, too, Laurel," Aurora said, bending down and smoothing her hair.

"Aurora?" Farren stepped out of the house, and his face broke into a smile the way it so often did when he saw her. "What are you doing here?"

"I need to talk with you," she said, hating the way his smile faltered, hating the uncertainty in his perfect brown eyes. She had told him once that she was his certainty—that no matter how unreliable his business or his health or his success may be, she was an immovable pillar he could count on. She hated that the Starmaker had turned her into a liar, into someone who broke promises, and she vowed then and there that the Starmaker would know she resented him for it down to her very core.

Aurora took Farren's hand and led him out into the fields, far enough away that his family couldn't hear them.

"Please stop walking," Farren said, his voice tight. "Tell me what has happened."

With tears in her eyes, Aurora recounted the morning to him: her encounter with the Starmaker and the sunlight in her blood, the way he had gone to her family behind her back and insisted she move to the castle. The way Aurora had agreed on the condition that he save Elsie's life.

As Aurora spoke, Farren's eyes widened, his deep bronze skin turning red like it always did when he was upset. He looked away from her and into the woods. It was better that way, better that Aurora didn't have to see the pain in his expression or the hurt she was causing. But then she thought that made her a coward, so she reached for Farren's face and brought his gaze back to hers.

"There is one more thing," she said, swallowing hard. "The Starmaker and I will be married."

For one awful moment, Farren said nothing, just stood there silently as tension pulled at his features. Then a terrible gasp caught in his throat. Aurora had never seen him cry before, and she was wholly unprepared for it.

"Why would he insist upon that?"

Aurora paused, took in a breath. "It was me," she said, voice shaking. "I insisted that he replace the glare line I am giving up by not marrying you."

"I could move with you," Farren said quickly. Frantically. "We could still marry."

"I would never do that to you. You can still have the life you've hoped for, and I know with absolute certainty that you will not find it in the castle, far removed from the things you love."

"But I love *you*," he said, his voice breaking.

"And I you," Aurora said, taking his hands. "But this is something I must do on my own. I will not let you sacrifice your dreams for me; I couldn't live with myself."

"There must be a way out of this," Farren said. "If we can find a cure for Elsie, then you won't have to go to the castle, and you and I can marry. Others have survived the Frost; Elsie can, too."

"Even if that were true, what of the rest of it? The Starmaker said I will die if I don't use the magic he believes I possess."

"How do you know he wasn't saying that so you would agree? We can go somewhere, just the two of us, and find a way to save

Elsie. And if your health takes a turn, we can come back and seek out the Starmaker."

Aurora didn't know the Starmaker, but she felt deep in her gut that he hadn't been lying. He hadn't seemed any happier about their arrangement than she was; perhaps it made her a fool, but she believed him.

"Farren—" Aurora began, but he cut her off.

"No," he said. "Don't do this. You don't have to go to him tomorrow—you can take some time. Come away with me and truly think about what you want."

"I don't have to think about it," she said, begging him to understand. "I know what I want, and what I want is the life you and I planned. That has never been in question. But I cannot put my sister at risk, and if what the Starmaker says is true, I cannot put all of Reverie at risk, either. It is too heavy a burden to bear."

Farren put his hands on her head and pulled her into a kiss, a passionate and urgent plea that Aurora wanted so badly to answer, but she could not. He rested his forehead against hers and closed his eyes. "Come away with me, Rora," he said again, softer now. "Meet me at our cave tonight, once everyone else is asleep. Please."

Her heart ached at the mention of the cave, a place Aurora had found when she was a child. It was dark and cold and covered in ice, but the floor was blanketed in wildflowers, vibrant and healthy blooms that were a testament to the magic that lived beneath the ground. Aurora used to go there to write, to dream up her own stories, but over time, the cave had turned from her place to theirs.

As Farren spoke, Aurora let herself imagine it, meeting in secret in the middle of the night to find a different solution with the man she loved. Huddling in the cave and thinking up ideas that didn't result in her moving far, far away. But it was just a fantasy, a way to delay the inevitable. Aurora had made a deal with the Starmaker, an agreement that would save her sister's life and secure the livelihood of her family. She wouldn't go back on her word.

"I'm sorry," she said, pulling away. "I'm so sorry, but I can't do that. I would never forgive myself if something happened to Elsie because I took too much time."

Farren looked at her, his brow creased, his eyes red. She wanted to comfort him, but there was nothing she could say that would make any difference. He had asked her to run away with him, and she had said no.

He nodded, wiped his eyes. "That's it, then?" he asked, his voice flat.

"It has to be. What else is there?"

For a long time, Farren said nothing, and Aurora wondered if that was how they'd leave things, a heavy silence that spoke for them both. But then he took her hand. "I'm sorry this is happening to you. It is an impossible position to be in."

The acknowledgment soothed something inside her, and she exhaled. "I'm sorry, too."

Aurora leaned in and kissed him on the cheek, breathing in his scent, his comfort and warmth, for the last time. Then she began her walk home. A few stray tears ran down her cheeks, but she knew she was doing the right thing. Walking away from

Farren was hard, but walking away from the life they had planned together was worse, and she let herself feel the pain of it the entire way home.

Then she squared her shoulders, took a deep breath, and pushed the pain away. Anger was a much sharper tool than sadness, and she would wield it with all her strength.

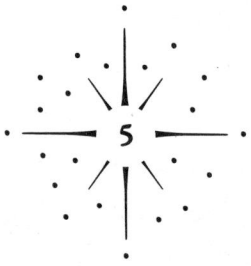

Falling Stars

Aurora couldn't sleep. She replayed the past twenty-four hours over and over in her mind, and in the quiet of her cottage, with the occasional pops and hisses from the fire, she could almost convince herself none of it had happened.

That none of it was real.

But if it had been only a dream, a terribly vivid dream, then Aurora would have been a wife by now, in her home with Farren, getting used to the sounds and smells of a new place. There would have been remnants of flowers in her long brown hair and a gold band on her ring finger and nerves in her stomach about sharing a bed with a man.

A safe love. The thought normally made her feel happy and calm, but in that moment she felt overwhelmingly sad that she wasn't willing to fight for Farren. She mourned the loss of their almost-life, carried it close to her chest so that she could fuel her anger with it.

After another hour of staring at the ceiling, Aurora sat up, frustrated. The fire cast a faint orange glow over the room that made shadows dance along the walls of the loft, and Aurora looked over at Elsie, asleep in the small bed beside her. Her breathing was labored, a faint hiss punctuating the top of every inhale, and Aurora wished she had made the Starmaker heal Elsie before he had left that day. He would be back soon, though, and Elsie would live. That was all that mattered.

Aurora was quiet as she crawled out of bed and slipped down the ladder. She waited at the bottom of the steps for any sounds from her brother or Mama, but the house was still. She tiptoed around, gathering heavy blankets and matches before finally pushing out the door.

"Sister?"

Aurora jumped and squinted into the darkness. "Aspen? What are you doing out here?"

"I was about to ask you the same thing," he said. He walked closer, and Aurora could see that his arms were full of firewood. "It is my night to feed the fire."

"I couldn't sleep," Aurora said. "I thought I might stargaze for a while to ease my worry."

"I'm sorry for what you're going through," Aspen said, and Aurora believed him. Aspen was careful when he spoke, and he didn't say things he did not mean. He had always been that way, and Aurora had come to rely on him for advice and wisdom.

"Thank you."

Aspen passed by her and stepped into the house without another word, and Aurora looked over at the forest behind their home. She couldn't see them in the darkness, but she knew rows of candy stripe phlox bordered the trees, a warning system that alerted the villagers when the Frost was creeping out beyond the cover of the woods. The flowers followed the entire forest edge, visible from every part of the village, vibrant blooms with petals of rich pink, the edges striped in white. They were beautiful, but on the day that Elsie had fallen ill, the ones behind their home had withered to a dull gray.

They were vibrant once again, though, and Aurora knew she would be safe here. She trudged through the snow to the stone fire pit that Evander had made when they were children. The stones were nearly black after years of use, and there was almost always enough ash and charred wood to get the fire going again without much trouble. There was a worn wooden pergola offering just enough cover that the pit and chairs remained free of snow, and Aurora grabbed her matches, producing a small fire in minutes that spat into the night. She pulled out a chair just enough to see the stars, sat down, and looked up.

The sky was clear. Aurora had always loved stories about the stars, and she had often braved the cold as a young girl to watch for the ones that fell. She'd thought that if she did it night after night, one would eventually fall directly beside her, and perhaps she could keep it, a special treasure just for her. Or maybe she would help hang it back in the sky, if that was what the star wanted—she didn't know how to hang a star, but she had been willing to try.

THE SUN AND THE STARMAKER

Aurora no longer believed that she might get to hold a star one day, but she still watched for the ones that shot across the sky. Her neck began to ache as she kept her gaze trained above her, and when a star began to fall, leaving a wake of glitter in the dark, her eyes welled up.

She jumped when she heard a sound and pulled her focus from the sky, blinking away her tears.

"I haven't been out here much since Evander married," Aspen said, pulling out a chair and draping himself in a blanket.

"It's a good night for it." Aurora kept her voice casual to match her brother's tone, but she was deeply moved that he had come back out to be with her. He was covered from head to toe in his warmest clothing, and his breaths sent white puffs into the night.

"Even better now, I would think," Aspen said, handing her a thermos of leftover cider from their trip to the market. Aurora eagerly took a sip, letting it warm her the whole way through.

"What is your reaction to everything that's happening?" Aurora asked. She didn't want Aspen to feel as though they couldn't speak of it, and she truly wanted to know. Perhaps talking with him would make her feel as though she wasn't carrying it all on her own.

"I think it is extraordinary," Aspen said with complete sincerity. "The Starmaker Rising..." He trailed off, shaking his head. "It is hard for me to comprehend."

"And for me."

Aspen looked at her then. "I know it feels like you don't have a choice in the matter, and I cannot fault you for that, as I would feel the same. But the truth is that there is always a choice, and you do not have to—rather, you *should* not—do this his way." He paused before continuing. "The Sun chose you for a reason, Aurora, and you owe it to yourself and to all of Reverie to take the entirety of who you are into your new role. You get to decide what your life as Starmaker will look like—no one else."

Aurora was stunned by his words, unable to speak for fear of losing herself to her emotions. She took a shaky breath. "Thank you for saying that. It was somehow exactly what I needed to hear."

"I'm glad," Aspen said, reaching over and squeezing her hand.

The door to the house closed, and Aurora looked up to see Elsie walking toward them, huddled in her blankets. Aurora stood, rushing over to her sister.

"You should not be out here," Aurora said, holding out her arm to take Elsie back inside. But her sister simply walked past her.

"The phlox was pink today, and I believe I am to be fully healed in a few hours' time," Elsie said, and Aurora almost laughed at how obstinate she was. How brave. Aurora had taken care of Elsie ever since Papa died, but she wasn't a child anymore, and it was probably time to stop treating her like one.

"Her logic is sound," Aspen said, getting up and pulling out a chair for Elsie.

"I suppose it is," Aurora agreed. She joined them and handed the thermos to Elsie. Just then, the door flew open once more, and Mama came out with the cake she had made for the wedding sitting unceremoniously on a large wooden carving board.

"Did you truly believe I would let you leave without helping us get through this cake?" Mama asked, setting the board on a small table in front of Aurora. She smoothed a hand over Aurora's hair before sitting down, then passed around forks as she told a story from Aurora's childhood. It was then that Aurora knew her mother would be okay, that she would be there for Aspen and Elsie in a way she had not been able to in the past.

It was the reassurance Aurora needed, and she felt some of the tension leave her body, knowing her family was here and safe and okay. More than okay.

All at once, they went for the cake, stabbing their forks through the layers, not trying to keep its beauty intact. It was such a ridiculous thing, the four of them sitting outside in the frigid night, each of them in so many clothes they could hardly move, passing around cider and eating forkfuls of cake in the earliest hours of the morning. The wood cracked and smoke rose into the night and they talked and told stories and laughed, all of them together, and Aurora let Aspen's words from earlier carve themselves onto her heart.

These people were the deepest parts of herself, and she would carry them with her to the castle, hold them close as she learned her magic, and weave the threads of her past into the tapestry of her future.

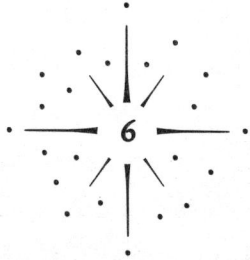

Poor Assumptions

Aurora stayed out for as long as she could, until her toes and cheeks tingled with too much cold, and then she followed her family back inside. It had been a beautiful night, a send-off she never could have pictured for herself, never could have planned, and she would treasure it for the rest of her life. But the dawn was fast approaching, and there was nothing to do but pack her trunk and prepare for the journey to the tallest peak, where the Starmaker's ice-covered castle sat high above Reverie.

She moved around the cottage slowly, trying to memorize every detail of what it felt like to live in this home that the light couldn't reach. She ran her fingers over the worn wooden table and slipped out of her socks to feel the rug beneath her feet. She smelled the faint woodsmoke clinging to the couch and chairs and listened to the ladder creak as she went up. Aurora had been sad about leaving when she'd thought she was marrying Farren, and the sorrow that accompanied her now that she was going to the castle left an enormous pit in her gut.

But while she was mournful, she was not afraid. The Starmaker believed she was important; it did not make sense for him to harm her. And so, when she could not put it off any longer, she opened her trunk and began packing it with steady hands.

"Let me help you," Elsie said, following Aurora up to the loft.

"I don't have much to take." Aurora could feel her sister's eyes on her, a question burning on her tongue. "What is it?" she asked, looking up from her folding.

"Do you really believe you are to pull the sunlight?" Elsie said the words quietly, as if they were sacred. Aurora supposed that made sense—up until yesterday, she too had viewed the Starmaker's role as wonderful and life-giving, because it was both of those things. But that was when she had believed the duty belonged to someone else, and now that the responsibility might be hers to carry, it didn't feel wonderful. It felt impossibly heavy.

"I don't know," Aurora said, sitting down beside her sister. "I saw the way my blood began to glow when I touched him, and I felt the heat inside of me. I wish I hadn't."

"Don't say that," Elsie said, taking her sister's hand. "Don't ever regret who you are."

Aurora shook her head. "It will be hard not to regret the thing that is taking me from you, but I'll try my best." She pulled her sister close and gave her a hug before packing the rest of her belongings.

"Take this," Elsie said, pulling the quilt they had sewn together when they were children off of the bed. "Something to make the castle feel like home."

Aurora wanted to tell her it wasn't necessary and that she was sure there would be plenty of quilts, but she really did want to take it with her. It would smell of Elsie and of home, of Aspen's mint tea leaves and Mama's rose-hip oil.

"Thank you." She folded the quilt and gently put it on top of her things, then latched the trunk shut.

When she got downstairs, the rest of her family was waiting for her, and Aurora was surprised to see Evander. "What are you doing here?" she exclaimed, rushing into his arms.

He hugged her tightly. "Aspen sent word to me yesterday." He pulled away and looked at her with what she could only describe as delight. "The Starmaker," he said, shaking his head. "I wanted to see you off."

"I'm so glad you came." She hugged him once more, not wanting to let go. She didn't see Evander nearly as often as she wanted, and she hadn't realized how much she had missed him until he was squeezing her close. "Where is Samuel?"

"He wanted to be here, but the roof developed a leak overnight. He's trying to fix it before it causes too much damage."

"Tell him I love him."

"He knows," Evander said. "And I will."

Aurora didn't know what else to say, so she turned to the rest of her family. They didn't look worried, nor were they happy. There was a heaviness in the air, a hopeful sorrow. Aurora had thought she wanted her family to be outraged for her, to fight for the life she had to give up, but this felt more appropriate, somehow. Easier.

"And so the Starmaker cast the light of the Sun over Reverie, an impossible magic born of an impossible love." It was her mother who spoke the words, the last line of a story her father used to tell by the fire after supper. The same story Aurora had told Elsie many times. It made a painful lump form in her throat, and she swallowed hard.

She hugged them all, holding on tight, whispering, "I love you," and hearing it in return.

She took a deep breath.

Then there was a single knock on the door.

Aspen moved to answer, but Aurora stopped him. "Let me," she said.

She walked to the door, slowly exhaled, and opened it. The Starmaker stood before her in all white, draped in layers of warm, luxurious fabrics. Intricate embroidery adorned his cloak, silver threads forming lines that fanned out from the collar, and though the hem touched the ground, it remained pristine. His golden eyes were points of brightness in the otherwise dark morning, and Aurora's cheeks flamed as she realized she was staring.

She remembered how irritable he had been the day before, the way he had shown her neither patience nor compassion when telling her of her fate, and she wondered at how a man so unpleasant could be so beautiful.

"I'm ready," she said, moving her eyes from his face and turning to her family once more.

Her brothers had managed to get her trunk down the ladder, and when she moved to grab it, the Starmaker cut in instead. "Allow me."

He picked up the trunk with ease and walked it out to the most beautiful sleigh Aurora had ever seen. The wood was dyed a dark navy that matched the night sky, and the trim was a brilliant gold that was somehow bright even in the darkness. Two lanterns hung on either side of the sleigh, and the seats were finished in white velvet with a large fur blanket draped over the cushions. The Starmaker secured the trunk to the back, then met Aurora at the door.

"Please come here," he said, looking inside the house at Elsie.

Elsie moved forward without hesitation, and the Starmaker held out his hands to her. She took them, and Aurora watched for any signs of her blood beginning to glow; if Elsie reacted the same way Aurora had to his touch, then she would know for sure that it was a mere effect of the Starmaker and not an indication of magic. Elsie continued to hold his hands, but there was no change in her veins, and though Aurora tried desperately to see even the slightest gleam, she could perceive no illumination beneath Elsie's skin.

The Starmaker closed his eyes and muttered words that Aurora could not understand, and then all at once, Elsie gasped. Aurora ran to her, shoving the Starmaker out of the way and holding on to her sister. "What happened? Are you all right?"

THE SUN AND THE STARMAKER

Elsie slowly opened her eyes and blinked. "I am well," she said, an awed tone to her voice. "Sister, I am well."

Aurora searched Elsie's face, and she could not deny the color that had returned to her cheeks or the clarity in her blue eyes. Elsie felt warm since the first time she'd been touched by the Frost, and Aurora knew that the Starmaker had kept his word.

"Thank you," she said, turning back to the Starmaker. She wanted to feel angry, to lash out at him for upending her life, but in that moment all she felt was deep, unwavering gratitude.

He nodded. "We must go."

Aurora gave Elsie one more hug and looked back at the rest of her family. Then she put on her green cloak and searched for her gloves before remembering she had lost one in the woods. She tucked her bare hands beneath the heavy wool of her cloak, feeling vulnerable.

"Wait," Aspen said. Aurora turned, but her brother was not looking at her. He was looking at the Starmaker.

"In this home, we have a deep respect for the Starmaker." Aspen paused. "But our love for Aurora is deeper."

Mama nodded in agreement, as did Elsie and Evander. They stood together in a line, watching the Starmaker, ensuring that he knew they would still look out for her. Still protect her. Still come to her aid whenever she needed them. Aurora knew what it meant for Aspen to say those words—his reverence for the Starmaker was fundamental to who he was, down to his very core—and it left her breathless.

Aurora didn't trust herself to speak again. Instead, she found her brother's gaze and silently mouthed *thank you*.

"I understand," the Starmaker said, looking at each one of Aurora's family members in turn.

Then they left.

Aurora walked outside to the sleigh, and four large snow deer stood at the front, patiently waiting to take them wherever the Starmaker asked. Aurora recognized the first deer in line as the stag she had seen in the woods. She hesitantly ran her hand down his nose and whispered, "I'm sorry." Then she walked to the side of the sleigh and put her foot on the step.

A hand reached out to help her, and she took it, looking down at it before moving her eyes to the Starmaker's face. He stood at her side, his touch like fire, the same as it had been the day before, and she knew her skin was turning golden.

"Do not fool yourself," she said to him. "You are no gentleman. You may carry my trunk and offer your hand as I step into your sleigh, but you are still the man who is forcing me into a life I do not want."

She let go and sat down on the soft bench, and for a moment, the Starmaker stayed where he was, his hand still frozen in midair as if her words had stunned him. Then he slowly walked around to the other side and sat beside her without a word.

Aurora looked over at her family as they stood outside the door, and then the Starmaker took the reins and the sleigh lurched forward, moving away from her home and the only life she had ever known. Her house receded into the distance, and a tear ran down Aurora's cheek. She wiped it away and realized the Starmaker was watching her; she did not pull her gaze from his and instead let him see her in her pain.

"It is not easy," he said, and Aurora waited for him to continue, but he was quiet.

The sleigh moved over the snow smoothly, and when Aurora looked back, she could no longer see her cottage, just the infinite darkness of the mountain where the Sun could not reach. She faced forward and did not look back again, burying her hands beneath the fur blanket and watching the world as it moved past them in a blur.

Everything was covered in snow, and the tree branches were heavy with the weight of it, drooping down toward the earth. The stars shone brightly overhead, and a crescent moon drifted toward the horizon, signaling the start of another day. She wondered if Farren was sleeping, warm in his bed, or if his night had also been restless and long. She hoped that one day he would understand, that he would hear of Elsie's recovery and forgive her. She hoped that he would marry and have the life he had always dreamt of. And as the sleigh carried her farther away from her home, she almost smiled, because even after everything, she was still hoping, and hope was a powerful thing.

Maybe, she thought, hope was everything.

The snow deer raced through the forest, and as they came out the other side, they began to climb the mountain, a steep trail that led to the castle at the top of the world. That was what Elsie had called it when she was younger—the castle at the top of the world—because it was the highest point on the northernmost mountain, suspended above everything. The entire structure appeared to be made of ice, and even in the darkness, Aurora could see the way it reflected the stars. She gripped the side of the sleigh as her body slid back in her seat, stopping against the velvet cushion behind her. The snow deer were steady as they climbed, and Aurora tried to trust them as the trail narrowed and the terrain became more rugged.

The castle loomed above them, and Aurora could now see that it was not built just of ice but also of ivory stone that shone like a beacon in the otherwise dark landscape. Rows of icicles hung from every balcony, and multiple spires stretched toward the heavens as if they could touch the stars. It was the closest Aurora had ever been to it, and though they still had quite a distance to go, she was stunned by its brilliance.

The snow deer took a sharp turn, and suddenly the sleigh was under the cover of trees once more. The snow wasn't as deep here, topped with a layer of ice that cracked and snapped all around them. Aurora shivered as a chill crept over her, and she pulled the blanket farther up her torso, but it didn't help. Her cloak had always been effective at keeping out the cold, but now it felt like lace, as if the air was going right through it. Aurora could feel the Starmaker's eyes on her, and she tried to calm her shivering, but it wouldn't stop.

Aurora was used to the cold, but this was unlike anything she had ever felt before. It crept along her skin and soaked into her body, as if her organs and bones were made entirely of ice, as if her heart were pumping glacier water instead of blood. A scream clawed up her throat, and her vision blurred, her grip on the blanket slipping and her mind going as dark as the night sky. She was so cold.

"Hold on to my hands."

His voice was urgent, and Aurora's eyes fluttered open as the world came back into focus. The Starmaker was sitting so close to her that their legs were touching, and she looked down to see her weak hands tucked into his. "Hold on to me," he said again, and Aurora tightened her grip.

Instantly her body was flooded with heat, the ice inside her colliding with a river of liquid sun, and she gasped as she came back to herself. Her head was pounding and her heart was racing, and she shivered uncontrollably as she tried to rid herself of the chill. It was as if the warmth and the cold were waging a war inside her, and she frantically looked around the woods, trying to find whatever had turned her body to ice. It must have been the Frost—the pain had been almost unbearable. But the snow deer pressed on, and there was nothing she could see except for the shadows of the trees as the sleigh glided past.

"Look at me," the Starmaker said, but Aurora couldn't focus; panic was building inside her. She was disoriented and afraid, her body still shaking. "Aurora," he said, and her eyes finally found his—it was the first time he had used her name.

Slowly, the Starmaker ran his hands up her arms, over her neck, and settled on either side of her face, his gold eyes almost glowing. He held her with firm yet gentle hands, and all at once the remaining cold left her body. The shivering stopped and her heart slowed. His expression gave nothing away, and when the tension in her body had eased, he dropped his hands and moved over on the seat, giving her back the space she'd wanted when they had started their journey.

"You will be susceptible to the Frost until your magic fully develops." He did not look at her when he spoke, and Aurora caught sight of his hand, restless on the edge of the sleigh.

"I thought your castle would be far from the Frost," she said, her voice small. She could still feel the ghost of his touch on her face, and she pulled the blanket closer to her.

"As it cannot harm me, I am closest to it."

He said nothing more, and they traveled in silence until the trail leveled out and the wildness of the woods gave way to a manicured path that was lined with white cherry blossoms. Aurora had never seen so many blooms in her life, and she wondered at how magical the Starmaker's land must be to support so many flowers. It was an incredible sight, and as they passed tree after tree in full bloom, the ache in Aurora's heart dulled slightly.

"It's beautiful," she whispered, but if the Starmaker heard her, he did not answer.

The snow deer came to a stop in front of a grand entrance with a large marble door that Aurora's cottage could have fit through. Several people stood on the steps, and it was a relief to discover that she wouldn't be alone with the Starmaker; perhaps there would be someone she could talk to, maybe even befriend. Reverie was still dark, but the castle was lit up, and though the lanterns were covered in ice, they cast a comforting glow over the massive estate. Aurora stared at it, unmoving, until the Starmaker cleared his throat and she realized he was already on the ground, offering a hand to her.

After a moment, she took it and stepped out of the sleigh and onto the soft snow.

"I am well-mannered, Miss Finch," the Starmaker said, looking at her coolly. "But I have never considered myself a gentleman." And with that, he dropped her hand and left Aurora standing in the cold.

✦

The Starmaker

In all his years, the Starmaker could not even begin to guess what he had done to deserve such a stubborn, strong-willed creature as his successor.

And not just his successor.

His *fiancée*.

The Starmaker scowled. He had been aghast when Aurora Finch had stated her conditions; he had assumed a simple "you will die if you do not do this" would be sufficient. It had been for him when his magic was discovered. But the girl had insisted on bartering as if they stood across from each other at a stall in the market. It was utterly preposterous.

If the Starmaker had not been so eager to find his successor, he would have at least attempted to negotiate before accepting her terms. But as it was, he could not risk her refusing him, and so the cost of his impatience was a bride.

Fool.

The Starmaker had no objection to healing the sister. In fact, he was happy to do so. But he could not think of anything he desired less than to take a wife. And not solely because he did not want one—though that was certainly a factor—but also because it would not be fair. But as this was not a marriage built on affection, the Starmaker supposed it didn't matter.

He looked over at the Starmaker Rising, clutching the fur blanket close to her chest, a tear running down her cheek. He remembered how hard it had been for him the day he'd left his own family.

"It is not easy," he said.

She did not respond, which was for the best. He had been awaiting his successor for many years and had long since decided that it would be kindest to pass their days together in as much silence as possible.

That was, of course, before he knew he would have to marry. *The Starmaker, a husband.* He shook his head at the thought, it was so absurd. But he was determined not to let the small, albeit unpleasant, inconvenience of marriage ruin what was otherwise a very welcome occurrence.

He had found his successor, and for that he was grateful.

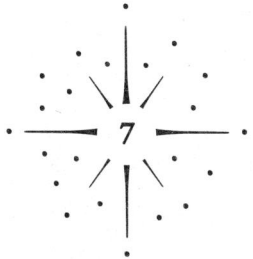

Rest

A urora watched the Starmaker as he left, sitting in the sleigh they had arrived in just moments before.

"He's late," a voice said, and Aurora startled, having forgotten there were other people outside.

"I'm sorry?" she said, turning toward the voice.

"He should have pulled the sunlight in by now." It was a woman who spoke, probably a few years older than Aurora, with soft brown eyes and dark curly hair that was pulled back into a bun. She wore glasses, and her rich beige skin turned pink over her nose the longer she stood in the cold. "I'm Ina. I manage the castle and will help you get settled." She had a calming presence that Aurora instantly liked.

"Thank you," Aurora said, stealing one more glance at

the trail, but the Starmaker was out of sight. "Are there consequences?" she asked, turning back to Ina. "For his being late?"

"Not for Reverie," Ina said, motioning to two other staff members who walked down the steps and retrieved Aurora's trunk from the sleigh. "There wouldn't be any problems for us unless he was extremely late. But it's quite painful for him."

"Painful?" Aurora followed Ina around a large tiered fountain with streams of frozen water arcing out from its center and deep orange roses caught in the ice. A white rabbit sat at the base of it, looking directly at her with big blue eyes, its fur shimmering just like the Starmaker's hair.

"His magic must be used; even a small buildup can cause his body to rise in temperature. You will learn all of this in time."

Ina ushered her through the large door, and the rabbit followed behind. Aurora meant to inquire about the animal, but when she stepped inside the castle, her words vanished on her tongue. While it was bitterly cold outside, the castle was warm despite its size. The foyer was enormous, with white marble flooring and a large stone statue that dominated the center of the room. It was carved from pure alabaster and showed two lovers leaning in for a kiss as hands behind each of them pulled them away from each other. A small light illuminated both of their faces in a golden glow, and Aurora was so transfixed by it that she didn't hear what Ina said next.

"Miss Finch?" Ina asked, coming up to her side.

"This statue," Aurora said. "It's beautiful."

"It has been here since the castle was built. The Sun gave it to

THE SUN AND THE STARMAKER

the first Starmaker as her parting gift; they loved each other very much even though theirs was an impossible love."

Aurora reached out to touch it, and the stone was warm. It hurt her to look at it, a love doomed from the start, but she couldn't pull her eyes away. "I've never seen anything like it."

"There is much to admire here," Ina said with pride in her voice. "Just don't be alarmed if you hear it crying."

"Crying?" Aurora asked in surprise.

"Over the years, more and more magic has seeped into the statue, and every once in a while, one or both of them will cry."

Aurora silently hoped she would never hear it; she couldn't imagine anything sadder.

"The castle is a magical place," Ina said, pulling Aurora from her thoughts. "It is so nice to have someone new to share it with. We're all very glad you're here."

Aurora looked at the woman, and though she did not reply, Ina's words eased something inside of her. She had lost so much in such a short time, had relinquished the life she now knew had never been hers, and the thought that her arrival was a joyous occasion to someone else was a balm for her aching heart. It was what she needed to put one foot in front of the other and step into this new world.

"Don't forget to look up," Ina said with a smile, and Aurora followed her gaze. The ceiling was not a ceiling at all, but rather a thin sheet of ice clear enough that she could see the stars, so close Aurora thought she could reach out and pluck them from the sky.

"Amazing," she said under her breath. While she would have given anything to be in the small house on the outskirts of Reverie, settling in as Farren's new wife, the beauty of the castle was undeniable. She wanted to hate it, to scowl at every room she walked into and resent its walls for keeping her in a place she did not wish to be, but she could no sooner despise it than she could the stars.

Aurora didn't want her awe getting back to the Starmaker, though, so she set her mouth in a hard line and decided to keep her wonder to herself as Ina showed her to her room. They were walking up a wide marble staircase when the entire castle lit up as sunlight streamed in through the windows. Aurora hadn't noticed how many there were, but it was as if the entire palace had been built to greet the Sun, not a single corner left in the dark. She gripped the gold railing as she took it all in, the space filling with rays of buttery light, coming alive with the breaking of day.

"I'm ready to see my room," Aurora said, turning away from the grand foyer and walking up the stairs. The rabbit followed them as far as the landing, then lay down on an intricate carpet woven with silver and gold thread. It seemed strange that the animal was given free rein of the castle, but Ina paid it no mind, so Aurora did the same.

"Of course," Ina said.

Aurora kept her eyes on the floor, not wanting to see any more of this place than she had to. She wondered what her family was doing, if they were all going about their normal chores now that she was gone or if they felt as stuck as she did. She wondered if they could feel her sorrow, if she had left a trail of it that wound down the mountain and led all the way back to her home, her own personal glare line.

THE SUN AND THE STARMAKER

Even with her eyes cast downward, Aurora could feel the opulence of the castle, the way every marble tile and crystal chandelier and ivory candlestick seemed to be touched by magic, the way every surface faintly glimmered. The hallway smelled fragrant, and Aurora looked up to see dozens of peach roses tucked in vases and resting on tabletops, far more flowers than she had gathered for her wedding day.

"Are there always this many flowers?" she asked, unable to silence her curiosity.

"Yes, miss. The Starmaker is very fond of flowers."

She wasn't expecting that, and she said nothing more until they arrived at a set of double doors at the end of the hallway, far away from the foyer. Ina opened both doors, and Aurora stopped at the threshold. The room was vast, with a large four-poster bed made of beautiful white oak, draped in a canopy of marigold silk. Across from the bed was a stone fireplace, and an armoire was already filled with the items from her trunk, plus many new dresses sewn from the finest of fabrics. There was a writing desk in the corner and another set of doors that led out onto a balcony that had been cleared of snow. Every surface was covered in candles and flowers, and Aurora closed her eyes, longing for the comfort of her cozy loft, for hushed conversations with her sister as the fire crackled below.

"Is the room not to your liking?" Ina asked, and Aurora almost laughed at the absurdity of the question.

"Isn't this all a bit much? Does the Starmaker truly believe he is worthy of this kind of extravagance?"

Ina bristled at the question; it was the first time her kind smile had slipped. "The castle was quite modest when it was built, but over the years, the magic in the land has turned it into this. I imagine the Starmaker had a similar reaction to yours when he first arrived. But I assure you that as you settle into this life and begin to see all of the hardship that comes with the magic in your blood, you will start to appreciate having a beautiful home in which to live out what can be a very difficult existence." Ina's words were stern, and she fixed her eyes on Aurora as she spoke. "Right now, you see extravagance, but the life of a Starmaker is one marked by sacrifice."

"I'm sorry. I did not mean to diminish what the Starmaker does for us." Aurora pulled her gaze from Ina's and looked around the room once more. "It is a lovely room. Thank you."

"I will leave you to get settled, and we will do a proper tour once you are rested." Ina paused before leaving. "The Starmaker informed us of your troubles on the journey; there is a hot bath waiting for you, should you need it."

Ina left, closing the doors behind her, and Aurora walked farther into the room. She couldn't deny how good a bath sounded, and she hurried into the washroom and saw a copper tub filled with hot water that spewed tendrils of steam into the air. There was a fragrant oil shimmering on the surface of the water that smelled of lavender, and peach rose petals floated on top. Aurora untied her cloak and slipped out of her wool dress, sighing as she lowered herself into the bath.

She closed her eyes and leaned her head back as Ina's words

swirled around in her mind. A life that was *very difficult, one marked by sacrifice.* It was then that Aurora realized how very little she knew about the Starmaker, and as she let the hot water seep into her skin and warm the places still cold from the journey, she promised herself she would learn as much as she could. It would not help her to make assumptions or avoid looking at the place that was to be her home; if there was truly no escape from the magic in her blood, then Aurora would face it head on.

She wasn't sure how long she stayed in the bath, but it remained steaming hot the entire time, and Aurora marveled at how much magic must be in the land the castle was built on, seeping up through the stone, enchanting the palace the whole way through. She knew the stories, knew that the bodies of the dead and buried Starmakers sustained the land and filled it with magic, but she was still surprised by the many ways in which that magic could manifest.

When Aurora finally pulled herself out of the tub, she dried off and found a long plush robe hanging from a crystal hook on the wall. She wrapped it around herself and poked her head out of the bathroom to ensure that she was still alone. The bedroom was empty, but there was a dress laid out on her bed with a handwritten note sitting on top:

Dinner is at seven p.m. Don't be late.

Aurora read the note multiple times, scowling at the message. Then she tossed it aside and collapsed onto the bed, exhausted from her sleepless night and harrowing journey. She closed her eyes and fell asleep at once.

When she woke, the room was dark. The light outside was gone, and Aurora stretched, her arm sliding across the note. She held it up and read it again, wanting to throw the paper into the fire and stay in her room; if the Starmaker couldn't be polite with his requests, Aurora had no intention of granting them. But her stomach grumbled as she considered what to do, and in the end, hunger won out. She slipped into the dress provided for her, an evening gown of green silk with gathered fabric at the bust and an empire waist with shimmering crystals circling her ribs, and she shook her head as she looked in the mirror. It was by far the fanciest article of clothing she'd ever worn, and it felt like such a waste to squander it on dinner. Still, she admired the way the silk moved with her, and she smoothed her fingers over the skirt that felt more like water than fabric. She ran a comb through her thick brown hair and pulled it back into a braid, and just as she turned away from the mirror, there was a knock.

Aurora took her time answering, breathing deeply as she watched the fire, calming herself before she saw the Starmaker again. When she finally opened the door, it was Ina who waited for her.

"I'll show you to dinner, Miss Finch," Ina said with a smile.

"Please call me Aurora," she said, following Ina down the hall.

"Very well, though soon you will be called Starmaker."

The words made a lump form in Aurora's throat, and her hands began to sweat. Ina had warned her that it would be a difficult life, but all she had seen so far was a luxurious castle with unimaginable comforts and a kind staff. The waiting was terrible, and she wanted to learn about her magic and what made this life such a hard one. Nerves were sprouting in her gut and spreading through her body, and she took several deep breaths as she walked down the staircase and past the foyer into a most impressive dining room.

A large crystal chandelier dangled from the high ceiling, where there was a hyperrealistic mural of pink roses soaring through a sea of stars. A long stone table with gold marbling was in the center of the room, surrounded by sixteen plush chairs upholstered in a rich blue velvet that shone beautifully in the light. It was now dark out, but there were hundreds of candles burning in the room, dripping wax onto various surfaces. And just like the hallway upstairs, the room was filled with fresh flowers.

"You're late," the Starmaker said from where he sat at the head of the table, a scowl on his face.

"My apologies for not having memorized the layout of this enormous palace yet," Aurora said, as she gave him a look to match his own.

"It was my fault, Your Radiance," Ina said.

"Now, that is clearly a lie. You have never been late a day in your life." The Starmaker's tone changed as he spoke to Ina. It was almost amiable, and his mouth pulled up at the corner when he looked at her.

Aurora thought it rather insulting that the Starmaker was seemingly capable of politeness and simply chose to withhold it from her. She shook her head and was about to sit down when she noticed a tuft of white on the chair beside him. She looked closer—it was the rabbit from earlier, propped up comfortably on a pillow with a tiny bowl before it. It was such an absurd image that she almost laughed.

"This is Constance," the Starmaker said, following Aurora's gaze. "She... comes with the castle."

Aurora found the introduction an odd one, but she simply nodded and walked to the opposite end of the table, where a staff member had pulled out a chair for her. Aurora sat down, and the Starmaker said nothing more as the staff brought out bowls of fragrant soup that made her mouth water. She tried not to seem too eager and carefully took a small spoonful, notes of apple and celery hitting her tongue.

"Thank you," she said to the man who had brought her soup, and he nodded but said nothing. Aurora went back to eating, but the loneliness that enveloped her was sharp and intense. Here she was in a room with several people, and yet no one spoke to her. "Excuse me for asking, but is it like this at every meal?"

The Starmaker looked up at her. "Like what?"

"Silent and uninviting."

"I am used to dining alone," the Starmaker said. "And I do not speak when I have nothing to say."

"In that case, I would like to take my dinner in my room." Aurora shoved back from the table, and the staff looked from her to the Starmaker and back again, but she held her head high and did not cower when the Starmaker stood and walked toward her.

THE SUN AND THE STARMAKER

"There will come a day when you will be the only one sitting here, Miss Finch, and you will think of how you'd give anything to look across the table and see another person."

"Then am I to assume that this dinner is for you?"

"No," the Starmaker said. "I am quite content with solitude. This dinner, and all the ones that come after it, are for you." He watched her for a moment longer, then turned on his heel and walked back to his side of the table, where he sat down and took a sip of wine.

Aurora followed the Starmaker back to his seat, ignoring the wide-eyed gaze of the rabbit. "Why don't you give me some helpful information instead of sweeping ambiguities? All I've heard since I arrived here is how difficult life will be for me, yet no one has given me any specific examples of what to expect."

The Starmaker blotted his mouth with his napkin, then slowly stood back up. He was mere inches from Aurora, and she could feel his gaze as it moved over her face, sending heat down her body. His gold eyes reflected the candlelight, and his white hair fell forward as he leaned closer.

"You will stop aging as soon as you come into your magic," he said, "and there will come a time not long from now when every person you've ever known, ever cared for, will be dead. You will spend your days illuminating a village that will know you only by your role, and you will bury your household staff and all your animals many times over as your life stretches out into infinity. You will force yourself to speak solely to remember the sound of your own voice, and one day you will have to reach into the farthest corners of your memory to recall what your name was before it was Starmaker. And finally, when someone else is born with the magic of the Sun, you will pass along all of your knowledge to them, and then you will die alone, only to be buried in the land so that your magic is not wasted." The Starmaker took a breath, his eyes never leaving Aurora's. "There will be no rest for you. Not even in death."

A heavy silence fell between them. Aurora's heart was beating fast, and her eyes had begun to burn as the Starmaker spoke. She wanted to reply, to say something that indicated she could handle what he'd described, but all she could hear were the words *there will be no rest for you.*

"Is that what you wanted, Miss Finch?" the Starmaker finally asked. Aurora could hear the derision in his voice, could feel the staff watching her. Her skin grew hot, and she could no longer keep the stinging in her eyes at bay. Her vision blurred as tears began to fall down her cheeks, and Aurora picked up her skirts and left the room without a word.

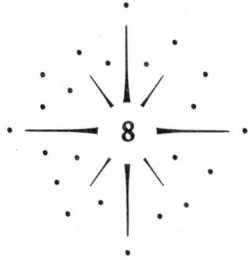

A Classic Instance of Fleeing

When she was sure she was out of view, Aurora ran. She rushed up the stairs and down the hall that led to her room, slamming the door shut behind her. She hoped every single person in the dining room heard it.

Someone had been there during the time she'd been gone; a fire crackled away, and all the candles were lit, casting warm shadows around the room. Aurora paced, walking in circles as her tears continued to fall, until finally even the effort of walking felt like too much, and she dropped to the floor in front of the hearth and watched the flames dance.

The Starmaker had given her exactly what she'd asked for—a straightforward picture of what her life would be like—and while she wanted so badly to feel comfortable with the images he'd offered, they terrified her. His words had awoken a violent need to avoid that unbearable fate at all costs; the very things she loved most about living, she would lose.

How could she live in a world without Mama's strength or Evander's wit? How could she survive without Aspen's gentleness or Elsie's courage? What was the worth of a story if she couldn't share it with the people she loved?

Aurora's chest ached from the pain of it all, from the absolute shock. She had never thought about the Starmaker's life before, ashamed as she was to admit it. She'd known that he was immortal until someone else displayed the Sun's magic, and she'd known he lived in an ice-covered castle and kept watch over all of Reverie, but she'd never considered the loneliness of his existence or how devastating it must be to outlive every person he'd ever cared for.

One day, she would be the one who outlived her family and friends, and she hoped there would be someone somewhere who would give more thought to her life than she had given to the current Starmaker's.

There was a soft knock on her door, and Aurora forced herself to stand. She briefly considered checking her appearance in the bathroom, but she cared little about what anyone in this castle thought of her. By the time she opened the door, though, whoever had come was gone, but they had left behind a tray full of food with a fresh rose resting to the side.

Aurora looked down the hall, but it was empty. She took the tray and sat back down in front of the fire, thankful to whoever had brought it. There was a small note resting beside the rose, written in delicate cursive:

THE SUN AND THE STARMAKER

It will get better.

It was only four words, but Aurora took the note and held it to her chest, closing her eyes and wishing on every star in the sky that it would come true. She didn't know how she would learn to accept the things the Starmaker had told her, or if she even could. His words had merely raised more questions to add to her already substantial list. But if today was the lowest point, if there was hope on the horizon, then Aurora would cling to that with both hands and refuse to let go.

She ate every last bite of food on the tray: decadent sauces covering the best game she'd ever had, bread that was still warm, and cheeses so rich they practically melted on her tongue. If her life was truly to be as bleak as the Starmaker had warned, at least she would eat well.

As she was finishing up the last piece of bread, something else caught her eye beneath the gilded ceramic plate: an envelope with her name on it. Aurora slowly pulled it free, and her heart caught in her throat when she turned it over, recognizing the navy blue wax seal on the back—it had to be from Farren. She couldn't understand how a letter had come for her already, but then she remembered the box in the village square, the entire thing made of ice with a crystal plaque that read TO THE STARMAKER. She had written to the Starmaker once when she was young, with wobbly script and hand-drawn snowflakes. But while she had passed the box many times in recent years, she had never thought to write again. It must have been filled with magic for the letter to have arrived so quickly.

Aurora broke the seal and saw Farren's familiar handwriting scrawled across the page. She ran her fingers over the paper, and her heart throbbed knowing he had done the same thing just hours earlier. At first she didn't read it, content just to hold it, to see the ink on the heavy paper and know that he was thinking of her. Perhaps she was scared to read it because the ache of wanting to go back home was already severe, and she knew his words had the power to worsen it. But in the end, she didn't have the strength to avoid it, and so she took a deep breath and began to read.

My dear Aurora,

I went to your cottage early this morning, hoping there was something I could do or say to change things, but you were already gone. Please forgive me for not fighting harder for you, though I will surely never forgive myself.

I know it is unfair of me after such a failure, but I am begging you not to marry him. I can get you out of this; just give me some time. It is my sole focus now, and I swear to you that I will not rest until you're back home. I implore you not to enter into something you cannot get out of.

I am coming, Aurora. Please wait.

Yours,
Farren

Aurora read the letter many times, her sorrow building with each pass. There was nothing Farren could do, nothing he could say, that would change things. She hated that he was holding on to such regret. But there was also a smaller, surprising emotion that nagged at her: irritation. She had made her choice, and as hard as it was, as impossible as it seemed, the choice was hers to make. Not Farren's.

She shook her head, scolding herself. He loved her, and that was why he was fighting. She couldn't fault him for that.

There was stationery sitting on the desk in the room, waiting to be used, and yet Aurora stayed where she was in front of the fire. There was nothing she could write to make any of this better, and she refused to send a reply strewn with insincerities.

There was a single knock on the door, this one stronger and more jarring than that of whoever had come before, and Aurora jumped. She got to her feet and wiped any remaining tears from her face, then answered. She was surprised to see the Starmaker, his broad shoulders and tall frame practically filling the whole doorway. She took a step back to give herself some space, but he seemed to take it as an invitation to enter, walking into the room in two long strides.

"If you've come to apologize, don't bother," Aurora said.

"I haven't," the Starmaker replied in a cool tone, and an embarrassed flush ran up Aurora's neck and settled in her cheeks.

"Then what are you doing here?"

"I had planned on going over the logistics of our days with you during dinner, which I was obviously unable to do given your premature departure, so I am here to go over them now." The Starmaker turned to her with an unreadable expression. "Do you think you can manage to get through it without fleeing?"

"I didn't *flee*," Aurora said, hoping the flush of her skin wasn't getting worse.

"No? I've lived for quite a while, Miss Finch, and from where I stood, it looked like a classic instance of fleeing." Aurora couldn't be certain, but it looked as if the corner of his mouth twitched just slightly; he was *enjoying* this.

"I assure you I am more than capable of going over a schedule."

"Good. Every day henceforth, you will accompany me to pull the sunlight into Reverie. We will begin our mornings at six o'clock, but you should plan to wake earlier so that you can eat before we depart. You will need your energy."

"Fine," Aurora said. "But before I begin following you around like a sick pup, I want you to prove to me that I have magic."

"Was the sunlight in your veins not proof enough?"

It should have been. Aurora knew that, especially when the Starmaker's touch had induced no such reaction in Elsie. But her homesickness and Farren's letter and her own stubbornness told her that she needed more, and so with an adamant tone she replied, "It was not."

"Very well," the Starmaker said, walking past her to the double doors that led onto the balcony. He opened them in one swift motion, and cold air invaded the room in an instant. He stepped outside and turned to Aurora, who was still standing by the fire. "I don't have all night, Miss Finch," he said, annoyance lacing his tone.

Aurora took her time, exaggerating the slowness of her steps as she made her way to the balcony. When she finally arrived, the Starmaker looked down at her with his mouth set in a hard line. "My amusement knows no bounds," he said, his voice dry.

"It was not for *your* amusement."

The Starmaker sighed and handed her a cloak before walking toward the stone balcony railing, looking out into the endless black night. The stars shone brightly overhead, and the moon was making its way across the sky. It was quiet and lovely, and Aurora wished she could enjoy the view without any thoughts of magic or marriage or immortality. If her life was long enough, perhaps she would someday.

She fastened the cloak around her neck and waited.

"When the Great Quake happened many years ago, it created the northernmost mountains on Earth, with peaks so high the Sun could not rise above them. Miraculously, this small village survived the quake, but as the days and weeks progressed without any light, people and animals began to die. It was during this time that the Frost formed, feeding off the living things the Sun could not protect."

"I believe I have already told you that I'm well-versed in our history," Aurora said.

"And yet you refuse to acknowledge that you are to be the next Starmaker, so I will proceed as if you know nothing." He paused as if waiting for Aurora to argue, but she was exhausted and didn't have it in her to fight. The Starmaker's face settled into an annoyingly satisfied expression, and he continued. "Reverie was the only village on Earth that the Sun was cut off from, and so she made herself human and journeyed to the mountain to inspect it for herself. All of our magic—mine and yours and that of every Starmaker who came before us—was born from the Sun falling in love with a human when she made that journey. She will speak to you when you have fully come into your magic; until then, you will speak to her and greet her as if she were your beloved."

Aurora took a step back and couldn't help the scoff that escaped her lips. "She picked the wrong person if that is what she desires. How am I to adore the thing that took my life from me?"

"You will not have a choice," the Starmaker said, turning to her. "As you feel her light in your veins, pumping through your body, the contempt you feel for her will fade. It is a complicated love, but love it is."

"I was taught to love the things that are good for me," Aurora said.

The Starmaker looked at her. "If that is the only love you have ever experienced, then I am sorry for you." His gaze hovered near her mouth as he spoke, and Aurora immediately felt defensive. How dare he make light of her love, of what she had given up to come here? But before she could protest, the Starmaker began to speak once more.

"Tonight you are taking the first step toward becoming the next Starmaker." He turned his eyes to the moon, and in a hushed voice that Aurora couldn't make out, the Starmaker began to speak to someone other than her. She realized in a rush that he was speaking to the Sun, and it killed her, the way his voice changed from stern to gentle, his impatience giving way to reverence. The Starmaker kept talking as he began rolling up his sleeves, the motion causing the muscles in his forearms to tense. When he had exposed his arms to the elbows, he whispered a final sentence, and all the blood coursing beneath his skin turned to gold.

Aurora stared, fighting against every impulse to reach out and touch his skin, to feel the heat of it. She blinked and looked away, assuring herself it was the magic, nothing more, that she wanted to touch.

The magic, she told herself again, more sternly.

"Do you agree that only the blood of a Starmaker could look like this on its own, without the touch of another?"

"Yes," Aurora said, breathless.

"Good. Then it is your turn. Introduce yourself to the Sun in any words you like." The Starmaker took several steps away from Aurora and placed his hands in his pockets.

Aurora almost laughed, it sounded so absurd, but the Starmaker was not laughing. And since she had been the one to insist on this, she would at least follow his instructions. She kept her voice low as she said her name, feeling awkward and unsure of what to say next, but she finally decided the truth was best.

"I do not wish to be here, nor do I wish to be the next Starmaker. If that is my fate, show me at once so that I may learn to accept it. If not, I would be very pleased to go home." Aurora said nothing more, watching the moon, waiting for something, anything, to happen.

And then it did.

All at once, a heat ran through her body, so intense that Aurora gasped. Shaking, she slipped her arms from her cloak and was met with the same glow she had seen in the Starmaker. She looked over at him, but he was too far away to have touched her, and she turned back to the moon with wide eyes and a racing heart.

"It isn't possible," she whispered, holding her arms out in front of her, watching the gold race beneath her skin.

"We've been over this," the Starmaker said, exhaling. "Are you satisfied?"

Aurora said nothing, pulling her cloak around her and walking into the bedroom without another word. The Starmaker followed, shutting the door behind him. "If that is all, then I will see you in the morning for breakfast."

"Fine," she said, turning away. A stinging sensation began in her upper arm, and she rubbed the area with her hand, trying to ease the burning.

"What is it?" he asked, staying where he was instead of leaving the room like she wanted.

"Nothing, my arm just stings a little."

The Starmaker walked toward the large gilded mirror leaning against the wall. "Come," he said.

"Why?"

He sighed. "Must you make everything more difficult than it ought to be?"

"No," Aurora said, walking over to meet him, "but it is a trait you seem to bring out in me."

THE SUN AND THE STARMAKER

"How fortunate I am." The Starmaker stood behind her and raised his arms to her shoulders. "May I?"

Aurora met his eyes in the mirror and nodded. Slowly, the Starmaker pulled the velvet cloak off her shoulders and turned her so that her right side was facing the glass. He tugged the sleeve of her dress down slightly, his fingertips just barely touching her skin. He studied her arm for a moment, then ran his thumb under what appeared to be a faint gold line. Aurora shivered and hated herself for it.

"There," he said.

"What is it?" Aurora asked, leaning closer to the mirror to get a better look.

The Starmaker unbuttoned the top of his shirt and slipped his right arm out of the fabric. Aurora tried to ignore the way his muscles tensed with the motion, tried to avert her eyes, but she couldn't seem to look away. The rest of him was as beautiful as his face, a cruelty that Aurora resented deeply. He then put his right arm next to hers so their reflections were side by side in the mirror. "It is the beginning of the Sun's mark; once you have fully come into your magic, it will look like mine."

Aurora stared at the Starmaker's skin, adorned with an intricate pattern of the Sun, rays coming out in lines that ran down his arm. It glowed the same as his veins, the same as hers.

"I do not wish to be branded by the Sun."

The Starmaker took a step back, slipping his arm into his shirt and buttoning it back up. "I would think you'd have realized by now that your wishes don't matter."

He left the room without another word, Aurora still studying her arm in the mirror. She wasn't sure how long she stood there, but then she remembered Farren's letter, discarded on the floor in front of the fire. She ran to get it, then sat down at her desk and frantically wrote a reply. Just two words, but she hoped with everything in her that he would heed them.

Don't come.

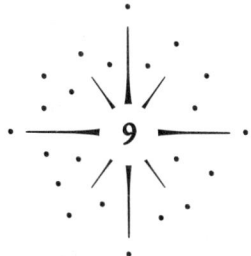

A Very Peculiar Door

Between the nap she'd taken earlier and the events of the day, Aurora was restless. She tossed and turned in her massive bed, throwing the covers off only to pull them back up, until finally she decided her time would be better spent elsewhere.

She slipped out of bed and pulled on her robe, though the room was perfectly comfortable. The fire was somehow still going, and she realized it must be due to magic, like so many of the oddities in the castle.

Aurora lit the candles on her desk and sat in the chair, eager to write to her family. It hadn't yet been a full day since she had left home, but she knew they would worry, and she wanted to put them at ease as soon as possible.

The writing desk was stocked with beautiful stationery,

thick paper with a slight sheen to it, THE STARMAKER RISING embossed in gold cursive at the top. She hadn't paid attention to the design when she'd written to Farren earlier, but now that she looked at it, it truly was lovely.

She pulled a pot of ink from the small drawer, along with a pen, and began to write.

Dear Mama, Elsie, and Aspen,

I made it to the castle, and it is every bit as magical and enchanted as you'd think. Perhaps even more so. It doesn't compare to our cottage, of course, but I will adjust somehow.

I'm writing to you now on my first night, unable to sleep, though please don't worry about me—I am being taken care of. I'm warm and well-fed, and the woman who manages the castle, Ina, is kind. I hope in time to call her my friend.

Once I am settled, I will ask the Starmaker about having you here for a visit. I would very much like to see you. Please pass my love to Evander and Samuel, and know that I am thinking of you all every minute of the day.

I love you. Please write when you can!

Aurora

Aurora looked over the words she had written. The letter read more hopeful than she felt, but she couldn't tell them about her conversation with the Starmaker over dinner or the way he lived such an isolated life that the years ahead frightened her. Perhaps one day, in person, she would be able to talk about it, but for now, she just wanted her family to know she was okay. Her letter would accomplish that, even if it was not entirely forthright.

She carefully folded the paper, placed it in an envelope, and took a beautiful gold wax from the drawer, melting it onto the back and stamping to seal the flap. She was sure Ina could send the letter for her in the morning, but Aurora was wide awake with several hours before breakfast, and so she decided she would try to find the mailbox herself. She needed to learn the layout of the castle anyway. She might as well do it in the middle of the night, when she wouldn't disturb anyone.

Aurora tied her robe snugly around her waist and found a pair of slippers in the armoire. She tucked the letter in her pocket along with the one she'd written to Farren, lit a candle, and closed the door behind her as quietly as possible. When she turned, she almost yelped.

Constance was sitting just outside her room, propped up on her hind legs, looking directly at Aurora. She didn't blink, her big blue eyes following Aurora's movements with a tired curiosity, as if Aurora wasn't being nearly interesting enough for her. She yawned. While Aurora was almost certain the animal was bored with her, she welcomed the company.

"Hi, Constance," she said in a whisper, kneeling on the ground. "I'm Aurora. I apologize that the Starmaker didn't properly introduce us earlier—he's rather grouchy, is he not?"

At that, Constance quirked her head to the side, and Aurora

held out her hand. The rabbit stretched forward, sniffing, then accepted one quick pet from Aurora before hopping back.

"I'd like to mail two letters," Aurora said, feeling slightly ridiculous for engaging in casual conversation with a rabbit, but the Starmaker wasn't one for chatting, and Aurora was lonely.

Lonely already, she thought, her chest tightening. She could feel a new wave of panic coming, the Starmaker's words from earlier roaring to life in her mind, but she forced them back down and took several deep breaths. One minute at a time. One hour. One day. That was all she could do.

"Okay, let's go," she said to Constance, standing up and walking down the hall. She stepped softly, expecting the floor to creak and groan like the ladder in her cottage, but it was quiet. She supposed that marble didn't settle the way wood did, but she'd never walked on a marble floor, so she hadn't known.

The flowers left a sweet smell in the air, and Aurora found herself more at ease now than she had been since she'd arrived at the castle. It was dark save for the candlelight, reminding her of home, and she was alone. She didn't have to react to anybody or mask her feelings; she could just be.

She took the stairs carefully, letting her hand slide along the smooth gold railing. And just as the castle seemed built to welcome the Sun, it reacted to the small flame of her candle in the same way, bouncing the soft light off nearby surfaces, reflecting it in every direction. Aurora looked around in awe, watching the deep orange light chase away even the darkest shadows. It was still dim enough that Aurora had to watch her steps and move carefully, but she no longer worried she'd crash into something and wake the whole castle.

Constance followed close behind her, and Aurora walked down the hallway and past the dining room in search of the kitchen. She would never feel at home here if she didn't know where the food was kept, and she pushed open a large wooden door to her right, knowing she had found it. She could smell bread and onions and the earthy aroma of freshly harvested vegetables before her candle even lit the room.

Sitting in the far corner was a mail chute made entirely of ice, just like the one in the village center, and Aurora suspected her letters would arrive at their respective destinations mere seconds after she sent them. She pulled the envelopes from her robe and dropped them in the box, listening for the soft thud of a landing, but there was only silence.

Aurora took her time in the kitchen, finding an apple and eating it down to the core before she felt ready to wander. She explored the entire first floor of the castle, filled with gorgeous drawing rooms and romantic artwork that hung from every wall and, of course, endless fresh flowers. She counted seven fireplaces, and there was a library that made her heart soar, the most stories she had ever seen in one place. It took her breath away.

It reminded her of the opportunity she'd lost at *Eternal Reverie*, and anger rose up inside her. She had never understood why her invitation to write had depended upon her marriage to Farren; if Mr. Glenn had let her contribute beforehand, perhaps he would have seen her talent and let her write for his paper regardless of her relationship to his son. But as it was, she'd never gotten the chance to prove herself, and she felt the loss acutely, deep in her chest.

Aurora continued on, stopping when she passed a large portrait hanging in the hallway. The small gold plaque beneath simply read THE FIRST STARMAKER, and the image showed him sitting outside on a throne of glass, surrounded by fresh snowfall. The artwork was like something from a dream, with soft lines and washed-out edges, the blues and whites almost hazy. The Starmaker's expression was soft—sorrowful, in a way—and the gold of his eyes shone bright against his warm brown skin. His hair was short but the same shimmering white as the current Starmaker's, and a rabbit that looked remarkably similar to Constance sat in his lap with a stoic expression.

Then, suddenly, it began to snow inside the painting.

Aurora blinked, sure she was seeing things, but hundreds of tiny snowflakes continued to fall from the top of the portrait. Snow accumulated on the Starmaker's head and shoulders, on the throne and the rabbit, and then a man appeared in the background, moving closer and closer until he reached the Starmaker and gently brushed the snow away. He shoveled the pathways around the Starmaker's throne, and when he was done, he receded into the distance until he vanished completely. The snow was no longer falling.

Admittedly, Aurora had not seen many portraits in her life, but she was sure she had never seen one like this.

She turned and reached the end of the first floor, where large glass doors let out onto a stone patio with a vast garden beyond. Aurora could have sworn she saw something moving in the distance, something white and glistening, but it was too dark to make out, and she decided to explore the grounds in daylight as soon as her schedule allowed. *If* her schedule allowed. She didn't know what her days would look like after pulling in the Sun.

When she finally felt ready for sleep, Aurora took a back staircase up to the second floor and wound through the maze of hallways, trying to find her room. She stopped when she passed by a very peculiar door.

It was just an ordinary door, a plain piece of worn wood with a tarnished brass knob, but that was precisely why it was odd. It was so normal. Too normal, given the rest of the castle. Aurora knew she shouldn't snoop, and even Constance had casually hopped past the door, but Aurora's curiosity got the best of her, and with a racing heart, she twisted the knob.

It was hard to open, not because it was locked—it wasn't— but because it was almost as if the door had grown into its frame, swollen shut after years of disuse. Aurora set down her candle and lodged her shoulder against the door, pushing her full weight into it. After several attempts, it finally opened, and Aurora stumbled into the room, nearly falling to the ground face-first. She took a deep breath and righted herself, then picked up her candle from the floor, illuminating the space.

She wasn't sure what she'd been expecting, but it certainly wasn't what she saw before her. It was a small unremarkable bedroom, more appropriately sized for Aurora's cottage than the castle. There was a narrow mattress on a plain wooden frame, a small desk, one bookcase, a cramped wardrobe, and one bedside table with a candlestick on top. Every horizontal surface was filled with plants, somehow still alive even though the rest of the room was covered in a thick layer of dust. Vibrant blooms of oranges and reds and violets provided the only color in the space, everything else dulled by age and grime. Aurora sneezed, and even Constance was aggressively twitching her nose from the doorway.

It didn't fit with the wonder and enchantment of the rest of the castle, but Aurora knew it was meaningful in some way. She just didn't know how.

She walked to the bookcase and ran her fingers over the spines, not caring that she was collecting dust on her skin and clothes. Rows of books on horticulture and astronomy lined the shelves, interspersed with the occasional collection of poetry. The faintest glint caught Aurora's eye, and she followed it to the very bottom shelf, where a picture frame had been turned upside down.

With unsteady hands, she reached for the frame, turning it over. She used her sleeve to clean the glass, careful not to cut herself on the large cracks that ran through it. The picture was of a family: a man, a woman, and two children. Aurora brought the frame closer to her face and realized with a start that the boy in the picture was the Starmaker. He had his arms wrapped around a girl Aurora assumed was his sister, similar large grins on both their faces. His hair wasn't silver but a dark, rich brown, and though it was hard to discern the color of his eyes, they certainly weren't gold.

THE SUN AND THE STARMAKER

It was the Starmaker when he had been mortal, and Aurora slowly scanned the room once more, realizing this must have been his bedroom as a boy, painstakingly moved to the castle from the house he'd been raised in. Tears burned in Aurora's eyes as she imagined the Starmaker sleeping in this small room tucked into this vast castle, unable to let go of the life he'd had.

She gently set the frame back where she'd found it and walked to the desk. There was a leather-bound journal resting on top, and after a moment's hesitation, Aurora opened the soft cover. It simply read THE FOURTH STARMAKER in elegant script, no other name, and the first entry began on the following page. A loose picture of a beautiful girl was tucked into the crease; she looked to be around Aurora's age, with a small smile and long blond hair. Aurora quickly shut the journal, knowing it was a complete violation to be looking at it, though her mind was flaming with curiosity. She turned back to Constance, who was watching her disapprovingly, and Aurora slowly stepped away from the desk.

"I didn't read anything," she said to the rabbit, though she wasn't sure if Constance believed her.

"He never lets us clean it." Aurora jumped at the voice, and Ina appeared in the doorway. "No one is allowed in here."

Aurora hurried out of the room, her cheeks burning. "I'm sorry. I was trying to find my way back to my room," she said, unable to meet Ina's eyes.

Ina tugged the door closed, and Aurora noticed the way she averted her gaze from the room. She fully respected the

Starmaker's request, and Aurora wished she had walked past the door without giving it a second glance.

"I'm not going to tell the Starmaker you were here because I don't think he would handle it well, knowing someone had been in this room," Ina said. "But I'd ask that you respect his privacy. He deserves it, as do you, and the rest of us."

"Of course," Aurora said, unable to imagine how she could feel any worse in that moment. "I truly am sorry."

Ina reached out and gently touched her hand. "I'm sure this day has been extremely difficult for you. Don't be too hard on yourself."

Ina showed Aurora back to her room, and as soon as she was alone, tears began streaming down her face as she pictured an immortal sorcerer in a tiny bed, trying desperately to sleep.

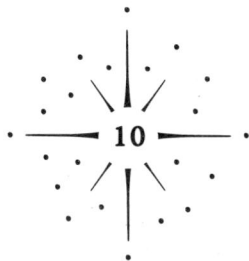

An Amusing Plight

When Aurora woke the next morning, having slept only a few hours, she was still full of regret. She should never have gone into the room, not only because it was such a clear violation of the Starmaker's wishes but also because the image of it had branded itself on her mind and she couldn't undo it. Something about it made a deep mourning stir inside her, an unexpected vision of loneliness and despair. She knew she should care more about having snooped in the first place, but she was most regretful of the torment that room would undoubtedly cause her any time she thought of it.

Aurora sat up in bed, bracing for the chill that usually settled in overnight, but there was no need. Her room was still warm, and there was a healthy fire crackling away in the hearth. She didn't relish the thought of someone coming into her room overnight to tend to the fire, but almost as soon as she thought it, she remembered it was magic that was sustaining the flames.

Other than the light from the fire, the room was dark and quiet. Aurora could not look over to the other side of the bed and see her sister, but it was a comfort knowing that Elsie had been healed. She would of course insist upon seeing Elsie soon, but for now, she was content knowing her sister was healthy and safe. And she hoped that with each new day, she would find other things to be content with. Aurora pulled the quilt they had sewn together all the way up to her chin, inhaling deeply.

There was a knock at the door, and Ina entered a moment later. Aurora's face flushed as she remembered their interaction just hours ago, and she wanted to apologize all over again, but before she could speak, Ina gave a slight nod of understanding. "Good morning," she said, lighting some candles and going over to the wardrobe. "Today is a fresh start, is it not?" Her eyes were kind and her smile gentle, and they eased some of Aurora's guilt.

"It is," Aurora said. "Thank you."

Ina turned to look at Aurora with total sincerity in her eyes. "There is nothing to thank me for, miss."

"Then might I ask you a favor instead?"

"Of course."

Aurora slipped out of bed. "I'm homesick and begging you to use my name."

Ina offered Aurora a sympathetic smile. "My apologies, Aurora."

THE SUN AND THE STARMAKER

"Thank you." Aurora walked to where Ina stood and pulled a thick wool dress from the wardrobe. It was a beautiful shade of blue, light and crisp just like the glacial lakes beyond Reverie, and Aurora let her fingers run over the fabric. Ina pulled out heavy stockings and a petticoat as well as boots lined in fur.

"These ought to keep you warm enough, but once you get comfortable with your magic, you won't need such heavy dresses. The sunlight in your blood will keep you warm."

"How long have you been here?" Aurora asked as she dressed, first pulling on the stockings, then the petticoat. She had previously believed that a fabric could not be both warm and soft, but it seemed she had been wrong.

"My whole life," Ina said. "My mother cared for the castle, as did my grandparents and their parents. One day, if I am blessed with children, I hope they will stay here, too."

"Where is your mother now?"

"She is back in the village with my father. He wanted to spend his remaining years in the house he grew up in, and my mother wanted to spend hers with him." Ina smiled to herself.

"Is it hard? Getting older while the Starmaker stays the same?"

"It is what I've always known," Ina said, grabbing the ties of Aurora's underskirts and pulling them tight. "The hardest thing will be watching the Starmaker die; I had hoped it wouldn't happen during my lifetime." Ina spoke the words as if she was talking to herself, then seemed to remember that Aurora was standing right in front of her. "Forgive me, I did not mean to imply that I'm dispirited by your arrival."

"That would make two of us if you are," Aurora said, turning to smile at Ina. "And I could sure use the company."

Ina laughed softly. "Thank you."

"Hopefully you will not have to say goodbye to him for many years," Aurora said, noticing the way Ina's gaze fell after she spoke the words.

"I hope not."

Aurora assumed it would be rather simple, that the Starmaker would begin to age as his magic diminished, dying many years later as an old man. She didn't relish the idea of marrying someone who would age while she stayed the same, but given that their union was solely for the benefit of a glare line, she figured she would hardly think of herself as married at all.

Ina held up the wool dress, and Aurora raised her arms above her head, wriggling into it. She was amazed at how well it fit her, the sleeves stopping at just the right point on her wrists, the bodice snug but not tight. "How is it that all of this clothing fits me without anyone ever taking my measurements?"

"The Sun herself chose you," Ina said, walking back to the wardrobe and pulling out the most beautiful cloak Aurora had ever beheld. It was velvet the color of Mama's baking sugar with soft white fur lining the hems, and the entire thing was embroidered with stars in silver thread. "As you will soon learn, this castle holds more magic than any of us can comprehend. When the Starmaker told us he'd found you, we came to this room to set it up and found the wardrobe already full."

"I see," was all Aurora could say. She did not like feeling as if her life was not her own, as if her fate had been determined by someone other than herself. How could she possibly love the Sun if she was given no choice in the matter?

When Aurora was done dressing, Ina led her down to the dining room, where the Starmaker was seated. Constance was in the chair beside his, and she looked at Aurora with lingering judgment. The Starmaker did not look at her at all. Aurora sat down at the opposite end of the table, shoving aside the morning paper, not wanting to see the column in *Eternal Reverie* that should have been hers.

"You know, it's customary to greet your guest when they enter a room," Aurora said as a member of the staff set a hot bowl of porridge before her, topped with ripe berries far larger than any she'd ever had at home.

"You are not my guest," the Starmaker said, taking a sip of tea before finally looking up at her. "You live here now, and there are things you'll learn as a resident of this house, the first being that I do not particularly enjoy mornings."

Aurora almost laughed. "But you wake at five every day."

"Yes," the Starmaker said. "A truly tragic consequence of my role." He looked back down at his meal, and Aurora did the same, though the exchange had eased some of the tension she'd been carrying. Everything about the Starmaker was resplendent, but the fact that he didn't like waking early was mundane, a trait befitting a man and not an immortal.

Aurora set her spoon down harder than she meant to. "I apologize, but have you really failed to get used to your routine in the hundreds of years you've been doing it?"

The Starmaker slowly looked up. He gave a sideways glance to his staff and shook his head, sighing.

"I have," he said.

Aurora couldn't help herself—she laughed long and loud, throwing her head back and closing her eyes. It was perhaps the best thing she'd heard since she'd arrived at the palace. She didn't care that no one laughed with her, that the staff looked at her in horror, or that the Starmaker's scowl grew deeper the longer she went on.

"For clarity's sake," she said, trying to compose herself, "you—the Starmaker, the person responsible for bringing daylight to Reverie—are saying you're not a *morning person*?" Another wave of laughter rolled through her, and she caught one of the staff members struggling to keep a straight face.

"I'm glad my plight amuses you so," the Starmaker said, his tone flat and dry and wholly devoid of amusement.

"Oh, I'm delighted by it," Aurora replied, picking up her spoon once more and digging into her breakfast. The Starmaker had felt so untouchable before, almost as if he were a god and she was just a girl lost in his presence. But in that moment, he was simply an exhausted man who wanted to sleep in and cared little for jokes at his expense. It made him real.

Aurora looked down at her porridge. She could feel the staff's eyes on her, but she didn't care. It was the first time she'd laughed since leaving her family, and it made her feel like herself again.

After several minutes, Ina appeared. "Your sleigh is ready, Your Radiance."

THE SUN AND THE STARMAKER

"Thank you, Ina." The Starmaker gave Constance several pets, then stood, turning toward Aurora. "It is time to go."

"But I'm not done with my breakfast," Aurora said, making no motion to stand.

"Perhaps you should have considered that before succumbing to your maniacal laughter."

Aurora took one more bite, blotted her mouth, and pushed back from the table, walking to where the Starmaker stood. "It was worth it."

"I am so tired," was all he said, more to himself than to Aurora, as he walked out of the dining room, through the foyer, and into the dark morning.

Aurora followed behind him, slipping on her gloves and pulling the hood of her cloak over her head to fight the cold. She wasn't paying attention and almost walked directly into the back of the Starmaker, who had stopped to look up. Aurora followed his gaze to the stars, inhaling deeply as she took in the absolute brilliance of a world beyond their reach.

"My cottage is the only house in Reverie that isn't touched by sunlight," Aurora said. She felt the Starmaker turn to look at her, but she kept her eyes on the sky. "It has never bothered me, the darkness. The cold. If it weren't for the threat of the Frost, I would have been more than content to live beyond the reaches of the light for the duration of my life."

"I too am fond of the darkness," he said, surprising her. "It is the only time I have for myself."

Aurora finally pulled her eyes from the stars and looked

at him. "Then I suppose it makes sense that you don't care for mornings."

The Starmaker didn't reply and instead walked to the snow deer and greeted them by running a hand down their noses, then he got into the sleigh. The deer Aurora had almost shot looked over at her, waiting, and she guiltily made her way to him, petting his head in penance.

"What is his name?" she asked, climbing into the sleigh.

"He doesn't have one," the Starmaker said as the deer took off, the sleigh gliding through a fresh dusting of snow.

"Why not?"

"Because a name is intimate, and it only makes things harder when they die."

Aurora found his words overwhelmingly sad, and she decided then and there that she would give the deer names, even if she was the only one who used them. Then she remembered the rabbit. "Constance has a name."

"Constance will never die," the Starmaker said, and while his tone suggested that he held no affection for the creature, Aurora had seen the way he had petted her at breakfast. "She was given to the first Starmaker by the Sun and will outlive us all, a fate she does not seem to mind."

So the rabbit Aurora had seen in the portrait *was* Constance. She thought of the way the animal's fur glinted in the light, almost otherworldly, and she smiled to herself. An immortal rabbit, the one breathing thing she would not outlive. It gave her incredible comfort, and Aurora vowed to earn Constance's affection after last night's mishap.

THE SUN AND THE STARMAKER

The Starmaker said nothing more, and Aurora pulled the blanket over her lap, twisting her hands in it as the deer pulled them down the path that led to the village. She closed her eyes and gripped the blanket tighter as they passed the area where the Frost had struck her the previous day, but she remained unharmed as they rushed through the trees and down the mountainside.

By the time the deer slowed to a walk, Aurora's face was so cold it felt as if it was coated in ice. "You will get used to the ride," the Starmaker said.

The deer stuck to a trail through the trees that bordered the village, and Aurora craned her neck to catch a glimpse of anything familiar. There were soft lights flickering in the distance, but that was all she could make out of Reverie, and she hoped that her family was tucked safely inside, sleeping soundly.

Once there were no longer lights in the distance, the deer wove out of the trees and onto a plateau just south of the village. Aurora knew this as the end of their world—the plateau gave way to a vast glacier that crept up to the edge of a stark drop-off. The peak on the other side was far enough away to create a deadly gap; there was no way down and no way up, and even though her village should have been lost to the hostile environment long ago, the Sun had come in and decided otherwise. It was the first gleam of gratitude Aurora had felt for the Sun since learning of her fate, and instead of rebelling against it, she let herself feel it.

The deer slowed to a stop at the edge of the glacier, and the Starmaker stepped out of the sleigh and wordlessly began walking. Aurora assumed she was meant to follow, so she stepped onto the ice and trudged after him. It was silent except for the crunch of the snowy landscape beneath their boots and the sound of the deer behind them, but the huffs of the animals soon faded into the quiet.

After a while, a large gold lamppost came into view, and at first Aurora thought she was seeing things. She blinked, but the lamppost stayed put, standing alone in the icy field, beautiful and magical and wholly unexpected. The Starmaker stopped and turned to Aurora, looking impatient as he waited for her to catch up.

"This will be similar to what we did last night, but it is much more intense," he said. "I won't lie to you: it is quite painful until you acclimate to the Sun's heat, but you will get used to it in time."

"It seems I will need to get used to many things," Aurora said dryly.

"As will I," the Starmaker mumbled, and Aurora almost asked what he meant, then realized he was referring to her.

She glared at him. "A little compassion wouldn't kill you," Aurora said. "You gave up a life once, too, or have you forgotten?"

The Starmaker turned to her. "I have not forgotten." It was all he said, and it enraged Aurora that he seemed entirely uninterested in making things easier for her. He had his childhood bedroom tucked away in the castle, and yet he acted as if Aurora should have no misgivings about her new circumstances.

"Perhaps your life wasn't worth mourning, but mine was. It wasn't perfect, but it was full and good, and it will take me time to let go of it."

"You know nothing of the life I gave up," the Starmaker said, his tone so severe that it sent a chill down Aurora's spine. She remembered the family photo, the way he had hugged his sister, the journal with the picture of the girl tucked inside. And while Aurora had been overwhelmed with empathy for him last night, she couldn't seem to find it again here now that he was being so cold.

"And I suppose you will say nothing of it, offering me no comfort or understanding."

"It is not my job to comfort you, Miss Finch. It is my job to teach you everything I know of this magic while I am still able. This entire mountain will soon be in your care, and the life you led before I met you is of little concern to me." He looked down at her as he spoke, his breath forming white clouds that drifted past her in the frigid morning.

"How can you claim to love this mountain when you care so little for the people who live here?"

"I care deeply, which is why I'm trying to help you move on. Do you truly think it would be better if I brought tea to your room so we could sit near the fire and you could tell me of your engagement to a boy you may never see again? Perhaps we could braid each other's hair as you regale me with stories of your childhood." He shook his head and pointed up the valley, toward the gentle lights glowing in the distance. "You are a Starmaker, Miss Finch, and it is time you act like one."

"If being a Starmaker entails being callous and cruel, then I am no Starmaker."

"It entails being present, but you are stubbornly stuck in the past."

"I arrived at the palace *yesterday*! That hardly qualifies as the past." Aurora was so frustrated by the Starmaker that she had to move, and though he had yet to draw the light over Reverie, she was heating up as if she'd been standing in the sun for hours.

"You have the fire of the Sun in your blood, and a clock began ticking the moment you touched me—you *must* use your magic. We can stand here and dwell on things over which we have no control, or we can forestall your death by calling the light." The Starmaker exhaled loudly and shoved his hand through his hair, and even in the darkness, it shimmered as if it were laced with starlight. "I suggest you choose the latter."

Aurora stopped moving and watched him, her heart beating wildly. She wanted to keep arguing, to yell at him until her voice went hoarse, but he had said *we*, and though perhaps she was being naive or wishful, she chose to believe that was his way of showing her compassion. And so she took it because she needed to.

"Everything is so dire with you," Aurora finally said. "But in case you are right and I'm on my way to certain death, I suppose we should begin."

The space between them was charged, and Aurora could sense their frustrations with each other colliding in the air, fighting like animals. She was sure they would still be there after her lesson, but for now she would concentrate on learning everything she needed to know about the journey that lay ahead of her. The Starmaker seemed to recognize the temporary reprieve, and he nodded, turning toward the village.

THE SUN AND THE STARMAKER

"Remember that your magic is the result of the relationship between you and the Sun. It's personal; there are no set recitations or spells. The Sun has deemed you worthy of conversing with her, so come to her with whatever suits you. We are the only way she can reach Reverie—it is the magic in our blood that creates an invisible tether between us, and that is the only thing sustaining our village." The Starmaker closed his eyes. "It is a heavy truth to carry, but it is alleviated by a lighter, more brilliant one: she wants us to survive."

When Aurora was a child, she had pictured the Sun as a princess in the sky, wearing a gold dress made of silk with a train of sunlight that illuminated the world. It all sounded so enchanting, and Aurora had marveled at the love the Sun must have felt for the original Starmaker, so fierce that she gave him magic to protect his home even though they could not be together.

It wasn't until Aurora was older that she had realized what a burden that kind of love must be, and it had made her feel traitorous when she wondered if the Sun thought her love for the Starmaker was worth enduring an eternity of separation and grief. Then Papa had died, and Aurora hadn't been able to bring herself to ask Mama the question that had haunted her: *Was it worth it?*

Aurora was glad she would never have to carry a burden like that, and she was even more thankful that the Sun had chosen to do so.

Even now, with everything that had happened, Aurora still cherished the stories. She was devoted to this mountain and captivated by the way it was sustained by magic that arose from an unimaginable love. The Starmaker's words rushed back to her then, and she felt her cheeks flush in the bitter cold.

If that is the only love you have ever experienced, then I am sorry for you.

The Starmaker began speaking, relieving Aurora of the thought, uttering words that she could not understand and wasn't sure she wanted to.

"Give me your hand," the Starmaker said in a low voice that held little of the sternness she had come to expect. At first Aurora didn't move, keeping her hands in her cloak, not wanting to touch him. He exhaled hard before turning to face her. "You and I need to be joined while you learn; you were able to call to the Sun on your own last night because the moon diminishes the power of the light, but now there is no moon acting as intermediary. There is a direct line between you and the Sun, and at the beginning I will need to pull the majority of the heat away from you. Otherwise you will be overwhelmed by it."

Aurora hesitated. She wasn't sure if she was more afraid of the pain or of officially beginning her role, and it felt almost impossible to give her hand to the Starmaker. She looked up the valley toward the lights and wondered if one of them belonged to Farren's house. Her cottage was too far away to see from here, but she pictured her family, cozy and warm, and missed them so much that it nearly took her breath away. It was that image—the one of her family—that gave her the strength she needed to move. She would do this for them.

Slowly, Aurora removed her hand from her cloak, and though it shook, she gave it to the Starmaker.

THE SUN AND THE STARMAKER

As soon as her hand brushed his, he gripped it tightly. "You will want to pull away from me when you first feel the heat," the Starmaker said. "Don't."

Aurora's heart slammed against her ribs, and she tried to still her body, but the shaking only got worse. She looked up at the mountain, past the village and toward the sharp, jagged peaks that blocked Reverie from the Sun. Everything was dark. Still. Quiet. Then, all at once, sunlight cut through the peaks and began rolling toward them. Aurora had never seen anything like it, and her eyes filled with tears at the sheer beauty of it. She watched with wonder as light slid over the village and moved across the valley where they stood. It was an avalanche of blazing yellow, magnificent to behold, and for one beat of her heart, she stopped shaking and just enjoyed the show.

Then the Sun reached her.

Heat shot through her body in an unbearable surge, searing agony that forced a scream from her lips as she squeezed her eyes shut against the pain. She tried to run, to pull her hand free of the Starmaker's grasp and get out of the light, but the harder she pulled, the tighter the Starmaker held on. The mountain was glistening, coming to life in the sunshine, but Aurora's vision blurred, and she could see nothing. She bit down on her cheek hard and tasted blood, and the fire inside her continued to rage.

She sank to her knees to get closer to the snow, and mercifully, the Starmaker knelt with her. She lay down on the ground on her stomach and buried her face in the cold, and still the Starmaker kept her hand firmly in his, even as she writhed on the earth. Then, finally, she stopped trying to pull away. The snow was the only thing keeping Aurora conscious, and she moved her free arm out of her cloak so her bare skin could touch it, and with that, her breathing began to slow.

It was only then that Aurora realized the Starmaker was rubbing her back, a soft circular motion like her mother used to make when she'd put her down for naps as a young girl. She didn't dare move or speak, scared that if the motion stopped, the pain would burn her alive, leaving nothing more than a husk on Reverie's glacier.

Aurora wasn't sure how long they stayed that way, but by the time she sat up, the pain had subsided and she felt as if she could breathe again. The Starmaker was quick to remove his palm from her back, then he slowly let go of her entirely. Her hand felt so cold without him holding it, and she moved it beneath her cloak.

The Starmaker stood, and Aurora watched as he walked toward the gold lamppost and stepped up onto the small platform at the base of it. The edge of the light was clutched firmly in his hand, and he hung it from a small hook in the lantern, securing its place over Reverie, stretching it out like a sheer piece of glimmering fabric between the Sun and the lamppost.

"The worst is over," he said as he made his way back to her. He did not help Aurora to her feet, and she wondered if she had imagined his hand on her back, if she'd been so delirious from the pain that she'd made the whole thing up as a way to cope. "Now that the sunlight covers Reverie, our biggest job is done for the day. We are also responsible for tending to any magic that has gone awry, and several times a week we will patrol the woods to ensure that the Frost isn't encroaching on the village."

Aurora stared at him, barely hearing the words he spoke. "I have never experienced pain like that before, and you expect me to move on as if nothing has happened?"

"I told you, the worst is over."

"If you think I will continue to come out here with you each and every day, you are quite mistaken."

The Starmaker turned to her, his golden eyes more vibrant in the daylight. "You will continue to do so, because you will die if you don't."

Aurora didn't want to believe him. She wanted to dismiss it as a scare tactic, a way to ensure that she stepped into her role as peacefully as possible, but after what she'd just felt, she knew he was right. This magic could kill her.

"A rather odd consequence if I am meant to develop an affection for the Sun, is it not?"

"Magic has a cost, as does everything else in the world worth having."

Aurora paused, watching the Starmaker. "And yet the *only* thing you have in your life is magic. It seems you have decided these other things you speak of are not worth their cost."

The Starmaker took a step closer to Aurora. "I have lived many lifetimes and paid many prices. To think you know me because you have spent a day in my castle would be a mistake."

"And to think you know me because I was chosen by the Sun would be a mistake."

"That is where we differ, Miss Finch," the Starmaker said, turning toward the sleigh. "I do not think of you at all."

The Starmaker

The Starmaker had never had a way with words, but even he knew *I do not think of you at all* had been a particularly bad choice. He was not used to being spoken to with such impertinence, and he found it deeply aggravating the way the Starmaker Rising made assumptions about who he was.

Still, the words had been unnecessary and—more notably—untrue.

Perhaps that was what aggravated him most.

He knew that she would come to hate him if he could not find a way to be more civil, and yet hatred was so far superior to the alternative that he could not bring himself to apologize. The Starmaker's own mentor had been brusque and impassive, and it had still been exceedingly difficult for him when the man had died. He could only imagine how much worse it would have been had the Starmaker felt an affinity for him. It was a cost, the Starmaker was sure, he'd been glad not to pay.

Of course, marrying the girl was not something he had planned on, but it would complicate things only if he let it, and he would not. Of that he was certain.

And so he said nothing to his fiancée, content to let her hate him.

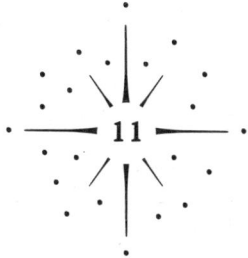

In Contract Only

Aurora did not speak to the Starmaker for the rest of the day, even as they patrolled the woods for the Frost and checked on the phlox bordering the village. The Starmaker spoke when he had knowledge to impart, but otherwise he did not seem to mind the silence. By the time they released the light for the day and journeyed back to the castle, the Starmaker had given up entirely, not even trying to teach her.

The sleigh had barely stopped moving before Aurora jumped out and hurried inside, not stopping even when Ina said her name as she passed. Aurora slammed her bedroom door and leaned against it, closing her eyes.

The Starmaker had said that the worst was over, but she didn't want to go through that pain ever again. She had suffered some nasty accidents before—slicing her knee open on a rock as she hunted, burning herself with oil in the kitchen, and missing a step coming down from the loft, breaking her ankle in the process. It all paled in comparison to what she had experienced that morning, and she didn't know how she could do it again.

Didn't know how she could possibly do it every day.

And the Starmaker's harshness—*I do not think of you at all*—made things so much worse.

There was a pot of tea waiting for her on the side table next to the fire, and a dress was laid out for her to wear to dinner. She peeked into the bathroom and saw a hot bath steaming away, and it was then that she understood Ina's words from the day before: she *did* appreciate having this place to come back to.

She sat by the fire and poured herself a cup of tea, noticing a letter resting on the tray. She hoped it wasn't from Farren, once again asking her to wait, but then she saw the unmistakable swoop of Elsie's handwriting and exhaled with relief. The back of the envelope was adorned with a deep magenta seal with silver flecks, a birthday gift that Aurora had given to her sister the previous year; she'd spent more than an hour in Reverie's stationery shop, trying to find the perfect color for Elsie, and she had loved it. Aurora tore open the letter.

Dear Aurora,

We were so pleased to hear from you in such a short time! Thank you for the letter. I miss you terribly and would be very happy to come visit at your earliest convenience.

THE SUN AND THE STARMAKER

Even Mama said she would see if she could get away from the house, which surprised me. I don't believe she has left for an extended period since Papa died.

We are doing well and eagerly await your next letter.

Love,
Elsie

P.S. If things aren't going well, you know you could say so, right?

Aurora drank her tea as she read, and when she folded the letter and set it back on the tray, the heaviness she'd been carrying from the day had eased slightly. The Starmaker may not care how she was faring, but her family did, and that was of great comfort to her.

Once her tea was done, she took a bath before getting ready for dinner. Aurora did not want to see the Starmaker again that day, but she was ravenous and felt as if she could eat the entire contents of the palace. Besides, this was supposedly her home now, and she refused to cower alone in her room. When her bath had warmed her from the frigid journey back to the castle, she slipped on the soft peach dress and readied herself.

Aurora made a point of arriving early to the dining room. She hated the way she felt as if she was intruding on the Starmaker, even when she arrived on time, and she wanted him to be the one walking in on her for a change. It was an added bonus that the room was empty, save for Constance, and she could sit alone and have a calm start to the evening before the meal began.

Constance looked at her from her usual place beside the Starmaker's chair, then hopped down the length of the table and jumped onto the seat next to Aurora's. She truly was a gorgeous rabbit, and Aurora tentatively held out her hand in penance for her behavior the night before. Constance looked at her for a moment before pressing her nose to Aurora's finger, and Aurora hoped that meant she was forgiven.

Just then, the door from the kitchen opened, and one of the staff made a choking noise. "I'm sorry, miss, I wasn't expecting you." He scanned the room, a look of horror settling on his face. "Was there no one here to greet you and get you seated?"

Aurora smiled at him. "I'm perfectly happy to seat myself. Tell me, what is your name?"

"Frederick," he said, visibly nervous.

"I'm Aurora. It's nice to formally meet you."

Frederick looked younger than Aurora, probably closer to Elsie's age, with short brown hair and immaculate posture. He stood with his hands behind his back, and the candlelight warmed his fair skin. He kept watching her, and finally Aurora rose to her feet.

"Would you feel better if you could help me get seated?" she asked.

Frederick looked relieved, and he hurried over and pulled her chair out for her, draping a linen napkin over her lap once she was sitting. "Thank you, Miss Finch."

"Please, call me Aurora," she said, and he looked unsure, but he nodded. He then noticed that Constance had changed places, and he quickly brought the rabbit her cushion and crystal bowl, taking it as seriously as he had Aurora's comfort. Aurora smiled to herself.

Just then, the Starmaker entered the room with long quick strides, but he stopped abruptly when he saw Aurora. "You're early."

"I would hate to keep Your Radiance waiting, as it seemed to displease you greatly when I arrived one minute past the hour last night."

He scowled at her. "Is it truly so difficult to arrive at the stated hour, neither early nor late?"

"You're early," Aurora pointed out.

"I like some time to myself before I'm expected to engage with"—he vaguely gestured toward her with his hand—"this."

The Starmaker then noticed where Constance was sitting, and he cocked his head to the side, giving the rabbit a long displeased look. He huffed, walking to his seat and sitting down before Frederick could help him, and Aurora had to stifle a laugh at how completely lost poor Frederick appeared. Finally, he walked back through the door to the kitchen with slumped shoulders and a look of dejection on his face.

"You've had quite a lot of time to yourself, have you not?"

The Starmaker sighed and looked up at her. "I have." He eyed her over his crystal goblet before taking a long drink of water. "My temperament is well suited to solitude."

"Now, that is something I believe entirely."

The Starmaker put his goblet down, and his mouth settled into a hard line. "I am trying, Miss Finch; perhaps you ought to do the same?"

Aurora's skin got hot as anger rose inside her. "If this is you trying, then I would hate to see you indifferent." She paused, shaking her head. "Between the two of us, I think it rather obvious that I am the one putting in effort."

"You certainly have an interesting idea of what constitutes effort. In case you have forgotten, you shut down immediately after pulling the light this morning and refused to let me teach you anything else. You make a show of how much you dislike being here. And you're stubborn and seem to take more enjoyment from irritating me than from the magic that your friends and family are quite literally dependent upon for survival."

"I will address two things," Aurora said, placing her hands on the table and staring down the Starmaker. "First, that *magic* felt as if it was killing me. I am not afraid of discomfort or even pain, but that was excruciating, and you did nothing to prepare me for it. If I am to learn to accept that kind of pain, then you can certainly learn to be patient." Aurora's words got more forceful as she spoke, and by the time she paused, she was breathing heavily. She took a long sip of water and tried to slow her racing heart.

"And the second?" the Starmaker asked coolly.

"I am perfectly capable of learning *and* irritating you; one does not preclude the other."

The Starmaker raised his brows. "Forgive me, I did not realize I was in the presence of such genius."

THE SUN AND THE STARMAKER

They glared at each other from across the table until Aurora finally looked away, noticing that Frederick, along with several other staff members, had come into the dining room but were seemingly frozen in place. Constance was the only one unfazed by the tension in the room, and she watched Aurora and the Starmaker as if they were the evening's entertainment.

No one dared interrupt the conversation, and Aurora leaned back in her chair and tried to release some of the fight coiling up inside her. "Frederick, I apologize for keeping you waiting. You may begin the dinner service."

At first Frederick didn't move, holding the silver tray as if it were a question instead of a meal. The Starmaker nodded. "Yes, Frederick, I find myself more famished than usual," he said, directing his words at Aurora.

As soon as the Starmaker and Aurora had been served, Frederick all but ran from the room, and Aurora dipped her head and began on the soup that sat in front of her. It seemed that all they could do was argue, but Aurora needed some answers, and so she tried to take the edge out of her voice when she addressed the Starmaker again. "You said the worst was over," she began, keeping her eyes on her dinner. "This morning, after you pulled the sunlight over Reverie. Is that true?"

The Starmaker didn't answer right away, and he seemed to be contemplating his words. "It is true," he finally said, "but I won't lie to you—it will be an uphill climb for a while."

"What does that mean?"

"It means that today was as painful as it gets. The Sun was

mapping your body, scanning you to learn the strength of your heart and the route of your blood. If you are to pull the sunlight, it's imperative that the Sun not overwhelm you."

"I'm fairly certain that's what happened this morning," Aurora said, her tone slipping back into contempt.

The Starmaker stopped eating, set his spoon down, and looked at Aurora with such intensity that it made her shift in her seat. "If the Sun had overwhelmed you, you would not be sitting here now."

Aurora tried not to react to his words, but a shiver crawled down her spine, and the hairs on the back of her neck stood on end. "I'm simply telling you how it felt."

"It will not feel that way again," the Starmaker said. "If you had not resorted to giving me the silent treatment—though I must acknowledge your remarkable maturity in moments of conflict—you would have learned that tomorrow will be easier, as will the day after that and the day after that. Make no mistake: it will not be *easy*, but the pain will lessen with each day you practice until one day, it will feel entirely bearable."

It took everything in Aurora not to respond to the *maturity* comment, though she furiously wanted to. "Will it always feel painful?"

The Starmaker leaned back in his chair as if he was truly considering her question. "It will always feel intense. Human bodies are not meant to handle that kind of heat, even heat that carries magic. But it doesn't feel painful to me anymore; it just feels like work."

Aurora nodded. She was good at doing work—living in a

THE SUN AND THE STARMAKER

cottage beyond the reach of the light required a lot of effort to survive. They always had to keep a fire burning, repairs to windows and doors and the roof had to be made immediately to keep out the Frost, and Aurora's mirrors were in constant need of cleaning and repositioning. Aurora was used to work, and if pulling the light began to feel like that for her, as it had for the Starmaker, then she thought she might have a chance of accomplishing what was required of her.

"Work I can do," Aurora said, and she meant it.

"Good."

Aurora was about to ask another question when Ina walked into the dining room and handed the Starmaker a stack of papers. "Here are the plans you asked for, Your Radiance," she said, giving Aurora a small smile.

"Thank you, Ina," the Starmaker said, and she left the room again.

"Plans?"

"For the wedding," he said, doing a rather poor job of masking his displeasure. While marriage had been Aurora's condition, she wasn't any happier about it than the Starmaker. But she knew how badly her family needed the glare line, and she was relieved that they would finally receive it. She hoped with everything inside of her that it would make their life in the dark just a little bit easier.

"Ah, yes. That. As you are the Starmaker, I assume you can get someone here quite easily to perform the ceremony." Aurora kept all hesitation from her voice, wanting the Starmaker to know she was fully committed to getting her family the line they needed.

"No," the Starmaker said, looking over the papers. "That will not do."

Aurora tried not to show the anger that roared back to life inside her. "If you're having trouble recalling, marriage was part of our agreement."

"My memory is quite well."

"Then are you suggesting that His Radiance, the great Starmaker, is not a man of his word?" Aurora's tone dripped with derision, but the Starmaker only looked bored.

"I am a man of my word, and I intend to marry you. But doing so here, just the two of us, will not do."

Understanding slammed into Aurora all at once, and her heart began to race. "Absolutely not. I refuse."

The Starmaker watched her from across the table, his eyes sparking to life with mischief, as if he took genuine pleasure in her outrage. "You want your family to get their glare line, and I refuse to marry in secret."

"It wouldn't be in secret," Aurora said, fumbling her words. "It would simply be private. Between the two of us."

"And what if I want to show you off?" the Starmaker asked, letting his gaze fall just below her face before finding her eyes again.

Aurora flushed and took a deep breath, trying to calm herself. She wasn't sure how she had lost her advantage so spectacularly, and she was desperate to get it back. "You are mocking me, and I don't appreciate it."

"I am doing nothing of the sort. You're a beautiful woman—did you think I hadn't noticed?"

THE SUN AND THE STARMAKER

The directness with which he spoke only angered her more, and she tried to ignore the way his words made her insides squirm with something that felt much too close to desire.

"I do not concern myself with your opinion of me."

"A fact that has been quite obvious since our encounter in the woods," the Starmaker said. He was agreeing with her, and yet it sounded like an affront. He took a casual sip of wine, and Aurora looked to Constance for help, but the rabbit only took a bite of her carrot.

"Why are you insisting on a spectacle?" Aurora asked, no longer trying to hide her frustration.

"Because marriage is a symbol of hope, and Reverie's Starmaker is about to die. Imagine what our union will do for the villagers. It will be written about in history books and children's stories. It will reinforce the magic of Reverie and be something to celebrate." The Starmaker paused. "I don't want this marriage, and I suspect you don't either; let us at least use it for the good of the mountain. To witness a marriage between the Starmaker and the Starmaker Rising would be remarkable indeed. Your family needs a glare line, and this mountain needs a story."

"We *have* our stories, and almost no one even knows I am the Starmaker Rising, a fact I would very much like to keep hidden for now."

"Miss Finch, the villagers will soon notice your absence. If you wish to keep your identity as the Starmaker Rising quiet, then you will need another explanation for your relocation. I may be cold at times, but I would rather like to avoid developing a reputation as a beastly ruler who plucks unsuspecting women from their homes. Marrying in a large ceremony will alleviate both of those concerns."

Aurora wanted to argue, but she knew he was right. If she wasn't ready for the entire mountain to learn that there was magic in her blood, then their union was the only other justification for her sudden move to the castle. A wedding would answer every question, and Aurora could hold on to her secret for as long as she wanted.

"As much as it pains me to admit this, I believe you're right," Aurora said, sighing. "Though I don't understand why your death ought to factor into this at all. Is it not true that once your magic has been transferred to me, you will simply start to age where you left off, as if you had never been immortal to begin with?"

The Starmaker looked uncomfortable, and he dropped his gaze to the table.

"I apologize," she said quickly. "I did not mean to make light of your eventual passing. I only meant to suggest that while it feels rather imminent to you, it will not feel that way to the villagers."

The Starmaker was quiet and looked to be thinking rather carefully about his next words. "Do not bother yourself with my passing, as this will be a marriage in contract only. From my perspective, the contract will be fulfilled once the ceremony is complete and the glare line has formed between the castle and your family's home."

The shift in conversation jarred her, and Aurora took a sip of her wine before speaking again. She flushed, knowing what he was implying, and though she would never admit it aloud, the thought *had* crossed her mind. He was devastatingly handsome, and while her brain found him infuriating most of the time, her body was all too aware of it. Still, she wasn't sure she was ready to share his bed, and she was glad to hear that he didn't expect it.

At least, her mind was glad; the message had yet to make it to the rest of her.

"I am to keep my own room?" she asked, reassuring herself that she had understood his meaning.

"Of course." The Starmaker said it like it was obvious, a ridiculous thing to even consider. "I much prefer my solitude to..." He trailed off as if he had realized his rudeness just in time.

"This?" Aurora supplied, gesturing toward herself.

The Starmaker nodded once but at least had the decency to look somewhat contrite. His voice was kinder when he next spoke. "This is not how I envisioned living out the remainder of my life, and I know the same is true for you. That, at the very least, is something we can agree upon." The Starmaker finished his meal and stood, giving Constance one more annoyed glance before turning to Aurora. "Ina will continue to take care of the wedding preparations so that we may focus on your magic."

He had begun to leave the room when Aurora pushed back from the table and hurried after him, catching his wrist. He slowly turned to her.

"Please do not make a fool of me," she said, so quietly that the words came out in a rough whisper. If she was to stand before all of Reverie in a grand ceremony and a ridiculous dress, she needed some assurance from him that it would, at the very least, appear genuine. If not for her sake, then for the sake of her family.

The Starmaker winced, a subtle movement that Aurora only noticed because of how close together they stood. For several breaths, they watched each other, neither of them stepping back to create more space, and Aurora hated how vulnerable the comment had been, how exposed it made her feel.

"Even if I desired to," he said, keeping his eyes on hers for a single beat of her heart, "I do not believe I could." Then he left, and Aurora stood in place, watching his back as he went.

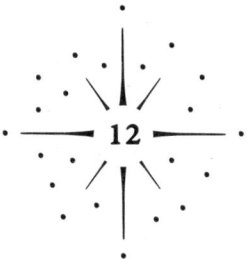

Snow Angel

A week passed, and the Starmaker was right: that first morning of pulling the sunlight was the worst. It remained painful, but with each day that passed, Aurora's body got more used to the jolt of heat that filled her veins. It wasn't comfortable, nor was it easy, but it was bearable, and that was a start.

It was the time after pulling the light and hanging it from the lamppost that Aurora looked forward to most. She spent hours wandering the mountain with the Starmaker, learning more about the land and the way the past Starmakers had made the mountain more and more magical over time. She knew that their bodies helped sustain the earth—that much she had learned from the stories and from visiting their graves with her parents when she was young—but she had no idea the extent of it. Their magic, slowly releasing into the ground over hundreds of years, was why Reverie could support practically any crop, why animals thrived and flowers bloomed year-round.

The only land more magical than the grave sites was the grounds of the castle, for the Sun herself had wept over the earth where the castle was built, feeding the dirt with her tears. That was why the palace was so healing; every injury Aurora sustained during practice was alleviated upon her return to it. She was amazed by how much magic was required simply to keep the Starmaker healthy enough to continue pulling the light.

The burial sites were in the most densely populated areas, which accounted for the lack of magic at Aurora's home; it was far from the Starmakers' graves. The land beneath her cottage would eventually absorb more magic once a Starmaker was buried closer to it, but until then, they were completely dependent upon the mirrors and glare lines.

There will be no rest for you. Not even in death.

The Starmaker told her that the mountain itself also needed new bodies to sustain its magic. It was part of the reason the Sun could not make the first Starmaker truly immortal. It wasn't enough that the land received light each day; it also needed magic to combat the harsh environment, including the Frost, and the Sun had waited as long as she possibly could before giving the first Starmaker to it. The Starmaker recounted this to Aurora with a seriousness that moved her—he told her to imagine how difficult it must have been for the Sun to cut her lover's existence short so that he could sustain the land he loved, knowing she would live an eternity with only his memory to hold on to.

Aurora wanted to feel indifferent to the suffering of the Sun, but she found she couldn't. It was a remarkable thing to endure, and if anything, it made Aurora love the stories even more.

"We must visit the village today," the Starmaker said after they had checked the health of the woods, making sure there were no signs of the Frost. "Tilly has wandered off the grounds of the castle, and we need to find her and bring her back."

"Tilly?" Aurora asked, not recognizing the name.

"The snow angel."

When Aurora still did not understand, the Starmaker sighed. "I assumed you would know her story, but now that I think of it, it has been many years since she last wandered off." The Starmaker stepped over a large tree trunk and exited the forest, walking toward the market. "Tilly was a young woman when I was the Starmaker Rising. One day, she ate a handful of yew seeds, not knowing they were lethal, then went out into the field in front of her home and made a snow angel. She died while in the snow, and after her body was taken away, the snow angel came to life. It was one of the first instances that demonstrated how powerful magic could be when it turned up in an unexpected place. We are now accustomed to magic going awry, but it was not always that way."

Aurora's eyes widened. "Is there truly a living snow angel on this mountain?"

"Yes," the Starmaker said. "She caused many problems at first, constantly going from home to home, trying to find herself. She didn't understand that her mind was no longer in her human body but in that of the snow, and she became agitated and confused. My mentor wanted to banish her to the woods, but I took responsibility for her, and she has lived on the castle grounds ever since."

Aurora could tell by the way he spoke that the Starmaker held an affection for the angel, something she would not have predicted. When he had told Aurora about other instances where magic had gone awry, he had always presented them as deeply annoying situations they had to deal with as Starmakers. The magic in the land was an incredible gift, and it was what enabled them to live in Reverie, but every once in a while, it went off course and wound up somewhere it ought not to be. But the Starmaker did not speak of Tilly with aggravation or exhaustion; he sounded genuinely worried for her.

"Tilly is still trying to find herself, and on rare occasions, she manages to get down into the village to look." The Starmaker's voice held a hint of sorrow, though it seemed to Aurora that he was trying to remain unbothered by the angel's predicament.

"That is perhaps the saddest thing I've ever heard," Aurora said, unable to keep the emotion from her voice.

"Yes. I have been trying to help her find peace for many years, but to no avail." The Starmaker paused. "It has haunted me my entire reign." The words were quiet, as if he had not meant to speak them aloud.

Aurora stopped walking then, and when the Starmaker did the same, she found his eyes. "She is fortunate to have you looking after her."

THE SUN AND THE STARMAKER

"I'm not sure that is a fair assessment. I have not proven to be a very effective caretaker, after all." The Starmaker turned and continued walking, and Aurora followed close behind. They were quiet the rest of the journey.

Before they had even entered the market, Aurora knew the snow angel was there. A huge crowd had formed in the village center, people shouting to one another and craning their necks. Children were up on their parents' shoulders, pointing, but they didn't seem scared. They seemed mesmerized.

"Oh, Tilly," the Starmaker said under his breath, quickening his steps.

Aurora thought he might be apprehensive about entering a crowd of so many people, as he rarely interacted with the villagers, but he did not hesitate at all. He rushed toward Tilly as if she were a toddler crawling toward the glacier edge, his face scrunched with tension and his arm outstretched.

"Excuse me," the Starmaker said when he reached the crowd. "Please excuse me, I must get through."

If there was one thing that could pull the villagers' attention away from a living snow angel, it was the Starmaker himself, close enough to touch. The crowd parted, and whispers of "Look!" and "The Starmaker!" began rolling through the sea of people, followed by a reverent hush. Aurora stayed a few steps behind him and pulled the hood of her cloak over her head, not wanting to be recognized, but it didn't matter; no one was paying attention to her.

The Starmaker made his way through the crowd with a patience Aurora knew he did not have, and she stepped into the space behind him, following his path to the snow angel. Finally, he reached her.

Tilly looked exactly like the snow angels Aurora and Elsie had made as children, except that she was as tall as Aurora. It was as if a cookie cutter had been pressed into freshly fallen snow, carving out an angel with smooth edges and perfectly defined features. Her wings were large, and the bottom of her gown rested gently on the earth. Tilly sparkled magnificently in the light, more even than the Starmaker's hair or Constance's fur, as if millions of tiny crystals had been packed into the snow that made her.

For a moment, Aurora just stared, entirely taken by the magic of it all, but then she quickly averted her eyes. She didn't want to make Tilly self-conscious.

"Hello, Tilly," the Starmaker said, his voice soft and gentle.

"Hello," she replied in a melodic tone that was as enchanting as the rest of her. "Can you help me? It seems I have misplaced myself."

"That's why I'm here," the Starmaker said. "To help you."

The crowd was silent now, the entire market hushed as the Starmaker spoke with Tilly. Merchants had stopped selling, the bells above shops had stopped ringing, and even the children had stopped playing.

"That's wonderful!" Tilly exclaimed. "I'm certain I'm around here somewhere. Have you seen me?"

The Starmaker's face softened as she spoke, and though he was being watched by dozens of people, he never took his eyes off her. "I see you, Tilly, right here, standing before me. You are

THE SUN AND THE STARMAKER

reflecting the sunlight, the most brilliant thing in this market. Your wings are spread wide, and your gown is swooping down to the ground in a full skirt. And though you are sparkling, you look sad." The Starmaker paused, and Aurora realized she'd been holding her breath as he spoke. "I see you, Tilly. If you come with me, I would like to help you see yourself."

The snow angel was quiet for a moment, and she looked around the market as if she was disoriented, her head darting in different directions before she focused once more on the Starmaker. "You see me?" she asked quietly.

"Clearer than a winter's morning."

The words seemed to calm Tilly just slightly, and she took a hesitant step toward the Starmaker, then another and another, until they were walking side by side through the crowd. Murmurs of "Thank you for the light" followed the Starmaker, but he kept his focus entirely on the angel.

Aurora waited until the crowd began to disperse, and then she walked in the same direction as the Starmaker and Tilly, running to catch up to them once they were out of the market. She met them back at the sleigh and watched as the Starmaker helped Tilly up onto the bench.

"Tilly, I'd like to introduce you to a friend of mine," the Starmaker said. "This is Aurora. She'll be spending the rest of the day with us."

"Lovely to make your acquaintance," Tilly said, and Aurora climbed into the sleigh, sitting beside her. "Perhaps you can help us with our search."

"I would be delighted," Aurora said.

The Starmaker took the reins, and the sounds of the market faded away as the sleigh moved swiftly across the snow, the glacier soon coming into view.

"Wait here for us," the Starmaker said to the angel when the snow deer had come to a stop. "We need to release the light, and then we can see to the matter of locating you."

"Very well," said Tilly, settling into the sleigh. "I will wait."

Aurora stepped down to the glacier and tried not to stare at the Starmaker as they walked toward the lamppost, but it was rather difficult. She had seen a different side of him, as if he were a prism that had turned just slightly, his normal white light bursting into a rainbow of colors.

"You are remarkable with her," Aurora said, trying to keep the heaviness from her voice.

"I am responsible for her," the Starmaker countered, but Aurora could hear the depth in his tone, the way he fought to sound apathetic.

"It is not a failing to care for her." Aurora couldn't understand why he refused to admit to his affection, as if it were some reprehensible thing he had to bury at all costs.

"It is my *biggest* failing," the Starmaker said, turning on her. Aurora stopped abruptly, her breath catching in her throat. "Up until recently, I was the only one on this mountain with magic, the only one who had the slightest chance of helping her, and yet I have not made this better. She has suffered for hundreds of years, and I have been unable to ease it."

THE SUN AND THE STARMAKER

"Do you truly think it would be better if she had no one who cared for her at all?"

The Starmaker shook his head, looking back toward the sleigh. "I give her hope over and over again when there is no hope. It's monstrous."

"Hope is essential for survival," Aurora said, her tone fierce. Hope was the only thing getting her through her new life—hope that things would get better, hope that she would come to appreciate the magic inside her, hope that she would learn to bear the grief of immortality. Without hope, she was nothing.

"Perhaps initially," the Starmaker said. "But everything has a limit, even hope, and I fear Tilly passed that point years ago. Now hope is nothing more than a cruelty."

The Starmaker continued walking, and it was clear to Aurora that he was done with the conversation. She wanted to argue with him because it was so difficult to accept what he was saying, accept that hope had limits, but she had lived only a tiny fraction of the time he had. Hope could very well become a cruelty and Aurora had yet to live long enough to discover that for herself.

A soft snow began to fall, and Aurora watched as the Starmaker stepped up to the lamppost and opened the lantern door, unhooking the light. Golden rays shot past them, rushing up the glacier, over the village, and out through the peaks of Reverie. Aurora still wasn't used to the speed with which the light vanished, but it was certainly a spectacle to behold.

There was so much Aurora hadn't seen given the location of her cottage, tucked quietly against a rock face covered in snow and ice, sitting comfortably in the darkness. She'd thought she had explored every inch of their village, but she had been wrong, and a small thrill ran through her as she imagined all the things she had yet to discover. Then something occurred to her: why hadn't she ever seen the way the light left? She had walked their mountain so many times that the map of it was written in her memory.

"Why are there never any spectators when you pull in the light and release it? That seems like something people would want to observe," Aurora said as they walked back to the sleigh.

"It is too dangerous," the Starmaker said. "All the heat is concentrated into a single point until we diffuse it over the village. If someone were to get in the way of it, they would die. Part of the magic of the land is that no one is aware of the light until it spreads out over the mountain, and no one can perceive the lamppost where we work."

"I was wondering why I had never seen it before," Aurora said, carefully traversing the glacier.

"It would have become visible to you after our encounter in the woods."

"The mountain holds much more magic than I realized," Aurora said, more to herself than the Starmaker, but he replied anyway.

"Far more than any of us can comprehend."

"Is that a comfort to you?"

"It is a fact," the Starmaker said, as if the very idea of taking comfort in such things was reserved for fools.

THE SUN AND THE STARMAKER

"Has anyone ever told you that you aren't very good company?" Aurora asked, facing him.

"I believe I've tried to tell you that on multiple occasions." The sleigh came into view, and Aurora was glad to see Tilly still seated, patiently awaiting their return. "Your listening skills require some work, as this constantly seems to bewilder you."

"I concede that I find it difficult to accept that someone could truly be as dour as you."

The Starmaker sighed but said nothing more, and they reached the sleigh in silence. Tilly turned toward the Starmaker, bending the top corner of her wing as if waving.

"Sorry to keep you waiting," the Starmaker said.

"It is quite all right."

The Starmaker and Aurora boarded the sleigh, and the snow deer took off toward the trail, leaving the glacier behind.

"I believe I saw you not long ago in the gardens," Aurora said, turning to face Tilly. "I'm glad we've had the chance to be properly introduced."

"Oh yes, I love the gardens," Tilly said. "At least, I think I do. My memory isn't what is used to be." Tilly paused as if considering something. "At least, I don't think it is."

"People change, you know. Even if you didn't like the gardens before, you can love them now. I used to do everything in my power to avoid waking up early, and now I love rising in the small hours of the morning, before the rest of the world is awake."

"How fortunate you are," the Starmaker mumbled, and Aurora couldn't help the smile pulling at her lips.

"My point, Tilly, is that not everything must be based on history. You can change your mind and change it back. You can decide what you like today, even if you hate it tomorrow. Don't get so caught up in who you were that you fail to see who you are."

"I don't believe I've thought about that before," Tilly said, as if she truly was trying to remember all the thoughts she'd ever had. "Once I find myself, I should like to ask."

Aurora found the snow angel's answer quite sad, but Tilly sounded rather content, and so Aurora tried her best to let it be. The deer rounded the final crest of the hill that led to the palace, and the Starmaker, Aurora, and Tilly sat in a comfortable quiet that matched the peacefulness of the evening.

When they arrived at the castle, Ina was waiting outside, and a look of relief washed over her when she saw that Tilly was with them. The sleigh came to a stop, and Tilly jumped out onto the snow, heading for the gardens without another glance at the Starmaker or Aurora. It seemed she did like the gardens very much; so much, in fact, that she was willing to put her search for herself on hold.

Aurora felt the Starmaker's eyes on her, and she turned to him before walking inside. "Tilly likes you," he said, as if surprised.

"As hard as it may be for you to understand, there are in fact several people who like me."

"That is not difficult for me to understand," the Starmaker replied, and it was Aurora's turn to be surprised. "But Tilly does not respond well to most people. She is slow to trust, and people tend to patronize her far more than simply speaking to her."

THE SUN AND THE STARMAKER

Aurora paused, choosing her words carefully. "I know that you have had many hopes dashed over the years," she said. "You and Tilly. But I have not lived nearly as long as either of you, and so I find myself with an abundance of hope. If you are amenable, I will hope for you both so that you no longer have to."

The Starmaker studied her, his eyes narrowing, and Aurora's skin flamed beneath his gaze. She wished she knew what he was thinking. Perhaps she had said the wrong thing, upset him in some way. But then he spoke. "I believe Tilly would like that very much." He paused. "And so would I."

Aurora nodded and turned to go inside, unable to forget the way the Starmaker had looked at her for the rest of the night.

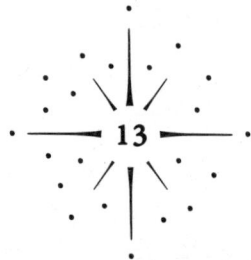

The Honor of Your Presence

Several days later, Aurora was sitting outside on a garden bench, bundled up in her thickest wool, watching the night sky. She had heard the stories of the northern lights, fabled ribbons of purple and green that danced across the night sky. It was said that the lights were a result of the Sun crying, when she was mourning her beloved so deeply that her tears fell through space and hit the Earth's atmosphere. Aurora had always wanted to see them, but they had never appeared in her eighteen years, and she had started to wonder if this was perhaps a story that was not rooted in truth.

Still, she couldn't give up looking for them.

It had been so long since the first Starmaker had lived, and Aurora couldn't imagine carrying that kind of pain for hundreds of years. Maybe the Sun had cried all the tears she could, and now there was nothing left. Aurora used to hear Mama crying at night, and though it had become a rare occurrence, she was ashamed that she had never knocked on the door to check on her, convincing herself that Mama wouldn't want her to. She wondered now if Mama was still crying over Papa, so many years later.

Just then, the doors to the garden opened and Ina stepped outside carrying a silver tray with an orange rose resting on top. She walked to the bench where Aurora sat, following her gaze to the sky.

"It is a beautiful night," she said.

"Indeed it is," Aurora agreed. "Ina, have you ever seen the northern lights?"

"I have not, but my mother did when she was a girl."

"Truly?" Aurora asked, her voice filled with excitement.

"Yes, she spoke of them often." Ina's voice was wistful as she watched the sky.

"Did she believe that the lights were caused by the Sun crying?"

"She did," Ina said. "And I'm inclined to believe it, too. The notion doesn't seem any less plausible to me than a living snow angel or a lamppost that holds sunlight."

Aurora smiled. "That is true, though I hope the Sun is not still grieving after all this time."

"I would not hope for such things, for the weight of her grief comes from the depth of her love, and that love is what keeps Reverie alive."

Aurora thought about that. "I suppose you're right."

"I would like to find a love like that one day." Aurora looked over to find Ina smiling. She didn't understand why anyone would want something so fragile, so capable of tearing one's entire life in two.

"Anyone would be lucky to be loved by you."

"Thank you, Aurora; that is very kind." Ina looked down at the tray she was holding, as if to remind herself of why she had come out to the garden in the first place. "A letter came for you today." She handed Aurora the envelope, then walked back inside, leaving Aurora alone once more.

Aurora looked at the lantern next to the bench, wishing she had brought a match with her. Almost as soon as she thought it, the lantern lit on its own, the orange flame casting just enough light for Aurora to read.

"Thank you," she said instinctively, then shook her head when she realized she'd said it to an object that could not hear her.

Aurora turned the letter over to see Elsie's magenta seal, and she eagerly tore open the envelope. Elsie's perfect cursive greeted her, and seeing her sister's handwriting provided her with more warmth than the castle's tea service or a hot bath ever could.

My dear sister,

Your wedding invitation was delivered today—the finest I've ever seen! Mama was pleased when it arrived, but I must admit that I did not receive it as well as she did. I know this was not part of your plan for your life, and I worry for your happiness.

THE SUN AND THE STARMAKER

I'm eager to see you and miss you far too much to put into words. If the Starmaker will allow it, I would very much like to visit you. I hope that he is treating you well and that your situation isn't as somber as I sometimes fear.

Please write to me again when you can.

I love you,
Elsie

Aurora read the letter several times, making sure she understood. She even moved closer to the lantern to confirm she was seeing it properly, but nothing changed the words on the page. Wedding invitations had been sent without her knowledge, and it was all Aurora could do to keep from screaming. She clutched the paper so tightly that her hand began to shake, and before she could think better of it, she rushed from the garden and into the castle in search of the Starmaker.

"Is there something I can help you with?" Frederick asked as Aurora hurried into the dining room, but the Starmaker was not there.

"Where is the Starmaker?"

"He is likely in his room, miss. Is everything okay?" he asked, eyeing the letter in Aurora's hand.

"Where is his room?" Aurora's words came out in a rush, and she knew her anger was rolling off of her in waves, but she couldn't help it.

Frederick checked the grand clock against the wall. "He will be preparing for sleep at this time," he said hesitantly. "Perhaps you can speak with him when you break your fast?"

"No, it cannot wait. Where is his room?" she asked again, not bothering to hide her irritation at having to ask twice.

Frederick didn't answer right away, clearly uncomfortable with the idea of letting Aurora interrupt the Starmaker. But finally he relented. "Take a right at the top of the stairs and follow the hallway all the way to the end. There will be a spiral staircase on your right: take that, and his door is at the top."

Aurora hurried out of the room, but not before Frederick could call out, "His Radiance does not like to be interrupted!"

"I do not care what His Radiance likes," Aurora answered, though she was sure Frederick could not hear her, as she was already halfway up the grand staircase. She clutched her wool skirts in her hands so she didn't trip and ran down the hallway until she reached the spiral staircase. Fresh flowers were everywhere, more and more numerous the closer to the Starmaker's room she got. Roses of every color adorned the furnishings, and Aurora had to be careful where she grabbed the glass railing, as it too was wrapped in vines with vibrant blooms the color of lemons.

Her heart was racing, and she had started to sweat, still in her outside garments, heat radiating through her. She felt as if the letter in her hand might incinerate and briefly wondered if her magic could do such a thing.

When Aurora reached the top of the stairs, she did not

THE SUN AND THE STARMAKER

hesitate. She grabbed the handle and threw the door open, rushing inside before stopping abruptly.

The Starmaker was standing in the middle of the room, soaking wet. He wore no shirt, and his pants were resting untied on his hips. Steam drifted from his bathroom and the scent of lavender hung in the air, and Aurora flushed when she realized she must have been mere seconds from finding him entirely unclothed. Large beads of water rolled down his chest and hung from his pearlescent hair before falling to the floor, and he gave her a look so severe that she wondered once again if their magic could set things on fire. If it could, she was sure she would turn to ash right there in the Starmaker's room.

"Do you not believe in knocking?" he asked, annoyance dripping from his voice like the water from his hair. The Sun's mark shone on his right biceps, the intricate design catching the dim light.

"Do you not believe in shirts?" Aurora asked, trying not to look at the way his body tensed and flexed as he tied the drawstring on his pants and reached for a thin white sleeping shirt hanging in his wardrobe. It wasn't what she had wanted to say, but she was terribly distracted, and with great effort, she forced her eyes to his face. "Care to explain this?" she asked, holding the letter out.

The Starmaker took his time slipping his right arm, then his left into his shirt. He slowly fastened each button, and Aurora loathed herself when disappointment rose inside her as he finished dressing. After an infuriatingly long while, he finally walked to where she stood and took the letter from her. He scanned the words, then looked up at her with a bored expression. "It sounds as if your sister misses you and would like to hear from you." He handed the letter back to Aurora, and she took it, exasperated.

"I am quite capable of reading," Aurora said, trying to keep her voice even.

"Then why don't you tell me what it is you'd like explained?" The Starmaker sounded entirely uninterested, and it enraged Aurora even more.

"How could you send out invitations without consulting me first?"

"As neither of us is particularly thrilled about our upcoming union, Ina has been seeing to the preparations so that we can focus on your learning. I believe I told you that." The Starmaker ran his hand through his hair, his fingers coming away wet. Aurora hated how beautiful he was, and she looked down so he wouldn't see the thought written all over her face.

"You should have asked me before sending them. You effectively announced our engagement without my permission."

The Starmaker pulled a rich navy robe from its hanger and slipped it on. "The wedding is four days from now, a fact you are well aware of. What did you expect?"

"Common courtesy," Aurora said, staring at him with utter frustration. "Though it seems that I once again overestimated your ability to be decent."

"Miss Finch, this conversation is wearing on me. What is it that you're truly upset about?"

THE SUN AND THE STARMAKER

"Who received an invitation?" Aurora asked, her voice breaking at the end. Her heart was racing, and she willed him to give any answer other than the one she expected.

"Everyone in Reverie."

Aurora shut her eyes against the words. She should have written to Farren, warned him this was coming. Apologized. Anything. She had told him before she'd left for the castle that she would marry the Starmaker, but Farren had written four letters to her since she had told him not to come, and she had not replied to a single one. He should have heard the news from her, but instead he'd received a lavish invitation as if he was just another villager.

"You sent Farren an invitation without giving me an opportunity to warn him."

"You've had ample opportunity. Is there not a desk equipped with stationery and ink in your room? Have you not had more than a fortnight to write to him?" The Starmaker picked up his teacup and looked inside, then scowled. "It seems to me as if you barged into my room to blame me for your own cowardice. My tea has run out, along with my patience." He looked toward the door, all but dismissing her.

"I didn't write to him because I thought it would be better."

"Better for whom? Do you really believe that he would prefer silence from you?" The Starmaker sat down in a large velvet chair—the only one in the room—and picked up a book. "You insist that you know of love, but your behavior suggests you know nothing of it." He opened his book and began to read, and Aurora watched him, incredulous.

"And you know nothing of compassion," she said, her voice shaking with anger.

"That's where you're wrong." The Starmaker looked back up, piercing her with his stare. "It is simply that my compassion lies not with you, but with him."

The words took her breath away, and she had to fight against the sting in her eyes. The worst part about it was that deep down, she knew the Starmaker was right. She had been a coward, and now Farren had received a wedding invitation that replaced the ones they had sent not a month earlier. They had hunched over his kitchen table, writing them all by hand, passing them to his little sisters so they could finish them off with silver bows. She remembered thinking how perfect their names looked together, side by side on the sky-blue paper.

Those invitations hardly felt real anymore, though the ache in her chest told her otherwise.

Aurora was upset and angry, and she was about to turn and leave when Constance poked her head out from behind the Starmaker's chair. The rabbit jumped through the table legs, but she had apparently misjudged the distance, for the entire side table wobbled before crashing to the floor. Constance darted into a far corner of the room, and the Starmaker let out a long sigh as he looked down at the mess. He lowered himself to the floor, eyeing the rabbit as he started to clean.

The last thing Aurora wanted to do was help the Starmaker, but there had always been work to be done at the cottage she grew up in, and it had created an irrepressible need in her to tackle whatever task was before her. And so she rushed toward the shattered teapot and cup, dropping to her knees and picking up the shards until a sharp fragment sliced straight through her palm.

Aurora sucked in a breath as blood pooled in her hand. She had never liked the sight of blood and had a rather unfortunate tendency to faint in its presence—a tragic habit given that she had two older brothers—and she took several deep breaths, trying to calm herself. The room began to spin, the Starmaker and the fire and the teapot morphing in her vision, and Aurora braced herself on the floor, struggling to remain conscious.

"Your hand is bleeding," the Starmaker said.

"What an astute observation," Aurora replied, her words blending into each other.

The Starmaker ignored her comment and grabbed several large pillows from his bed. "Let me help you."

He knelt and carefully arranged the pillows on the rug behind her, and after a very long moment during which Aurora wondered if he was rethinking his offer, he wrapped his arm around her back and helped her lie down. The spinning was getting worse, and she clutched the Starmaker's shoulder as her vision blurred. He stiffened beneath her touch but did not move away.

"I," she began before pausing to take a breath, "do not care for blood when it is outside a body."

"You don't say." When Aurora was settled on the pillows, the Starmaker slowly released his hold on her. "Wait here while I retrieve some bandages."

The Starmaker disappeared into his bathroom, and Aurora

rolled onto her side, inhaling deeply. She was concentrating on the silver-and-gold rug on the floor, following single threads with her eyes to distract herself, when Constance came into view. She looked mildly contrite, and Aurora reached out to pet her with her uninjured hand.

After several seconds, the rabbit hopped away, and the Starmaker's bare feet appeared on the rug. Aurora was surprised when he sat down directly beside her, placing a wooden bowl filled with water on the floor and dipping a white cloth into it before holding out his hand.

"Allow me," he said, and Aurora hesitantly put her hand in his. He blotted the cut, his movements patient and slow, as if he would stay there for hours if her injury required it. He wrung out the cloth and washed the cut again before reaching for a small glass jar. "This salve will sting, but it will have you healed by morning."

"You're being rather nice considering the fact that you called me a coward just moments ago," Aurora said.

The Starmaker paused, keeping his eyes on her injury. "I said you were acting with cowardice, *not* that you were a coward. There is a difference."

Aurora exhaled in frustration. "It is still an insult."

"It is," the Starmaker said. "I am simply making the point that one ought to be precise with one's words, insulting or otherwise."

Aurora's mouth gaped open, and it took her several moments to find her words. "You utterly exhaust me."

The Starmaker went back to work on her hand. He dipped

his middle finger into the salve, then slowly slid it over her cut, the rest of his fingers brushing against her palm. She began to feel dizzy once more, and she told herself it was a reaction to the blood, not his touch, that had caused it.

"And what do you imagine you do to me?" he asked, looking up at her, holding her gaze.

Aurora didn't answer right away, instead going over the past several weeks in her mind. She let out a small laugh. "It seems we have something in common, then."

The Starmaker shook his head, grabbed a clean bandage, and wrapped it around Aurora's palm. Aurora couldn't be sure, but it seemed as if he was taking more time than was strictly necessary, and when he finished wrapping her hand and didn't let go, Aurora was certain.

"We challenge each other," the Starmaker said, finally releasing his hold on her.

"I suppose we do."

They watched each other for several moments, and then the Starmaker helped her sit up. He stood, taking a large step back. "It's getting late," he said.

Aurora blinked, coming back to herself. "Yes," she agreed, but her mind was still on his touch and his eyes and the way he'd said *we challenge each other*. "Thank you for the help."

The Starmaker nodded, and Aurora stood, picking up Elsie's letter and moving to the door. She paused as she pressed down on the handle. "You should know," she said, turning back to him, "that I never back down from a challenge."

It was too dim to see clearly, but Aurora could have sworn that a faint grin tugged at the corner of the Starmaker's mouth. Then she left the room, and the image was gone.

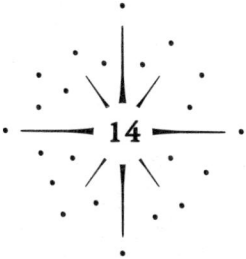

A Decent Husband

Aurora awoke as she always did, comfortable and warm and missing her sister so much it hurt. So when she saw Elsie sitting on her bed, watching her, Aurora wondered if perhaps she was stuck in a dream. She blinked several times and sat up, but her sister remained where she was, laughing.

"Elsie?" Aurora asked, her voice barely a whisper, scared that she was seeing things, that her homesickness was playing tricks on her mind.

"Good morning, sister," Elsie said, and Aurora shot across the bed, tackling her in a hug.

"What are you doing here?" Aurora exclaimed into her sister's hair, not ready to let go of her yet.

"I will tell you as soon as I can breathe."

Aurora finally relented, rolling back onto her heels. There

was a large silver cart in the middle of the room covered in decadent food, scones and jams and berries overflowing onto a vibrant pink cloth, and a large teapot was nestled between the pastries with two cups beside it.

"What is all this?" Aurora asked.

"It's for your wedding day, of course. The Starmaker arranged everything, and he asked me to give you this."

Elsie handed Aurora a letter, written on heavy parchment that shimmered like sunlight on snow. Aurora looked at her sister, then carefully removed the wax seal, marbled gold with a design of the sun that matched the mark on the Starmaker's arm.

Aurora,

I know this is not the wedding you want. At the very least, please allow me to take care of the sunlight so that you may spend the day with your sister.

I may not be very good company, but I will be a decent husband. That I can promise.

I will see you at seven.

Don't be late.

Yours,
The Starmaker

Aurora felt her sister's eyes on her as she read. The letter was so unlike him, and it almost irritated her that he was being gentle with her today. It would be easier if he was unfeeling and cold. Anger was not as difficult a feeling as sadness, not as unbearable as regret. She did not need his kindness, but as she looked at her sister, she realized that perhaps she was wrong. Perhaps she needed it very much.

"Tell me everything," Aurora said, setting the letter aside and pulling her sister over to the chairs by the fire. They piled their plates high with as many pastries as they could hold, then sat across from each other, and Aurora could hardly tear her eyes away from Elsie, so thankful she was there.

"The Starmaker wrote to me four nights ago," Elsie began between bites. "He asked if I would be willing to come to the castle and spend your wedding day with you, to which I promptly agreed." Elsie looked around the room, one hand poised in midair, ready to take another bite of her scone. "This place is an impossibility," she said.

"An improbability," Aurora replied, but when her sister gave her a questioning look, she simply shook her head. Her mind was caught on what Elsie had said: that the Starmaker had written to her four nights prior. That was the night Aurora had confronted him about the invitations, and she wondered if the Starmaker had not been truthful when he'd said his compassion did not lie with her. Or perhaps his sentiments had changed after he had tended to her injury. She didn't know, nor did she understand why it mattered. But it did.

Aurora pushed her thoughts aside. "It is truly special. I cannot tell you that these past weeks have been easy, because the truth is that they have been the absolute hardest of my life. I'm beginning to believe that the only way any Starmaker survives it is by having such a magical place to retreat to."

"Does he not treat you well?"

"He treats me..." Aurora trailed off, unsure how to answer. "For all the sun in his blood, he is a cold place to land. He is frustrating and lacks compassion, and I spend most of my days angry with him. In fact, I don't know that I've ever met anyone who exasperates me more." She shook her head, looking into the fire. "But for all his faults, of which there are many—*many*," Aurora emphasized, "he is fiercely devoted to this mountain. And sometimes, in the most surprising moments, I find myself wondering if we understand each other more than we let on." Aurora hadn't planned on saying the last part, but as soon as she did, the words seemed to fit, as if they were a missing piece of a puzzle she'd been trying to solve.

Elsie had an odd expression on her face—almost a smile, but not quite. "He said the same of you, you know."

"You spoke with him?"

"He is the one who came to get me this morning," Elsie said, and Aurora couldn't hide her surprise.

"I assumed he had sent someone from the palace to do that."

"Then perhaps you don't know him as well as you think you do." Elsie stood and grabbed another pastry from the cart.

Aurora wanted to move the conversation along, but her curiosity got the better of her, and she had to ask. "What did he say about me?"

THE SUN AND THE STARMAKER

"He said that you are extremely stubborn and go out of your way to irritate him." Elsie raised her eyebrows, smirking. "But he also said that he understood why the Sun chose you."

"He did?" Aurora asked.

"He said that what you're doing is very difficult and that most people would not be able to bear it. He said you are strong."

Aurora shook her head, frustrated. "It would be nice if he would say those things to me for once."

"Perhaps he will if you stop trying to irritate him for sport." Elsie spoke in a scolding tone, but then she laughed, loud and free, and then Aurora was laughing, too.

When she had laughed until her stomach hurt, she finished her tea and looked at her sister, a somber expression settling over her face. "How is Farren?" she asked softly.

"It has been hard on him," Elsie said. "He believes the Starmaker to be a cruel ruler who forced you into this role. Aspen and I have both tried to talk with him, to explain that the Starmaker is not who put the magic in your blood, but I suspect having someone to blame is easier than not."

"I should have written to him, explained everything," Aurora said. She sank to the floor and grabbed a blanket, lying down in front of the fire. Elsie joined her, and Aurora covered them both with the throw. "I didn't know what to say, so I hardly said anything. I told him not to come here because I thought it would be better that way. But I was being a coward, which the Starmaker was more than willing to point out to me."

Aurora could hear the Starmaker protesting in her mind,

explaining that he had *not* called her a coward, the thought taking her back to the night in his room.

"You can reach out to him at any time," Elsie said, and Aurora felt guilty when she realized how quickly her thoughts had turned from Farren to the Starmaker. "It might help for him to hear it from you."

"You're right." Aurora lay on her back and looked up at the ceiling. "I'll write to him after the wedding and tell him everything."

"Don't put it off for too long. Poison can grow from blame."

"I won't," Aurora promised.

Just then there was a soft thud against the door, and Aurora got up to answer. When she didn't see anyone, she looked down, and there was Constance, watching her with big blue eyes. Aurora laughed.

"Please come in," she said, opening the door wide. Constance hopped in and went to where Elsie was lying before the fire.

"Who is this?" Elsie asked in delight, reaching out to pet the animal.

"Constance," Aurora replied. "She is a resident here." She took her place on the rug once more, pulling the corner of the blanket back over her legs. "How is everyone else?"

"We are adjusting," Elsie said, continuing to pet Constance. "Mama is extremely proud of you. She can hardly believe her daughter was chosen by the Sun. It has made her talk about Papa more, for some reason. It's nice." She smiled. "But it's hard not having you at home, and we all worry about you. How difficult this must be for you."

THE SUN AND THE STARMAKER

"It is," Aurora said. She wanted to put on a brave face for her sister, to tell her that things were going well and that she was settling into her role. But she couldn't bear the thought of feigning strength in front of one more person, and so she was honest. "Most days I'm overwhelmed that this is to be my life, and on the hardest days, I wonder how I will survive it at all. But it is also a wondrous sort of magic. It's hard to explain, but when I'm connected to the Sun, it's as if I see the world through a different lens. I have never felt as grateful for the natural world as I do when I'm pulling the sunlight." Aurora rolled onto her side to face her sister. "I think it's changing me for the better, and in rare moments, it's hard for me to regret that."

"I can tell," Elsie said. "I can see it in you."

"What do you see?"

"Strength. You have always been strong, of course. But this is different. I don't want to minimize what you're going through, and if you asked me to abduct you and take you far away from here, I would do it in a heartbeat." Elsie paused. "But you look as if you've found yourself."

Aurora's eyes began to sting, and she looked away.

"Before, you were so focused on the rest of us that you never paid yourself any mind. And I suppose that's a good quality if you are to be the caretaker of this mountain. But you kept yourself so busy that it almost became a shield, though I must admit I never understood what exactly you were shielding yourself from." Elsie looked at Aurora, her eyes bright. "In stepping into this role, it seems as if you are becoming who you were always meant to be, and while perhaps you are afraid, you are also radiant."

Aurora couldn't help the tears that fell down her cheeks, and she reached for her sister. "Thank you for saying that," she said.

Elsie was crying, too, and she clutched Aurora with both hands. "I have always known that you are my guardian angel. Soon you will be that for all of Reverie, and we are so lucky to have you."

Aurora laughed, wiping at her tears. "But you would abduct me if I asked, hm?"

"Without question," Elsie said with fire in her eyes. "I would do absolutely anything for you."

"I know." Aurora went quiet, and an ache began in her chest, so severe it took her breath away. Looking at Elsie, she realized this was the youngest she would ever see her sister. Elsie was getting older every day, and even if her life was long, it would never be long enough, not when Aurora's continued to stretch out before her. It was then that she almost asked her sister to do it, to kidnap her so she wouldn't have to live without her. How could she possibly endure such a thing? She covered her face and cried, and for a moment she worried she wouldn't be able to stop.

Elsie rubbed Aurora's head, gently pulled her hands from her eyes. "Tell me what you're thinking."

"I'm thinking that of all the hard things this life entails, outliving you will be the hardest by far."

"Oh, sister," Elsie said, pulling her close. "We will not have to say goodbye for a very long time."

"However long we get, it won't be long enough."

THE SUN AND THE STARMAKER

"No," Elsie said, dropping her head onto Aurora's shoulder. "It won't be."

Just then, the gold handkerchief on Aurora's side table drifted through the air toward her and Elsie, startling them both. It wiped Aurora's cheeks first, then Elsie's, before gliding back to the table.

Elsie laughed in disbelief. "So this is what it's like to live on magical land."

"The castle is the most magical place of all, and I doubt I will ever get used to it. In fact, I hope I don't."

There was a knock at the door, and Ina entered a moment later to find Elsie and Aurora wiping the remaining tears from their faces. "Are you all right?" she asked, looking at Aurora with concern.

"We're okay. We have just missed one another."

"Then what a joy it is that you have come to stay with us," Ina said to Elsie. "You look very much like your sister."

Aurora smiled. Ina had welcomed her from the moment she'd set foot in the castle, and she had been patient as Aurora had adjusted to her new life. Aurora was thankful for her, and one day, when she was more settled, she would tell her so.

"Except I don't have strands of white in my hair," Elsie said, running her fingers down Aurora's braid. "It's beautiful."

"I'm surprised by how fast it's turning," Aurora said. "Same with this." She pulled her sleeping gown off her shoulder and showed Elsie the Sun's mark, lines of gold that were growing more pronounced with each day that passed. "The Starmaker told me that one day, when I fully come into my magic, my hair will turn entirely pearlescent, and the mark will be complete."

Elsie ran her fingers over the tattoo, breathing in. "It's remarkable," she said. "It shimmers like the light."

"We'll have to cover both for the wedding," Ina said, "if you do not wish for the village to know that you are the Starmaker Rising."

"I would appreciate that."

"Then shall we begin our preparations?" Ina asked, and Aurora nodded.

"I suppose so. This is your event, so you just tell me what to do and when."

Ina frowned. "Are you not even a little excited to marry?"

Aurora paused, trying to find the right words. She knew that Ina loved the Starmaker like family, and she didn't want to offend her. "I am very eager to see my family, and I'm excited to see how you've transformed the village center." She said it as enthusiastically as she could, but she knew it wasn't the answer Ina was looking for.

"I don't want to overstep, but if love is what you desire, I do believe you'll find it here." Ina offered her a gentle smile, and Aurora couldn't help but smile back. It was such a kind thing to say, but it felt so out of place, and Aurora wondered if they were thinking of the same person. The Starmaker was guarded and distant, not even naming his animals for fear of getting too close. Love was the last thing she would find in him, but she didn't have the heart to argue. Then Ina continued. "Maybe not in the traditional sense, but this castle was built on love, and it fills the walls to the brim. It is here, if you are willing to look."

THE SUN AND THE STARMAKER

It was then that Aurora realized Ina had not been talking about the Starmaker at all, and she felt her cheeks burn with embarrassment. "Thank you, Ina," she said, a little too quickly. "Now, what can I do?"

Ina was back in planning mode once again, and she ushered Aurora into the bathroom. "Take your bath, and I will be back in one hour with your stylists."

"Stylists?" Aurora asked, looking from Ina to her sister. Elsie shrugged.

"Of course. You did not think you would ready yourself on your wedding day, did you?"

Aurora looked at Ina with an expression that said she had thought exactly that. "I am happy to do it myself."

Ina took her by the shoulders and gently turned her so that she was facing the mirror.

"My dear, you are about to marry the Starmaker. You must shine."

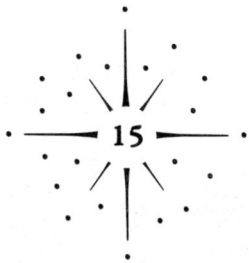

Clarity

Aurora had never been poked and prodded so much in her life, and she was relieved when it was finally time to board the sleigh to the village. She had been terrified to look in the mirror when the stylists had finished, but it had turned out she need not have worried. She still looked like herself, just a little less rough around the edges. And while she was deeply uncomfortable with the scale of the event, she had fallen in love with the dress Ina had chosen.

Aurora stepped into the sleigh, careful not to catch her skirts with her shoe. The icy blue gown was so pale it could be mistaken for white, with a tight bodice that was covered in thousands of crystals. It fell to the floor in layers of silk chiffon that moved together like liquid, and the delicate long sleeves were crafted from the same sheer fabric that was woven just tightly enough to obscure the mark of the Sun on her arm. Dozens of silk-covered buttons ran down her back from her neck to her tailbone, and the skirt's top layer was longer than the rest, creating a small train.

Aurora sat down in the sleigh slowly, afraid of harming the dress, and then Elsie and Ina climbed in next to her, and the snow deer took off for the village. Elsie held Aurora's hand the whole way, and when the lights of Reverie came into view, Aurora's grip tightened and her palms began to sweat.

The village center had been transformed. The streetlamps had been wrapped in twinkling white lights, and the cobblestone pathways were lined with hundreds of floral arrangements, white roses and blue poppies wrapped around glass lanterns that held flickering candles. The evergreens had cleared the cobbles that morning, and hundreds of lightning bugs flitted overhead to combat the darkness. There was a soft snow falling, and it dusted the paths and lanterns in a frosty white.

The Starmaker had let the light slip between the peaks hours ago, and there were dozens of iron stands holding copper bowls that burned with vibrant orange flames. All the walkways led to the center of Reverie, a large open circle where the market was usually held, but today the stalls had been cleared for the wedding. There was a platform made of ice in the center with so many chairs arranged around it that Aurora's breath caught in her lungs when she saw them, realizing how many people would be there. Between the chairs were narrow aisles where glass poles stood, and sheer fabric draped from pole to pole, woven with soft lights that cast a beautiful glow over the area.

Snow clung to rooftops and trees, sparkling in the moonlight, and the flowers caught falling snowflakes that glistened on their petals. The air smelled sweet and fresh, and Aurora inhaled deeply to steady herself.

It was every bit as magical as the Starmaker's wedding ought to be, and for a single moment, Aurora wondered how a marriage with such a lovely beginning could possibly be a bad one. She had been dreading this day even though she had insisted upon it, but it was impossible not be overcome by the beauty of it all.

The village center was already full of people, almost every chair claimed, and Aurora knew that the Starmaker had been right: this night would surely be counted among the mountain's stories.

"I'm going to take my seat," Elsie said, giving Aurora a hug.

"Come find me after." Aurora held on to her sister and closed her eyes, trying hopelessly to calm her racing heart.

"I will. Promise."

Elsie left, and Aurora stayed in the sleigh just beyond the lights of the village, waiting with Ina. Then, before she was ready, a string quartet began playing, and it was time.

Aurora had yet to see the Starmaker, and as she stepped from the sleigh and onto the path, she craned her neck, hoping to catch a glimpse of him. There was a pause in the music, and then another song began and everyone stood, blocking Aurora's view. She faltered, her head too light as if she might faint at any moment, and she told herself to breathe. All she had to do was breathe.

People murmured as Aurora passed, but she tried not to

THE SUN AND THE STARMAKER

notice. She had wanted to keep her identity as the Starmaker Rising hidden, and so her family and Farren had kept it a secret. Her family had done so because it was what Aurora wanted, but Farren, she suspected, still hoped that she might leave the castle and come back to him. Aurora wanted to preserve a sense of isolation so that she could learn her magic without feeling the weight of the whole village upon her, and she wondered now if that had been a mistake. She forced herself to look up, to meet her neighbors' eyes, but no one appeared to be looking at her with judgment. Instead, they were smiling kindly and blotting their eyes with the lace handkerchiefs that had been placed upon each seat. They were happy for her, and it moved her to her core.

Aurora took a step forward, then another, each one leading her closer to the Starmaker. She gripped her bouquet tightly, a gorgeous arrangement of roses so white they matched the freshly fallen snow, and she tried to stay calm as every head turned to watch her. She had never wanted attention, had never wanted to be anyone's focus, and yet all of Reverie had shown up to watch the Starmaker marry and to get a glimpse of his bride.

She paused.

That was all she was right now: the Starmaker's bride. She wasn't Aurora Finch or the Starmaker Rising, wasn't a sister or a daughter or a writer. She was being wholly consumed by the Starmaker's gravity, and she understood then that while this would certainly be *a* story the villagers told, it wouldn't be a true one.

Aurora forced herself to keep going, and she finally got close enough to see the Starmaker. His eyes locked on hers instantly and didn't look away. His jaw was tense and his stance rigid, but when Aurora met his gaze, she saw his shoulders dip, as if he had finally let out a breath he'd been holding.

Aurora realized then that they were in this together. Marrying may have been her requirement, but it was one she had been forced to make by circumstances that were far beyond her control—circumstances that were far beyond the Starmaker's as well. Every other person was there to witness something spectacular, but for Aurora and the Starmaker, this was a life that had been written for them in the stars, and they were simply being pulled along through the infinite night sky.

Aurora took a shaky breath, but she couldn't get her mind to quiet. Nothing felt right, and suddenly she was angry, not only for herself but for the Starmaker as well. Their stories *mattered*, and yet they were telling a lie for the sake of a glare line and an acceptable reason for her to have moved to the castle.

It wasn't real. None of it was real. And if there was one thing Aurora was sure of, it was that she had not given up her life to star in someone else's fiction. She wouldn't do it.

She began walking again, all the way to the icy platform where the Starmaker stood. He offered her his hand, and she took it as she stepped onto a silver rug to face him. She could feel her resentment of him fading, receding into the distance like the life she'd once planned for herself. It became hazy while he sharpened before her until she saw him with extreme clarity. He had once been mortal, a boy who had journaled and read poetry and collected books about plants and stars. He had once been in love, had once had a family, had once been a person instead of a role.

Aurora was certain that the Starmaker would be irritated at best if he knew she was outraged on his behalf. She almost laughed herself. But she would one day take his place, and while they were to protect the mountain and keep the village safe, there was nothing that said they must lose themselves to it.

The Starmaker was resplendent in a white suit and light-blue cloak the same color as Aurora's dress. His straight hair fell just beyond his shoulders, glimmering beneath the stars, and his eyes were bright as he watched her. It was all fake, the way he looked at her and the way he gently held her hands, and Aurora could no longer force her emotions aside.

Anger turned to panic, her breaths coming too quick, too shallow. She tried to focus on her family and how much they needed the glare line, but the thought couldn't settle amidst her distress. Nothing could, and all she could think in that moment was that she needed to get out of there. Aurora pulled her hands from the Starmaker's and found Elsie in the crowd, who was healthy, entirely healed from the Frost.

The Starmaker had upheld his side of the agreement, but Aurora couldn't do it, couldn't go through with the very thing she had required of him. *She* had demanded they marry, and yet she couldn't do it.

"Aurora," the Starmaker said, his voice tight, so quiet only she could hear. "What are you doing?"

"I'm sorry." She looked at him and tried to make him see everything she was feeling. But there were so many people watching, a priest who was impatient to start, and a distance between them she wasn't sure even the most genuine of emotions could bridge. She had to be quick, to say something the Starmaker would understand. "My sister is healed, and I have moved to the castle to learn your magic. But this is something I cannot do."

And with that, Aurora jumped from the platform and ran as fast as she could, leaving the Starmaker standing alone before all of Reverie. She paused at the end of the aisle, turning to see him one more time, frozen in place and entirely stunned. Then she forced herself to move. With every step she took, her panic eased, fading away, and by the time she finally reached the sleigh, she was entirely rid of it. She knew it would return when the reality of her choice came crashing down on her, but that was a problem she would deal with later. For now, she felt free.

Aurora could hear the chaos erupting behind her, the chairs scraping against the ground as people stood and craned their necks, trying to get a look at her or the Starmaker or both. Voices got louder and louder, but Aurora kept her eyes ahead. She took the reins, and the snow deer began to run, pulling her far, far away.

It was the best she'd felt since she'd encountered the Starmaker in the woods, and with the wedding at her back and the wind in her hair, she smiled.

The Starmaker

It had been many years since the Starmaker had been genuinely surprised, and even longer since he had been mortified. But in a matter of seconds, Aurora Finch had managed to accomplish both.

The Starmaker was acutely aware of all the people watching him, and he knew he needed to come up with something to say, but he'd been stunned into silence. Sweat formed on the back of his neck, and he clenched his jaw. He had never relished speaking publicly, and now he had to account for why he had been left at the altar with no bride in sight.

The *audacity* of that girl.

He knew he should be angry, and he was. In fact, he was furious, but that was part of the problem. His body was pulsing with senses he had long since forgotten, as if his nervous system was waking after a very long nap. He couldn't think straight. He couldn't think at all.

It was maddening.

It was...

...invigorating.

All at once, the Starmaker remembered, truly remembered, how remarkable it was to live.

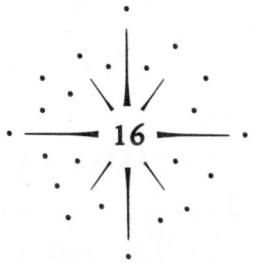

Very Old Wine

When Aurora arrived at the castle, there was no one outside to greet her. The staff was in the village for the wedding, and Aurora was thankful to have the palace to herself. The journey back had been exhilarating, but now that she was here, her adrenaline was fading and she realized how truly exhausted she was.

Aurora walked the empty hallways to her room, relishing the way her footsteps echoed as she went. She wasn't proud that it had taken her until the last possible moment to understand that she couldn't go through with the wedding, but she also couldn't bring herself to regret it.

Aurora reached her bedroom, shutting the door behind her and resting her back against the wood. She closed her eyes and took several deep breaths, blowing them out through her mouth.

She knew she needed to write to her family and explain herself to the Starmaker, and she would. But for now, all she wanted to do was sleep.

She finally opened her eyes and nearly screamed.

"Aurora," Farren said, standing in middle of the room. "I didn't mean to frighten you."

Aurora's eyes were wide. "What are you doing here?" she asked in a rush, looking over her shoulder as if the Starmaker would appear at any moment.

"I came here to see your new life. I thought it might help me move on." Farren shook his head and looked at the floor. "I didn't want to go to the wedding, and I figured it would be fairly easy to get inside the castle since everyone was at the ceremony." He shrugged; then something seemed to occur to him, and he stood up straighter. "Why are you back so soon?"

"I didn't marry the Starmaker," Aurora said, a dull ache beginning in her head.

"I knew it." A smile pulled at Farren's lips, and he rushed toward her. He took her face in his hands and murmured how much he'd missed her, and at first, Aurora closed her eyes and covered his hands with hers. Farren filled her senses, newspaper ink and woodsmoke and a hint of sweat, so familiar. What she wasn't expecting, though, was how weak her reaction to him was. The familiarity with which he touched her, even his scent, didn't seem to fit anymore, and instead of being comforting, it made her tense. She needed room to breathe, and she took a step back.

"You knew what?"

"That you wouldn't marry him." Farren's voice was a mix of relief and hope, and Aurora realized he thought she'd run from the wedding for him.

The pain in her head was getting worse, and she rubbed her temples. "Farren, I'm sorry I didn't write to you sooner. I should have, should have explained everything. It wasn't fair, what I did to you."

"You don't have to explain—" Farren began, reaching for her once more, and Aurora took another step back.

"It wasn't fair, but what I did tonight... I didn't do it for us." Aurora said the words as gently as possible, but she could see the way they struck Farren, the way his face fell and his brow furrowed. "I was panicked and angry, and I couldn't go through with the wedding."

"I don't understand," Farren said, his deep brown eyes searching her face. "You don't want to be with me?" He asked the question so plainly that it broke Aurora's heart, and she knew that the kindest thing she could do was be honest with him.

"I did before, and I still mourn that loss. But I do not want to be frozen in time while you progress ever onward. That is not a life I wish for myself."

"I don't care about that," Farren said, cutting her off.

"But I do. And I need you to hear me when I say it. I'm sorry for all that has happened, and I know we would have had a beautiful life together. But it doesn't fit anymore, and as hard as it is, we both need to accept that."

"I don't want to accept that," Farren said. "I won't."

"You must." Aurora sighed, needing to move, and she began to walk around the room. She was frustrated with him, frustrated that he wasn't listening, frustrated that he was speaking over her and ignoring what she was saying.

"We can make it fit," Farren insisted, and Aurora couldn't understand why he was fighting so hard for this. For her. For them.

She realized suddenly that what had been a safe love for her—a love where she would never have to live in fear of the grief that had stolen her mother and haunted the Sun—might not have been a safe love for him. Maybe for Farren, it had been something stronger. Something greater.

An overwhelming sadness spread through her chest as she wondered whether her love for Farren had been more about fear than hope. More about preservation than dreams. If a love born of fear was even love at all.

"I'm sorry," Aurora said again, and she truly meant it. "I'm so sorry. But I've made up my mind, and I hope that one day, you will understand."

"This isn't you." Farren shook his head, his words turning sharp. "He did this to you. Changed you. I know your heart, Aurora, and this isn't it."

Aurora walked to where Farren stood, looked him directly in the eye. "My heart is no longer your concern, nor is it so malleable as to be changed by the whims of another. This *is* me, and these are my choices."

"I refuse to believe it," Farren said, his tone so different from how it had been just moments before. Mean, almost.

"And that is your right. But it is not my responsibility to make you believe things about which I am being rather clear."

Aurora knew then that she *had* changed. She was not the person she'd been on the day she'd met the Starmaker, nor was she the girl who had accepted Farren's proposal. Before, she would have sat with Farren for as long as was necessary, let him interrupt and even insult her if that was what he needed in order to move on. But she wouldn't do that now, and she grew impatient as she realized that she'd rather be arguing with the Starmaker than safely loving Farren.

"I think it's best if you go," Aurora said softly.

Farren nodded, taking a step toward the door. "I'm sorry for coming. It wasn't my intent to upset you."

"You don't have to apologize. I should have written to you."

"I'm not sure it would have made a difference," Farren said honestly, and Aurora understood. He had needed to hear it from her in person, and she couldn't fault him for that. "I'll go now."

"Not through the castle," Aurora said. She didn't know if the Starmaker was back or not, but she didn't want him to see Farren. She didn't want anyone to, though she wasn't sure why she felt that way.

Farren's expression soured, but he said nothing, just walked to the balcony and opened the door in silence. Aurora followed, standing behind him as he climbed over the railing.

"Farren," she said. He turned to look at her. "Be careful on your way home. The Frost is active in these woods."

He nodded, jumped onto the large branch of an apple tree,

THE SUN AND THE STARMAKER

then made his way to the ground, swallowed up by the darkness of night.

Aurora stood where she was for several minutes before finally making her way back inside. Her gown felt impossibly heavy, but she couldn't get it off by herself, and she wasn't ready to face Ina, so she went to her desk and began to write. It was the only thing she knew to do, and she filled sheet after sheet, getting her thoughts down. She wrote about Farren and the wedding and her magic. She wrote about the castle and immortality and her family. She wrote about the Starmaker, and once she started, she couldn't stop.

The Starmaker this and the Starmaker that.

The Starmaker, the Starmaker, the Starmaker, over and over again.

When she was done journaling, she wrote to her family, apologizing for the mess she had undoubtedly caused them and promising she would visit them soon. She assured them she was okay—more than okay, really—told them she loved them, and sealed the letter. She knew she had made things more difficult for them by not securing the glare line they needed, and thick guilt sat heavy in her gut. But it was the shame that really sent her spiraling. Making life easier for her family should have been reason enough to marry, and she'd truly thought that it was, but she had been wrong. Perhaps she could get them more mirrors, something to help ease the burden her panicked choice had put upon them.

By then it was late, and Aurora was restless and hungry. She was sure the Starmaker and the staff were back at the castle, but no one had bothered her, for which she was grateful. Aurora quietly opened the door and stuck her head out, listening for any activity in the hallways, but the castle was silent. It had been a long day for everyone, and they were likely all in bed, as she should be. But she knew she wouldn't be able to sleep, and so she replaced her wedding shoes with slippers, lit a candle, and made her way to the kitchen.

As she was about to turn into the room, Constance hopped out, and Aurora had to sidestep so as not to run into her.

"Can't sleep either, hm?" she asked the rabbit, entering the kitchen. Then she stopped.

The Starmaker was standing with his back to her, grabbing a plate from the shelf. He slowly turned and his eyes met hers, rendering her breathless.

"I'm sorry," she said, frozen where she was. "I didn't think anyone would be up at this hour."

"I was counting on the same thing," he said.

Aurora paused. "Should I go?"

He held her gaze for a moment longer before turning his attention to the kitchen island. A gorgeous spread of sweets and cake was sitting untouched, and Aurora felt another pang of guilt as she realized the staff must have worked all day to put this together before the ceremony.

"No," he finally said. "I think it would make the staff very happy to know their efforts were not wasted."

Aurora hesitantly walked into the kitchen, then grabbed a plate. She tried not to seem overeager, but she was ravenous, and

THE SUN AND THE STARMAKER

in the end, she piled her plate with as much food as it would hold. The Starmaker raised an eyebrow but said nothing.

"I didn't have dinner," she said, and then felt ridiculous; of course she hadn't. She had left the wedding long before the reception had even begun.

"I remember." The Starmaker put more food on his plate as well. "I was there, you know."

Aurora slid onto a stool at the island, slowly exhaling. "I owe you an explanation."

He didn't say anything, didn't even look at her, which Aurora took as an invitation to continue.

"I have loved the stories of Reverie ever since I was a little girl. I learned them all by heart, and I knew from a young age that I wanted to be a writer. I wanted to be able to tell stories like the ones I heard as a child." Aurora paused, taking a bite of a devilishly sweet pastry. "Before our encounter in the woods, I was to wed Farren, whose family owns and operates *Eternal Reverie*. His father promised me a column once I married his son."

"Are you going to tell me your whole life story?" the Starmaker asked with annoyance.

Aurora rolled her eyes. "You're so impatient," she said. "Just listen."

The Starmaker waved his hand through the air as if he could not care less whether she continued or not.

"When I saw you standing at the altar, I got angry, so angry that you were being forced to play a part you did not want. Angry that we both were. And then that anger turned to panic, and I couldn't calm myself down, couldn't ignore my instinct to run." Aurora shook her head, still so full of that feeling, surprised by the intensity of it even now. "We are Starmakers, and our stories are going to be told for generations; at the very least, shouldn't they be true? Don't we deserve that?"

The Starmaker was quiet, and Aurora wasn't sure he would answer her. Then he spoke. "I don't know," he said wearily, and she could tell it was a sincere response. "I'm not sure I know who I am anymore, aside from the Starmaker."

It was one of the most honest things he'd ever said to her, and it made her chest ache with both sadness and understanding. She thought back to his childhood room, the way it looked as if no one had set foot in it for years.

"Well, for starters, you're grouchy. You're not a morning person. You prefer silence to casual conversation and have a soft spot for animals. You also quite enjoy your tea, flowers, and poetry. And every time the snow deer pull us down that particularly steep drop on the way to the glacier, you get an excited look on your face as if it's the most fun you've ever had." Aurora said it lightly, trying to ease the weight of his admission, but the Starmaker watched her with confusion. Then his expression shifted, and he looked genuinely moved. But it was gone almost as soon as it appeared, leaving Aurora questioning if she'd even seen it at all.

"I do love that drop," he admitted. "Otherwise it's not a very charitable description, is it?"

"Then how about this: you make me feel as if I can be extraordinary." Aurora was stunned when the words tumbled from her mouth, and she wished instantly that she could take them back. She couldn't believe she had said it out loud, and she looked away, mortified. Leaving him at the altar and rejecting Farren in the same night had made her bold; bolder, she thought, than she ought to be.

But the words were also true. From their very first day together, the Starmaker's only expectation of her was that she be great; he had never treated her as if she were anything else, and it had empowered her in a way she had never experienced before.

The Starmaker shifted in his seat, and she could feel his eyes on her. "You are extraordinary," he said plainly, as if it was the most obvious thing in the world. "The Sun chose you for a reason."

"As she did you," Aurora said. "It would be a tragedy if you forgot all the reasons you were chosen."

"Hm," was all he said in response, reaching for a bottle of ice wine sitting in a silver bucket. The Starmaker hesitated. "Would you like a glass?" he finally asked, pulling two from the shelf. "I've been saving it, and now seems as good a time as any. This particular bottle is from my wedding."

"You were married?" Aurora asked, unable to hide her shock.

"Almost," the Starmaker said. "I called it off. I had the decency to tell her before the ceremony, of course, but it was months after I'd come into my magic, and I knew it wouldn't be the marriage I had once hoped for. She still wanted to proceed, but I had no desire to watch her fade away someday."

It reminded Aurora of her conversation with Farren, and she understood. She understood entirely. "Up until this moment, I've always assumed marriage was something I wanted. But I'm realizing now that what I really wanted wasn't marriage at all, but rather the life it could afford me." Aurora said it softly, as if she should be ashamed. She thought about how she had mourned losing her position with *Eternal Reverie* more than her life with Farren, and now she knew why.

"If I were not the Starmaker, I would have liked to be a husband. To wholly belong to another." The words were so quiet Aurora barely heard them, and yet they caused something deep inside her to stir. She couldn't make sense of it, so she changed the subject instead, needing to focus on something else.

"I'm sorry I didn't tell you before the ceremony."

"As am I," the Starmaker said, pouring two glasses of wine and handing one to Aurora. "Especially because it forced me to announce that you are the Starmaker Rising."

Aurora gaped at him. She knew it wasn't fair of her to be hurt, not when she had left him standing there alone, but she couldn't help it. "You agreed that you wouldn't."

"Yes, just as you agreed that we'd marry—insisted, really. But I had to explain why you moved to the castle so suddenly, and this is the perfect reason; your family won't become the subject of gossip and the castle won't lose the faith of those it protects." He paused, met her eyes. "I am sorry."

"You weren't *forced* to do that. You could have said anything." Aurora's voice began to rise, and she tried to stay calm, but the weight of the entire mountain was pressing down on her shoulders, crushing her.

"I wasn't given much time to prepare," the Starmaker said, matching her tone.

"You are the Starmaker! They would have believed anything you told them," Aurora said, standing, hating that she felt betrayed by him. He had handled being left at the altar better than she was handling this, and she knew it. And so did he.

"The jilted Starmaker," he corrected, and Aurora didn't know why, didn't even feel it coming, but she laughed, a truly unhinged thing that could only be described as a cackle. The Starmaker stared at her as if he couldn't believe the sound that had just come from her lips, and then he was laughing, too.

Aurora clutched her stomach and laughed so hard she cried, and when she had no energy left, she sat back down.

"I didn't get the chance to tell you earlier, but you look beautiful." The Starmaker's voice was low, and Aurora watched him, unable to breathe. His gaze trailed down her face and over her neck, sweeping across the bodice of her dress, which glistened in the dim candlelight.

"I can't get it off," she finally admitted. "It's so tight and I'm so full, and all I want is to be free of this dress." She paused. "Will you help me?"

The Starmaker swallowed, his jaw tensing. "Help you...?"

"Unbutton my dress. I don't want to wake Ina, and I'll never be able to sleep in this. It doesn't need to be a big deal; I simply cannot reach the back on my own."

The Starmaker said nothing for several breaths, and then he nodded.

Aurora stood, walking to where the Starmaker was seated. She turned her back to him and pulled her hair over her shoulder, waiting.

And waiting.

And waiting.

Finally, the Starmaker's fingers brushed her skin, gently undoing button after button. She could feel his exhales whispering across her back, and she shivered, hoping the Starmaker couldn't see the goose bumps that were forming along her spine. She had told him it wasn't a big deal, that she only needed help, but her body hadn't fully internalized the message, and her breaths became shallow as an ache began deep in her center.

His fingers made it all the way down to her tailbone, caressing her skin ever so softly, and Aurora felt unsteady on her feet. The Starmaker cleared his throat. "Done," he said in a hoarse whisper.

Aurora turned slowly, holding her dress up in front. Their eyes met, and she had the sudden urge to press her lips to his, to learn how he tasted. To learn how he felt. It wasn't so much a want as a need, and Aurora was dizzy with desire.

The Starmaker's eyes were dark, searching her face, catching on her lips. Then he abruptly blinked and turned his head, grabbing the counter as if he needed the extra support.

Aurora came back to herself, taking a deep breath and reaching for her wine, wholly unprepared for what had just passed between them.

"To challenging each other," she said, tipping her glass to him, desperate to clear the air of the moment.

THE SUN AND THE STARMAKER

The Starmaker raised his drink as well. Their glasses touched, and Aurora took a long sip, eager for the sweet chill of dessert wine to slide down her throat and ease her stirring gut. Instead, a wretched sourness hit her tongue, and Aurora violently turned her head, spewing the beverage all over the kitchen.

The Starmaker's wedding wine—the precious liquid he had been saving for hundreds of years—was running down Aurora's chin and dripping onto the counter. She took in the mess before her, utterly shocked. Everything was covered, and she fought the urge to walk from the room without a single word. What a tragic turn of events. She could feel her cheeks flaming, and she turned to the Starmaker, mortified.

He stared at her, slowly raising his glass to his nose. "Hm," he murmured to himself. "I guess dessert wine *can* go bad."

He set down his glass without taking a sip, stood, and walked to Aurora. "You've got something just here," he said. He slowly brought his thumb to her jaw and rubbed it across her chin, lingering for just a breath. Then he turned and walked out of the room, leaving Aurora holding up her wine-stained dress, drowning in embarrassment.

Everything was silent.

Then she heard his laughter burst forth and bounce off the castle walls, reaching her all the way back in the kitchen.

Melting Snow

Aurora briefly considered skipping breakfast and never leaving her room again, but the only thing worse than having to show her face to the Starmaker would be hiding away. She took a deep breath, steadied herself, and walked into the dining room with her head held high.

The Starmaker was already seated, eating his breakfast with Constance beside him, and he glanced up at Aurora when she walked in. He said nothing, but she caught the faintest twitch of his lips.

She glared at him.

Frederick and Ina stood against the wall, eyes moving between Aurora and the Starmaker, clearly uncertain of how to react. "The Starmaker and I spoke last night," Aurora said. "I assure you we are fine."

THE SUN AND THE STARMAKER

"That's very good to hear, miss," Ina said, and Aurora gave her a pointed look. "I apologize. Aurora."

"Thank you. And Ina, I must apologize to you. The wedding you arranged was truly beautiful, and I'm very sorry that all your hard work was overshadowed by my premature departure. You did an incredible job with it."

Ina looked moved, and she gave Aurora a small smile. "Thank you, Aurora. I'm very glad you liked it."

Frederick hurried over and pulled out Aurora's chair for her, and she sat down, looking at the Starmaker. He avoided her eyes, concentrating very intently on the food in front of him, his face straining.

"Go on, then," Aurora said dryly. "Get it out."

The Starmaker let out one long loud laugh, then cleared his throat and blotted his mouth with a napkin. "My apologies," he said.

Ina and Frederick looked deeply confused.

Aurora turned her attention to her breakfast, but her mood soured when she saw the headline on the front page of *Eternal Reverie*.

STARMAKER LEFT AT THE ALTAR BY ICE-COLD BRIDE

"Clever," she said under her breath. All of Reverie now knew that she was the Starmaker Rising, and *this* was the headline they'd printed? The article didn't have a byline, but Aurora was sure it was Farren who'd written it. She'd thought their conversation had been as amicable as possible, but it seemed she had been wrong.

"Surely you could have written something better than this drivel," the Starmaker said, and Aurora looked up in surprise. He'd actually managed to make her feel better.

"I could have," she agreed.

They were quiet as they ate their breakfast, and then they put on their cloaks and boarded the sleigh. "Would it be okay with you if we visit my family today after pulling in the light? I feel I should see them after yesterday's events."

"I suppose so. It would be beneficial to check on the woods that far back, too—see how the phlox is doing."

The Starmaker was back to his normal self, but there seemed to be a level of comfort between them that hadn't been there before. Perhaps that was the natural progression of things when one embarrassed oneself so spectacularly, but either way, Aurora was grateful for it.

She was glad she would soon see her family. It wasn't just the wedding and all of Reverie knowing about her new role that was weighing on her, but her magic as well. She had stopped making any meaningful progress, and she worried there was something wrong, that she wasn't strong enough to take on her new role. Visiting her family's cottage would undoubtedly make her feel better, and she hoped it might help her figure out the key to moving forward.

After another frustrating morning of trying and failing to hold more light than she previously had, Aurora was eager to leave the glacier behind and head to her cottage beyond the reach of the Sun.

"I can feel it inside you," the Starmaker said when they got back in the sleigh. "My magic. As more of it transfers from me to you, as more of it *lives* in you, I feel it." The Starmaker spoke quietly, and he did not look at her. "When we were pulling the light just now, your frustration ran through me as if it were my own. I don't understand it," he said, almost breathless. He paused. "It seems we are connected now."

Even if Aurora hadn't already been fighting against her changing feelings, his words would have all but ensured that there was a shift between them. She couldn't name it, couldn't even describe it, yet she knew it had happened. She forced her eyes from him and took a breath, big and deep, as if she'd gone without air for too long.

"I do not like to think of it," Aurora said. "Taking your magic." She knew that as soon as all of it transferred to her, he would be mortal, susceptible to all the things he had once been protected from—aging and illness and death. It tore at her insides.

"It is the way things are," he said simply.

"It may be easy for you to accept, but remember that you have had years to get comfortable with what will happen, while I have had mere weeks."

The Starmaker exhaled, looking out at the trees as they passed by in a blur. "I suppose you are right."

Just then, the words he had spoken when they'd met in the woods came rushing back to her, and a sharp pain began in her chest as she remembered them: *I've been waiting a long while for you.* She didn't know how she hadn't recognized it before, and she looked at the Starmaker as if seeing him for the first time.

He *wanted* his reign to be over. He was ready to pass on his magic and responsibilities, and Aurora suddenly saw how truly tired he was.

They wanted different things: Aurora hoped she could take as long as she needed to learn how to be the next Starmaker, while the Starmaker wanted to prepare her as quickly as possible. It made so much sense to her now, their constant frustrations and annoyances with each other—they were working toward different goals, and the realization caused a seismic shock inside her.

Aurora had spent most of her eighteen years mapping out the safest path for her life, and she had done a brilliant job of it. But as she watched the Starmaker, she felt that safety slipping away like melting snow, and the tighter she held on to it, the faster it vanished.

"You are staring," the Starmaker said, not bothering to face her.

He was right, but Aurora couldn't help herself. He was stunning, impossible to turn from even though it hurt to look at him. Finally—and with some effort—she pulled her gaze away, but she couldn't stop thinking about her revelation, couldn't stop her mind from spinning.

The Starmaker had welcomed Aurora's arrival, even knowing he would lose his immortality to her. And suddenly, when Aurora looked out toward the horizon, all she could see was unbearable grief and loneliness. How could the future hold anything else when the Starmaker was so eager to end his reign?

Aurora was thankful when her cottage appeared in the

THE SUN AND THE STARMAKER

distance, and she practically launched herself from the sleigh when they were close enough. The door opened just in time, and Aurora ran directly into Elsie's arms.

"Are you okay?" Elsie whispered as Aurora's grip tightened, and at first Aurora didn't answer. She just held on to her sister.

"I'm okay," she said, finally pulling away when Mama appeared from the kitchen, drying her hands on a towel.

"What are you doing here, darling? Is everything all right?" she asked, ushering Aurora inside. She followed her mother, then turned to see the Starmaker standing in the doorway, clearly unsure if he should enter.

"Come inside," Aurora said, and hesitantly, he took a step. Aurora turned to her mother. "Everything is fine. We need to check on the woods behind the house, and I wanted to stop by and make sure you were okay after yesterday."

"So you are well, then?"

"Yes, of course," Aurora said.

Her mother's expression changed then from one of concern to one of displeasure. "I'm only asking because I cannot fathom why you would embarrass yourself and your family so thoroughly if you are well, as you say."

Aurora looked at her mother with surprise. She hadn't expected her family to be happy about what had happened, but she hadn't expected this, either. "I'm sorry. I thought I could go through with it, but I was wrong. I wish I had known sooner so I could have spared us all the spectacle."

Aurora caught sight of *Eternal Reverie* on the table and

quickly looked away, but the headline continued to flash in her mind. Just then, Aspen walked in the door, looking from Aurora to the Starmaker and back again.

"Is everything okay?"

"Yes," Aurora said with exasperation, then gave Aspen an apologetic look. "I'm sorry, I wasn't expecting to be asked that question so many times upon my arrival."

"Surely you can't blame us," her mother said, shaking her head. "Honestly, Aurora, what were you thinking?"

"It didn't feel genuine," Aurora said, and she could hear how unsatisfying the answer was. How weak. "I got mad, and I panicked. I'm so sorry you won't get your glare line."

"You made an agreement with the Starmaker, and you went back on your word. Not only to him but to all of us." She didn't sound mad, though. She sounded discouraged, and it was then that Aurora understood how much her mother had been counting on a line to the castle.

"I'm sorry, Mama."

"It is not an easy thing, what your daughter is doing." Aurora was shocked to hear the Starmaker's voice behind her; she had almost forgotten he was there. "We will check on your phlox regularly and do what we can to ensure that you remain safe from the Frost. You have my word."

Aurora stared at him, not believing what she was hearing. Was he...coming to her defense? After she had utterly humiliated him?

"You're right, of course," Mama said after several moments,

THE SUN AND THE STARMAKER

her voice softer now. "I suppose I got swept up in the excitement of it all."

"I can hardly blame you," Aurora said. "That was kind of the point."

"I should have been thinking about what it was like for you up there rather than getting caught up in what it was like for us down here. We had visitors every day who wanted to talk about the union, and I wasn't used to that kind of attention. I'm sorry, Aurora."

Aurora shook her head. "Don't be. I understand."

Elsie offered them tea, and they all sat at the table together. It was strange to see the Starmaker in her home, sitting at the table where she'd had countless family meals as if he'd been there a hundred times before. He wasn't comfortable, exactly, but he was trying. He smiled at the appropriate times and nodded as he listened, and it did something weird to Aurora's heart, as if it were beating in an entirely new rhythm.

She didn't understand why he was doing this, and it was unsettling.

Unsettling, and somehow exactly what she needed.

When they were done, Aurora hugged her family and promised to write soon, and then she wandered through the woods with the Starmaker before heading back to the sleigh. Everything looked as it should, and the guilt Aurora felt over depriving them of the glare line eased slightly. Then she had a thought she couldn't ignore.

"There's something I want to show you," she said.

The Starmaker didn't say anything, simply nodded, and Aurora took the reins. The snow deer began to pull, and after several minutes, more than a hundred mirrors appeared in the distance, reflecting light so bright that both the Starmaker and Aurora had to cover their eyes. Even the snow deer turned their heads to avoid staring directly at them.

Once the Starmaker's surprise wore off, he sat up in his seat and craned his neck to get a better look. "What is this?" he asked.

"It is how my family grows certain crops. We lease this slice of pasture from our neighbors and reflect the light onto our property. It isn't ideal, of course, but it makes a significant difference to the utility of our land."

"Clever," he said, and he actually sounded impressed. "Very clever."

"I have always loved mirrors, and one day I thought, *Why not use them to benefit my family?*"

The Starmaker looked at her. "This was your idea?"

"It was." Aurora had been tending to the mirrors for so long that they had become part of her routine, but seeing them through the Starmaker's eyes made them new again, and Aurora felt a deep sense of pride as she looked at them all. "It took me years to build up my collection, but I think it came together rather nicely."

"It is remarkable," the Starmaker said, and Aurora smiled at him. "It is no wonder the Sun chose you."

Aurora knew he meant it in a positive way, but it only served to remind her of what a terrible job she was doing each morning as she tried to pull in the light. She sat back on the bench, frustrated.

THE SUN AND THE STARMAKER

"It seems I am much better at reflecting the light than I am at pulling it."

"It will come with time," the Starmaker said. "We likely have only a few more sessions before your fever sets in, anyway. Perhaps the break will be good for you."

"Fever?" Aurora asked. It was the first she was hearing of it.

The Starmaker grabbed the reins and turned the snow deer back toward the glacier. "The magic in your blood is increasing your body temperature the more you use it. At first, it will feel like a normal fever, and you will experience chills and sweats. But soon you will acclimate."

"Is it dangerous?"

"No, but you will become quite ill for a few days. The fever will worsen as your body temperature rises, and you will be extremely weak. But the castle has healing properties that will help your body adjust, and soon you will be fine."

Aurora turned away. "Even more to look forward to," she said.

The village came into view in the distance, and Aurora could see the market bustling with activity. But the longer she looked, the more a deep sadness settled inside her, a heavy feeling she couldn't shake. She watched the crowds of people talking and laughing, and she realized that she would outlive each and every one of them. It felt like a blow to the abdomen, knocking the wind right out of her, and she bent at the waist, completely caught off guard by the brutality of it.

The Starmaker looked over at her, bending to meet her eyes. "What is it?" he asked, but Aurora could barely hear him over the pounding of her pulse in her ears. He pulled back on the reins, and the snow deer slowed to a stop.

Her mother and brothers and Elsie—she would have to say goodbye to them one by one, and she didn't think she could survive it. An impossible weight pressed down on her chest and wrapped around her sternum, making it difficult to breathe.

"How do you bear it?" she asked in gasps, clutching her arms tightly around her middle, trying to keep from falling apart.

"Bear what?" He sounded confused, and he followed her gaze to the center of the village.

"There will come a day when every single person in that market will be dead. When every single person I love will be gone. And I'll still be here." The words shook as they fell from her mouth, and Aurora tried hard to keep from crying. The realization had come on so suddenly, and now that it had, she could think of nothing else.

She tried to tell herself that she was not the only one who would experience loss in her life, that part of being human was loving and losing and grieving. Enduring, somehow. She told herself that every person who had come before her had gone through their own tragedies, that she herself had survived when she had lost Papa. But her heart slammed against her ribs and her head throbbed and she couldn't pull herself out of the pit she had fallen in.

The trees were quiet, their snowy branches absorbing the distant sounds of the market, and soon the only thing Aurora could hear was her own heartbeat. The Starmaker inched closer to her,

THE SUN AND THE STARMAKER

and he reached out his hands before suddenly pulling them back, seemingly at war with himself over something.

"Look at me," he said, awkwardly holding his hands in front of his chest as if he was unsure of where to put them. Aurora's breaths were quick and shallow, and she was suddenly aware of how little control she had over herself, but she did as he said.

The Starmaker seemed to make a decision then, and slowly, so very slowly, he took her hand and placed it against his chest, pressing firmly. "Breathe with me."

His breaths were exaggerated, and he let them out slowly as Aurora did the same, following his lead. His heart was a slow and steady rhythm that soothed the frenzied beat of her own, and he never took his eyes off her, breathing with her until Aurora felt herself coming back, climbing her way out of the panic.

"You will bear it," the Starmaker said simply, "because you are able to."

"How do you know that?" Aurora asked, her voice trembling.

"Because you were born for this. You have the fire of the Sun in your blood, Aurora, and with it a strength that defies logic. It won't be easy, and there will be days when you forget that your heart is still beating, but you will find meaning and purpose in other things. In *lasting* things."

"Like what?" Aurora asked, needing something real to hold on to. "Where do you find meaning?"

"I find it in the mountain I'm protecting. In the flowers that continue to bloom year after year after year. I find it in the stars and the moon and the very real sunlight that's in my veins. Even an eternity would not be enough time to discover all of the riches of this world." The Starmaker took a deep breath and exhaled, long and slow. Aurora did the same. "It is a different kind of love from what you feel for your family. But it is love, and if you let it, it will sustain you."

Aurora closed her eyes, noticing that her heartbeat now matched the Starmaker's. "I'm scared," she whispered.

"I know." The Starmaker pushed her hand harder against his chest, but Aurora still refused to look at him, keeping her eyes closed.

"Were you afraid?" she asked, finally meeting his gaze.

The Starmaker slowly removed his hand from hers and slid over on the bench, creating space between them that Aurora did not ask for or want. "I was terrified."

"What made it better?"

"Time," the Starmaker said, a softness to his voice that didn't match the rest of him. "Something you have in abundance."

Aurora nodded. She wasn't sure she believed that it would ever get better, but for now, her heart was steady and her breathing was deep, and she felt in control of herself once more. "Thank you," she said, hoping her tone conveyed how much she meant it.

"You're welcome." He took the reins once more, and the snow deer began to pull, and for a reason she couldn't name, Aurora wished that her hand was still tucked beneath his, feeling the beat of his heart. Wished she could have made the moment last just a little bit longer. But she was quickly learning that nothing could last forever, not even the Starmaker.

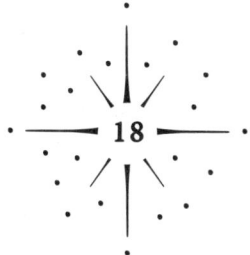

Ruins

The next morning, Aurora stood on the glacier, dreading the arrival of light. It was hard for her to believe that she would one day carry the Sun on her own, as it was near impossible for her to even do a decent job of helping the Starmaker. She knew he wanted her to hold more and more of the light, but she was staying stagnant, each day only able to bear what she had carried the day before.

Aurora couldn't figure it out. She wanted to get better, to make a breakthrough, and she suspected that the more progress she made with pulling the light, the more progress she'd make with settling into the rest of her life. But progress was eluding her, and as she stood on the glacier next to the Starmaker, she prepared herself for another day of disappointment.

Aurora shivered as she looked up the face of the mountain

toward the massive peaks in the distant dark. It was a clear morning, with deep, fresh snow that had fallen overnight, and her nose and cheeks were surely turning red from the cold. She was far enough away that she couldn't hear the huffing of the deer, and aside from her breathing and the Starmaker's, the snow swallowed all sound.

"Are you ready?" the Starmaker asked, glancing toward her. She still wasn't used to the sight of him, the way he looked like he was made of stardust instead of muscle and bone, and she thought it horribly unfair that her mind wasn't capable of ignoring it.

"Have I ever once answered that question with a yes?" Aurora asked.

The Starmaker sighed. "You have not," he conceded. "But it would hardly be polite to start without asking first."

"When have you ever cared about being polite?"

"Perhaps it started when I began to feel my magic living in you," he said, and Aurora laughed.

"So not very long, then."

"Would you prefer that I be rude?"

Aurora gaped at him, but he remained entirely expressionless. She couldn't tell if he was being derisive or if he was truly unaware of how often he *was* rude.

"What?" he asked, watching her.

"Nothing," Aurora said, keeping her tone dry. "I'm quite used to you at this point, but if you think being polite will help me progress, then we can certainly try it."

The Starmaker studied her face, and it appeared as if he was

THE SUN AND THE STARMAKER

thinking rather deeply about her implication that his normal state was one of incivility. He frowned. "Let's begin."

"Let's begin," she agreed.

The Starmaker gave her one more glance, and when she did not take the opportunity to apologize, he scowled and turned away from her.

The Starmaker began whispering his greetings to the Sun, and as he did, he held out his hand. Aurora took it and braced herself for the onslaught of warmth, squeezing her eyes shut and telling herself that she could do this. Telling herself that she was ready to take on more of the light. But as golden rays shot through the peaks and slid down the mountain straight toward the glacier, her confidence wavered.

She opened her eyes to an avalanche of light, crashing into them in a rush of heat, and she held tightly to the Starmaker. She whimpered in pain as she pulled the rays from him, pulling and pulling and pulling until her entire body felt as if it would incinerate on the spot. She held as much as she could, shaking from head to toe with the weight of it. When they had called enough light to cover all of Reverie, they turned and walked to the lamppost together, pulling the blanket of warmth with them. Each of Aurora's steps was harder than the last, and by the time they hung the edge of the light from the hook in the lantern, Aurora was sweating profusely and her breathing was ragged. She dropped to the snow and clutched her chest, and the Starmaker closed the lantern door, then sat down beside her.

"How did I do?" she asked, keeping her gaze on the ground,

not wanting to see disappointment on the Starmaker's infuriatingly beautiful face.

"The same," he said, and Aurora nodded, still trying to catch her breath. "Your fever is about to set in," the Starmaker continued. "We will close out the week together, and then you will take a break as your body acclimates to its new temperature."

"Is that why I'm not progressing?" Aurora asked, hope rising within her. "The fever?"

"I suspect not," the Starmaker said. "It hasn't yet set in, and until it does, you are strong enough for this. I carried more of the light each day until my fever came."

Aurora groaned in frustration. "Then perhaps the Sun has made a mistake and I am not to be your successor after all."

"The Sun does not make mistakes."

"Then you may very well live forever if I can't figure this out."

"You will learn," the Starmaker said, standing and offering Aurora his hand. She reached out and took it, not letting go until she was sure she was steady on her feet.

"You said we are connected now." Aurora watched the Starmaker, blinking as if she had to adjust to the way he looked in the light. His eyes were a brighter gold, his hair shimmering like the sun-dappled snow, so brilliant she had to stop herself from reaching out to touch it. She shook her head, trying to remember what she'd wanted to ask. "What did you mean by that?"

"I can feel my magic running through your veins," the Starmaker said, and the confidence with which he usually spoke was replaced with something else. Not aversion, exactly, but she could tell the feeling was deeply uncomfortable for him. "When you have a particularly strong reaction to something or when we're actively pulling the Sun, I can feel your emotions. I didn't notice it at first, but as more of my magic has transferred to you, it has become more apparent."

Aurora held her breath as he spoke; there was something heavy and intimate in his words, making her stomach drop and her center cramp as if she were in free fall. She had to look away from him, scared that he would feel the reaction she was having.

"Was it that way for your mentor with you?" she asked, keeping her voice as even as possible.

"If it was, he never spoke of it."

Aurora nodded and looked up toward Reverie, anywhere but at the Starmaker's face, forcing herself to relax, to not give anything away. "Well, it's fortunate for you that I have excellent control over my emotions."

The Starmaker quirked a brow. "You're a bit reactive, are you not?"

"I'm engaged with my conversations and experiences, if that's what you mean."

"No, I don't think that is what I mean."

Aurora sighed and looked back to the light hanging from the lamppost. "I suspect this will become much less bearable for you if I cannot progress with my magic."

The Starmaker followed her gaze to the lamppost and beyond. "Come with me," he said, beginning to walk. "There is something you should see."

He trudged past the lamppost toward the edge of the glacier, which dipped into a gentle decline until it abruptly dropped off the mountain, the very end of their world. Aurora slowed her steps, terrified of stumbling and sliding off the cliff. That would be quite the fall, even for an immortal Starmaker.

"At what age did you discover your magic?" Aurora asked, following as he veered to the right, toward a small break in the glacier with what looked like scattered boulders in the distance. Aurora had never seen them before, but of course she hadn't—no one ever ventured this far out, and until today, Aurora had assumed even Starmakers had their limit at the lamppost.

"I was nineteen."

"I know there was someone you loved," Aurora said hesitantly. "Did you ever regret calling off the wedding?"

The Starmaker stopped, turning to look at her. "No," he said. "It was the right decision for both of us. She went on to marry and have children, and I believe she was happy with the way her life turned out."

"I'm glad."

He looked as if he was going to continue walking, but then he spoke again. "If you are concerned that you will regret ending your relationship with Mr. Glenn, then you should see him. Talk with him. I do not wish for you to live with regret, not when you will have such a long time to reflect upon it." The Starmaker paused, as if carefully considering his next words. "And you do not have to sneak him in. The castle is your home now as much as it is mine; he need not jump off of balconies and hide in the night."

THE SUN AND THE STARMAKER

Aurora was entirely caught off guard, and she thought there was a note of tension in his last sentence, though she could have imagined it. "Nothing happened," she said quickly, unsure why she felt the need to say it at all. Still, she wanted him to know.

"I do not care what happened."

"Farren was waiting for me in my room when I got back to the palace; he thought I hadn't gone through with the wedding so that he and I could be together." Aurora was bewildered by the turn the conversation had taken; she had not been thinking of Farren at all, but given that the Starmaker knew of his visit to the castle on the night of their wedding, she was glad to have the chance to tell him the truth.

"As I said, I have no interest in what happened."

"I want to tell you anyway," Aurora said, frustrated. If he was going to bring it up, then she at least deserved the decency of a proper response.

"Must you always be this stubborn?"

Aurora ignored the question. "I told Farren to leave because I didn't want to be with him; I wanted to be arguing with you instead."

The Starmaker inhaled sharply. "And why is that?"

"Because being angry at you is the only thing I'm good at anymore."

The Starmaker's mouth pulled up at one side, a hint of amusement playing on his lips, but it was gone almost as soon as she saw it. "You certainly possess a knack for it," he said, never taking his eyes off hers.

"I don't regret it," Aurora whispered. "Ending things with Farren."

The Starmaker nodded, an expression settling on his face that Aurora couldn't parse. He turned and began walking again, and Aurora followed. The conversation felt important somehow, and she replayed it in her mind as they traversed the glacier. They walked for what felt like hours, but it could have been shorter; Aurora wasn't sure, what with her thoughts entirely devoted to the longing that had bloomed within her, foolishly insisting that she should tell the Starmaker every feeling she had ever had. She couldn't understand why she wanted that, and she pulled her cloak closer to her chest, continuing on.

As they got closer to their destination, Aurora realized that what had looked like large rocks were actually ruins. She shoved her thoughts aside and focused on what the Starmaker wanted to show her.

She came to a stop beside him. There were many buildings to look at, none of them more than stone skeletons, barely recognizable. Aurora walked up to the wall closest to her, the entire surface covered in a pale white film that almost looked like scarring. She took off her glove and ran her fingers over it, the surface cold and rough, exceedingly dull compared to the rest of their surroundings. Reverie was full of glittering colors, pinks and oranges and blues, flowers blooming year-round and sunlight glistening on every surface; it felt wholly like a magical village, brilliant and enchanting, a wondrous spectacle that was as cozy as it was beautiful. But this place was entirely devoid of that.

THE SUN AND THE STARMAKER

"What is all this?" Aurora asked.

"These dwellings used to border the village square," the Starmaker said. "All of them were taken by the Frost before the first Starmaker began his reign. Over time, as the glacier moved down the face of the mountain, it took the buildings with it." His eyes were distant as he took in the loss laid out before them. "Sometimes I come here to remind myself why it matters so much."

"*It?*" Aurora asked.

The Starmaker gestured up the mountain. "The light, the magic. The endless life. As the days stretch on and bleed into each other, it's easy to forget that there is a very real threat that can be held at bay only by the magic in our blood. You and me, Aurora," the Starmaker said. "That's it."

Aurora took in the dozens of ruins before her, and something in the distance caught her eye. She carefully stepped around the stone walls, a maze of devastation, then bent over and picked up a single bloom: a dull-gray candy stripe phlox, perfectly preserved in ice.

A shiver ran down her spine as she remembered the flowers that had turned gray behind her home right before Elsie had been touched by the Frost. She tucked the phlox into her cloak and made her way back to where the Starmaker stood.

"You and me," she said, and before she even realized what she was doing, she reached out and laced her fingers with his.

Aurora felt him flinch, and he looked down at their hands before slowly finding her eyes. He shifted on his feet, and Aurora was suddenly aware of how bold she'd been. The Starmaker wouldn't even name his animals for fear of intimacy, and here she was holding his hand willingly, not because the magic demanded it. Not for any other reason than that she'd wanted to.

"For now," he said, pulling his hand from hers and clearing his throat. He looked up toward Reverie, then began the long walk back to the lamppost, not once glancing over his shoulder to see if Aurora was following.

Embarrassment rolled through her, and she stood still, not wanting to risk the Starmaker feeling her reaction to the way he'd rejected her. She didn't know what had come over her; he had all but encouraged her to continue her relationship with Farren, and she had reached for his hand. How foolish she'd been.

Aurora took a deep breath and began her walk back up the glacier, still holding on to the dead candy stripe phlox.

For now, the Starmaker had said, his words replaying in her mind over and over again, and no matter how hard she tried, Aurora could not make them stop.

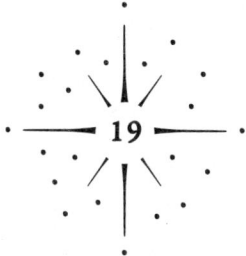

Unfortunate Longings

Aurora studied herself in the mirror. The mark of the Sun on her arm was getting bigger, the design filling in as she had more lessons with the Starmaker. She didn't hate it as much as she had at first, and she had come to think the way the image glowed with magic was beautiful. Her hair was also changing, more and more strands of white the same as the Starmaker's streaking her brown waves, shimmering in the light.

Aurora had asked him the purpose of the physical changes, and he'd said the Sun wanted all of Reverie to know her beloved at a single glance. It was something that had been passed on to each Starmaker, a physical representation of the Sun's love for a human.

The more stories Aurora heard, the more she wondered if her love for Farren had truly been love at all. She wanted to believe it had been, and she knew there were many different kinds of love, but she had started to ache for what the Sun and the first Starmaker had shared. She had always been fascinated by the tragedy of the stories, and she'd told herself she would never want a love like that. But maybe her fascination wasn't fascination at all—maybe it was longing. Maybe the stories were where Aurora felt safest to entrust her deepest desires.

The thought greatly unsettled her.

Perhaps it was the Sun's light in her blood that had awoken that yearning within her. She wondered if it was possible that the Sun's love for the original Starmaker had entered her bloodstream along with her magic, rendering Aurora's previous contentment hollow.

When Aurora said as much to the Starmaker one day as they were riding to the glacier, getting ready to pull in the light, he answered without hesitation. "I have always believed that to be true," he said. "Magic makes the world painfully beautiful, and with that comes an intense longing, as we know we will never fully appreciate the depth of it. No matter how much we want to, there is far too much for us to comprehend."

"Are you scared to start aging?" Aurora asked, her voice quiet. There was something in the Starmaker's tone that made her think he was reflecting on his limited years, and though she didn't want to be rude, she wanted to know.

"No," the Starmaker said, avoiding her gaze. "I am ready."

"I wonder if it is that way for all of us when our time comes," Aurora said, watching the trees as they passed.

"It was not that way for my mentor." He rarely spoke of the third

Starmaker, and Aurora turned to look at him. "He did not want to die, and I believe he would have been content to live forever."

"Oh," she said, unsure of how to answer. "That is sad in its own way."

Aurora wasn't convinced she believed what she'd said, though. She couldn't imagine ever being ready to lose her life; she was still at the beginning of hers and hungry for all the mountain had to offer. Scared, but hungry. Losing that hunger, Aurora decided, would be far sadder than not wanting to die.

The Starmaker's voice interrupted her contemplation. "It was honest. But I would much prefer peace over regret."

"I suppose that's all we can hope for."

The Starmaker said nothing more, and they rode the rest of the way in silence. When they arrived at the glacier, Aurora got out of the sleigh, then the Starmaker, and they walked to the lamppost side by side. It was a routine they had fallen into over the weeks, one that brought immense comfort to Aurora. She had begun all her days at the cottage in the same way, and finding a similar steadiness in her new life was a small joy she didn't take for granted.

Aurora came to a stop when they reached the lamppost, her heart starting to race as she anticipated what was to come. Then she was struck with a thought, one so surprising that it took her breath away: what if she wasn't progressing because she didn't want the Starmaker to become mortal? What if she was trying to keep him here with her, scared to lose the one person who could truly understand her in this life?

As soon as she thought it, she knew there were truths woven within, for her eyes began burning, and she had to squeeze them shut, not wanting the Starmaker to see her sudden emotion.

She didn't want to lose him.

It was a ridiculous desire to be sure, one that she had to push from her mind at once. The cruel reality was that her very existence was hastening the Starmaker toward the end of his. Her magic strengthening meant his getting weaker, and her life extending meant his getting shorter. They were inextricably linked, and in the end, only one of them would survive: her.

It occurred to her then how deeply afraid she was of grief. An immortal who was terrified of losing the people around her—the sick humor of it twisted her stomach too tight.

The only thing that gave her comfort was knowing she had time to come to terms with the Starmaker's eventual death. She didn't have to accept it right away. He had stopped aging at nineteen, which meant that once he was mortal again, he would have many years of life ahead of him. She clung to that fact as if it was a lifeline, and she refused to let go.

Still, though, there was the smallest whisper in the back of her mind, the faintest voice saying, *I wish he didn't have to age at all.*

"I'm ready to begin," she said, trying to keep her voice steady.

"It will keep happening." The Starmaker looked at her with an unreadable expression.

"What will?"

"The hollowing out of your insides when you think of what's to come."

THE SUN AND THE STARMAKER

She slowly brought her eyes to his. "Will it ever stop?"

"No, but it won't happen as often. You will get used to your reality. But in many ways, your life will be marked by death, and that never gets easier."

"Do you miss your mentor?" Aurora didn't dare give voice to the thoughts she was having, but she would ask around them as if they were fire, as if touching them would burn her but getting close would keep her warm.

The Starmaker's expression changed ever so slightly. He looked softer, in a way. Or perhaps he pitied her; that would be far worse.

"I did not know him well," the Starmaker finally said. "But I felt a profound loneliness when he was gone."

When Aurora could no longer bear to meet the Starmaker's eyes, she blinked and turned away. "Let's not keep the Sun waiting," she said.

The Starmaker nodded, looking toward the sharp peaks of Reverie. Without the light of the Sun, they were just shadows, so faint Aurora wouldn't have known they were there if she hadn't memorized their every line as a girl. She used to sit in the center of the village and trace the peaks with her fingers, closing one eye and then the other, bringing them into focus. Aurora wondered if that was one of the reasons the Sun had chosen her as the next Starmaker, if her love for the mountain and the stories made her the perfect fit.

The theory made her feel better, in a way.

Aurora squared her shoulders and looked toward the peaks,

preparing herself to usher in the daylight. It didn't feel natural yet, but she was finding a rhythm that she hoped would soon enable her to progress. She knew the Starmaker was holding back, still taking on most of the light himself so as not to overwhelm her, and while she suspected she finally understood her lack of improvement, she couldn't push herself that morning.

As light burst between the peaks and flooded over Reverie, Aurora tried to ignore the Starmaker's tight jaw and the subtle shaking of his body. She didn't know if they were signs of his frustration with her or indications that he was getting weaker as Aurora took more of his magic. She hoped for the first but feared it was the second, and she held his hand tightly, trying to steady him. But as soon as the Sun reached them, he quickly pulled his hand from hers and stepped up onto the lamppost, hanging the light.

"Are you well?" Aurora asked.

"Do not concern yourself with me," he said, stepping down to the snow. "You need to focus on yourself."

"I am perfectly capable of doing both," she said, but as soon as the words left her mouth, she feared she had lied. The Starmaker raised his brows, and in that moment, she knew that he too was aware of the falsehood. She shook her head and turned away, wanting the privacy of her room and the heat of her fire.

"I'm glad to hear it," he said, but the doubt in his voice echoed her own.

She stepped into the sleigh and the Starmaker followed, and the snow deer pulled them toward the village. There was a peculiar case of magic gone awry they had to deal with, and Aurora was glad for the distraction, as odd as it was. They had received reports of a streetlamp that had begun to sing a lullaby so potent that anyone who heard it fell asleep instantly, and while Aurora knew it was serious, she was eager to see it.

"While we are in the village, I would like to take a few minutes to shop," Aurora said, hoping the change of topic would clear some of the tension between them. "You may wait in the sleigh if you prefer, but I would like to get a gift for Tilly."

The Starmaker looked at her in surprise. "A gift?"

"I thought of it when I was showing you my collection of mirrors. I'd like to get Tilly a looking glass so that she can see herself whenever she wants. It occurred to me that since she spends all her time outside, she likely never sees her own reflection, and I wonder if that's part of the reason she feels so stuck—she doesn't recognize herself in her current form."

"That's an interesting thought," the Starmaker said, and while his voice was neutral, he looked genuinely moved that Aurora had been thinking of the snow angel. "It's certainly worth a try." He paused. "If you don't mind, I think I might like to help you pick out the mirror."

Aurora fought the smile that pulled at her lips, the warmth that bloomed in her chest. "I don't mind at all."

They were quiet the rest of the way to the village. The Starmaker stopped the snow deer a good distance from the market, and Aurora gave him a questioning look.

"They don't have magic in them. If they hear the streetlamp's lullaby, they will be susceptible to it just as the villagers are."

They stepped out of the sleigh and hurried to the market to deal with the magic gone awry, and Aurora stopped when they reached the streetlamp. Dozens of people were fast asleep on the cobblestones, some of them piled on top of each other and many with scrapes on their hands or cheeks from how they had landed when they'd fallen. It was snowing, and the villagers who had been asleep the longest were covered in layers of white.

The Starmaker gave the streetlamp a very irritated look, but it did not seem to notice and continued to sing.

"Have you ever seen this before?" Aurora asked, not quite believing her eyes.

"This is not the first time magic has found its way into a streetlamp, but it has never caused a problem like this before."

"And we are able to stand the lullaby because of the magic in our blood?"

"Yes," the Starmaker replied. He shook his head. "I haven't the slightest idea how to solve this."

He walked up to the streetlamp, which softly sang its lullaby, seemingly unfazed by his presence.

Tucked in a mountain, a blanket of peaks,
darkness and starlight for all those who seek
the deepest of slumbers,
tranquility, too,
I sing so that you may waken anew.
Now, what if I told you
my song never stops

THE SUN AND THE STARMAKER

and forever you'll stay on the stones where you've dropped?
Days turn to years—it sounds rather bleak,
but you ought not worry, for you are asleep!

The Starmaker let out the longest, deepest sigh Aurora had ever heard, and she fought the urge to laugh.

"You are rather annoying, are you not?" the Starmaker asked, but the streetlamp seemed unbothered and continued its lullaby.

The Starmaker attempted several things to quiet the lamp, first trying to suck the magic out of it, then trying to overwhelm it with too much. Neither worked, though, and the Starmaker became more impatient.

"As if this task isn't unpleasant enough, we must listen to this dreadful song while we work. Unbelievable," the Starmaker muttered to himself.

While he was fully distracted by the lamp, Aurora went in search of a paper and pencil, which she found at the nearest stall, whose merchant was fast asleep. Aurora promised to return them when she was done, even though he was not awake to hear her, then hurried back to where the Starmaker stood, his arms crossed, scowling up at the lamp.

"What are you doing?" he asked, watching as Aurora scrawled words on the paper. When she was done, she held it out for him to see.

"Why would you want the lyrics to such a god-awful song?"

Aurora didn't think it was *that* bad, but she didn't dare tell the Starmaker that. "I don't. But what if we sang the lullaby back to it? We have far more magic than the lamppost—I bet we could sing it to sleep for good."

"That is..." The Starmaker trailed off, an irritated expression on his face. "A very good idea. I should have thought of it."

"I'm not sure how you could possibly think clearly when you find the song as irritating as you do."

"It is *atrocious*," the Starmaker said, closing his eyes as if doing so could block out the sound. "Let's give it a try."

Aurora held the lyrics for both of them to see, and they began singing. The streetlamp started to sing louder, a bit of panic entering its voice, and so Aurora and the Starmaker sang louder as well. After several seconds of this, they were all practically shouting, but then the streetlamp's words began to slow and blend together until it sounded as if it were singing underwater.

Finally, it fell asleep.

Aurora and the Starmaker kept singing until they were sure the lamp was fully out, not wanting to risk it waking again. After several minutes, they stopped and sat down on the bench next to the lamp, waiting to see what would happen.

Slowly, the people scattered on the ground began to stir, disoriented and confused and very, very groggy. Aurora spoke to the villagers, explaining what had happened, and asked that they alert the castle at once if they heard so much as another note from the lamppost.

The Starmaker joined her, and the villagers bowed and thanked him for the light before stumbling on with their days. The lamp showed no signs of waking, and so Aurora and the

THE SUN AND THE STARMAKER

Starmaker walked through the market in search of a looking glass for Tilly.

Aurora thought all the mirrors were lovely, but the Starmaker insisted on looking at each and every one so that he could ensure they were selecting the best. When they found one with a gold frame engraved with roses and lightning bugs that held crystals where they would otherwise glow, the Starmaker inspected it closely, looking over every inch before declaring that it was perfect and Tilly would love it. Once they had made their purchase, they checked on the lamp on their way to the snow deer, but it remained asleep.

By the time they got back to sleigh, Aurora was exhausted. It was a good exhaustion, though—the kind that comes from a day full of contentment. It had felt so normal walking through the market with the Starmaker, picking out a gift for Tilly, tending to the lamp; it had been so *nice*. And it was then that Aurora realized it wasn't just arguing that she wanted to do with the Starmaker; it was everything else, too.

I wish he didn't have to age at all.

The Starmaker groaned then, tearing Aurora from her thoughts. "What is it?" she asked, worried they had forgotten something or that there was some new problem requiring their attention.

"That ridiculous song is ingrained in my mind, and I fear it may never leave." He sounded thoroughly stricken by the idea, and Aurora couldn't help it—she laughed.

The Starmaker

After dinner, when the castle was quiet, the Starmaker walked the halls until he came to a plain wooden door. It had been many years since he had set foot in the room, but the Starmaker Rising's arrival had made him reflective, and he stopped, hesitating before pushing the door open.

It was exactly as he remembered: a replica of the bedroom he'd had before the magic in his blood had been discovered. When he had first arrived at the castle, he had been unable to sleep, a horrible insomnia taking hold of him. It had been his sister's idea to bring his room to the castle so that he might rest. She had always been creative in a way the Starmaker was not.

At first, he had balked at the idea, ashamed by the depth of his struggles. But as the sleepless nights had gotten worse, he'd become desperate, and he'd moved all of his belongings into the castle until he had perfectly replicated his room at home.

It was such an exact match that when he was in it, he could almost convince himself that his parents and sister were sleeping soundly on the other side of the wall. Slowly, he had learned how to sleep again.

He was delighted to see that the plants he'd left behind were still thriving, that the magic had continued to sustain them even in a forgotten room covered in dust. He gently touched the leaves and smelled the blooms, and for a moment, he was no longer the

THE SUN AND THE STARMAKER

Starmaker. He was a nineteen-year-old boy, unable to sleep, terrified of the role he was expected to fill.

The Starmaker had developed a deep appreciation for the life he led, but looking around the room, he remembered what it had been like to have endless possibility on the horizon, to look toward the future with anticipation and eagerness. He walked to his old writing desk, and it was there that he saw his worn journal, but something about it was off.

He studied the pattern of dust on the desk, realizing that the journal had been moved just slightly, and he shook his head. *Of course* Aurora had found the room and gone through his things. He should have known.

The Starmaker frowned.

He picked up the journal and flipped through the pages to the very last entry he'd written more than a century ago. He'd stopped writing midsentence, and looking at it, the Starmaker was taken back to that night so many years past, when he'd realized that every entry he'd written since becoming the Starmaker—and every sentence he could possibly write in the future—would all read the same. So he had stopped writing altogether, closed the journal, and never picked it up again.

How tragic it was that he now felt as if he could fill entire pages, every word infused with newness, with unfamiliar pangs he had long since forgotten.

He stared at his final entry, wondering if his life could have gone another way. He had decided many years ago that solitude was most compatible with being a Starmaker, yet it was clear that the Starmaker Rising would choose a different path. And though he wasn't sure why, he was confident she would do well.

The Starmaker closed the journal and set it back on the desk, leaving the room in two strides and slamming the door shut behind him. Going to the market with Aurora had been *fun*, a word he had not used in ages. Even with the streetlamp singing that wretched lullaby, he had enjoyed himself. And while they had shopped for a looking glass for Tilly, he had forgotten he was the Starmaker. The whole experience had been so painfully human.

As the Starmaker walked the halls of his castle, a quiet resentment began to stir in his gut. For the first time in his very long life, he wondered if loneliness was really the cost of magic or if it was a price he'd needlessly paid.

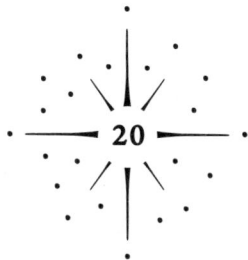

20

Vivid Imagination

Aurora was quiet all through breakfast, unsure of how to act around the Starmaker. She was certain he could hear her thoughts, certain he could feel the secrets within her in the beating of her heart and the knots in her stomach. Every time she exhaled, she was scared the words *I don't want to lose you* would echo through the room in a deafening scream. That morning's issue of *Eternal Reverie* stared back at her, mocking her.

BOLTING BRIDE TO BE NEXT STARMAKER

Another reminder of what she was trying so hard to avoid.

She didn't know why she cared so much. Most of the time she didn't even like the Starmaker. But every once in a while—and, if she was being honest, more regularly of late—a glance or something he said would make him temporarily tolerable. Pleasant, even. It infuriated her, and it seemed that anger was the only emotion she was capable of showing, and so she sat silently at the opposite end of the table, keeping her eyes on the bowl in front of her. Constance sat beside her, ignoring her own bowl in favor of watching Aurora, as if the animal, too, was reading her thoughts.

Aurora glared at her.

The Starmaker watched her with curiosity but said nothing, and it was perhaps the first time that Aurora was thankful he was fond of wordless meals.

After breakfast, Aurora hurried in front of the Starmaker and got situated in the sleigh, pulling a thick blanket up over her torso to keep warm. When he sat down beside her, she did not meet his eyes and instead kept her gaze straight ahead. The snow deer began moving, and Aurora was glad for the sound of their hooves in the snow and the wind in her hair.

"Are you cross with me?" the Starmaker asked, the first words he'd spoken to her since he'd greeted her at breakfast. It seemed the Starmaker could tire of silence after all.

Aurora didn't want to answer because she didn't know what to say. How could she tell him that her magic wasn't progressing because she didn't want him to become mortal? How could she admit that she didn't know how to accept it?

She couldn't—aside from the obvious reasons, she didn't want the Starmaker to think she was saying something she wasn't. She didn't want him to think she had feelings for him when really her feelings were all tied up in the utter loneliness of the life ahead of her. She was almost certain of it.

"I'm just thinking about how I can do better today."

"And what have you come up with?" the Starmaker asked, not sounding even remotely convinced in her ability to do so.

Aurora sighed. She couldn't tell him about her most inconvenient realization, but she could tell him something true. "When my sister was touched by the Frost, I dedicated every waking hour to her care. I researched herbs to give her and made sure a fire was always going. I gave her my portions of stew to ensure that her gut would be warm, and I pulled up her blankets each night when they came off as she slept." Aurora watched the shadows that passed by the sleigh. "During my worst moments, I wished I had never known my sister at all."

"Why are you telling me this?"

"Because for as long as I've loved my sister, I've lived in terror of losing her."

Understanding seemed to pass over the Starmaker's face. "And now it is a guarantee."

Aurora swallowed hard. "Yes." She paused, looking up at the Starmaker. "And when that happens, there will not be a single soul to help me through it." *Not even you*, she thought.

The Starmaker was quiet for a long time before speaking again. "You are strong enough to survive it."

"How do you know?" Aurora asked, so softly she wasn't sure if she had spoken the words aloud.

"Because you're stubborn, and while it is one of your more aggravating qualities, it will serve you well in this life."

Aurora was stunned. "*Those* are your words of encouragement? That I'm stubborn?"

"Yes," the Starmaker said. "The fact that you don't like the answer doesn't make it any less true."

"You may be the least comforting person I've ever met."

"You say that now, but tonight, when you are lying in your bed unable to sleep, you will think back to this conversation and realize that I'm right."

"I assure you, I will not be thinking about you in my bed."

The Starmaker gave her a sideways glance. Though it was hard to tell in the darkness, she could have sworn a smirk pulled at the corner of his mouth, but before she could be sure, his face settled again into its usual sharp, humorless lines. "That is not what I meant." He paused. "If it were, you would know."

Without warning, vivid images of the Starmaker tangled in her sheets sprang to life in her mind, and the harder she tried not to think about them, the more insistent they became. She saw herself running her fingers over his Sun's mark, saw him reaching for her jaw and pressing his mouth to hers, feeling his warmth in the deepest parts of herself. She saw it with such clarity that she had to close her eyes against it, which only made things worse. She was horrified when she caught herself wondering what he tasted like, what his bare skin felt like to touch.

A blush was spreading across Aurora's cheeks, and she was flustered by the way his words and the images they'd conjured

THE SUN AND THE STARMAKER

skipped around in her core like stones over water. She gripped the blanket tighter and tilted her head to the sky, studying the trees with such vigor that her neck began to ache. She wished on every star in the sky that he couldn't feel the quickening of her heart, but even if that was the case, she knew that her stretching silence told the Starmaker exactly what she was thinking, and for a brief moment, she considered launching herself from the sleigh.

"You need a release," the Starmaker said.

Aurora's jaw fell open, and a furious heat sparked in her center that made her squirm in her seat. "I beg your pardon?" she choked out.

"Something that enables you to let go of your fear of grief so that you may live in the present."

Aurora tried to remove the stunned expression from her face and let the Starmaker's intended meaning douse the fire in her gut, as he was clearly not experiencing the visions of heavy breathing and hungry touches that Aurora was. But she was too slow, and the Starmaker spoke again. "You need to make more progress, Aurora."

"I know that," she snapped, exhaling sharply.

"Fine."

The snow deer slowed when they reached the glacier, and by the time Aurora stepped out of the sleigh and walked to the lamppost in the center of the ice field, she had managed to slow her heart back to normal, though not without effort. The cold of the morning helped, and when the Starmaker took her hand and stretched his free arm toward the peaks of Reverie, Aurora was ready to receive her portion of the light.

He paused. "Perhaps we should give Tilly her gift tonight?"

Aurora was surprised by the question, and it made her heart ache, how much he loved the angel. "I would like that."

The Starmaker nodded, and Aurora was about to close her eyes when something moved in the shadow of the trees, distracting her—perhaps a wild animal or one of the snow deer. But then the Starmaker began speaking, and Aurora was pulled back to the glacier. His voice was like magic itself, causing her eyes to flutter closed and her body to tense as she awaited the Sun, a reflex she had no control over. Then, in one brilliant moment, light poured between the peaks and raced over Reverie to greet the Starmaker. Aurora felt his hand tense in hers, and she knew instantly that something wasn't right.

She opened her eyes just in time to see the light pass through the Starmaker as if he didn't even exist, nothing more than air—and it all barreled straight into her chest, along with even more of the Starmaker's magic. The force of it sent her flying through the air, her entire body burning from the heat. With her connection to the Starmaker lost, the Sun snapped back to him, but the damage was already done.

Once, when Aurora was young, she had knocked a pot of boiling water off the stove, and some of it had splashed onto her arm. Her skin had turned red and angry, rising up in protest, and Aurora had cried for hours, the pain incessant. She felt the same pain now, except it wasn't only on her arm—it was everywhere, her skin and her muscles and her organs and bones. She gasped, her vision blurring as the world spun around her. The Starmaker ran toward her, but his steps were stilted and uneven, and she realized in a rush that he, too, was hurt.

So much of his magic had already passed to Aurora—too much—and yet the Sun had slammed into him with such strength that he would have needed all of it to handle the blow. It was a wonder he was standing at all, and watching him, Aurora knew they were running out of time. If she couldn't learn to hold more of the light soon, the Starmaker would be entirely drained of his magic before Aurora was capable of caring for Reverie on her own.

The Starmaker continued toward her, taking one labored step after the next, and Aurora could see how painful it was for him. She tried to get to him, to push herself off the ground and rush to his side, but she was too weak, and she watched as the Starmaker fell to his knees and collapsed on the ground. Aurora called out to him, but the sound was so small that the snow swallowed it up, never meeting the Starmaker's ears. She thought she was reaching for him, but she wasn't sure. The world spun faster and faster until finally, the whole thing went dark.

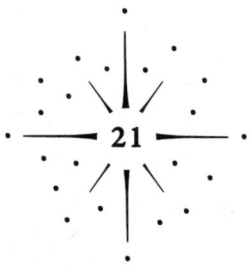

Seven White Wolves

The sound of mumbling made its way into Aurora's mind, waking her. Her head felt as if it weighed as much as a boulder, and not a second after she woke, the burning sensation came back with startling force. She cried out, but it sounded more like a whimper; her voice was hoarse, as if it hadn't been used in days.

She tried to get her eyes to open, and after several seconds, they finally obeyed. Aurora blinked, expecting to see firelight dancing over the walls and marigold silk hanging above her head. But instead, there was stone above her and hard earth beneath her. Every surface was covered in ice except for the wildflowers upon which she lay, and she realized in a panic that she was in the cave she had found when she was a child, the one she had shared with Farren. Her head was throbbing, and she was sure

THE SUN AND THE STARMAKER

her fever had set in because while every part of her burned, she was freezing.

Aurora tried to put the pieces together, to remember how she had gotten to the cave and who she was with, but her mind was as dark as a moonless sky. Then, in a rush, visions of the Sun passing though the Starmaker filled her head, and she winced at the memory. She saw the light and the Starmaker's magic filling her body, saw herself barreling through the air and crashing to the snow-covered earth. She saw the Starmaker stumble, then collapse in a motionless heap.

She had to get to him.

Aurora pushed herself onto her elbows, squeezing her eyes shut against the way the cave spun. It was as if the world had tilted while she'd slept and she had to relearn its axis.

"Hello?" she asked, the word barely a whisper. She tried again, this time louder: "Hello?"

The mumbling stopped, and a moment later Aurora saw two legs in the opening of the cave. Farren stooped and came inside.

"Hi, Rora."

"Don't call me that," she said, her voice straining with the effort. She wasn't sure who she had been expecting, but it wasn't Farren, and her fear gave way to frustration. "Where is the Starmaker?"

"After he hurled you across the glacier, I stopped keeping tabs on him." Farren's voice was even, but there was tension in it that wasn't like him.

Aurora realized it had been Farren she'd seen in the woods,

and she wished she had taken the time to investigate before pulling in the light. If she hadn't gotten distracted, she would be back at the palace with the Starmaker right now; she would know the state of his health and not be worrying for him.

She tried to sit up, but her entire body revolted, and she slammed back down. It felt as if a fire was raging inside her, and she remembered what Ina had told her about the pain the Starmaker felt when he was late to pull in the light. Panic rose within her as she realized how very far away she was from the healing magic of the castle and how very little magic ran through the ground this far out.

"How long have I been here?" Aurora asked, once again trying to sit. Farren rushed over and helped her up, but she pushed him away, not wanting him near her. She shoved her hair out of her face, waiting for his answer.

"Two days," Farren said.

"Two days!" Aurora tried to stand, and after several attempts, she finally got to her feet. She stumbled out of the cave, bracing herself against the stone, and looked up at the sky, trying to determine the time of day. It was dark out, with no trace of the Sun. "Has there been light the past two days?" Aurora asked, holding her breath.

Farren didn't answer her right away, and Aurora couldn't help but feel that he was doing it on purpose. "Yes," he finally said.

Aurora breathed out as she was flooded with relief. The Starmaker was okay. But it was surely not easy for him to pull the light on his own, not with so much of his magic living in Aurora's veins. It was then that a second unwelcome thought entered her mind, nagging at her: he had told her she needed to make more progress on their way to the glacier that day, and anger rose inside her as she wondered if he had deliberately pushed her too hard—if he had been the one to overwhelm her with pain, and not the Sun, as she had assumed.

"I must get back to the palace at once," Aurora said. She retied her cloak so it hung close to her body, but when she tried to take a step, the spinning returned. She leaned against the mouth of the cave and wiped the sweat from her brow before trying once more, but Farren stepped in front of her.

"You can't go back there," he said. "He hurt you, and I will not let it happen again."

"Does anyone know you're here? I thought I heard whispers when I woke—who were you speaking with?"

Farren's mouth set in a hard line. "No one. I tend to talk to myself when I'm in stressful situations."

"*You're* in a stressful situation?" Aurora shook her head, looking from Farren to the path beyond, wondering how she would get back to the castle. "I am not some damsel who needs rescuing. I am the Starmaker Rising, and the only thing I need you to do is get out of my way so that I may leave."

"No," Farren said with resolve.

Aurora tried to stay calm, but between the pain and the fever, she felt as if she was moments away from losing consciousness again. She stood up straighter, trying not to show how weak she was.

"Why are you doing this? We spoke after the wedding, and I thought you understood. What else do you need?"

"I accept that we are no longer together, but does that mean I'm not to look after you anymore?"

"Yes!" Aurora said, her voice rising. "I'm no longer your concern, and I don't need you looking after me."

"Clearly you do," Farren retorted. "You're hurt, Rora. Badly. You were unresponsive for two days, and you looked so awful that I thought I'd have to inform your family of your demise."

"Did it ever occur to you that perhaps carting me off into the woods and tossing me on the ground in an ice cave may have made things worse?" Aurora asked, impatience sharpening the edges of her words. "I am well cared for at the palace, and while I admit that this magic is painful and harder to master than I thought, it is not threatening my life." Aurora narrowed her eyes, fixing Farren with a glare. "At least not when I'm using it regularly. It will kill me if I fail to practice, which I should have been doing the past two days."

"Or perhaps that is a clever lie the Starmaker told you to get you to stay at the castle," Farren said. "Look at you—you can hardly stand. Do you truly believe this magic is helping you?"

It was at that point Aurora would have appreciated a mirror, or perhaps some clear water to gaze into, but since neither option was available, she could only assume that she looked terrible.

"It is not your job to protect me, and I would very much like to return to the castle," she said. "Yours are not the actions of a man in love, and I have no desire to be caught up in whatever twisted logic you have used to justify your behavior. You're better than this, Farren."

"I *was* better than this. Then my fiancée left me to marry a total stranger without so much as a second thought."

Aurora let out an exasperated sigh. The spinning was getting worse, and her hand shook as she gripped the stone, scared she would fall over without the extra support. She was in dire need of a hot bath and a warm meal, and while she spoke with confidence, she had no idea how she'd gather the strength to get back to the castle alone.

"First of all, the Starmaker and I are not married, though that has nothing to do with you, as I believe I made clear." Farren looked away when she said it, hurt, but Aurora had run out of patience. "Second, this isn't about who I marry. It's about the magic in my veins and this mountain and every single person who calls Reverie home. I didn't choose this, but I accept it. You need to do the same."

"Then help me," Farren said, looking uncomfortable.

"And how do you suggest I do that?" Aurora winced as the burning sensation got stronger, but she tried not to let it show. She was angry, and even though Farren had told her that the Starmaker was still bringing in daylight, Aurora was worried for him. The last she'd seen, he'd been crumpled on the snow, just out of reach. She wanted—no, *needed*—to see him.

Aurora tried to map out the route from the ice cave to the castle in her mind, but it was far and she was weak. And the thought of walking through the dark forest, where she knew the Frost was active, sent a shiver down her spine—she had no protection against it except for the magic in her veins, and she was in no position to use it. Still, she had to try.

"I need to see that you're happy and safe," Farren said.

"I don't owe you that." Aurora felt dizzy. "You are not the judge of my happiness or my safety." She paused, looking at the cave and the surrounding trees. *"Clearly."*

"You are safer here with me than in the middle of a glacier, being thrown across the ice."

Aurora closed her eyes. She was done arguing with him. "You may write your headlines and drown in your bitterness, but you are *never* to come for me again."

With that, she gathered every ounce of strength she had, intending to pass Farren and begin her long walk to the castle. But as soon as she took her first step, her body gave out and she collapsed on the ground.

Farren rushed to her, taking hold of her hand. "You need a doctor," he said, frantically looking around, as if he was finally questioning whether isolating the Starmaker Rising was truly a good idea.

"What I need is to go to the palace and use my magic," Aurora managed to get out, propping herself upright. She was sweating too much, and she could feel damp beads lining her forehead and covering the back of her neck.

Then she heard something in the distance. She forced herself to stay conscious, and she tried to pull away from Farren, scared that some of his friends were coming as backup. The fever and the magic raged within her, and she began to worry that she might never make it back to the castle. She tried to conjure her magic, hoping it would give her enough strength to walk, but she was too weak.

"Please," Farren said, his voice urgent, "don't make me go home empty-handed."

"What are you talking about?" Aurora asked. She pulled against Farren's grasp, but he didn't let go, and she finally gave up, sinking into the snowy earth. She was all out of strength, and she took a deep breath, staring up into the night sky.

"My home may not be in the darkness, but we, too, were expecting a glare line."

Aurora's head was spinning, and she couldn't follow what he was saying. "But the paper is doing well and provides a good living. Why would you need a glare line to the least magical home in all of Reverie?"

"It *was* doing well. It turns out the villagers aren't very tolerant of disparaging headlines about the Starmaker Rising. We've lost almost ten percent of our readership over the past two days, and my father is furious with me." Farren shoved a hand through his hair. "But we have needed the line for a while. All of our crops die, and we can't figure it out. A glare line to your home—where you somehow manage to grow food in the most hostile of environments—would help a great deal." He paused. "It didn't matter as much before, but now that the paper isn't bringing in what it used to, we must work our land."

"Farren, I am struggling to feel sympathy for you at the moment. Please get to the point." A branch broke in the distance, and Farren's grip tightened as he looked at Aurora with panicked eyes.

"I want you to create a glare line between our homes."

"What?" Aurora asked. "Did you truly bring me all the way out here to intimidate me into giving you a glare line?"

"It's only fair. You left me with no recourse, gave me no say in our relationship ending."

"Just as I don't have a say in whether I'm the next Starmaker!" Aurora looked at Farren, hoping the strength of her voice could make up for the physical strength she lacked. "I do not have that kind of power; glare lines are created by the Sun and her alone. But even if I did have that ability, I would not use it for you. You kidnapped me, you have put me at risk, and you are holding my wrist so tightly it hurts."

"My father," Farren started, a choking sound escaping his mouth. "He is irate. I need to go home with something. Please."

"I will not help you. Do not ask me again."

Aurora had often read stories about how quickly one could fall in love, but she was discovering that the reverse was true as well. Any lingering feelings she had for Farren vanished in an instant, entirely gone, almost as if she had never loved him at all.

The woods around them suddenly filled with low, deep growls, and Aurora once again tried and failed to sit up. Then seven white wolves came into view, teeth bared, circling them with slow, deliberate steps.

"These wolves will do exactly as I ask." The Starmaker's voice was patient, ensuring that each syllable was perfectly timed. It poured over Aurora like a warm bath, and she craned her neck to see him. When her gaze found his, she thought he was the best thing she'd ever laid eyes upon. He continued, "Release her at once, and then explain to me why I shouldn't have your arm ripped from your body."

Farren's hand fell, finally letting her go, and Aurora rubbed her wrist. She hoped that Farren had held on to her out of panic; he had always been somewhat afraid of his father, and Aurora knew how hard it would be for Farren to return home and face him. But still, he had crossed so many lines, and Aurora would never be able to see him the way she once had.

The Starmaker was watching her carefully, his eyes moving over her, looking for injuries.

"I am well," she said to him, her voice soft. "But I could use some help up."

He reached her in two long strides, picking her up off the ground with ease, cradling her in his arms. Aurora could see the relief in his eyes now that he held her, but it vanished as soon as he looked at Farren once more.

"Well?" the Starmaker asked.

"You're the one who hurt her," Farren said, practically growling the words. "I saw what happened on the glacier. I was trying to *help* her."

"All you have done is keep the Starmaker Rising dangerously cold and unacceptably hungry."

Aurora tried to stay present, but it was so hard, and her entire body went slack in the Starmaker's arms.

"Do not pretend you care for her," Farren said, resentment dripping from the words.

The Starmaker tightened his hold on Aurora. She tried to

keep her eyes open, but she was so tired. "I would not dare insult her with such a deceit."

Aurora could feel the rise and fall of his chest, could feel the tension in his arms and shoulders. He had been worried, and it was written in every muscle and every movement. She rolled her head back to look up at him, into his fierce golden eyes, and for one beat of her heart, it was just the two of them. Farren and the wolves and the cave faded away until only Aurora and the Starmaker remained, watching each other in a field of snow.

"Take me home," Aurora said, the final word hanging in the space between them like the scent of the Starmaker's most fragrant roses. Sweet and strong and bright.

He nodded, then looked up at Farren. "If you ever come near her again without her express permission, I will throw you into the darkest part of the forest where the wolves and the Frost will compete for your flesh." The Starmaker's voice was so calm, so cold, that it made Aurora shiver. He turned without another word, Aurora's eyelids heavy and her head pounding.

"Please don't let me go," she said to the Starmaker.

"I am here for as long as you want me," he said, his voice stern but soft, as if he was taking a vow.

The sleigh came into view, and the wolves ran ahead as the Starmaker slid onto the bench, keeping Aurora tightly in his arms. He covered her with a cloak and then a blanket, and when her head settled against his chest, she felt his hand smooth her hair.

"What if I said forever?" she asked as her eyes closed. She had not intended to speak the words aloud, but the way the Starmaker stilled when she said them told her she had done so, and in that moment, she found she didn't care.

✦

The Starmaker

Adrenaline coursed through the Starmaker's veins as he carried Aurora back to the sleigh. His heart pounded in his chest, slamming against his ribs in a frenzy.

He had never felt more alive.

He scowled, but he could not bring himself to loosen his hold on her.

This was very bad indeed.

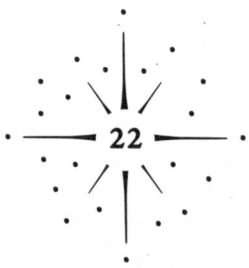

Denial

Aurora woke to a tapping sound. Her head was throbbing, and it felt like minutes passed before she was able to open her eyes. Her body was covered in a salve that had all but taken away the burning she had felt the day before, but she was exhausted and frail, and the fever was taking its toll, her bedsheets soaked in sweat. The tapping continued, and she turned her head to see the Starmaker sitting next to her bed, staring into the fire. There was an open book on his lap, and his fingers moved restlessly against the worn pages.

"What are you reading?" she asked, her voice hoarse with sleep.

The Starmaker jumped, promptly closing the book and moving toward her bedside. "I was not getting much reading done," he admitted. "How are you?"

THE SUN AND THE STARMAKER

"Tired, and my head hurts, but the burns feel much better."

He nodded but still looked concerned. His brow was furrowed, and the tension he'd carried yesterday still pulled at his shoulders and spine, stretching him into a too-tight version of himself, one that might snap in half at any moment. His normally shimmering hair was dull, and the skin beneath his eyes was dark. Aurora tried to push herself up, but the motion caused the room to spin, and she slowly lay back down.

"Rest," he said.

"We need to talk first." Aurora couldn't get past her suspicion that he had shunted more light to her than she could hold in hopes of forcing her to progress. She was so relieved he was safe and so angry that he had put them both at risk. "Please be honest with me. Did you deliberately overwhelm me with light?"

The Starmaker didn't answer at first. He clenched his jaw and looked past Aurora, toward the balcony doors and the world beyond. He shook his head, and when he turned back to her, he seemed... mad. "Do you truly think so little of me that you believe I would harm you in that way? In *any* way?"

Aurora was surprised by how forcefully he spoke, and she made herself sit up. "You lectured me on the way to the glacier about how I needed to progress, and then *that* happened. What was I supposed to think?"

The Starmaker didn't respond right away. "You're right," he finally said. "I have not given you reason to think otherwise."

Aurora thought that was it, that the conversation was over and the Starmaker would leave the room, but instead he stayed seated beside her and looked her in the eyes. "I grew up in a very devout home, Aurora, and I have never believed in anything as much as I believe in you."

Aurora was stunned. The words seemed to unlock something inside of her, as if they were a key she had been searching for tirelessly. She inhaled deeply and reached out her hand to the Starmaker, realizing then how badly she wanted to use his name. Not his title, not the word the world knew him by, but his given name. "What is your name?" she asked.

The question caught the Starmaker off guard, and he visibly recoiled. "I am the Starmaker," he said, but his tone gave away that he knew exactly what she was asking.

"Your given name," she clarified, sitting up taller.

The Starmaker shook his head, avoiding her gaze. "It doesn't matter. It has been so long since I've heard it, I'd hardly recognize it."

"I'd like to know," Aurora pressed. It felt important to her, intimate, and in that moment, she wanted to learn his name more than she'd ever wanted anything. It was then that she realized he wouldn't tell her, though, precisely because of the intimacy of it.

"I'm sorry," the Starmaker said, standing and moving away from the bed. "It is not something I have shared with anyone since the last of my kin passed away. I felt that part of me should be buried with them."

It struck Aurora as painfully sad that the human part of the Starmaker was gone—no longer a man or a son or a brother, just the one who pulled the light. Perhaps it was easier for him that way; maybe remembering that part of himself was too hard.

THE SUN AND THE STARMAKER

Aurora knew she would come up with her own ways to bear the grief of this life, and she would not judge the Starmaker for his.

"I understand," she said. "Why don't you tell me what happened on the glacier instead?"

The Starmaker looked relieved that she had let her question go so easily, and he stopped pacing. "I've been thinking about it since it happened, and I believe that the Sun has decided you are ready. I tried to stop the light from reaching you, but I was not strong enough."

Aurora was about to push back against his assertion about the Sun, but the way he said those last words—*I was not strong enough*—made her pause. He sounded surprised, but he spoke with finality, and Aurora realized that he was turning mortal again.

The end of his life was beginning.

"It is starting," Aurora said softly.

The Starmaker sat back down in his chair, and Aurora inspected him for any sign of aging, but she found none. He was tired and disheveled, but he was still the unfairly beautiful Starmaker he'd always been—no new wrinkles or papery skin, no graying hair or slowing steps. He was perfect, a truth Aurora hated to admit but could not deny.

"The Sun has decided you are ready," he said again. "It won't be long now before you're pulling the light on your own."

"The Sun is clearly mistaken," Aurora said, trying to fight the panic rising in her throat. "You saw me—I was unconscious for days. There's no way I'm ready."

"She will make you ready," the Starmaker said. It was possible Aurora was imagining it, but she thought he was working very hard to keep fear out of his voice. "And I will do my best to support you in every way I can so that you are not hurt like that again."

"I felt it," she said, closing her eyes and reliving the memory. "It wasn't just the light that reached for me—it was more of your magic moving through me."

"I felt it, too." The Starmaker paused, and Aurora opened her eyes to look at him. "We must get you comfortable with holding more light; my magic will continue transferring to you, and as that happens, I will be less capable of helping you."

"And what if the Sun transfers all of your magic to me before I am able to hold the light?"

The Starmaker shook his head. "That won't happen."

"And if it does?"

He sighed. "I'm not sure," he said finally. "I suppose that would mean Reverie would remain in the dark until you could carry it all."

"I don't understand why your magic would move to me before I'm ready."

"Nor do I," the Starmaker said, and they were both quiet. Aurora didn't have the energy to keep questioning the Sun or her magic or anything else, so instead, she said simply, "Thank you for helping me. I know that morning on the glacier wasn't easy for you, either."

The Starmaker didn't reply, but neither did he move away,

and Aurora watched him as he seemed to war with himself over something.

"What is it?" she asked.

The Starmaker stood and began pacing again, taking several turns around her room before coming to a halt beside her bed. "I was worried about you, Aurora. It was torture not knowing where you were or if you were safe. I didn't like it."

Aurora almost laughed at the way he said the final sentence with disgust. "I'm sure it was very hard for you not knowing if your successor was safe."

"I was not worried for my successor," the Starmaker said, practically spitting the word. "I was worried for *you*, Aurora." He swallowed hard. "You."

As soon as he said it, the space between them became charged, as if the words had changed the chemistry of the air itself and every particle was reacting to them the way Aurora's stomach was. Her heart picked up speed, and the Starmaker's eyes were so intense that she had to force herself to keep her gaze steady, not wanting to look away.

"I was worried for you, too," she said quietly. "You were the first thing I thought of when I woke, and when Farren told me the light had come while I'd been out, it was the sweetest relief I'd ever felt. I wanted nothing more than to get to you and make sure you were okay."

"A stark change from seeking me out to argue with me." The Starmaker laughed, a low rumble that began in his chest.

"I can do both."

"Yes," the Starmaker said. "It seems you can." He paused. "You should get some rest."

Aurora lay back on her pillow, and the Starmaker pulled up her quilt, even though she was sufficiently covered. His movements were slow, and he took his time tucking the quilt beneath her shoulders. His hands lingered there as if he was unsure what he wanted to do next, and Aurora's breath caught in her throat as she watched him.

She had been frustrated with him for so many reasons since they met, but perhaps the biggest was that she was no longer interested in keeping space between them. Her fingers itched with the desire to reach up and pull him down to her, to cover herself in the weight of him, to feel the press of his lips on hers. He would not be here forever, and he would weaken as his body began to age, but he was here now. He was here, and so was she, and in that moment she was not convinced that wanting him was foolish.

Slowly, she pulled her arm free of her blankets and took hold of the Starmaker's wrist. "What if you stayed?" she asked, not taking her eyes off his.

"I'm not tired." The words were rough, and Aurora wondered if it was her exhaustion that was making her dizzy, or if it was the pain or the fever, or if it was the Starmaker himself, pulling her into his orbit.

"I did not mean for sleeping."

His jaw tensed and his body went rigid. "Aurora," he began, his voice hoarse, "I cannot. The last thing you need is to care for another person who will inevitably leave you."

THE SUN AND THE STARMAKER

"Who said anything about caring?"

Aurora watched as his mouth pulled up on one side, a devilish smirk that made her desire even stronger. "Do you not care for me?" he asked, bending over as he spoke the words, his face just inches from hers. "Not even slightly?"

Aurora pushed herself up on her elbows again, closing the space between them, her lips practically brushing his. "I'm rather frustrated with you at the moment."

The Starmaker's eyes danced in the firelight, amusement playing on his face. When he pressed his lips to hers, it wasn't hungry or restless the way Aurora had envisioned it. Instead, it was patient. Gentle. Loving, even.

His lips were soft and warm and tasted of tea, and all Aurora could think was *more*. More kisses, more touches, more moments that sent her far away from her role as Starmaker Rising. There was a voice inside her whispering that this—*he*—was the greatest adventure she'd ever been on, that being held by him was perhaps the most at home she'd ever felt. She pulled him closer, but he merely brushed one more kiss against her lips before standing. He watched her with his golden eyes, reflecting the Sun back at her when all she wanted was to forget about the light.

"I want you," the Starmaker said, so plainly it broke Aurora's heart. She'd been trying so hard to guard herself, terrified of what loving one more person would mean, terrified of the way grief could destroy her. Just three words, but they were honest and true, and Aurora was angry at him for voicing something she was desperately trying to deny.

She was always angry at him.

"It is complicated to want you. Your very existence is ending mine, and yet I would rather die having known you than live a thousand lives as strangers." The Starmaker walked toward the door, but he turned to look at her once more before leaving. "You have a very long life ahead of you. I would never forgive myself for making it harder."

Then he was gone, shutting the door softly behind him. Aurora stared at the space he'd stood in, stunned by his words and his gentleness and his care. Her mind was racing, and she had an incredible urge to cry.

He was the Starmaker, and she was the Starmaker Rising; they could never be together, and Aurora couldn't escape the heartbreaking truth that she was killing him just as he was bringing her to life.

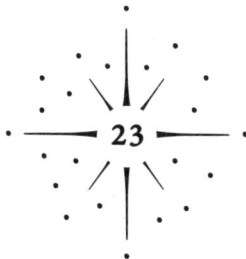

The Heart Seldom Yields

Aurora was feeling better, but as soon as her mother heard what had happened with Farren, she insisted on coming to the castle. The Starmaker accompanied her through the dark woods, requiring him to wake much earlier than normal, and though Aurora knew he was silently cursing the intolerable hour, he did not complain. It made her feel cared for, ridiculous as it was—such an overwrought reaction to a mundane occurrence.

Aurora had told her mother it wasn't necessary for her to come, and yet when she burst through the door and rushed toward the bed, Aurora's eyes filled with tears.

"Hi, Mama," she said, swallowing hard.

"I got here as soon as I could." Her mother ran a palm over her hair and studied her face, rested the back of her hand against

Aurora's skin. She nodded, seemingly satisfied that Aurora was not in imminent danger. "Tell me what happened."

Aurora had written to her family about the fever and the cave, but now that her mother was in front of her, sitting beside her on her bed, she told her every detail. She didn't want her family to hate Farren, but it wasn't her responsibility to lie for him, and she didn't hold back. It was therapeutic in a way she wasn't expecting, and she realized how much she'd missed being able to talk with her mother about what was going on in her life.

"I can't believe Farren did such a thing," Mama said, her hand wrapped tightly around Aurora's. "You could have died in that cave." It had been a long time since Aurora had seen her mother so upset, and she had almost forgotten that Mama had fire inside her along with her usual softness.

"I'm glad it wasn't worse."

"Farren is the one who should be glad; the Starmaker could hardly hide his fury while answering my questions on the journey. He was scowling the whole way here."

"That's just his face," Aurora said, shifting on the bed, but her mother shook her head.

"He has grown to care for you, darling. Surely you must see that."

Aurora wasn't sure how to answer. It was true that there had been a shift in their relationship, and the Starmaker wasn't as cold as he had once been, but he still kept her at a distance no matter how hard Aurora tried to get closer. She closed her eyes against the memory of their kiss, the lingering desire inside her that she couldn't forget. She wanted more of him.

No, that wasn't quite right.

She wanted *all* of him, could feel in the depths of her soul that she wanted an epic love after all. It was a devastating realization, and Aurora was shocked when her vision once again blurred.

"What is it?" Mama asked, wiping Aurora's cheek.

Aurora paused, sucked in a breath. "I think I care for him a great deal." She said the words so quietly that her mother had to lean in to hear them, and then a sob broke free from Aurora's throat.

"Oh, my darling," Mama said, pulling Aurora in close, wrapping her arms around her. "I know you do."

"But I cannot," Aurora said, taking a deep breath, trying to steady herself. "I don't want to go through what you did with Papa."

It was then that Aurora's mother pulled away and looked her in the eyes, radiating a fierceness that Aurora seldom saw. "Don't you say that. Don't ever say that."

"Why not? It almost killed you, losing him."

Mama's eyes were wet now, too, and the handkerchief on the side table sprung into action, darting through the air and wiping her cheeks first before doing the same to Aurora.

"Not now," Aurora whispered gently, and the handkerchief drifted back to the table with far less enthusiasm than it had taken off with.

Mama smiled at the gold cloth before the intensity in her expression returned. "It was the worst time of my life," she said. "I wish I could have been more present for you and your siblings. I wish so badly that I could have been there in the way you needed me to be, and I will regret that always. But one thing I don't regret, could *never* regret, is loving your father." She paused, taking both of Aurora's hands. "And if I had to do it over again, I would love him again, choose him again, because our life together was worth it. I got to experience an exceptional love, and the pain I felt when he died and continue to feel today doesn't erase that—it reflects it."

There was something breaking inside of Aurora, as if all of her organs and bones were rearranging themselves to make space for what her mother was saying. Aurora had been sure that it wasn't worth it, loving someone like that, but her mother spoke with such conviction that it took Aurora's breath away. She had lived through the worst possible outcome, and yet she still believed it was worth it.

Aurora knew then that the Sun would say the same, that falling in love with a human had been worth the pain. She could feel it in the magic in her blood, and she wondered how she had gotten it so wrong.

"I miss Papa," Aurora said, looking at her mother through her tears. "I miss him so much."

"I know you do, and he would be so proud of the person you've become." Her mother tucked a strand of hair behind her ear. "It would pain him to think you were closing yourself off from love because of him. There was no one in all of Reverie more romantic than your father."

"The Sun might have something to say about that," Aurora said, a small laugh escaping her lips.

"Perhaps she would," Mama said. "But I believe it all the same." She squeezed Aurora's hands. "Please do not be so fearful of what may come that you fail to enjoy the present. I know it may seem like your future is inevitable, but it is up to you to decide how it will look—how full your life will be, how much love it will hold, how much happiness and laughter and joy. Please do not deny yourself those things because you are afraid of the pain they may leave in their absence. Life includes pain, my darling, and you cannot escape or outwit it."

"I'm learning that," Aurora said.

"Yes, it seems that you are," her mother agreed.

They were quiet for several minutes, long enough for Aurora's breathing to return to normal and her eyes to dry. There was still a small voice whispering in the back of her mind, telling her that she wasn't as strong as her mother or the Sun, warning her that she couldn't bear that kind of loss. But if becoming the Starmaker Rising had taught her anything, it was that she was stronger than she thought.

Strong enough, perhaps, to love with abandon.

At some point, Aurora fell asleep, and she woke to the scent of her mother's lentil stew. It was the same stew she made whenever anyone in their home was ill, and Aurora would recognize the smell anywhere. Between that and her childhood quilt that was tucked tightly around her, she was almost convinced she was back at the cottage.

Her eyes fluttered open, and her mother was sitting on the edge of the bed with a tray that held a large bowl of soup and some fresh bread.

"The cook offered to make something for you, but I said that would not do." Mama smiled, waiting for Aurora to sit before setting the tray on her lap.

"Thank you," Aurora said, eagerly taking a spoonful. As she'd gotten better, her appetite had grown, and she had to pace herself so as not to devour her meal all at once.

"I will write down the recipe for the cook so that you may have it whenever you are feeling unwell."

Aurora didn't think her mother was referring to times far in the future, long after she was gone, but her words still hit Aurora in her chest, and she took a deep breath to dull the ache.

"I would like that."

"Your sister was so upset that she couldn't come with me, and both she and Aspen send their love. I wrote to them while you slept, and they will be glad to know you're improving."

"And Evander and Samuel? Are they well?"

Mama paused. "I haven't seen your brother since the morning you left for the castle, but Aspen assures me he and Samuel are both doing well."

Aurora heard the hurt in her mother's voice, and she regretted the question. "I'm sorry, Mama. I shouldn't have asked."

"It is not your responsibility to shield me from the consequences of my own actions." Mama said it with a sad smile, casting her eyes downward. "Evander had just lost his father—you all had—and I couldn't support him through it. I couldn't support any of you. That is my own fault and something I will have to live with for the rest of my life."

"You did your best," Aurora said, grabbing her mother's hand.

"It wasn't enough." Her voice shook, and she took a deep breath and blotted her eyes. "I will keep trying to be there for him now, though. And perhaps one day he will let me."

Aurora had never before had such an open conversation with her mother, and she was struck by how much her mother had been carrying. How aware she was of the shift in their family after Papa had died, and how she blamed herself for the rift between her and Evander. The clarity with which she spoke moved Aurora greatly, and she thought her mother even stronger now than she had before.

"The Starmaker checked on you several times while you slept," her mother said, changing the subject. "He came back to the castle as soon as he'd pulled the light."

Aurora tried not to react to her mother's words, but there was a warmth that bloomed inside her, spreading outward. "He did?"

Her mother nodded, smoothing back a stray piece of white hair that had caught on Aurora's eyelashes. "I do not think you are the only one who cares a great deal."

Aurora looked away, out the balcony doors to the snow-covered trees in the distance. "He does not want to care for me."

"And nor do you for him, but the heart seldom yields to what one's mind desires."

"Yes," Aurora said, "a rather aggravating trait." It was something the Starmaker would have said, and she almost laughed.

"Indeed it is," her mother agreed, standing and picking up the tray. "Rest now. There is much to come."

Aurora wasn't sure what her mother meant, but she lay back down and her eyelids got heavy and she didn't get the chance to ask.

As she slept, she dreamt of the Starmaker. He held both of her hands, his beautiful face leaning into hers, his lips just barely brushing her own. They stood on the top of the highest peak, beneath a black velvet sky drenched in starlight. She smiled as his mouth met hers.

Then he was torn away, hands slipping from her grasp, sucked into the endless night while Aurora screamed after him.

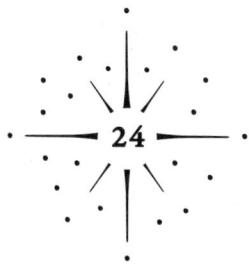

Reflections

On the first day Aurora was well enough to move about the castle on her own, the Starmaker approached her with hurried strides.

"Now that you are back to standing, I thought we could give Tilly her gift." He said the words with a seriousness that suggested he was talking about a disease or a famine, not a present, and Aurora tried her best to match her expression to his tone.

"I suppose you are right," she said with exaggerated sadness, but the Starmaker did not seem to notice her jest.

"I'm glad you agree." He had been holding one hand behind his back, and he brought it out to reveal the looking glass they had picked for the angel. "Let's go."

He turned on his heel, walking down the hallway with great urgency. They passed the portrait that Aurora had noticed her first night at the castle, but there was no snow in it now; this time, a glorious light was shining brightly from the corner, so intense it hurt Aurora's eyes. She paused to inspect the painting, and the Starmaker didn't realize she had stopped until he was holding the door to the patio open for her. He let out a sigh and met her back at the portrait.

"The weather changes every day," he said, following her gaze.

"Amazing."

Much to Aurora's delight, the groundskeeper once again appeared from behind the hedges, this time carrying a parasol so large that he stumbled and tripped as he walked toward the throne. When he reached it, he set the parasol up to the side, ensuring that the Starmaker and Constance were shaded. Once he was satisfied with the placement, he receded into the distance again, and Aurora watched until she could no longer see him.

"I once saw the groundskeeper swept up and tossed aside by a blizzard. I was terribly worried for him, but he was back the next day, cleaning up after the storm."

"I might just have to stop by this portrait every day," Aurora said, finally pulling her eyes from the painting.

"I used to," the Starmaker said, then winced as if he regretted the words.

"Used to?"

"I apologize," he answered, shoving a hand through his hair. "At some point, I realized that I had seen every weather scenario I could possibly see, and it started to feel repetitive."

"Oh," was all Aurora could say, her delight fading.

THE SUN AND THE STARMAKER

"But I hope you do visit it every day. Every single day." The Starmaker shook his head. "I am realizing now that my life has felt monotonous because I decided years ago that was how it would be. I didn't allow myself the pleasure of new experiences or new people." He paused, his gaze drifting down the hall as if he was looking for something just out of reach. "You will do much better than I."

Aurora was quiet for a moment. "You do not have to apologize for how you have coped with this life."

"I do when it steals some of the joy from yours."

"Then you are forgiven, and if it makes you feel better, I assure you I will visit this portrait every single day."

The Starmaker nodded. "That would make me feel better."

"Then consider it a promise." Aurora's disappointment faded away, and instead, a quiet determination moved through her. She would live her life as the Starmaker on her own terms, in her own way. She remembered Aspen's words to her before she had left for the castle, how he had told her that she should take the entirety of who she was with her, and she wondered at how her brother always knew the right thing to say, always had wisdom that far surpassed his age.

The Starmaker looked visibly relieved, and they walked out to the garden side by side. It did not take long to find Tilly, as she was right out front, bent over some rosebushes.

"I have decided that I like the smell of roses very much," said the angel, and it made Aurora's heart burst. If she was determining what she did and did not like, then perhaps she was slowly beginning to accept her new self.

"It is one of my favorite things, too," the Starmaker said, and that seemed to make Tilly happy.

"We have a gift for you," Aurora said, and the snow angel made her way to where Aurora and the Starmaker stood. He handed over the package, and Tilly carefully unwrapped the paper with the tip of her wing.

"Aurora thought you might enjoy being able to see yourself," the Starmaker said.

"But I am missing," Tilly replied with confusion.

"No," the Starmaker said gently. "You are right here." He reached out and turned the mirror over so that the glass was facing her, then slowly brought it up to her face.

Tilly gasped, and she looked so distraught that Aurora wondered if her idea had been terribly flawed. She reached out to take the looking glass from Tilly, not wanting to cause the angel any more distress, but the Starmaker pushed down on her arm and mouthed *wait*.

The seconds that followed were excruciating. They watched as Tilly stared into the looking glass, her wings turning in and her head bowing as if she couldn't bear the sight of herself. "How do you know this is me?" she asked.

"Look," Aurora said, taking the mirror from Tilly and showing the angel her own reflection before moving the mirror in front of the Starmaker. "It reflects whatever is in front of it."

Tilly tilted her head to the side, watching intently as Aurora moved the looking glass over the roses and finally back to Tilly. "This is you," Aurora said gently, handing the mirror back to the angel.

THE SUN AND THE STARMAKER

Tilly looked from Aurora to the Starmaker, and he nodded in agreement. Then she slowly brought the mirror to her face.

"I like how much I sparkle," she said, turning her head back and forth so that her snow caught the light. "Neither of you sparkles the way I do."

"No, we don't," the Starmaker said, his voice catching. He cleared his throat, and Aurora's eyes burned with the threat of tears.

"Whenever you feel lost, you can look in the mirror and see that you are exactly as you should be," she said.

Tilly nodded at Aurora's words but kept the looking glass firmly in front of her. "What if I feel lost all the time?"

"You can look in the mirror as often as you like. It is yours to keep, and perhaps as time goes on, you won't feel quite so lost," Aurora said.

"This is the best gift I've ever been given," Tilly said quietly, finally looking up from the mirror to Aurora and the Starmaker. "At least, I think it is."

Aurora did not want to take all the credit for the gift, but the Starmaker seemed unable to speak, so Aurora smiled at the angel. "We are so glad you like it."

When Tilly had run off with the looking glass and Aurora and the Starmaker were back inside, he took in a long deep inhale. "That was," he said, pausing to find the right words, "one of the very best moments of my life."

"And you have lived a very long one," Aurora pointed out.

"I have," the Starmaker agreed. "Thank you for what you did for her. And for me."

Aurora smiled. "You're welcome."

"Now, if you don't mind, there is one more thing that requires your attention."

"You know I am recovering from a grave illness," she said, figuring she had earned at least another day or two of rest. Her mother had returned home early that morning, and it was now up to Aurora to voice what she did and did not have the energy for. It was immensely comforting that even though she was grown and living away from home, her mother would always treat her like her daughter.

"I am aware, but I believe you will find this an acceptable alternative to lying in bed."

Aurora was skeptical of that, but her curiosity got the best of her. "Then let's see it."

The Starmaker led the way to the second floor, then down a long hallway to a spiral staircase. It was similar to the one leading to the Starmaker's room, but it was much taller, and even when Aurora craned her neck, she could not see the top.

"Are you truly insisting that I climb this?"

"I am," the Starmaker said apologetically, "but we can go as slowly as you need."

Aurora gave the Starmaker an irritated glance, but she started to climb, taking her time as she went higher and higher. The Starmaker stayed close behind her, and every once in a while, when she paused or missed a step, his hand immediately found the small of her back. During one such moment, she thought about how easy it would be to ease her back into his chest, how good it would feel

THE SUN AND THE STARMAKER

to rest against him. She had almost convinced herself that what had passed between them in her bedroom had been a dream, that the warmth of his lips on hers had been an apparition she had conjured in her feverish state. But her body was all too aware that it had been real, and it reminded her constantly that it had happened and—more frustratingly—had not happened again.

Aurora sighed and continued her climb, and after what felt like hours, she finally reached the top. The Starmaker opened the door for her, and she stepped into a small circular room that was cluttered with all sorts of things: plants and books, candlesticks and dinnerware. A large rug was rolled up and propped against the wall, and a tall broom stood beside it. The Starmaker quickly closed the door behind them.

"Be careful in here," he said.

"What is all this?"

"Every item you see is a case of magic gone awry, and as much as I've tried to fix them, these things are too unruly to have out in the open. That plant, for example, bites," the Starmaker said, motioning to a gorgeous red flower surrounded by green leaves. "Hard," he added. "That sled in the corner cannot move horizontally across the ground; it can only climb vertically, putting anything inside it at risk of falling."

"What about the mirror?" Aurora asked, and the Starmaker motioned for her to look into it. When she did, though, it appeared ordinary. She turned to the Starmaker, who was leaning against the wall, arms crossed, watching her. Perhaps it was the climb up the stairs or the small space that was getting to her head, but she couldn't understand how he looked so perfect doing something as unremarkable as standing still. "It looks normal," she said, turning back to the mirror.

"Just wait."

Aurora watched herself in the mirror, and then suddenly, her reflection began to speak. "I can't understand how he looks so perfect doing something as unremarkable as standing still."

Aurora gaped at her reflection, then dove out of view of the mirror.

"Most people do not enjoy their thoughts being spoken aloud," the Starmaker said, and though his tone remained even, she could see he was fighting very hard to suppress a grin.

"You could have been a gentleman and simply told me what the mirror does."

"I believe I warned you that I am no gentleman."

Aurora took a deep breath, trying not to let her humiliation consume her. "What is it you brought me here to see?" she asked, aching for a change of subject.

"It isn't in here," he said, turning to a glass door that led out onto a balcony. "It's outside."

He opened the door, and when Aurora stepped through it, she gasped. Mirrors hung from every baluster, and even more sat atop the balcony railing, leaning against the castle. They were all huge, far larger than the biggest one in Aurora's collection, and every one of them was pointing the same direction, down toward Reverie. They reflected so much light that Aurora could practically feel the heat radiating off of them, a brilliant display that made her breath catch in her throat. She had never seen so much light concentrated in one place, save for when she pulled in the sunlight with the Starmaker each morning.

"None of them can read your mind," the Starmaker said, and Aurora ignored the amusement in his voice.

"They're beautiful."

"They are all angled directly at your cottage," he said. "It was not easy finding a path that would work, but I'm rather pleased with the result."

Aurora looked at him, unable to process what he was saying. "You did this for my family?" she asked.

"I know you've been worried about them since they didn't get the glare line they were expecting. I wanted to help ease that burden somehow."

Aurora didn't know how to respond. She was scared that if she opened her mouth, she would cry or say something so heavy she couldn't take it back. She was completely overcome, and she wondered if the Starmaker could feel it, feel the weight of every unspoken word rushing through the magic living inside her.

There was a glimmer far off in the distance, at the base of the peak, and Aurora squinted to see it more clearly. She had never noticed it before, and she wondered if it was some kind of optical illusion. The Starmaker followed her gaze, clearing his throat.

"I took one mirror to the cottage. I know how much you miss Elsie, your whole family. That mirror reflects the light that we are reflecting down. Think of it as a hello of sorts, something you can look at whenever the missing feels too great."

Aurora was stunned, and she stared at the Starmaker, not quite believing what he had done for her.

"I might love you," she whispered, realizing too late that she had spoken the words aloud.

The Starmaker did not react, not even a flinch, and Aurora wondered if she had said it so quietly that he had not heard. She couldn't decide if she wanted that or not.

"Perhaps you can write to your family and tell them about the mirrors. I would be keen to know if they make a difference." The Starmaker's voice was normal, and Aurora realized he definitely hadn't heard her, and for a reason she couldn't name, she felt disappointment wake inside her.

"Of course," she said, trying her best to keep her voice even. "Of course I will. They will be most thankful, as am I."

The Starmaker looked at her then. "They are just mirrors, but I found I needed a distraction while you were ill."

"They are not just mirrors," Aurora said, her voice quiet.

The Starmaker's eyes were full of an emotion she didn't recognize, one that darkened the usually vibrant gold, and it was suddenly difficult for her to breathe. "No," he finally said. "They are not."

✦

The Starmaker

The Starmaker had forced himself not to react, not to move, not to speak. After the last of his family had died, he had made peace with the fact that there was no one left who loved him and that there never would be again.

I might love you, Aurora had said, proving him wrong.

The Starmaker knew that Aurora had a deep fear of grief, and before he could even take a breath, a thought came to him so forcefully that it was all he had heard since.

I might ruin you.

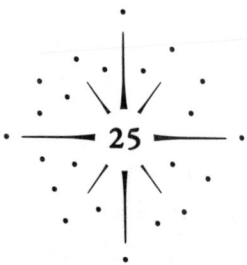

Dying Star

Later that night, Aurora woke to a shuffling sound beyond her balcony. She tried to ignore it and fall back to sleep, but it continued, and her curiosity got the best of her. The fire had died down to a few stray flames, and Aurora pulled on her robe and tucked her feet into her slippers before venturing outside.

She stood on the balcony and wrapped her arms around her waist, watching as her breath drifted off into the cold night. A crescent moon hung in the sky, and distant stars peppered the darkness as if someone had stood at the top of the world and tossed a handful of diamonds up in the air, never to come back down.

The sound that had woken her continued, and Aurora walked to the railing and looked down. It reminded her of her very first night at the castle, when she had asked the Starmaker to prove that there was magic in her blood. That night seemed so long ago, as if she had lived many different lifetimes since then. Maybe, in a sense, she had.

Aurora scanned the gardens until she saw the Starmaker pushing a wheelbarrow toward his greenhouse, leaving a trail in the snow behind him. She thought about calling out to him, but he was already far past her room, a comfortable enough distance that he could pretend he didn't hear her even if he did.

Aurora laughed at the thought.

She turned back inside and shut the door softly behind her. She climbed into bed and closed her eyes, but she was wide awake and knew that sleep would not find her again.

I might love you.

Aurora still couldn't believe she had said the words aloud, but the thought that continued to swirl in her mind hours later was how she wished the Starmaker had heard her, how she didn't know if she would ever summon the courage to say such a thing again. She didn't even care how he would respond; she simply wanted him to know.

Aurora turned on her back and looked up at the ceiling, wondering what the Starmaker was doing in his greenhouse, what sorts of plants he was tending. She had never actually been there, though it was where the Starmaker spent many of his free hours.

After several more minutes of lying there, Aurora threw off the covers, wrapped herself in her robe once more, and shoved her feet into her boots. She went to her wardrobe for her cloak, then found herself moving quietly down the hall, descending the stairs, and heading out into the early morning.

It wasn't necessarily her intention to follow the Starmaker, but that was precisely what she did, walking beside the trail he had left in the snow, many paw prints dotting the ground beside his footprints. Tilly sat on a bench in the gardens, holding her looking glass out in front of her. Aurora stopped and watched her for several moments, her heart aching as the angel tilted her head to the left, then the right, then back again.

Aurora continued walking, and the greenhouse came into view in the distance, a warm light glowing from within. The outside was coated in frost that sparkled in the moonlight, and she slowed her steps, worrying that she was about to barge into the Starmaker's sacred place. Interrupting him had never bothered her before, but things were different now. She didn't know exactly what had changed, but Aurora found that she was trying not to annoy him, which was hardly realistic.

When she reached the door, she opened it without hesitation.

The Starmaker's back was to her, and he didn't look up or turn when she entered. "To what do I owe the pleasure?" he asked, his tone dripping with sarcasm, and Aurora smiled to herself. Something had changed, but not everything.

"You disturbed me, so I felt it was only fair to return the favor."

He sighed, stopped what he was doing, and made a show of slowly turning around. He cocked his head to the side and brushed the dirt off his hands. "If I did disturb you, it was unintentional.

THE SUN AND THE STARMAKER

This," he said, motioning to Aurora, "seems rather deliberate, does it not?"

"I couldn't sleep," she said, walking farther into the greenhouse. The door closed softly behind her, and she looked up, the glass hazy from the frost. The greenhouse smelled sweet and earthy, filled with every color and species of rose Aurora could imagine, and the sight of them moved her deeply. She saw years of work in the tiny space, hours of tending seeds and pruning stems and ensuring that each plant received enough water, and it had paid off, for the blooms were vibrant, each one larger than her fist. There was hardly enough room for both Aurora and the Starmaker to stand, and she moved carefully, shuffling around the roses so as not to harm them.

"Nor I," the Starmaker said, turning back to his work, and Aurora watched as his hair fell over his shoulders. She didn't say anything, so overcome by the beauty of the roses and the quiet of the night and the small amount of space that separated them.

"Aurora, tell me what you're doing here or leave me in peace," the Starmaker said, but there was a pain in his voice that hadn't been there before, as if he was mourning his flowers. The thought took her breath away, a swift, hard punch to her center, and a small gasp escaped her lips.

As if he was mourning his flowers.

Aurora tried to reach back into her memory, to find the specific moment she had learned that a Starmaker began to age once their successor was found, living out the rest of their life as a mortal. But as hard as she tried, she couldn't locate it, and her stomach dropped when she realized it must have been an assumption. It was a plausible one, of course, but as she looked at the Starmaker now and thought of how eager he had been to give Tilly her gift, Aurora knew her assumption was incorrect. She just didn't know *how* incorrect.

"You are doing it again," the Starmaker said, not bothering to look at her.

"Doing what?" she asked, her voice coming out hoarse.

"Mourning things that have yet to happen."

His back was still turned to her, but Aurora kept her eyes on him, watching his every movement as if something in the way he tended to his roses might give her the answers she sought. "How long did you get with your mentor before he died?" She said the words so quietly, and yet they seemed to take up all the space in the greenhouse, hanging in the air like early morning fog.

The Starmaker's hands went still in the soil. "Long enough," he said.

"What does that mean?"

"It means exactly what I said. I will not pretend to know what the Sun has in store for me."

"You are not making things better for me by lying," Aurora said, her voice rising. She didn't want to fight, but she felt as if the whole world was shaking beneath her, and she needed something steady to hold on to.

"I am not lying."

"You are being intentionally vague, which ought to be the same thing."

THE SUN AND THE STARMAKER

"Has it ever occurred to you that perhaps I don't enjoy discussing the end of my life?" The Starmaker exhaled, long and slow. The faint moonlight reflected off his hair and skin, casting him in a soft blue glow that made him appear as if he consisted entirely of starlight. Looking at him was like watching a dying star, painful and beautiful and impossible to turn away from.

"But you said you were ready." Aurora's voice was small, and she hated how despondent she sounded.

The Starmaker did not reply and instead went back to his flowers. But Aurora didn't need a response to know his time was coming, and she tried to calm the dread building inside her, the overwhelming sadness. She took a deep breath and told herself that she needed to learn more before panicking, and if the Starmaker would not be honest with her about his fate, then she would find the information elsewhere. But for now, in these earliest hours of the morning, she would not fight with him.

Aurora walked slowly to where he stood and gently placed both hands on his back. His muscles tensed beneath her touch, his spine straightening, a low breath escaping his lungs. "If you will not talk to me, then perhaps you will show me."

The Starmaker turned his head, his eyes finding hers over his shoulder. "What is it you're asking for?"

"I want to learn," she said softly. She moved her hands away from his back, trailing her fingers over his shoulder and down his arm, meeting his hands in the dirt. "I do not think I can bear to lose your flowers, too. Show me how to care for them in your absence."

The Starmaker's expression was entirely unreadable. Half of

his face was in shadow, and his slanted cheekbones and the sharp edge of his jaw were somehow more pronounced in the darkness. "They can be rather finicky," he said.

"A trait they picked up from you, no doubt."

The Starmaker turned away so Aurora could not see his face. "I am meticulous. It is not the same thing," he said, the words barely audible, as if he had spoken them for himself alone.

"I want to learn," she said again.

The Starmaker paused, a delicate silence stretching out between them. Then, "I want to teach you."

He kept his back to her, and Aurora reached out and touched his chin, slowly turning his face toward her. "Why will you not look at me?"

When the Starmaker finally met her eyes, Aurora wished she had let him be. He looked so pained. So tortured. "Because every time I do, it makes me want to live so badly I can hardly breathe."

Aurora was overwhelmed by the words, by the bitterness that clung to them, by the way he said them with such restraint it was as if a single syllable might make the entire mountain crumble. "Then close your eyes."

"Aurora—"

"Close your eyes," she said again, and this time, he did. Aurora's mind refused to quiet, and she could easily name at least ten reasons why this was a spectacularly bad idea, but she couldn't bring herself to care. Not then. Not with the light of the moon on his face and the sound of his confession lingering in the space between them.

When Aurora kissed him, it was like feeling the warmth of

THE SUN AND THE STARMAKER

the Sun for the very first time, and all she wanted was more of it. But the Starmaker remained stiff, unmoving, and Aurora pulled back, afraid that she had pushed him too far.

Then all at once, he came to life.

"Get back here," he said, taking her face in both hands, pulling her into him as if she were the air and he hadn't taken a breath in years. She gasped when his tongue stroked hers, and he wove his hands through her hair and gently tugged, tipping her chin up and revealing her neck. He kissed the corner of her mouth, her jaw, her collarbone, burying his face in her skin, inhaling her as if she were life itself instead of the end of it.

Aurora awakened with want, and she felt as if she would never be whole again, as if she would never know peace until every part of her had been touched by him and every part of him had been touched by her. It couldn't be healthy, and Aurora remembered when he had told her he was sorry that she had only ever experienced love that was good for her.

She knew now what he meant. It wasn't necessarily that it was bad. The problem was that she needed him, insatiable and endless, and the more she got, the more she wanted. She would never feel satisfied again.

The Starmaker found Aurora's mouth once more, his kiss warm and lips soft and tongue teasing, and she sighed into him when his hand moved up her rib cage and over the swell of her breast.

Then he stopped, took a sudden step back. Aurora couldn't keep up, her head still stuck in their kiss, in the way he had touched her.

"We can't," he said, his breathing heavy, gripping the edge of the table behind him as if he needed to physically hold himself back. "It isn't fair to you."

"I am more than capable of determining what is fair," Aurora said, closing the space between them once more, bringing her mouth to his ear. "I want this," she whispered, and his whole body shuddered when her lips brushed his skin.

"I want this, too," the Starmaker said, as if he was in pain, his voice strained and low. "I want this, too," he said again, taking hold of her waist and pulling her closer, and then he kissed her with an urgency that matched her own. Aurora's body pulsed with desire, a longing she had never known before, and she arched into the Starmaker, wanting to get closer. She untucked his shirt and ran her hands over his stomach, his muscles tightening beneath her touch, his skin hot as fire.

The Starmaker groaned and guided her toward the table, pressing into her, and she could feel how much he wanted her, how desperate he was to make her his own. Aurora was amazed by the need aching in her belly, the warmth blooming beneath her nightgown, and instead of fearing her hunger, she felt emboldened by it.

Aurora wrapped her arms around his neck and curved into him, and the Starmaker's breathing quickened when her hips rolled against his. He reached for the tie on her cloak as Aurora tipped her head back, and he kissed along her neck, greedy at first, and then slower,

slower,

slower,

until finally, he stopped altogether.

He rested his head on her shoulder and took several deep breaths, and Aurora felt a hint of sweat on his neck when she pulled her hands away.

"I'm sorry," he said, raising his head to look at her. "You caught me in a moment of weakness."

Aurora wanted to tell him that she was weak for him all the time, but she knew by the way he tensed his jaw and narrowed his eyes that he had finally found the resolve he'd been looking for.

"I want you to feel good about your choices," she said softly, stepping away from him.

"*Good* is not the word I'd use," the Starmaker said with lingering frustration. "*Conflicted* is more accurate, but I appreciate the sentiment." He sighed, long and heavy. "If you are still interested, I would like to show you how to tend to the roses."

Aurora's chest ached, and she blinked against the sting in her eyes. "Yes," she said. "I would like that very much."

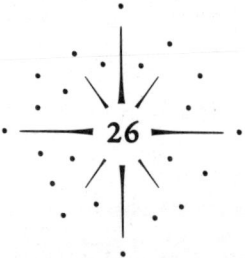

Tragic Symmetry

When it was time to pull the light into Reverie, it was as if nothing had happened in the greenhouse. The Starmaker went back to his usual exhausted grouchiness, and Aurora knew he regretted what they'd done, that he worried he had made his inevitable departure harder on her. And though they had shared a soft, gentle morning as he'd taught her how to care for his roses, that had passed, and now he wouldn't meet her eyes. His tone was harsh and clipped, and he sat as far from her as possible on the sleigh bench, as if he was trying to make her despise him again.

"You cannot make me hate you," Aurora said when they arrived at the glacier, stepping out of the sleigh. She looked up at him. "It will not work."

"Your stubbornness is getting in your way." The Starmaker

THE SUN AND THE STARMAKER

jumped to the ground and stalked toward the lamppost without another word, and it infuriated Aurora the way he always chose when conversations were over.

Without thinking, she picked up a pile of snow, packed it in her hands, and threw it at the Starmaker's back as hard as she could. "Do not walk away from me!" she shouted, following after him.

The Starmaker stopped, and it felt as if he took a full turn of the Earth to face her. "That was a very poor decision."

"At least it was one I made myself," Aurora seethed. "You seem to make all the other ones for me."

The Starmaker slowly walked toward her, stopping mere inches from her face. "Perhaps that is because you aren't very good at making them."

"I'm rather happy with the choices I've made; you are the one who seems to be struggling."

The Starmaker shook his head, shoving a hand through his hair. "What do you want me to say, Aurora? That the only thing I can think about is kissing you again? That it is taking every shred of strength I possess not to pull you to the ground and touch the places I failed to get to last night?" He sighed, looking off into the distance. "You are the last thing in the world I should want."

The Starmaker turned back toward the lamppost, walking quickly, and Aurora trailed behind him. She hated how tortured he was, how clearly he was berating himself over what had happened. She wished she could convince him that she would be okay, that what she needed was for him to *be* with her, not to walk away as if their time together were infinite.

She met him at the lamppost and said nothing. And as they went through the ritual of pulling in the light, the Starmaker's suspicions about what had happened when they'd last been on the glacier together were proven correct. The Sun had decided that Aurora was ready, no longer tolerant of her lack of improvement. Aurora had thought she would have to fight to catch up to the magic that was already inside her, and she was terrified she wouldn't be ready by the time the Starmaker's magic fully transferred to her. But she was wrong.

That morning, Aurora pulled more light than she ever had before, even though she tried to resist it. Even though she deliberately dropped the thread and shunted it back to the Starmaker. She was getting stronger even as she tried to prevent it, and it would not be long before she could hold the light of an entire day by herself, sealing the Starmaker's fate along with her own.

She had tried so hard to progress with her magic, and now that she finally was, she wanted nothing more than to slow down.

After Reverie was covered in light, they went to check the forest for any signs of the Frost, and the Starmaker relaxed somewhat as the day went on. Aurora was glad, for she wanted to talk with him, to learn everything she could about him.

The Starmaker would be remembered, certainly. The villagers would construct an elaborate grave for him where they would go to pray for generations. There would be no shortage of flowers at his final resting place, nor would there ever come a time when he was no longer revered. But remembering someone for their role was not the same as remembering them for who they were.

THE SUN AND THE STARMAKER

Reverie would remember him as the fourth Starmaker, but Aurora would remember him as the person he was beyond the light of the Sun. That was why she wanted to know his given name, but he still refused to share it, even though she had asked several times since that morning in her room. But she knew other things, had collected bits and pieces of who he was as if they were precious gems, and she would hold them in her heart, where they would live as long as she did.

"Tell me," Aurora said as they walked deeper into the woods, "If you were not the Starmaker, how would your perfect day unfold?"

The Starmaker looked at her, his mouth set in a straight line, his eyebrows slightly raised. "I am the Starmaker."

"I know that," Aurora said. "But if you were not."

"If I were not," the Starmaker said, his voice drifting off into the trees as if he were recounting a dream, "I suppose I would sleep in, take my breakfast in the courtyard garden, and spend time with the animals."

"Have you always loved animals?" Aurora asked. It was a quality that surprised her, given how opposed he was to intimacy. The bond a person shared with an animal was strong and deep, and it seemed he would want to avoid those attachments the same way he did with humans.

"No," the Starmaker said. "I used to think they were wretched things."

"That is more consistent with your personality," Aurora pointed out, and the Starmaker grunted beside her.

"They do not know me as the Starmaker, nor do they care about my magic," he said. "They see me as a man, and they have helped me keep my humanity during this very long life. I will be very sad to leave them."

His words seemed to hang in the air, and Aurora could practically see them rearranging themselves before her, *I will be very sad to leave them* morphing into *I am dying*.

"Will they not die first?" Aurora asked, trying to keep her tone as casual as possible. "Animals have painfully short life-spans."

The Starmaker did not look at her, but Aurora saw his jaw tense. "I will always have animals," he finally said, "and I know how difficult it will be for me to leave them whenever my time comes."

Aurora did not press the issue, and the rest of their day was pleasant. Once they were back at the castle and done with their dinner, the Starmaker disappeared to his room, and Aurora pulled Fredrick aside.

"Frederick," she said to the young butler, "please make sure the deer have been properly fed. I will be going back out."

"Right away," he said, but before he could leave, Aurora touched his jacket.

"I would appreciate your discretion," she said in a low voice. "The Starmaker will not be accompanying me."

Frederick shifted on his feet, looking nervously around the room. It was just the two of them, but Aurora could sense his unease, as if she'd asked him to murder the Starmaker in front of the entire village. Red splotches spread over his cheeks, and she almost felt bad for asking him at all.

"It is nothing untoward," she said, trying to reassure him. "I only wish to visit the bookshop in the village."

"The Starmaker's library is a fine one," Frederick said, lighting up. "I'm sure whatever you're looking for can be found there."

"It cannot," Aurora said, heading toward the grand staircase. "I am going to my room to change, and I expect the sleigh to be ready upon my return."

"Certainly," Frederick said, and while he did a poor job of hiding his discomfort, he strode down the hall to see to her wishes.

Aurora washed her face, smoothed her hair, and picked out a cloak that was not so splendid, hoping she could go about the village unnoticed. Once she was ready, she made her way back to the entrance of the palace, thankful when the only person she saw was Frederick, waiting for her out front.

"Miss, I should like to accompany you," he said, his eyes pleading with her.

"Frederick, I assure you I am quite capable of going to town and back on my own."

"I have no doubt that you are," Frederick said, tugging on his overcoat. "But with the Frost encroaching, and your recent..."

"Kidnapping?" she supplied.

"Yes, with that, I would feel more comfortable going with you."

"Come on, then," Aurora said, stepping around him and into the sleigh. "I don't wish to be gone too long."

Frederick ran around the sleigh to the other side, and the snow deer took off at a run, rushing them down the mountainside. Frederick held on to the sleigh with both hands and looked like he might be sick, and by the time they pulled up beneath the glittering lights of the village, his skin had taken on an ashen hue.

"You look unwell," Aurora said, studying him.

"I am fine," he replied, and then his eyes went wide and he jumped out of the sleigh. "I will meet you at the bookshop!" he called over his shoulder, breaking into a jog. Though she felt bad about his upset stomach, his illness fit perfectly into her plans, as she had no intention of allowing him into the shop with her.

Aurora drove the sleigh into a narrow alleyway near the bookshop, petted the snow deer, and assured them she would be swift. She walked around the stone building to the entrance, keeping the hood of her cloak up so as to remain as inconspicuous as possible. The bookshop was small, with a sky-blue door and a steeply pitched roof, lanterns dangling from the edge and emitting a soft orange glow. A small bell chimed above her head when she opened the door, and she squinted against the yellow light. The shop owner hurried over to her, taking her hand.

"It is not every day you see the Starmaker Rising," the old man said. "It is an honor."

"Please, Mr. Burgess. I am still the girl who insisted on reading every book on your shelves," she said, though she was moved by his greeting.

He studied her face, a small smile on his lips. "I suppose you are."

"Thank you for accommodating my request, and on such short notice."

"Not at all. The evening is seldom busy."

THE SUN AND THE STARMAKER

Mr. Burgess locked the door and led Aurora to a cozy table in the back. "Might I offer you some tea?"

"Please," she said, sitting in an old chair that creaked beneath her weight.

When they both had their tea, Aurora took a breath and tried to compose herself before she asked her questions.

"This shop has been in your family for generations, is that correct?" she began.

"That's right. My great-great-great-grandfather opened it. It was one of the very first shops in town."

"Quite fitting for a village built on stories," Aurora said, smiling and taking a sip of her tea.

Mr. Burgess's eyes glinted behind his wire-rimmed glasses, and his face lit up. "Quite right," he said excitedly.

"Am I correct in assuming that this shop was first opened under the reign of the third Starmaker?"

"You are," he said, his voice holding a note of curiosity.

"I am wondering what you can tell me about his death." Aurora tried to ask the question as delicately as possible. The villagers cared little for the morbid or bleak, and Aurora could not recall a single instance of someone talking about the realities of a Starmaker's life.

Mr. Burgess frowned and furrowed his brow, looking over the stacks of books in his small shop. "Little has been written on the subject, I'm afraid. We know the date of the last Day of Darkness, so I can tell you the date of his passing, but I know nothing of the specifics."

The shopkeeper stood and ran his fingers over leather spines until he found the volume he wanted. When he sat back down across from Aurora, he opened the book, but it violently slammed itself shut.

"Oh, don't start with this," Mr. Burgess muttered, forcing the book open once more, but as soon as he began turning pages, the cover closed again, snapping shut around his hand. "My apologies," he said to Aurora, now taking hold of the front cover and forcing it open with both hands. He quickly pinned it to the table with his elbow, and though the book tried valiantly to close, it was not strong enough. Mr. Burgess gave a triumphant huff, flipping through the pages until he found what he was looking for, but Aurora didn't need a date, and she kept pressing.

"Do you know how much time passed between the end of the third Starmaker's reign and the Day of Darkness?"

The shopkeeper seemed to understand what she was asking him and looked up from the book, which seized the opportunity to slam shut victoriously. "That would be tricky indeed to discern. A Starmaker's reign officially ends *on* the Day of Darkness, and the following day is the official beginning of the next."

"But the current Starmaker must have come fully into his magic before his predecessor's death," Aurora said.

"That is true," the shopkeeper agreed. "But since it is considered disrespectful to celebrate the Starmaker Rising before the Day of Darkness, the texts do not cover the Starmaker's earliest days."

Aurora looked at Mr. Burgess and slowly lowered her hood

THE SUN AND THE STARMAKER

to reveal her hair, almost entirely turned to glittering white. The shopkeeper raised a trembling hand to his mouth. "Sir, I'm less interested in what your books say and more interested to hear your family's stories. Your ancestors built their lives around the lore of Reverie; surely there are stories that were passed down in your home but never printed?"

Mr. Burgess stared at her for several seconds, seemingly unable to speak. "It has happened so quickly," he whispered.

"Far quicker than I would have liked." So little was known of Starmakers' personal lives that even when *Eternal Reverie* had announced her as the Starmaker Rising, no one could have guessed when her reign would begin or when the Starmaker would die. It was one of the mysteries of the mountain, and while Aurora generally appreciated the lack of knowledge surrounding her role, she did not want to be kept in the dark herself. "You do have stories, don't you?"

Mr. Burgess slowly nodded, clearing his throat. "Of course."

"If you don't mind, I would like to hear them."

He took a sip of tea, the cup shaking slightly in his hand. "There is a saying in my family: *In order to begin, there must be an end*. It is what we say in times of mourning and grief. The Starmaker is the greatest symbol of hope we have, and yet each one must end for another to rise." The shopkeeper paused, gently tapping his fingers on the table. "Since a Starmaker's rise overlaps with their predecessor's last days, it is only ever whispered about so as not to be seen as dishonorable."

Aurora nodded. She wouldn't want her rise to overshadow the

Starmaker's end, and she was glad to hear that it wouldn't. "And when do you suspect those last days will be?"

"There is more to the saying," the old man said. "*Just as the dawn shares a day with the dusk, so too does a beginning share a day with an end.* I do not know the exact origins of these phrases, but I believe they come from a tale of the death of the first Starmaker." He paused, taking his glasses off and looking at Aurora with sadness in his eyes. "It is my belief that the Starmaker's end will occur on the very day you fully come into your magic."

Aurora stared at him, sure he had misunderstood. He must not have heard her question correctly. "I am not asking when he will become mortal; I am asking when he will die."

"I understand," Mr. Burgess said, nodding. "I believe he will die when the last of his magic transfers to you, when you are able to pull in the light and hold it entirely on your own."

"But I can almost do that now!" Aurora said, her voice rising.

"I'm sorry." The old man finished his cup of tea. "I'm sure this must be very difficult to hear." He paused, watching her, and suddenly he inhaled sharply, as if fully grasping why she had come to his shop in the first place. "You care for him, don't you?"

Aurora couldn't bring herself to speak, but her eyes filled with tears as she looked at the shopkeeper.

"A Starmaker and a Starmaker Rising falling in love!" he exclaimed, almost as if he was telling a story. "It holds a tragic symmetry with the tale of the Sun and the original Starmaker."

"Yes, I am aware," Aurora said, unable to hide her panic.

Mr. Burgess seemed to come back to himself, his voice taking on a much softer tone. "There is nothing in my books that confirms this belief; it is just what I have gleaned from my family's stories. That is all."

As soon as he had said it, though, Aurora had known in her gut that he was right. The Starmaker had never corrected her when she'd spoken of him becoming mortal, nor had he ever given her a clear answer about when he would die. Understanding came crashing down on her like the weight of the whole sky, every star and planet and sun pressing into her at once. He had been trying to protect her; this whole time, even on the days he was irritated, even through his exhaustion and as he reckoned with his imminent death, he had been trying to protect her.

And in so doing, he had lied to her over and over again.

"Thank you," Aurora said, standing. "I appreciate your help, as well as your discretion."

"Of course," Mr. Burgess said, leading her to the door. "I wish I had better news to share with you."

She gave him a weak smile. "As do I."

Aurora left the shop and climbed into her sleigh, where Frederick was waiting. He began to speak, but she did not hear it, and something on her face must have told him that she was too distracted to converse, for he fell silent.

The Starmaker did not have years. He did not have months. He might not even have weeks, and Aurora's entire body went cold from the truth of it. He was dying, and that was simply not something Aurora could accept. Silent tears ran down her face the entire way back to the castle, and she wrapped her arms around her chest to keep herself from breaking open, to keep her heart from spilling out onto the frozen earth.

But it was no use.

A ticking clock had begun in the back of her mind—*tick tick tick*—and one day soon, it would stop.

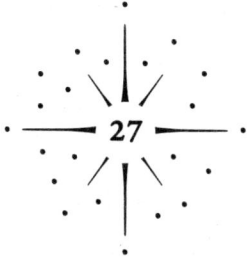

Beginning and End

Aurora did not intend to confront the Starmaker right away. When she arrived back at the castle, she went straight to her room and did not speak to anyone, not even when Frederick asked if she was all right or when Ina said she'd been worried. But after hours of pacing in her bedroom, unable to quiet her mind, she could not wait any longer.

She threw on a long silk robe over her sleeping gown and stormed to the Starmaker's room. If she could not sleep, then neither would he.

When she reached the narrow staircase, Aurora took the steps two at a time and burst through the door without a single knock. The Starmaker wasn't in bed, though, and Aurora swallowed the disappointment of not waking him. Instead, he was sitting by the fire, reading a book of poetry and nursing a cup of tea. Constance was resting in his lap, and Aurora tried to ignore the ache it created in her chest.

"This is undoubtedly my least favorite habit of yours," the Starmaker said, not looking up from his poem.

"I know your secret," Aurora said, walking over to him and taking the book from his hands. Constance jumped to the floor, and the Starmaker sighed, finally meeting Aurora's eyes. It didn't make any sense how vibrant he was, how healthy he looked. He seemed every bit the immortal, and it was hard to reconcile his appearance with the truth that he was dying.

"And what secret is that?" he asked, the firelight casting shadows on his face.

"That you will die as soon as I fully come into my magic." She could barely get the words out, and she was embarrassed by the way her voice shook. She wanted to stay angry at him, to tear around his room and scream and shout, but the admission took everything out of her, and she sank down to the floor.

"You may take my chair," the Starmaker said.

"I do not want your *chair*."

He studied her for a long time, not saying a word. He took slow sips of his tea until it was gone, then settled back into his seat, and Aurora was unsure if he didn't know what to say, if he was upset, or if he truly was just annoyed at having been interrupted.

"We are going to need more tea," the Starmaker said, and after he rang his bell, neither of them spoke until a staff member delivered a silver cart with a full tea service and biscuits. Aurora poured herself a full cup, took two biscuits, then sat back down and waited.

"Yes," he finally said, the single word piercing Aurora like an ice pick through her ribs. "I will die when you fully come into your magic."

"How could you not tell me?" she asked, her voice nothing more than a whisper, unable to hide the betrayal she felt, the utter helplessness. Constance hopped over and came to rest at her feet.

"I wanted to protect you," he said, the gentleness in his voice rousing her anger once more. She didn't want him to be gentle, not now. She wanted him to be obnoxiously steadfast in his belief that he had done her a service; at least then it would be easier to stay mad.

"You have done nothing but make this harder on me." Aurora's voice was rising, and she hoped he could see the fury in her eyes.

"That was not my intent. My mentor told me almost immediately when he would die, and I wished he hadn't. It slowed my progress with my magic, I made both of us ill by resisting it longer than I should have, and in the end, I spent more time mourning him than getting to know him. I should have used that time to ask questions and try to understand the life I was stepping into. You have done that, Aurora, and I don't know that you would have had I been honest about the transfer of magic."

"*Transfer?*" Aurora asked, disgusted by the word. "You mean your life for mine. Your *death*. Don't dress it up in nicer language on my account."

"Yes, my death," the Starmaker said. "This is how it has always been and how it must be."

"No." Aurora set her plate and tea aside, getting on her knees in front of the Starmaker. Tears welled in her eyes and fell down her cheeks as she took his hands in hers and grasped them tightly. She looked up at him, his beautiful face blurred through her tears, but she did not care that he saw her cry.

"No," she said again. "I will let this mountain crumble before I will lose you."

The Starmaker slowly slid off his chair, sinking down to his knees on the floor so he was eye to eye with Aurora. He pulled his hand free and pushed her hair back from her face. "You won't," he said, and Aurora wanted so badly to argue with him, to tell him he was wrong.

"I will not watch you die."

"You will not have a choice," he said, the sternness she knew so well finding its way into his tone.

"We'll see about that."

"Aurora." The Starmaker spoke her name in a whisper, and he searched her face as if he was looking for a solution to an unsolvable puzzle, the very key to life itself. His fingers trailed down her cheek and onto her neck. "So stubborn."

"Do not placate me," she said, even as she leaned into his touch.

"And what would you have me do instead?" he murmured, pressing his forehead to hers.

Aurora closed her eyes, trying to stop her tears, trying to block out the visions of the Starmaker's breath fading away to nothing. "Kiss me," she said.

THE SUN AND THE STARMAKER

She wasn't sure if he would do it or not, but almost as soon as she said it, his mouth was on hers. The first thing she noticed was salt on her tongue, and it felt oddly intimate that the Starmaker was tasting her tears. He kissed her softly, and she wrapped her arms around his neck, holding on as if she could prevent him from going if only she held tightly enough.

She would hold on and on and on, and not let go.

"This cannot be the end," Aurora said, her voice shaking, her fingers in his hair.

"It is your beginning," he said simply.

"Don't you dare act like this is somehow favorable for me," she replied, her voice rising again. She hated how calm he was being, how steady he was when she felt as if an earthquake was rocking her core, leaving all of her pieces scattered.

The Starmaker shook his head, and Aurora could see him working through it all, wondering how it had come to this, how he had ended up on the floor of his bedroom, clinging to the very person who was destroying him.

Aurora was quiet, slowly gathering the courage to ask what she needed to know. "Tell me how it will happen," she finally said.

The Starmaker looked conflicted, as if he was trying to deduce whether telling her would make it easier on her or far worse.

"Please tell me," she said.

The Starmaker sighed. "It will happen when we perform the ritual transferring my remaining magic to you. It will not be violent or gory, just quiet. The castle will send a sleigh to the glacier with a casket to collect my body, and it will be held in the sanctuary until my burial. My body will remain as it is now, the remnants of magic enough to sustain it." The Starmaker looked down, and Aurora knew he was remembering when he'd lost his own mentor. "It will be as peaceful an end as anyone could hope for."

"I am glad for that."

"As am I," he said, hesitating before he continued. "It will be difficult, but you will learn to live without me."

"I will not," Aurora said, her anger returning. She sat up and looked at the Starmaker with staunch defiance. She would never let him go, not unless the Sun herself appeared as a human once more and tore the Starmaker from Aurora's arms. And even then, she would not let it happen without a fight.

"You must," the Starmaker said, standing up and pacing around the room. Aurora was taken aback by the way his voice turned angry, aggressive, but she did not yield. She stood up as well and watched him as he shoved his hand through his ice-colored hair. Hers was almost a perfect match now; only one section of brown remained.

"If you must be angry, it ought to be at the Sun, not me," she said, crossing her arms.

At that, the Starmaker stalked toward her, his face so close that she could brush his skin with her lips if she tilted her head just right. "Shall we speak of anger?" he asked, seething. "I was ready to die, Aurora. I had accepted my fate before you came along, and for that, I am angry with you. I'm irate. You took what little peace I had and ruined it, and I may never forgive you."

"Fine," Aurora said, getting even closer, refusing to back

down. "Don't. Be irate. Be unforgiving. Hate me and curse my name to the ends of this mountain. Anything is better than your readiness to step into your grave."

"What would you have me do?" the Starmaker asked through gritted teeth, fire in his eyes. "This is the way it is, and I could no sooner change it than steal the stars from the sky."

Aurora stared at him in disbelief. "I don't know, but you have to do something. *Anything.* This entire mountain is drenched in magic, is only able to exist because of it. You may end up failing, but do you not owe it to yourself to try?"

"I owe it to myself to live out the remainder of my life in as much contentment as possible. I do not want to die screaming about how things could have been, and I certainly will not spend my limited time searching for a solution that does not exist." The Starmaker sat on the edge of his bed, putting his head in his hands. He exhaled, frustrated and slow. "Why must everything be a fight with you?"

"Because you are worth fighting for, and if you will not try everything you can to stay on this Earth with me, then I will do it myself."

The Starmaker shook his head, looking up at her. "Do you not think I want that? Do you not think I lie awake at night, utterly wrecked that the only person I would ever want an eternity with is the very one who is bringing forth the end of my life?" His eyes pleaded with her, and he looked so pained. "I cannot spend the remainder of my days enraged that we did not get enough time, though you must know it is a regret I will carry to my grave."

Aurora felt all of the fight leave her at once, and she slowly walked to the Starmaker, sitting down on the bed next to him. Constance was lying in front of the fire, a little rabbit silhouette that watched them intently, and as ridiculous as it was, her presence made Aurora feel better. She took the Starmaker's hand in hers and ran her fingers over his knuckles.

"You rest," she finally said, meeting his eyes. "I have no such scruples about being enraged."

The Starmaker laughed at that, a defeated, sad sound. "No, I should not think you would."

Aurora lay back, pulling the Starmaker with her, and they silently stared at the ceiling. After a while, he fell asleep, but Aurora was restless, looking at the mural above her while she listened to the Starmaker breathe. It was vast, covering the entirety of the ceiling, a painting depicting the Sun and the first Starmaker lying together on Reverie's glacier, covered in light. It was a romantic, whimsical image, but the longer Aurora looked at it, the angrier she got. Theirs was not the only love story that mattered.

The painting shifted then, the Sun fading away, leaving the Starmaker on his own. He slowly stood and wandered the glacier, looking as if he had lost something. Then he stopped and tilted his head toward the sky, staring after the Sun, tears streaming down his face. When one fell from the ceiling and landed on Aurora's cheek, she could not watch any longer.

She turned away and closed her eyes, succumbing to a fitful sleep.

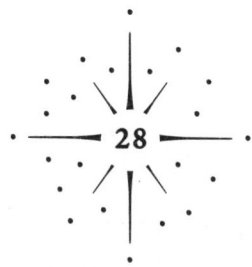

Waking Up Slow

Aurora and the Starmaker spent the following nights together, whispering to one another as Constance shot them irritable glances for keeping her awake. They did not touch in all the ways Aurora yearned for, but they held one another as they spoke of their fears and their dreams and their longings. Aurora was in a constant state of agitation, never close enough to the Starmaker, never forgetting what was to come, and never letting go of her anger at a situation that was entirely beyond her control.

Her mother had told her that loving her father had been worth it, and Aurora wanted to believe her. She wanted to believe her so badly that it became a physical ache in her chest, living inside her and going with her wherever she went.

This morning, it was with her on the glacier.

Aurora held on to the lamppost after hanging the day's light as she stepped back down and looked up the mountain toward the peaks. Her breath shook and her heart raced, and she wiped the edge of her cloak across her brow.

Today had been a trial to see if Aurora could carry the weight of the Sun before the official ritual that would transfer the rest of the Starmaker's magic to her, and she had done it alone. If she hadn't been able to bear the weight on her own, the light would have ricocheted back up the mountain, leaving the village covered in a blanket of night. But deep down, as much as she hadn't wanted it to be true, Aurora had known she was ready. And while it had been difficult and exhausting, she had been right.

When the light had rushed down the mountain and slammed into her, Aurora had fallen back into the snow, crushed by the weight of it. But she hadn't let go, gritting her teeth and summoning all of her energy so she could stand back up. It had been a slow, agonizing walk to the lamppost, but she'd done it, and when she had hung the light from the hook, a tear had slipped down her cheek.

As Aurora trudged through the snow back to the sleigh, she looked toward the woods in the distance, hoping they were healthy. She had been pushing off the ritual so she could have more time with the Starmaker, and they had not been patrolling the woods for the Frost as often as they should have. They preferred instead to go back to the castle after hanging the light, spending their days drinking tea and tending to the garden and talking for hours. And today was no exception. Aurora held tight to the

THE SUN AND THE STARMAKER

railing of the sleigh as the snow deer pulled her up the mountain for a few precious hours with the Starmaker.

There was a nagging feeling in her gut, telling her she should turn back and do what she was meant to do. But Aurora ignored it, knowing she would have plenty of time to push back the Frost. She had meticulously planned this day, and she was eager to surprise the Starmaker.

When the snow deer pulled up to the castle, Ina was waiting out front with a smile on her face, and she gave Aurora a knowing glance.

"Has he woken?" Aurora asked, jumping out of the sleigh and rushing up the stairs.

"Not yet," Ina replied, her eyes dancing in the early morning light.

Aurora squeezed her hands, then ran through the entryway and up the grand staircase, all the way to the Starmaker's door. She was out of breath, and she took several seconds to calm herself, then quietly went in.

The room was dark save for a dying fire that popped and crackled. Constance was at the foot of the bed, and she looked up at Aurora, who put a finger to her lips. The animal seemed to understand, and she stayed still as she watched Aurora walk into the room.

When Aurora had woken that morning, she had slipped out of the Starmaker's bed as quietly as she could, giving the staff stern instructions not to wake him. Her pillow was still indented, and the Starmaker's arm was stretched over her side of the bed, and for a moment Aurora just watched him, her heart expanding and breaking to see him this way. He was reaching for her even in sleep, and she wondered if that was how she would sleep for the rest of her life, reaching for someone who was no longer there.

She shoved the thought aside, then slowly walked to where the Starmaker slept, sitting on the edge of the bed. She rested her hand on his shoulder, gently running her fingers up and down his arm until he began to stir. His eyes blinked open, and he lazily grabbed Aurora's hand, rolling over to face her.

"I have a surprise for you," she said, smiling at him and kissing him on his forehead before walking to the enormous windows and opening the shades. Light streamed into the room, and the Starmaker sat up, a look of pure bewilderment on his face. "I did the trial on my own this morning," Aurora said, and the Starmaker just stared at her, clearly not understanding. "You slept in."

His eyes grew wide, and then he laughed, a big full-body laugh that echoed through the room and went straight for her heart. The Starmaker pulled her on top of him and laughed into her hair, wrapping his arms around her and kissing her, a long deep kiss that reverberated throughout her body. She kissed him back as tears welled in her eyes because it was such a perfect moment, and she wanted to pause time so she could live in it just a little longer.

But time was their enemy, and so Aurora reluctantly pulled away, stood, and offered him her hand. "Come," she said. "There is more."

THE SUN AND THE STARMAKER

Once the Starmaker had dressed for the day, Aurora led him out of his room, down the stairs, and through the castle.

"Are you in any pain from not pulling the light?" she asked, passing the portrait of the first Starmaker. Today, it was overcast in the painting, and the groundskeeper stayed in the background, trimming the hedges.

"No," the Starmaker said. "I don't have enough magic left to create a substantial buildup."

Aurora had assumed that was the case when she had planned the day, but it was still a harsh reminder of their situation, and she shoved the thought aside, intent upon enjoying the day.

"Where are we going?" the Starmaker asked.

Aurora could hear the excitement in his voice, even as he tried to mask it with indifference. She smiled to herself, shaking her head. He truly couldn't help himself.

"The courtyard," Aurora said, opening the door that led to the gardens, motioning to the table that had been set for them. "For breakfast."

The Starmaker's face brightened, and he hurried past her and down the steps to the elaborate meal awaiting them. There was a silver-and-white rug over the cobblestones with a glass table sitting on top. Snow covered the ground and all of the trees, but eight lanterns circled the table with big flames that provided ample heat. Large white blankets draped each chair, and peach roses covered all of the surfaces absent of food. Even a cushion and bowl had been perfectly placed at the table for Constance.

It was gorgeous, and Aurora looked at Ina, who had joined them.

"Thank you," she whispered, and Ina smiled.

"It is a lovely thing you're doing."

Aurora looked over to the Starmaker, who was already sitting down. He picked up a rose from the table and twirled it in his fingers, and he seemed so content that it broke Aurora's heart. Then she caught sight of Constance hopping around the base of the table, and she was delighted that the rabbit had decided to join them.

The Starmaker reached beneath his chair, scratching behind her ears.

Aurora walked down the steps and joined the Starmaker at the table, draping her lap with a blanket and pouring herself a cup of tea.

"Thank you," the Starmaker said, looking at her with adoration. "You have given me more than I ever thought possible."

"It's just breakfast," Aurora said, but her voice was heavy with emotion.

"That is not what I meant."

"I know."

The Starmaker took a sip of tea, leaning back in his chair and closing his eyes. "I have always loved it out here," he said.

"It's beautiful."

The Starmaker looked as if he wanted to say something, but he swallowed whatever it was and glanced toward the gardens instead. Just then, Tilly poked her head out from behind a hedge, and when she saw them, she ran over to the table, holding her looking glass.

"Look!" she exclaimed, standing next to the Starmaker, extending the mirror as far as she could with her wing. "Do you see me?"

"I do," the Starmaker said, peering into the mirror.

"Yes, of course you do," she said, laughing, "because that is me in the mirror!"

Aurora could tell that the Starmaker was trying to remain casual so as not to make Tilly self-conscious, but she watched as he swallowed and blinked several times. "It most certainly is."

Tilly was beaming, and she skipped off with her looking glass in hand, disappearing into the garden.

"There are moments when I am overwhelmed with frustration that you managed to do more for Tilly in a single day than I did during my entire reign," the Starmaker said, looking in the direction the angel had gone, "but right now, I cannot bring myself to feel even the least bit sad." He shook his head. "Thank you. I would never have forgiven myself if I'd left her before she found peace."

"She is truly special," Aurora said. "I will always look after her, I promise."

"I know you will."

The Starmaker fidgeted in his seat, and Aurora knew there was something he needed to say. "What is it?" she asked.

"I don't want to spend this morning on morose conversation," he said, "but I would like to know how the trial went, if you are willing to share."

It was a reasonable question, and Aurora needed to tell him, but it was so hard to talk about without thinking of everything it meant. She decided to get through it as quickly as possible. "As you can see, there is plenty of light," she said. "It was very tiring and very heavy, but I was able to bear it on my own."

The Starmaker nodded and took another sip of tea. "Then all that is left is the final transfer."

"Yes," Aurora said, her voice breaking. The Starmaker looked at her then, and she could see that it pained him just as much as it did her.

"Enough of that," he said, letting the strain leave his face and taking a deep breath of the clear morning air. "Let us enjoy this fine breakfast you planned for us."

And amazingly, they did. They fell into conversation as if nothing was looming in the distance, as if they had every reason to believe that their story was just getting started. Aurora laughed as she recounted childhood memories and listened as the Starmaker shared stories of his own, eager to hear whatever he wanted to say.

After they had filled their bellies with eggs and breads and sweets, Aurora stood and took the Starmaker's hand, leading him into the garden. She had found for him an extremely rare species of rose, one with petals like ice that shimmered in the light.

"Where did you find this?" he asked, his voice full of wonder.

"The nursery in the village. They said it had appeared for the first time a few weeks ago. The owner did warn me to be careful just in case the glittering petals aren't the only peculiar thing about it. Hopefully it doesn't bite," she said, remembering the red flower up in the castle.

"This is remarkable," he said.

"Plant it wherever you'd like." Aurora handed it to him, and his face lit up as he took the rosebush, gently holding it as if it were a fragile pup just freed from its mother's womb. He cradled it close to his chest as he walked around, looking for the perfect spot, and when he finally found it, he turned to Aurora.

"Plant it with me?" he asked.

Aurora nodded, and they knelt on the ground, digging a hole with their hands and dropping the plant in together. They covered the roots up with dirt, and astonishingly, another rose bloomed right before their eyes.

"Unbelievable," Aurora whispered, reaching out to touch it.

"There is so much magic here," the Starmaker said, looking around him. "It is everywhere."

"I love getting to see it through your eyes." And Aurora meant it. He was composed and dispassionate most of the time, but not out here. Out here he was like a child who had just seen his first falling star.

"It is one of the rare things in my life that thrills me more the longer I am around it," he said, then paused, looking at her. "You are another."

"You find me thrilling?" Aurora asked, tilting her head to the side, giving him a skeptical glance.

"In the beginning, I would have characterized it differently," he admitted. "But I do not think there is any other way to describe it now. When we met, I had been Starmaker for so long that I had disengaged from my life, and you forced me back to the present." He took her jaw with his dirt-covered hand and kissed her as another rose bloomed, then spoke in a low voice. "So yes, Aurora. You thrill me."

"Then just wait until you see what we're doing next," she said, pulling him up to standing and heading out toward the field beyond the barns. She'd had the staff gather together as many of the animals as they could, the wolves and snow deer and horses and goats. Even Constance was there, all of them ready to play with the Starmaker.

He stopped when they got to the field, looking at Aurora in disbelief before taking off at a run. He jumped around the field and played with the animals, lay on the ground and let the wolves pounce on him, cradled Constance in his arms. Then Tilly came to see what all the commotion was about, and she too joined in the fun. Ina watched from a distance, and Aurora saw her shoulders move up and down as she cried.

After he had spent time with each one of his animals, the Starmaker joined Aurora once more, looking at her as if she had given him everything, the whole world.

"I know I told you this would be my perfect day," the Starmaker said, "but it was somehow even better than I could have imagined."

"There is one more thing, if you're willing."

"What else could there possibly be?" he asked, searching her face, trying to uncover all of her secrets.

There was just one left, though.

Aurora paused, took in a breath. "Marry me?"

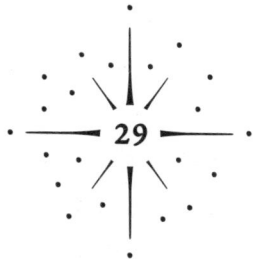

29

A Midnight Wedding

The Starmaker

"Okay."

The Starmaker responded instantly, before he even had time to think about the question or his answer or the consequences.

He said *okay* because he wanted to marry Aurora Finch, because the only thing in the world he wanted more than to marry her was to have a life with her, and since he could not have both, he would, with hunger and greed and fervor, take one.

"Okay," he said again.

Aurora smiled, taking his hands. "Okay."

✦

Later that night, beneath the light of the moon and a thousand stars, Aurora walked down the garden path to marry the Starmaker. She wore a white silk dress that brushed the earth as she moved, and when it caught the wind, it fluttered out behind her. It was plain, with long billowing sleeves, a deep neckline, and a flowing silhouette that made her feel free. There were no crystals or lace or embroidery, and Aurora was fairly certain it was meant for sleeping, but it was perfect, exactly what she wanted to wear. Ina had helped her weave pink flowers into her loose shimmering-white braid and had dusted her cheekbones with a silver mineral that sparkled faintly against her skin.

The night of their failed nuptials, the Starmaker's voice had been soft when he'd spoken of wholly belonging to another. Aurora remembered her reaction to the words, the way she'd felt each one in the very depths of her soul. She hadn't understood it at the time, but she now knew it was because the Starmaker had voiced a desire she had buried so deep within herself that she hadn't known it was there.

She had wanted to wholly belong to another.

And now she did.

Aurora held a single white rose from the plant she had given the Starmaker earlier, and the bloom twinkled like the stars and the fresh snowfall around them. A row of candles had been pushed into the ground, illuminating her path, and the crisp night air was heavy with silence.

The Starmaker waited for her in the middle of the gardens, the priest their only witness, though Aurora was certain Tilly was watching from somewhere out of view. When Aurora met the Starmaker's eyes, she was overcome. He was bathed in moonlight, and he watched her with a gravity unlike anything she had experienced, as if she was being seen for the very first time. His stance was rigid, his jaw tight, and his lips parted at the sight of her.

When she reached his side, he held out both hands, and Aurora took them in hers. She turned to face him, and he inhaled sharply. Aurora drew closer, as if she was the air that filled his lungs, and with clear, wide eyes, she gazed into his.

He was *glorious*.

And he was hers.

The Starmaker's eyes turned red and wet, and a look of utter shock passed over his features. He slowly raised a hand to his face, wiped his cheek, then looked at his tearstained fingers. "You..." he started, then trailed off. He took Aurora's hand once more, and she felt the tears on his skin. "I am undone by you."

Aurora inhaled, her chest aching, unsure if her ribs could contain her expanding heart. "And I by you."

The priest began to speak, leading them through the vows that would join them together for the rest of their days and follow them into the earth. They were the same vows Aurora's parents had spoken, and Aurora repeated them with veneration, binding her soul to the Starmaker's with the same promises that had bound the great loves that came before her.

"I will love you with the warmth of the Sun and the light of the moon," she began, the stars overhead shining brightly. "I will carry you with the strength of the mountain and keep your soul tucked close to mine. And when we return to the dust of the stars, I will whisper your name in the endless after so that I may find you even in death. Always will I come for you, and always will I stay."

When Aurora finished, the Starmaker said the same words, his voice unsteady, as if it might break at any moment. His composure never slipped, but for Aurora, it did.

The village jeweler had been able to accommodate their sudden request, and so they were able to exchange rings as well as vows. The Starmaker placed a band of vibrant sapphires onto Aurora's finger, rich blue stones the color of the sky just before the moon rose. His was a simple white gold band with a single inlaid sapphire at the top, a perfect match to the gems in Aurora's ring. She had thought it was beautiful when she had chosen it from the bands the jeweler had set before her, but seeing it on the Starmaker was something else entirely. She ran her thumb over the top of it, assuring herself it was real.

"All that remains is for you to kiss your bride," the priest said, and Aurora looked up at the Starmaker, watching his perfect face. She was scared of loving him, of what losing him would do to her. But in the end, she'd been more scared of never knowing him at all, never knowing who she was capable of becoming with him by her side. She understood now that she was exactly where she was meant to be, and that if she was granted a thousand lifetimes, in each and every one, she would choose the path that led her here, to the Starmaker.

"My bride," the Starmaker whispered, taking her face in his hands and kissing her slowly. He touched her with reverence, his mouth moving over hers with absolute devotion. Her breath caught when his tongue found hers, and when he deepened the kiss, she leaned into him, afraid her legs might give way beneath her.

The Starmaker pulled back just slightly, brushing his lips over her jaw and up to her ear. "I've been waiting a long while for you."

They were the same words he had said to her when they'd first met in the woods, yet they were entirely new, heavy with a different meaning. He kissed her ear and her jaw before finding her mouth once more, and it was a wonder that Aurora was still able to stand at all.

When the Starmaker pulled away, she could feel his reluctance, but then they were walking inside the castle, and Ina was showering them with rose petals, and they shared crystal flutes of sparkling wine, a pear tart Ina had made, and glasses of ice wine that had not gone bad.

After they had celebrated with the staff, they made their way to the Starmaker's room, and not even Constance was allowed inside. The Starmaker held Aurora's hand and led her to the bed, and she sat down, keeping her eyes on his. He gently slipped the silk from her shoulders, kissing her collarbone and her neck and the corner of her mouth. His lips lingered on her skin, and then he pulled back and looked at her, tucking a strand of hair behind her ear.

"My name is Caspian," he said, the word catching in his mouth as if he'd forgotten how to say it.

"Caspian," Aurora repeated, and it hit her straight in her gut because it was so him, so perfectly him, that it hurt her to say. It felt significant and wonderful on her tongue.

She stood to kiss him, the echo of his name still present on her lips. Then she slowly took off his shirt, trailing her mouth down his chest and stomach, sitting back on the bed and stopping at his hips. She looked up at him, her fingers tracing the button on his trousers.

"Tell me what you want," she said.

He swallowed hard, watching her. "I want to touch you while you say my name." His voice was hoarse, and Aurora knew what it had taken for him to speak his desire aloud, to be vulnerable in that way.

Keeping her eyes on his, Aurora let her dress fall to the floor and lay back on the bed, shifting out of the rest of her garments. Caspian's gaze slowly ran over the length of her body, and Aurora forced herself to be still, wanting him to see all of her. She took a deep breath, exhaling slowly, trying to calm her racing heart. Then Caspian found her eyes once more.

"I am captivated by you," he whispered.

Aurora reached for him, and he stepped out of his pants before joining her on the bed. Every part of him was as beautiful as the last, and she traced her fingers down his neck and over his chest, committing him to memory. He kissed her, and as he did, Aurora took his hand and placed it over her heart, inhaling into his touch, watching him as he reacted to his name on her tongue.

"Caspian."

Aurora burned with longing and nerves and need, but more than anything, with a love she had never thought would be hers, a love she had told herself she would never want. But with her hand over his and his mouth on hers, she understood that she had never had a choice in the matter. Loving Caspian was as inevitable as breathing, and whenever she had tried to fight against it, she was left gasping for air.

Aurora tipped her head back, and Caspian kissed the length of her neck, over her collarbone, and down her sternum, following her rib cage around her heart. He was where she felt most at home, and while she used to believe that love could only be either all-consuming or safe, she had been wrong. It could be both.

Caspian's mouth moved over her breast, finding the most sensitive part, and Aurora's breath caught in her throat.

"Caspian."

He groaned when she said his name, replacing his mouth with his hand, trailing his lips back to hers. The universe itself was not vast enough to contain the love Aurora had for this man, and yet she felt perfectly safe, as if she was curled up by the fire in her family's cottage, her heart steady and her mind calm.

He slowed then, kissing her as if they had all the time in the world—gentle and deliberate and soft, as if they were eternal. Unhurriedly, Caspian slid his hand down her ribs, brushing over her stomach and pausing at her hip.

"Tell me if you want me to stop," he said, the very thought making her desperate.

"Don't you dare," she breathed, arching into his touch.

He drew circles around her hips before finally trailing his fingers down, brushing the place between her legs, and Aurora said his name on a gasp. She felt him react to her with the way he deepened his kiss and the way his body tensed, needing her as much as she needed him.

Still, he took his time, applying a soft pressure that made her mind foggy and her body warm, and he pulled back to watch her as pleasure built deep in her core. Caspian overwhelmed her senses until he was all she could taste, all she see, all she could feel, and somehow it still wasn't enough. She needed more, gripping the sheets and pushing into him until an urgent heat concentrated into one single point beneath his touch.

All at once, she let herself go, warmth flooding her, as she looked at Caspian and whispered his name over and over again.

Caspian slowly kissed her neck, her ear, trailing his mouth along her jaw, then pausing just above her lips. His eyes were heavy with awe, gazing deep into hers.

"You brought me back to life," he said.

Aurora grasped the back of his neck, pulling him in for a kiss, pressing her tongue against his, and sliding her palms down his chest. She rested her hands on his hips, gripping him tight and pulling him closer, and as he slowly fit his body to hers, a low moan escaped his lips. Aurora ran her fingers through his hair and clutched his back, opened her eyes to watch his face so she could memorize the way it felt to be his.

Caspian kissed her deeply, his breaths coming faster. Aurora understood the weight of his words because he had brought her to life as well, opened up the entire universe before her just as she was ready to settle for the smallest piece. Aurora had not expected the longing that would awaken in her gut when she

THE SUN AND THE STARMAKER

saw the wonders of the world, and the more she discovered, the more she *wanted*. She wanted to live an extraordinary life with an extraordinary love on this extraordinary mountain.

She wanted an extraordinary story to tell.

She wanted it all.

Aurora kissed Caspian with her hands tangled in his hair, trailing her mouth along his jaw and whispering his name in his ear. Her lips were warm against his skin, and when he lost himself to her, he buried his face in her neck and exhaled long and slow, his body collapsing into hers.

For a while they were silent, their deep breaths the only sounds. Aurora said his name once more, and he looked at her with tears in his eyes, a small disbelieving smile forming on his face.

"I did not think I would ever hear it again."

He kissed her in the stillness, and a small laugh escaped his lips. Aurora thought it was the best thing she'd ever heard.

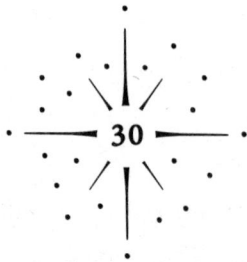

Illusion

Aurora had been right to worry about the woods, for she received a letter from Elsie the next day informing her that the candy stripe phlox behind their home was once again turning gray. Aurora had not considered the glare line when she had asked Caspian to marry her, but she took comfort in knowing that a line was now forming between the cottage and the castle, offering at least some protection from the Frost. Her family would be safe when they were indoors, but the line needed time to soak into the land and protect their crops.

When Evander had married, his line had been complete within a fortnight, and Aurora hoped it would be the same for hers. She had written to Elsie and told her to be patient, hinting at something wonderful, but she wanted to wait to share the news in person. That day had arrived, and Aurora was eager to see her family.

THE SUN AND THE STARMAKER

After they pulled the light over Reverie, she and Caspian got back in the sleigh, and the snow deer took them past the village, toward the dark woods that sat at the base of the peaks.

"Do you think we will ever be rid of the Frost?" Aurora asked Caspian, her hand tucked in his.

"Ever is a rather long time," he replied, but she could tell he was pondering it. "I do believe we'll be rid of it. It formed because of an unimaginable cold that gripped the mountain before the Sun made herself human, but one day, there will be enough Starmakers buried in the land to fend off the cold that the Frost needs to survive."

He paused, and Aurora wondered if he was thinking of what he'd told her that first night at the castle: *There will be no rest for you. Not even in death.*

Aurora thought his hand tensed slightly around hers, but she could have been imagining it. She hoped she was.

The snow deer slowed as Aurora's cottage came into view, and her worries faded as the door opened and Elsie ran outside. Aurora jumped from the sleigh to greet her sister, hugging her tightly, then waited for Caspian to join her. They walked inside together.

Mama rushed over and kissed Aurora on the cheek, and Aspen came in a moment later, dropping firewood on the hearth and taking Aurora in his arms.

"It is good to see you, sister," he said, and Aurora hugged him tightly.

"And you."

Aspen greeted Caspian as well, and Mama offered them tea. When everyone had a steaming cup in front of them, Aurora took Caspian's hand. "We have something to tell you," she said, surprised when her voice shook with emotion. She cleared her throat and slipped off her glove, holding out her hand for her family to see.

Mama jumped up from her seat, looking first at Aurora and then back to the ring, her eyes filling with tears. "When?" she asked.

"Three nights ago," Caspian said, squeezing Aurora's hand. "You may be surprised to hear that it was your daughter's idea."

"A rather good one, I'd say," Elsie exclaimed, wrapping her arms around Aurora.

"I tend to agree with you," he said, a small smile tugging at his lips, and it filled Aurora with warmth, seeing him joke with her family. Then Elsie threw her arms around Caspian's neck, and Aurora couldn't keep her tears at bay. A look of surprise crossed his face, and he tensed up, but then he slowly relaxed and patted her on the back.

Aspen shook Caspian's hand and congratulated them both, and then the front door opened and Evander and Samuel walked in. "Surprise!" Evander said.

Aurora ran to him, wrapping her arms around him and holding him tight, then did the same to Samuel. "What are you doing here?"

"Elsie wrote to us, letting us know of your upcoming visit. I hated not being able to see you off, but at least I'm here now," Samuel said, winking at Aurora.

"Then this is the perfect opportunity to introduce you to my husband," Aurora said, her voice catching on the last word. The word seemed to have a similar effect on Caspian, and for a single breath, they looked at each other, the rest of the room fading away.

"Husband?" Samuel asked, pulling Aurora out of her reverie. She excitedly nodded and recounted the ceremony, telling them about the moonlight and the priest and the palpable happiness that had bloomed in her chest.

"Welcome to our family," Mama said, and Aurora watched Caspian, who looked away, whispering the word *family* under his breath as if he couldn't remember what the word meant.

Then he nodded and, with a heavy voice, said, "Thank you."

Aurora wanted to stay the whole day, to help Mama with dinner and set the table and hear about all the things she had missed since moving to the castle, but they still had to monitor the forests, and so she reluctantly said goodbye to her family and promised to visit again soon.

As the sleigh pulled away from the cottage, Aurora noticed that Evander and Samuel were still inside, and she smiled to herself.

Soon the home was out of view, and the snow deer pulled them closer to the dark woods. Even at a distance, Aurora could see a break in the border of pink petals, but phlox was particularly sensitive to the Frost, and she hoped it was nothing more than an early warning sign, something she and Caspian could easily heed.

The snow deer came to a stop when they reached the edge of the trees. Caspian took his time getting out of the sleigh, and Aurora pretended not to notice, jumping down to the snowy earth and following behind him. He was in good spirits, and Aurora was trying her best not to analyze his every movement, his every step, to make sure he would not die *today*—that was a certain way to sour his mood. Caspian had told her many times that he could not die until they performed the ritual that would transfer his remaining magic to her, but Aurora worried for him still.

They both stopped when they reached the phlox, surveying the flowers that stretched out in either direction. Aurora brought her hand to her mouth, unable to speak. Patches of gray were everywhere, not just at the farthest reaches of the forest but closer to the village as well. She gently took a bloom in her hands, studying it. It was completely devoid of color, looking as if it belonged in a charcoal drawing, not in vibrant Reverie. It reminded her of the one she had seen in the ruins, and she shivered.

"What is happening?" she asked quietly, keeping her voice down as if everyone in the village might hear her.

Caspian didn't answer right away. Instead, he walked farther into the woods, inspecting the forest floor, running his fingers over bark, feeling the needles on branches as if he spoke a language that only he and the trees understood. It was beautiful to watch, and Aurora followed close behind him, trying to learn as much as she could.

After they had walked for what felt like hours, Caspian sat beneath a large pine, leaning his back against its trunk and closing his eyes. He looked pained, and Aurora knelt down beside him.

"Are you feeling all right?" she asked.

"I am fine," he replied, keeping his eyes closed. "The trees, however, are not."

THE SUN AND THE STARMAKER

"But we are pulling the light each day," Aurora said. "And while we could have been more vigilant with our patrols, surely we didn't miss so many that the Frost was able to advance this much."

Caspian opened his eyes, staring into the distance as understanding crossed his face. He shook his head slightly, and his expression settled into one that was grim and tense.

"What is it?" Aurora asked. Her heart sped up, and her chest ached as she waited for his response. He rocked forward onto his knees and set his hands on the earth. The canopy above was covered in snow, but the ground was clear, and as the Frost mostly kept to the depths of the forest, the soil here was untouched.

"How does the Sun know to choose a new Starmaker?" he asked, so quietly she wasn't sure if he actually wanted her to answer. He got up and began surveying the trees again, every step deliberate.

"Please tell me what you're thinking," Aurora begged, unable to handle the unease stirring in her gut.

Caspian stopped and turned to face her. "She chooses a new Starmaker when the land requires it."

"What does that mean?"

"The bodies of the previous Starmakers protect against the Frost, and the living Starmaker pulls in the light." Caspian paused, dire determination on his face. "I have let this go on for too long."

It wasn't his fault, though. Pulling the light had become a frustrating dance in which Caspian tried to give her his remaining magic—the ritual that would complete Aurora's transition to Starmaker—and Aurora staunchly refused it. The trial had proven to her that she could carry the entirety of the light on her own, but until all of Caspian's magic was in her veins, he would not die. It had been difficult to reject what little power he had left, but she had done it, and he was still here with her. If anything, she was the one to blame.

"I don't understand," Aurora said, almost pleading. "Surely one Starmaker cannot make such a difference?" She felt hopeless, and she racked her brain for another solution, anything to give them more time.

"Four Starmakers. I will be the fourth, and the magic in the land is much more potent when properly fed."

"Fed?"

"The mountain needs another body," Caspian said, and Aurora looked at him in disgust. "I concede that was a poor choice of words, but the point stands. Once all of my magic is transferred to you, my body will still be covered in the remnants of it the way tea stains the inside of a pot. It won't be nearly enough to pull the light, but it will be enough to give the land what it needs. When I am buried, those remnants will seep into the earth and fight the Frost."

Aurora sighed, looking out into the vast woods, knowing there was nothing more to be done.

"We can't put it off any longer," Caspian said gently, but something in his tone told Aurora he would not be argued with. "We are fortunate that it hasn't yet spread beyond the phlox, but it will. It is only a matter of time."

Aurora said nothing. She couldn't bring herself to agree with him even though she knew he was right. This was the way their magic worked, and the entire mountain was dependent upon it. She nodded, and they began their walk back to the sleigh.

They didn't rush, and Aurora could tell that Caspian was appreciating his surroundings, knowing that this would be the last time he ever walked these woods. He wandered from tree to tree, gazing up at the sky, feeling the bark against his palms and the cold breeze on his skin. Aurora wanted to look away, to let him have these intimate moments to himself, but she couldn't bear to. She was experiencing him the way he was experiencing the woods, committing each detail to memory, the curve of his spine and the angle of his jaw and the way his lips parted slightly when he looked up. She was jealous of every last second he had on this mountain, and she wanted them all to herself.

Caspian finally made his way out of the woods, past the candy stripe phlox to the sleigh where the snow deer were waiting. Aurora followed, so focused on him that she didn't see the broken branch hanging over the flowers. It caught her across the neck, and Aurora winced, bringing her hand to a long gash on her skin. Her fingers came away bloody, and she watched as a single drop ran down her palm and hit the earth. She immediately felt lightheaded, and she took a steadying breath.

"Are you okay?" Caspian asked, moving to her aid. He reached beneath his cloak and pulled out a handkerchief, first cleaning the blood from her hand, then her neck.

"I am," Aurora said, looking up at the trees and breathing deeply until she finally felt steady on her feet. Caspian offered her his arm, and she took it, slowly making her way back to the sleigh.

Once they were both seated, he ran the cloth over her neck once more, not seeming to mind the blood.

"I was so distracted by your beauty that I walked straight into a branch," Aurora said.

Caspian laughed at that, taking her hand in his as the snow deer pulled them to the glacier to let go of the light. Aurora looked back to the woods once more, and though they were getting farther away, she could have sworn a single flower turned from gray to pink.

"You think I'm beautiful?" Caspian asked, the corner of his mouth tugging upward, and she turned back to him.

"I do," Aurora said, "though I don't believe it is an opinion, but rather a fact."

"If that is true, it is certainly one I have never heard before."

Aurora stared at him, shocked. "How is that possible?"

Caspian was quiet for a moment, as if he was truly pondering the question. "I suppose because it has been quite a while since I've spent time with anyone who would feel comfortable saying such a thing to me."

"Then let me tell you again how beautiful you are."

Caspian shook his head, giving Aurora a look that said she was utterly ridiculous, but she could see his cheeks going slightly pink, and she realized that he was embarrassed. She was wholly unprepared for the way it made her eyes burn with the threat of tears, for the painful lump that formed in her throat.

Her stoic, indomitable Starmaker was embarrassed.

When the snow deer came to a stop at the glacier, Aurora practically threw herself out of the sleigh, not wanting Caspian to

THE SUN AND THE STARMAKER

see how strongly she was reacting. She wondered if he could feel it or if he was now too weak to sense the magic in her at all.

The thought made her unbearably sad.

"You wait here," Aurora said. "I can let go of the light."

"No." Caspian stood and joined her. "I want to do it."

Aurora nodded, and they walked to the lamppost in silence. Caspian stepped up and opened the glass door, and for several breaths, he just looked at it. Then he slowly raised his arm, unhooked the light, and sent it sailing back up the mountain and between the peaks until nothing but darkness remained.

When they got back to the castle, they invited the entire staff to dine with them, and when they retired to his room for the evening, they once again asked Constance to rest elsewhere. Neither of them slept; they talked and they kissed; they touched and they held each other. They even laughed.

But as time so often did, it moved too quickly, and soon it was morning again. The mountain needed a body, and the village needed a Starmaker whose magic was complete.

Caspian's arms were wrapped tightly around her, and her legs were tangled with his as he kissed her forehead. His breath tickled her skin, and Aurora could almost convince herself that it was a normal morning, that they would come back here that night after they had pulled the light for the day. But it was just an illusion.

Caspian let her go, moving farther and farther away as he slid out of bed—

too far—

and it was the coldest Aurora had ever felt.

Caspian

Caspian had been ready to die. He had been preparing for it for many years, and he had accepted it. He had *welcomed* it. Throughout all his preparations, he had always been certain of one thing: he would die alone. He was certain because he had made the decision long ago.

Then Aurora had shown up and decimated his meticulously laid plans.

Caspian had always known he would outlive every person he ever cared for, but in a twisted turn of fate, he had fallen in love at the end of his life, and now he would be the one to say goodbye first.

He was not ready for that.

He quietly made his way to his childhood bedroom and picked up the journal he had abandoned years ago. He turned to the first blank page and began to write. At first, he didn't know what to say, but then the words came furiously, and he tried to keep up as best he could.

He wrote to her and for her and because of her, knowing she would find it. And when he finally laid down his pen, a single tear rolled down his cheek and onto the last page, smearing the ink.

God, he hated to leave her.

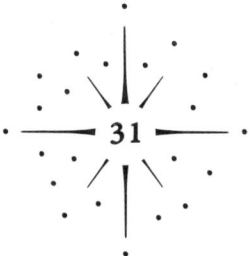

The Endless After

Aurora dressed slowly, watching herself in the mirror. Only a few strands of her hair remained brown, and her blue eyes swirled with gold. Her Sun's mark caught the candlelight, and the design shimmered against her fair skin, nearly complete. There was an almost imperceptible gap at the very top, and Aurora knew that by the end of the day, that gap would be gone, and so too would Caspian.

Her eyes burned, but Aurora refused to cry. She worried that if she started, she would not stop, and so she would have to save it for later, when she had the time she needed for her tears to run dry.

When Aurora reached the dining room, she was startled to find everyone who worked at the castle gathered there. Caspian was speaking to each and every person, expressing his gratitude for the way they had cared for him and his home. He was almost to the end of the line, and when he came to Ina, Aurora had to turn away, the pain on Ina's face too much to bear.

"We've known this day was coming," Caspian said, addressing everyone in the room, his voice even and calm as if he were handing out a list of chores for the day instead of saying his final goodbye. "It has been my absolute honor to serve not only as your Starmaker but as your friend. I have had an exceptional life, and I am grateful."

Aurora was still standing in the entryway, not wanting to interrupt but unable to make herself leave, and Caspian turned to her. "You have a new Starmaker now, one who is more than worthy of the title. My only regret is not getting to see her reign."

Everyone in the room turned their eyes to Aurora, but she could feel herself losing her composure, and she took a shaky breath, trying to hold herself together. "I'm sorry," she whispered, looking at Caspian. "I can't do this."

She left the room, retrieving her cloak and gloves, and walked outside to the waiting sleigh. She moved to each snow deer in turn, petting their snouts and running her fingers through their fur, trying to focus on anything other than the ritual awaiting her. She walked around the castle and picked a bundle of roses, tucking them beneath her cloak, and when she finally stepped into the sleigh and pulled the blanket over her lap, Caspian was exiting the palace along with all of the household staff. Aurora watched as they lined up on the steps to see their Starmaker off, and it made the ache in her chest scream.

"You should have addressed them," Caspian said when he was seated on the bench beside her.

"I know," she whispered. "But I couldn't find the right thing to say."

"There is no right thing." He took her hand beneath the blanket. "Most of them won't remember the words you speak, anyway; they will remember how you made them feel. Do not let your silence speak for you."

Aurora nodded. "I will make it right when I arrive back at the palace."

With that, the snow deer began to pull, the sleigh gliding away from the castle. Aurora looked back then to see all of the staff waving after them, and when Caspian turned and put one hand in the air, she had to swallow her tears.

"Will you promise me something?" he asked when they were out of view of the palace, turning to face her. Aurora kept her eyes on the trail ahead, and Caspian gently placed his fingertips on her chin and forced her to look at him. "Please do not deny me my favorite thing to look at."

Aurora blinked. She swallowed hard and raised her eyes to his. "What is it?"

"Do not let my choices influence your own. I chose isolation because it was what I could live with." He paused, his eyes sad. "But it turns out that what I needed most was you. *You*, Aurora. You showed me what it was to live when I had forgotten."

"Caspian," Aurora began, but he kept speaking.

"Promise me you won't forget."

With tears in her eyes, she nodded. "I promise."

They were quiet for the remainder of the ride. Aurora sensed that was what Caspian wanted, and he watched as they glided past the trees, taking in their surroundings as if it were his first time seeing them. Aurora had to turn her face away. He acted resigned to what was to come while she was desperate to change it, and though she was glad that he'd be able to die with peace in his heart, she was outraged that it seemed so easy for him to leave her.

All of his affairs were in order, down to the exact location he was to be buried, where his body would feed the land for years to come. Villagers would visit his grave and leave him flowers, thanking him for his reign as well as the magic he continued to give to the mountain. He would be remembered for what he was instead of who he was, but Aurora would remember him for both.

When the sleigh came to a stop on the glacier, the snow deer began to whine as if they too knew what was about to happen. Caspian stepped out and gently petted each of his deer, placing his forehead against their snouts and closing his eyes. Aurora's chest felt as if it was on fire, and she stayed motionless as she waited for him, not wanting to take away from the moments she was not meant to be part of.

"Aurora," Caspian said, and she blinked at him. He had stepped away from the deer, and he was watching her with careful eyes. "I am ready."

"And what if I am not?" She said the words through gritted teeth, and she wasn't sure if Caspian heard her or not. But then he

THE SUN AND THE STARMAKER

walked over to her and pulled her hand from her cloak, holding it in his.

"You will be okay." He said it with finality, then began his walk to the lamppost for the last time. Aurora walked with him and did not pull her hand from his because she knew she would regret it if she did. But she wanted to fight against all of this, to tear her hand away and race into the woods where none of this could touch her, find a place where she could hide from the inevitable. As if such a place existed.

Caspian looked up at the lamppost and ran his free hand over the cold metal, and Aurora felt broken because she couldn't understand his love for the Sun or for the magic, couldn't understand how he had accepted his fate. She would never say it out loud, but in some ways she envied him, and in that moment she was terrified that she would spend the rest of her very long life angry and resentful.

She didn't want that, but she also didn't know how to prevent it. She *was* angry, and she wouldn't pretend that she wasn't.

"I wept," Caspian said, pulling Aurora from her thoughts. "On the day my mentor died, I fell to my knees and wept. I did not know him the way you know me, but I assure you that whatever it is you're feeling, I felt some fraction of it, too."

Aurora looked at him then, her eyes burning. "Why are you telling me this?"

"Because I was exhausted and ready to pass the mountain to the next Starmaker. Connection has never been a talent of mine, and you somehow forced it to happen against my will. But now..."

He trailed off, looking up at the sky. A light snow had started to fall, and several flakes landed on his eyelashes. Aurora had the incredible urge to dust them off and keep them in her pocket, though such fantasies were foolish. They were no more lasting than the Starmaker.

"But now?"

"You aren't alone, Aurora. I have stood exactly where you are and felt all the despair and hopelessness and anger that you are feeling now. I survived it, and so can you."

Aurora could no longer hold back her tears, and they fell freely even as she tried to blink them away.

"You are so strong," Caspian said, brushing a stray piece of hair behind her ear.

"I don't want to do this." Aurora pulled her eyes from his, wiping her cheeks on her cloak. "I don't want you to say your goodbyes wrapped in words you think will hearten me."

"I am not being insincere."

"No," Aurora said, walking in circles around the lamppost, staring down at the footprints she was leaving behind in the snow. "But you are being polished and rehearsed. Be present with me. Feel whatever it is you feel, and I will do the same."

Caspian nodded once. "Fine," he said, his composure breaking. "Then I must tell you that the only solace I take in dying is knowing that my magic will help sustain the earth you walk upon, and my deepest hope is that you feel it with every step you take."

Aurora moved closer to him, so close she could feel his breath upon her skin, could feel his exhales as if they were her own. "And

I must tell you that death is not strong enough to keep me from you, and every step I take will be in search of the gate that will lead me back to you."

Caspian grimaced, and Aurora knew it was because he did not want her to spend her days looking for something that did not exist. But he did not reprimand her or object. Instead, he put his hands on either side of her face, looked into her eyes, and said, "If anyone can defy death, it is you."

He pulled her into him, kissing her with the passion and longing of all the kisses they would not have. Aurora melted into him, ignoring the way her tears dripped off her chin like winter rain, ignoring the way his kiss was saying goodbye when she still could not accept it. Caspian pressed his lips to her eyelids, her cheeks, her jaw, her neck, and when he finally pulled away, his eyes were red and wet. He trailed his fingers down her face, wiping away her tears, and with a heavy breath, he lowered his arm.

For one beat of Aurora's heart, they were both still, frozen to the ground beneath them. Then Caspian took her hand, and they turned to face the peaks of Reverie together. There was nothing more to say, and when Caspian called to the Sun for the final time, Aurora was ready. The light burst between the peaks in a brilliant glimmer, vibrant rays stretching over the snow-covered landscape, illuminating the village center and coming straight for them. Aurora watched Caspian as he caught the light with complete composure, even though the weight of it was too much for him now.

"I will love you forever," she whispered.

"Then perhaps I am immortal after all."

They held on to each other tightly as Aurora readied herself for the Sun, but she did not speak of magic or duty or warmth. Instead, she spoke her truth: "I hate you for taking him from me."

The Sun's voice surrounded Aurora, and even as she glared at the light, she could not deny the beauty of it, the way the sound seemed to magnify every other sense until she was seeing Reverie through a different lens. She heard the seeds beneath the earth as they grew, the roots of the trees as they reached out to each other, and the heartbeats of beasts as they welcomed the morning light. She heard it all, everything, the world and the stars beyond, all wrapped up in the Sun's celestial voice.

The Sun sets on one
to rise on another.

Aurora swallowed a sob. The remaining light rushed toward them, and she gasped as the rest of Caspian's magic entered her bloodstream. It was a powerful surge that echoed through her body, and somewhere deep inside her, she recognized it as his. It felt like him—cold and warm, stoic and deliberate, impatient and reverent. Challenging. Gentle. She accepted it all, hoping she would never forget, not for a single moment, that the magic she possessed had once belonged to the man she loved, had once flowed through his veins and moved through his heart.

Aurora took a deep breath, preparing herself for what was to come.

THE SUN AND THE STARMAKER

She felt the exact moment Caspian let go of her hand, and her arm flailed, trying to find him once more. She frantically grasped for him, but he took a step back, just out of reach. "Please," she whispered, but there was nothing he could do; he was no longer able to pull the light with her. It was Aurora's job now, and she held it all on her own. It was heavy and overwhelming, and she wanted to collapse beneath the weight of it, but the truth was that she was strong enough to carry it.

She forced herself to turn away from him, beginning the long walk to the lamppost. She could feel his eyes on her as she moved, each step harder than the last, until finally she reached the bronze post. She stepped up onto the platform, turning back to look at him, and he watched her with clear eyes. Then he clutched his chest with his hand.

No.

With all of her strength, Aurora lifted the golden rays of the sun and heaved them onto the hook in the lantern. It was the final step in the ritual, and Aurora slammed the glass door shut and jumped back to the ground.

Caspian.

He was on his knees, and Aurora ran to him, dropping into the snow beside him. He fell to the side, his head landing in her lap, and Aurora cradled him gently.

"I'm here," she said, her voice shaking. "I'm not going anywhere."

"Whisper my name in the endless after..." His voice was weak, and his breaths were ragged, as if the words had taken whatever life remained in him.

"I will," she promised, bending close so he could hear her. "I will," she said again, her lips against his ear, repeating it over and over.

He met her eyes, touched her lips. "Find me even in death."

The sunlight got brighter then, warmth colliding with the falling snow. Everything was so quiet; not even the animals in the forest or the deer at the sleigh stirred. It was as if the entire mountain held its breath.

"Caspian," she gasped, holding him close. Then the light in his eyes dimmed and his chest no longer rose, and all at once he was gone.

This new dawn brings with it new life.
You and you alone call out to me.
I am the Sun.
You are the Starmaker.
Today your reign begins.

Aurora bent over Caspian, his head still in her lap, and wept.

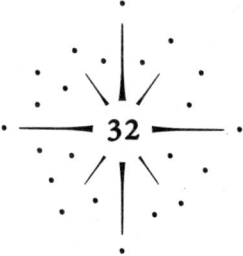

Darkness

The day following the Starmaker's death was marked by darkness. Aurora did not pull the Sun, and Reverie remained under a black cloudless night, the stars and the moon casting the only light on the mountain. It was customary to mark the Starmaker's passing in this way, and when the villagers realized what it meant, they closed their shops and emptied out of the market until even the square was blanketed in the thick of night. The only stirring came from the bells, ringing out from the center of the square in mourning. Aurora could hear them all the way from her room in the palace, and she kept her balcony doors open to let in the sound.

Aurora had stayed with Caspian until the very last second, until the castle staff had arrived on the glacier, pulling him from her and laying him to rest in his marble casket. She had cried over him as she'd set the peach roses she had gathered on his chest, saving just one to place on the glacier where he had taken his last breath. *I will find you even in death*, she had promised, and then the staff closed the casket and took it back to the castle, where it would lie in the small sanctuary beyond the gardens, awaiting burial.

Aurora closed her eyes against the memories. A single day of mourning did not feel like enough to mark Caspian's life, his unwavering protection of Reverie. She wondered how long would feel adequate, and she realized there was no amount of time that would properly convey her grief over losing him.

Not a day.

Not a month.

Not a year or one hundred years more.

Aurora sat on her bed with her knees pulled to her chest, her quilt draped over her legs, listening to the sound of the bells. Constance sat at the foot of the bed, watching her with her enormous blue eyes, and Aurora swore she saw grief in them. A tray of food sat untouched on the desk, and the gold handkerchief was always at the ready, standing upright on the side table. Ina had dropped off a sampling of the many letters that had arrived that day. Perhaps Aurora would read them eventually, when the intense grip of pain subsided and she felt like she could breathe again.

Perhaps.

When her room began to feel too small, Aurora dressed in her warmest wool and went outside to be with the animals. They too seemed to understand that Caspian was gone, and they whined as she made her way from the deer to the rabbits to the squirrels. Before she reached the wolves, one of them howled, and the rest of them joined in. The sound mixed with that of the bells, the most sorrowful thing Aurora had ever heard, and it echoed through the trees and off the mountain peaks, covering all of Reverie in its anguish.

She wandered the grounds for a long time. The gold handkerchief followed close behind her, and when she could no longer stand it, she snatched it from the air and shoved it deep into her pocket. She touched the flowers and visited the greenhouse, and when she went to check on the rosebush she had planted with Caspian, she saw that it was in full bloom, sparkling white petals that were somehow vibrant even in the dark.

There is so much magic here.

Aurora roamed the gardens until her head ached from the sweet scent of flowers, then trudged through the snow to the small sanctuary. First she sat and leaned her back against the entrance, and then she stood and walked in tireless circles around the structure. She kept her hand on the stone, hoping Caspian could feel her presence. It was cold and dark in the small space, and she didn't want him to be alone.

Aurora was about to go back to the palace when she caught sight of Caspian's stag far off in the distance, the one she had tried to kill that first day in the woods. The memory felt like a knife, and before she knew what she was doing, she ran toward him, and then the stag was running, too. Aurora's heart was pumping, the cold air blowing her hair back and stinging her lungs, but it felt so good to *run*. She was getting closer to the stag, and she picked up her skirts, her legs burning with the effort, moving as fast as she could until there was no more distance between them. Then she abruptly stopped, and so did the stag.

The stag bowed his head, shoved his snout into Aurora's chest, then dropped to his knees and curled up on the snow. Aurora did the same, and the stag shifted toward her so that she was resting on his side. She lay there for a long while, looking up at the stars, feeling her life stretch out before her. So much time. So many years. So much grief.

She understood why Caspian had guarded himself, why he'd had walls so high they were nearly impossible to climb. Why he wouldn't even name his animals for fear of intimacy. She remembered then that she had decided to name the deer but had yet to do it. Now was as good a time as any, and it felt fitting to name the stag first.

She turned her head to see his face, feeling the rise and fall of his chest with each breath he took. She was as struck by him then as she'd been the first time she'd seen him, so tall and serene and beautiful. He did not seem to mind the darkness. He lifted his head to look at her, and Aurora saw the stars reflected in his eyes, even a falling one that drifted from one eye to the other. He put his head back down, and she ran her hand over his fur.

She decided to call him Fate.

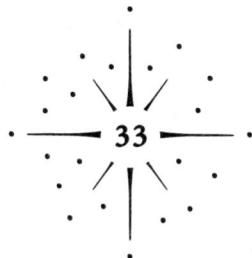

A Discovery

Aurora had not given it enough thought at the time, the way the candy stripe phlox had turned from gray to pink on the day she had called Caspian beautiful. She had been light-headed from her bleeding cut and distracted by the Starmaker, and the changing flower had not mystified her as it ought to have. But now it demanded her attention, waking her from a restless sleep in the dead of night.

Why had it changed?

The most likely explanation was that it had been a trick of her mind. They'd been pulling away in a sleigh when she'd seen it, after all, and the petals were small, so she surely hadn't been looking at the same bloom as she had been when she'd cut her neck. Perfectly reasonable.

And yet she couldn't let go of it, and so she got out of bed, dressed in a rush, and had the sleigh prepared for her.

Aurora was calm as the snow deer pulled her to the edge of the woods where the phlox stretched out endlessly in either direction. The moon was full, creating enough light to illuminate the plants, and she didn't stop the deer until she had reached the house she grew up in.

She kept her distance, not wanting to wake her family, and the ache in her chest seemed to pulse in time with the soft orange glow of the fire inside. For a while, she just stood and watched it, but the nagging in her mind was incessant, and she finally turned away and walked to the phlox behind the house.

Aurora stopped at a patch of candy stripe that was entirely gray, set her lantern down, and pulled a red rose from her cloak. The bloom was large and fragrant, and when Aurora touched a thorn to her finger, a single drop of blood appeared. She took several deep breaths, trying not to look as the drop got bigger. She knelt on the ground and shoved the snow aside, holding her finger above the roots, and then the drop fell to the earth.

She pulled a cloth from her cloak and quickly wiped her finger clean, and then she waited.

At first nothing happening, and Aurora tried to fight the disappointment in her gut. At least she had tried. But then color seeped into the plant, the stems turning green before her eyes, faint but real. Then, all at once, the petals burst to life, vibrant pink and crisp white crawling across the blooms in a show that took Aurora's breath away.

THE SUN AND THE STARMAKER

She shook her head, not quite believing what she was seeing; perhaps she was dizzier from the blood than she'd realized. It had been only a drop, after all. Was there truly that much magic inside her? She walked several paces away and repeated the process, and sure enough, color returned to the flowers.

Aurora realized in a rush that her blood could feed the earth, fighting back the Frost. And because the magic in her veins was so potent, only a tiny amount was necessary. The mountain didn't need Caspian—it could survive on her alone.

Aurora rushed back to the sleigh, her body vibrating with what she had learned. She had never wanted any of this; she had dreamt of a comfortable life for herself and those she loved, but Caspian had awoken something in her, a desire for more. She wanted to leave her mark on the world, wanted her own stories told throughout the ages. There were many who believed that loneliness was the cost of an extraordinary life, but Aurora could not accept that.

She *would* not accept that.

The Sun had fallen in love with a human she could never be with, but Aurora was no Sun. And she would not spend her many years alone. Her stories would not be those of a heartbreaking, doomed love, but rather a love so strong it would outlive death.

Aurora hadn't meant to bypass the glacier, to go straight to the castle instead of first pulling the light. But her mind was racing, and all she could think about was getting to Caspian's library and reading every page of every book until she discovered a way to bring him back.

It was Caspian who had said there was so much magic here—that it was *everywhere*—and Aurora was intent on using it.

She'd thought she had accepted their fate, believed she could move forward and do what was required of her. But she had been wrong. Seeing the phlox come back to life had induced a kind of frenzy inside of her, a panicked hope that perhaps she wouldn't have to accept things as they were after all. Her hope built and built and built, and by the time she reached the castle, it had grown so big it was impossible to see past, blocking out everything except her desire to bring Caspian back.

When she walked inside the grand entrance, it was dim and quiet, the only sound that of the statue's hushed crying. She looked up at it: the Sun and the Starmaker carved from stone, being pulled from each other, an impossible distance between them. The statue didn't often cry, but it had done so constantly since Caspian's death.

Aurora turned away and lit a candle, hurrying to the library with soft footsteps. She had many hours of work ahead of her, and she did not want to be interrupted by the staff. The hallways were silent, awaiting the arrival of the light, and Aurora resented the way the palace was still so magical, still so vibrant.

Perhaps that was why she failed to pull the sunlight that day: because she felt the whole mountain should still be in mourning, just as she was. It wasn't a conscious decision, though—rather more like a task that had slipped through the cracks of her mind. And once it happened the first time, it made the second and third and fourth easier. There was a nagging in the back of her mind, telling her she was forgetting something, but she was so focused on the books in the library that she did not give it the attention it deserved.

On the fifth day, Aurora was splayed out on the soft rug, surrounded by piles of books. She was reading everything she could on the magic of Reverie, the connection to the Sun, and the way the land had changed when each Starmaker was buried. At her request, Mr. Burgess sent her new books each morning to supplement the materials in Caspian's library, and Aurora turned page after page, looking for anything that hinted at a living Starmaker giving their blood to the mountain, but there was nothing.

There had to be. She just hadn't found it yet.

Aurora was so caught up in her reading that she didn't hear the way the staff whispered, worried they may never see the light again. Ina brought her plates of food, and Aurora ate just enough to keep her mind going. When she slept, it was in the library on a pile of blankets, and only for a few hours at a time. She read and wrote and read and wrote, and when she needed a break, she stood and walked in circles, never leaving the room.

Aurora paid no attention to the way her body was failing without the use of her magic, ignoring the pain as if it were simply an itch. Constance stayed close by, hopping nervously around the library, watching Aurora as if ensuring she didn't fade away.

When Ina came with supper on the seventh night, Aurora did not look up from her reading. Ina set the tray down, but she did not leave. She stood before Aurora until the Starmaker finally noticed her, blinking up at her as if trying to adjust to the light.

"What is it, Ina?" she asked, dipping her head once more to her book.

"It is the light, Your Radiance." Ina's voice was gentle and hesitant, and she knelt down in front of Aurora. "We have not seen it in quite a while."

Aurora rubbed her eyes. Her vision was blurry from all the reading she'd done, and she hadn't realized how badly her head was aching. "I will get to it," she said, taking a piece of bread from the tray and gulping it down in two bites. "I just need to finish what I'm doing first."

"May I ask what it is you're doing?"

Aurora answered without looking up. "No."

Ina swallowed. "Your Radiance, you are the Starmaker. Surely there is nothing more important than that."

Aurora looked at Ina with such intensity that her eyes blazed more than the crackling fire. "What I am is a grieving widow. Now, please leave me be."

Ina did not move for several breaths, but Aurora had already gone back to her reading and did not notice when she was once again alone. When she couldn't find any information on whether the blood of a living Starmaker could indeed sustain the land, at least for a time, she began reading up on immortality. It was a complicated matter; the Sun—a truly immortal being—had given a human part of her immortality. And that immortality transferred from Starmaker to Starmaker, a seemingly movable force that could be shared like a pot of tea.

It had to mean something.

THE SUN AND THE STARMAKER

Aurora rubbed her temples, her head throbbing. She continued to pore over book after book, scribbling down half ideas and sparks of inspiration, anything that could lead her to a breakthrough.

Immortality. Blood. Transferable. Body. Magic. Glare Lines. Phlox.

The more she read, the less the ache in her chest took her breath away. The more she wrote, the less the stabbing in her gut mattered. It was her own kind of medicine, and she was dulling the pain as much as she could.

When a fresh set of books arrived at the palace from the bookshop, Aurora tore into them immediately, and a small white envelope fell from the stack. She picked it up, hoping the owner had some family lore to share or some whispers he had heard that might help her, but it was nothing of the sort.

Your Radiance,

I am writing to you on behalf of many shopkeepers from the village square. We cannot adequately convey the depth of our condolences for the loss of our fourth Starmaker, may he rest in warmth. While it is surely not our place to suggest how you should grieve, we must make you aware that with the loss of the light, the Frost is creeping out beyond the forest, and it is only a matter of time before it reaches not only the village square but homes and livestock as well. All of our candy stripe phlox are now gray.

This will be my last delivery of books for the time being. I hope you find what you are seeking, but more urgently, I hope you remember your place in Reverie and bring us some much-needed light.

Yours in service,
Oliver T. Burgess

Aurora shook her head and tossed the note aside. How could the people who claimed to have loved the Starmaker urge her to do the very thing that had killed him? Pulling the light had brought Caspian to his end, and going back to that glacier and hanging the light from the lamppost felt almost as impossible as Reverie's existence in the first place.

She wanted to ask Caspian how he'd done it, how he'd gotten up just two days after his mentor's death to pull in the light, and it felt so unfair that she could not. He was the only one who could help her, yet he was lying unmoving in a marble casket, awaiting burial.

Aurora got back to work. She fought against the pain ravaging her insides because she couldn't distinguish it from her grief, and she didn't understand how weak she was becoming because her mind would not allow her to think of it.

She was not sure how much more time passed before the door of the library swung open and Elsie walked in with a fierce expression on her face. It could have been hours, or it could have been days.

"Elsie?" Aurora asked, blinking at the figure standing in the doorway, wondering if perhaps she was imagining it. She couldn't remember the last time she had slept, and it was plausible that her mind was tricking her.

"Yes, sister, it's me. Now get up."

"I'm sorry?"

"Get up," Elsie said again, moving to Aurora's spot on the floor and yanking her up by her arm.

"Why are you doing this?" Aurora's words sounded almost like a cry, and when she got to her feet, her sister had to steady her. She swayed left, then right as all the blood rushed away from her head, and she fell back to the floor.

"Because our home is closest to the woods. It is *our* home and *our* family that will be touched by the Frost first." Elsie spoke to her sister as if she weren't piled in a heap on the floor, pulling her to standing once again. Aurora tried to resist, tried to sink back to the ground, but Elsie held on tight.

"Don't tell me you're as worked up over a little darkness as everyone else. It has only been a few days; the Frost does not move that quickly."

Elsie looked shocked, but her expression softened as she studied Aurora's appearance, her sister's tangled hair and the dark circles beneath her eyes. "Sister, it has been more than a fortnight."

"What?" Aurora asked, looking helplessly around the library, taking in all the books scattered across the floor, the blankets that served as a bed. "Impossible," she whispered, though she wasn't convinced. She tried to think back over the hours and days since Caspian's death, but they all seemed to run into each other, just one long stretch of night.

Elsie pulled her sister close, wrapping her arms around Aurora so tightly that Aurora could feel herself being forced back together, and when she tried to resist, to hold on to her anger and apathy, Elsie held her tighter still.

"Leave me alone!" Aurora shouted, trying to break free, but Elsie's grip was strong.

"I will not leave you," Elsie said.

"You will! That is the problem. You and Mama and Aspen and Evander will all leave, and I will be left with no one." Aurora struggled against her sister's hold until she no longer had the strength, until all of the fight drained out of her. "I will lose you all." Aurora gasped, and then a violent sob tore from her throat and echoed through the library, bouncing off the walls. Elsie ran her hand over Aurora's hair and whispered softly in her ear, clutching her as she sobbed, and Aurora clung to her because she was sure she could not stand on her own.

When Aurora had no more tears to cry, she slowly pulled away, and Elsie led her out of the library and back to her bedroom. "You need to sleep," she said.

"The Sun," Aurora replied, staring out her balcony doors at the endless night sky. "I need to pull the Sun." It was then that she realized how ill she felt, and she knew it was the magic building up in her system, causing her body to shut down. She was thankful to be at the castle, surrounded by magic that kept her alive, but even magic had its limits. If Elsie had not come, Aurora wondered if she would have let her magic kill her without ever even knowing what was happening.

"Yes, you do. But after you sleep."

"Will you still be here when I wake?"

"Yes."

"Promise?"

"I promise."

It was only then that Aurora climbed into her bed, pulled up the covers, and closed her eyes. She did not dream that night, not of Caspian or the Sun or the Frost. Instead, as she slept, her mind worked through each and every page she had read, filing away the important bits for safekeeping.

Eternally Yours

When Aurora woke, her sister was sitting in a chair next to her bed, reading. It was the same chair Caspian had used when he had brought her home from the cave, and the memory sat heavily on her chest.

"Elsie?" she asked, rubbing the sleep from her eyes.

"You slept well," Elsie said, closing her book. "You moved so little I even checked to make sure you were breathing."

Aurora nodded. "I feel better."

"Good, because I have something for you," her sister replied, holding out a large bright red tomato.

Aurora was confused, and she stared at Elsie's offering as if it was a clue to a puzzle she didn't know she was solving. "A tomato?" she asked.

"Yes." Elsie was smiling, and she forced the fruit into her

sister's hand. "We grew it. The glare line that has formed between our cottage and the castle has changed our land. Between the glare and the mirrors, it is practically as if we are in the path of the light."

Aurora sat up in bed, studying the tomato, turning it over in her hands. "You grew this? On our land?" she asked, her voice quiet, her eyes burning.

"With a lot of help from the love you shared with the Starmaker," Elsie said, taking Aurora's hand. "The glare line has been marvelous." Elsie paused and gave her sister a meaningful look. "You did it, Aurora. You grew Papa's favorite fruit."

Aurora sucked in a breath, hardly believing it. "Are there more?"

"There will be," Elsie said, "but this is the first. It is only right that you have it."

"We will have it together," Aurora said, keeping the fruit tucked close to her chest.

She looked out the balcony doors at the darkness still covering Reverie, and a new wave of shame rolled over her. "I'm deeply sorry for how I've behaved." Aurora couldn't bring herself to meet Elsie's eyes. She had vowed to keep Reverie safe, and instead, she had put it at risk at the first opportunity. She did not deserve the trust she'd been given.

"I know you are."

"How can I possibly undo the damage I've caused?"

"By doing your job, sister. Pull the light today and tomorrow and the day after that. Bury the Starmaker and fight back the Frost. People are quicker to forgive than you think."

Aurora exhaled and rubbed her temples, trying to diminish the ache in her head. "I hope you're right."

"I am. There is a bath waiting for you, and I'll let Ina know to prepare a proper breakfast today."

Aurora winced at the mention of Ina and how profoundly she'd let her down. She would make it up to her—she would make it up to all of them.

"Thank you," Aurora said, squeezing her sister's hand. "Thank you for coming."

"I'm sorry it took me so long," Elsie said, shaking her head. "I wanted to come straightaway, but Mama was ill, and our brothers were tending the fields. I could not leave her."

"Is she well now? Was it...?" Aurora trailed off, scared to ask the question. "Was it the Frost?"

"No," Elsie said, and Aurora breathed out in relief. "A fever. She is better now."

Aurora nodded.

"Get yourself cleaned up and eat some breakfast. You have work to do."

Aurora looked at the tomato in her hands. "Perhaps you could ask Ina to have something special prepared using this?"

"Of course." Elsie took the tomato and slipped out of the room, leaving Aurora alone.

She was about to get in the bath when she noticed a faint knocking sound coming from inside the armoire. She opened the door, and one of her wool dresses was moving, the waist darting out in every direction. Aurora hesitantly removed the dress from its hanger, inspecting the fabric, when suddenly the gold handkerchief flew out from the pocket and bolted around the room.

Aurora jumped back, startled. She remembered how the handkerchief had followed her on the Day of Darkness, and how she had shoved it deep into her pocket when she could no longer handle being trailed. That had been more than a fortnight ago, and Aurora felt terrible.

"I'm so sorry," she said to the handkerchief. "I greatly appreciate you and will do a much better job of showing it in the future. I hope with time you will forgive me."

The handkerchief seemed to calm down as Aurora spoke, and it flitted around her head and brushed her cheek before coming to rest on the side table. Aurora exhaled in relief, thankful the cloth was quick to forgive, and readied herself for the bath.

The hot water felt so good against her aching body, but she forced herself to move quickly, to make up for the hours and days she had lost. She closed her eyes and whispered an apology to Caspian, telling him that she had tried to find something—anything—that would bring him back but that she had failed. And in the process, she had failed all of Reverie as well.

In the end, Caspian had been right: the thing she needed to learn was how to live without him. She shook her head in the water, her eyes burning. She still didn't know how to do that, but she knew she couldn't hold on to him at the expense of her duties and responsibilities. She knew she couldn't hold on to him if it meant letting go of everything else. Their story deserved a better ending than that.

"I'm sorry," she whispered again. She allowed herself several breaths, then stood up, dried off, and pulled herself together. She brushed her white hair and pinned it back from her clean face, and when she stepped into her bedroom, her sister was back and had laid out a dress for her.

"You look good," Elsie said, but Aurora frowned.

"You do not have to be nice to me," she said, grabbing her dress and stepping behind the partition. "I do not deserve your kindness."

"You do," Elsie insisted, her voice rising. "You just lost your husband, a man you loved very much, and the survival of an entire mountain is now on your shoulders. You deserve much more than kindness."

Aurora draped her robe over the partition and stepped back out when she was dressed, looking at her sister. "I miss him so much."

"I know."

Aurora took a deep breath, readying herself to face her household staff. "Will you come to breakfast with me?"

"I would love to," Elsie said, but as they walked, Aurora had a sudden vision of Caspian's childhood room. She was not the only one who had struggled with becoming Starmaker; Caspian had as well, and though he had dealt with it much better than she, it eased something inside her chest.

You aren't alone. He had told her that on the glacier, and while she hadn't wanted to hear it then, she was now so glad he had said it.

"Can we stop somewhere on our way to breakfast? I promise it'll be brief." Aurora couldn't explain it, but it felt important to visit Caspian's room, to feel that connection to him, to know that he had struggled and had continued on despite it.

"Of course," Elsie said.

Aurora led them down the hallways to the worn plain door. She looked up at it, resting her hand on the wood, pausing just a moment before going inside. Then she turned to her sister.

"I'll be right out," she said, pushing through the door and into the room.

Aurora inhaled deeply, scanning the small space, sitting down on the tiny bed. The room had felt painfully sad the first time she had seen it, but it seemed cozy now, and it made her feel closer to Caspian, seeing the ways he had dealt with becoming the Starmaker.

He had survived it, and so would she.

Aurora gave herself several more moments, and then she stood, knowing there was much to do. But Caspian's journal caught her eye, and she walked to the desk, running her fingers over the leather. Then she stopped. A pen was resting next to the spine, and though it had been a while since she'd last been here, she was almost certain that there had not been a pen before. She looked at it skeptically, as if it might jump up at any moment. She told herself to ignore it, but she could not, and she grabbed the journal in a rush.

She frantically flipped to the last entry, holding her breath, and saw pages full of fresh ink. She knew Elsie was waiting for her, but she had to skim Caspian's words, know what he was thinking.

She told herself it was a violation, but she was tired and her resolve was weak. She found the first word of the new entry, and her eyes burned with tears.

Aurora.

She gasped. He had written to her. She took an unsteady breath as she began to read.

Aurora,

Perhaps the least surprising discovery I have made in the entirety of my life was that you have already been in this room.

Aurora laughed, wiping the tears from her cheeks. She could hear his voice perfectly, and the pain in her chest screamed.

I will not pretend to know what to say, because I do not. Leaving you will undoubtedly be the hardest thing I ever do, and the truth is that I'm frightened. I had forgotten what it was to be alive, and you forced me to remember, and in so doing, I found a crushing will to live. I am desperate to stay with you. I am angry I cannot.

Immortality is a fickle thing. It is given, and it is taken away. It expands to infinity and contracts to nothing. It is the Sun's gift to us, but as it turns out, it is revocable.

THE SUN AND THE STARMAKER

Perhaps that is the way of all things. I knew what to expect—that one day it would be taken from me—and yet I find myself stunned.

I am yours, Aurora; I have been yours ever since I pulled that arrow from your bow, and one day, when you are ready, I hope you will put your pen to paper and write of a Starmaker falling in love with the Starmaker Rising. You have always loved a good story, have you not? Ours is my favorite; may it outlive us both.

I will meet you in the endless after.
Don't be late.

Eternally yours,
Caspian

The ink was smeared at the end, and Aurora ran her fingers over it, wondering if it was one of her tears that had done it, or maybe one of his. She closed the journal and tucked it close to her chest, carrying it from the room.

"Are you all right?" Elsie asked when Aurora found her in the hall, taking her arm.

"He wrote to me," she said, and Elsie squeezed her tight.

Aurora took several deep breaths, and by the time they reached the dining hall, her tears had stopped and she was ready to take on the day. All of the palace staff were in the room, and shame found her once more, a furious heat running up her neck and settling in her cheeks. But she wouldn't turn away this time or ignore the pain she had caused them. She wanted to make things right.

She remembered what Caspian had told her: that her words were not what mattered most, but rather how she made them feel. She took a deep breath as Ina stepped forward.

"How nice it is to see you, Your Radiance."

"And you, Ina," Aurora said. She looked around the room, meeting the eyes of everyone there. "There is no excuse for my behavior over the past fortnight. I know I have caused you all a lot of worry and anguish, and for that I am endlessly sorry. I am here now, and I will try my hardest to earn back your trust. I humbly ask your forgiveness—it does not have to be today or tomorrow, but eventually, I hope that my actions will prove to you that I take my role as your Starmaker seriously, and I will never let another day pass without pulling the light. You have my word."

"It is good to have you back, Your Radiance," Frederick said, stepping over to Aurora's chair and pulling it out for her. She smiled at him.

"Thank you, Frederick."

Elsie sat to one side of Aurora, Constance to the other, and they ate quickly, filling their stomachs with sweet biscuits, ham, and the best tomato they had ever eaten. Except for Constance, of course, who ate hay. When Aurora could not eat any more, she gave her sister a hug and told her she would see her when she returned. She gave Elsie Caspian's journal and asked that she place it in her room for safekeeping, then walked down the long hallway and outside to where her sleigh was waiting. Ina handed her

THE SUN AND THE STARMAKER

the bundle of roses she had requested, and Aurora tied her cloak around her neck, set the roses in the sleigh, and petted her snow deer. Just as she was about to board, Tilly appeared.

"Hi, Tilly," Aurora said, noticing the looking glass in her wing. Aurora hadn't seen the angel without it since she'd first received it, and it made Aurora's heart swell. She had messed up greatly in so many ways, but at least there was something she had done right.

"You must look," Tilly said, holding up the mirror to Aurora. "Whenever you feel lost, you can look in the mirror and see that you are exactly as you should be."

Aurora tried to keep her composure as Tilly repeated the exact words Aurora had spoken when she had given the angel the gift, and she blinked several times. She stood next to Tilly, looking at her reflection in the mirror.

"What do you see?" she asked the angel.

Tilly was quiet, studying Aurora's reflection with intense concentration, and Aurora was almost afraid of what the angel would say. Then she stepped back, looked Aurora in the eyes, and said simply, "I see the Starmaker."

Any hope of keeping her composure vanished with the angel's words, and several tears slipped down Aurora's cheeks. She quickly wiped them away and swallowed hard. "Thank you, Tilly," she said.

The angel smiled, then stood next to Ina as Aurora stepped into the sleigh, sitting on the bench she used to share with Caspian.

She took a deep breath, and the deer began to pull.

I am the Starmaker, she said to herself. *Today my reign begins.*

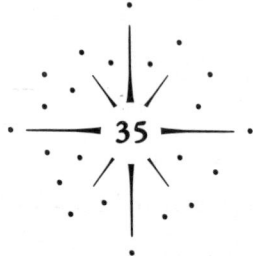

Even a God Can Forget

The woods did not look normal. Even in the darkness, Aurora could tell that something wasn't right. The trees were bent at odd angles, and they didn't move freely in the wind. There were no animals bounding through the brambles or scurrying up the trunks; there was only silence.

The snow deer went faster than usual, sprinting down the trail as if they were being chased. A few of them whined as they went. There was a biting cold in the air that made Aurora's skin crawl; it was an unnatural cold, and she knew it was the Frost taking over the forest. She only hoped that she wasn't too late and that Caspian's burial would push it back again, away from the village, away from the people, and away from her family. If not, there was always her blood; she would make things right one way or another.

THE SUN AND THE STARMAKER

Aurora was relieved when they came out of the woods and glided around the village center, down to where the glacier waited. She squeezed her eyes shut against the memories that flooded her mind of the last time she was here, bent over Caspian as he took his last breath. She wondered if her life would be long enough for those memories to fade, if one day they would not be the first thing she thought of when she saw this place. She wondered if she wanted that.

The snow deer came to a stop where they always did, at the start of the glacier. It seemed the time away had not disrupted their routine, and Aurora ran her hand over their fur as she passed them and walked toward the lamppost. The glacier creaked as she trudged over the ice and snow, but she trusted it, just as she always had. She moved deliberately toward the post; it was nothing more than a shadow in the dark morning, but she knew the route well, and she could find it in a blizzard if she had to.

She thought she would feel lonely or detached from her duties, but instead she felt more emboldened with each step she took. She wasn't forgetting Caspian's life, but rather extending it by continuing to do what he had always done. She did not care for the Sun, not the way Caspian had assured her she would, but she cared for him and his legacy. She cared for Reverie and this mountain. And she cared for herself. She knew what kinds of stories she wanted told about her, and they were not ones of failure or defeat. They were ones of boldness and adventure and love.

She'd had those things with Caspian, and she would create them again on her own.

As the lamppost came into view, something didn't look right, and she narrowed her eyes in the darkness, trying to see more clearly. The glacier was uneven around the base of the post, and Aurora quickened her steps. When she got closer, she knelt to inspect what had happened, and she was stunned to see a rose lying before her. And not just one rose—dozens of them, their vines rooting down beneath the ice, surrounding the lamppost in an impossible garden.

Aurora remembered the single rose she had left behind after Caspian's death. This was a more beautiful tribute to his life than she ever could have imagined. In a field of ice, somehow his roses had taken root and bloomed.

She stood back up, laughing as she pulled the fresh bundle of roses from her cloak. They were his favorite, and she had wanted a piece of Caspian with her as she began the next chapter of her life. Little did she know she would get an entire field of them, beautiful in the snow, surrounding the gold metal of the lamppost as if they had always been there.

Aurora set the roses at the base of the lantern and took a deep breath. It was time.

She turned to face the peaks of Reverie, the jagged rock faces looming large in the distance. It was as if she was greeting an old friend, and for a single breath, she took in the view—mostly shadows, but still shimmering with magic. She closed her eyes, held out her arms, and began her conversation with the Sun.

Caspian had said that Aurora would come to love her, that she wouldn't have a choice, but so far he had been wrong. Aurora respected the Sun and had a deep appreciation for her role in keeping Reverie safe, but love it was not. And so she decided to be honest. Perhaps it was a bad idea, telling the divine that she did not love her, but the Sun would surely know if she wasn't being sincere.

Before she could speak, though, she was surrounded by the Sun's voice.

I've been waiting for you. The voice filled Aurora's head with its sweetness, made the mountain come alive with its melody. The Sun did not sound angry or impatient, but calm.

"It was not easy for me to lose Caspian," Aurora said, reaching for the light, but it seemed the Sun wanted to have a conversation before letting Aurora take anything from her.

Clearly. You put all of Reverie at risk because of your grief.

"I know," Aurora said. "And I will have to live with that shame for the rest of my life."

You are the Starmaker, Aurora Finch, and with that comes immense responsibility. You cannot let this happen again.

"I *know*," Aurora replied more forcefully. "I am here, and I am ready to right the harm I have caused. I will be here tomorrow and the day after that and the day after that; I swear it."

I certainly hope so. This mountain of yours is built on a delicate system of light and magic; it is not strong enough to tolerate such disruptions.

Aurora scoffed and opened her eyes, staring into the darkness. She wasn't sure why the comment made her so angry, but it did; the Sun had spoken as if Reverie and all its people would simply perish if the wind blew in the wrong direction. "It is still here, is it not? Our mountain is strong and dares to survive even when everything is against it."

It survives because my love for a human compelled me to save it.

Aurora shook her head. "Then you more than anyone should understand what it is to grieve and the great strength it requires to live in the midst of it. I would have thought you would offer some sympathy or encouragement, but instead you have only reprimanded me. If you are quite done, I would very much like to bring in the light."

There was no reply, and when Aurora reached for the light once more, she was able to grab hold of it. She closed her eyes and pulled, heaving it through the peaks and letting it pour over Reverie like rain, touching everything. She pulled it closer and closer, and when it finally crawled over the glacier and into her hands, she turned and stepped up to the lamppost, opening the glass door and hanging the light from the hook in the lantern. She closed the door and hopped off the step, turning to look at her village.

She heard cheering in the distance, and she tried not to let the sound drown her in shame. She was here. She was making up for her transgressions. She was making it right. Aurora wasn't sure if she would ever forgive herself for abandoning Reverie when it needed her most, but she wanted to try.

She sat at the base of the post, surrounded by roses, and watched the village soak up the light, watched the snow sparkle and the buildings glimmer, everything coming back to life as if waking from the deepest sleep. Aurora replayed her conversation with the Sun, wondering if the other Starmakers had ever conversed with her the way she just had. Caspian had always made it sound like he was the speaker and the Sun merely listened, but that certainly hadn't been the case today.

There was something gnawing at her mind, and Aurora couldn't figure out what it was. She closed her eyes and focused, but the thought was just out of reach, and every time she felt as if she was getting close, it slipped away again. She replayed the conversation over and over, but to no avail—each time left her more frustrated than the last. She had spoken with the Sun, had a real, honest dialogue with a god, and instead of feeling awestruck or overwhelmed, she was terribly sad.

Why was she sad? The Sun had been harsh with her, but Aurora had deserved it. And though she would have appreciated some compassion or grace, she was owed neither. But there was something about the way the Sun had spoken that had left her feeling hopeless.

Aurora stood and walked across the jagged landscape, her boots crunching on the ice beneath her. She tried her best to avoid the roses, not wanting to crush them, and made her way to the snow deer. It was time to check on the phlox.

When Aurora had boarded the sleigh and the deer had taken off at a run, she thought back to all the research she had done in the past fortnight. It hadn't given her the answers she sought, but perhaps deep down she had always known there was no defying death. She wondered if all of the reading and panicked research had simply been an attempt to avoid grief, a way to fill the hole that had opened in her chest when Caspian had died.

She realized then that what she had done wasn't all that dissimilar from what the Sun had done with the original Starmaker. The Sun had come up with a plan to keep him alive, had poured herself into finding a way to save him as well as his home. The only difference was that the Sun had boundless magic, so her plan had worked. Why hadn't she recognized that same reaction in Aurora, that all-consuming panic that had made her determined to find another way?

They weren't so different, Aurora and the Sun. Aurora was no god, but she had simply wanted the same thing the Sun had wanted: to save the person she loved.

The snow deer came to a stop just outside the row of phlox, and Aurora stepped out of the sleigh. Over breakfast, she had asked Ina to schedule Caspian's burial for two days from now, and she hoped that giving her blood to the mountain would help keep the Frost at bay until then. She knelt on the snow-covered ground next to the plants, pulled a rose from her cloak, and pricked her finger with a thorn. One single drop of blood fell to the earth, and just as she had come to expect, the phlox turned vibrant and bright, as if it had never been touched by the Frost at all. She repeated the process in several places, and the candy stripes regained their color. It eased some of the tension in her shoulders, and she took a deep breath. With the village illuminated and the phlox bursting with lively pinks, Aurora knew that the mountain was going to be okay.

She walked deeper into the trees, remembering the last time she had been here with Caspian and all that had happened since.

THE SUN AND THE STARMAKER

The texts she had read over the last fortnight had all emphasized that the mountain was built upon a relationship: the Sun and a human who would become the first Starmaker. Companionships of every kind were celebrated, the village itself built upon love and respect and longing.

But Caspian had written that he'd forgotten what it was to be alive. What a tragic outcome for the one who'd brought life to the mountain. Aurora had to believe that the Sun hadn't wanted that.

She stopped walking, understanding in a rush why her conversation with the Sun had upset her so much. It was because nothing in the Sun's words had implied that she knew what it was to love, what it was to be desperate to change things. It was almost as if she had forgotten, just as Caspian had.

"You don't remember," Aurora whispered, looking up to the sky.

She thought about how she had never seen the northern lights, the result of the Sun's tears, and how Ina had said that the Sun's grief came from the depth of her love. If Aurora was correct and the Sun did not remember, it was very bad indeed, for the whole of Reverie's survival depended on the Sun's magic. If the Sun could not remember why she had saved the village in the first place, then there was no guarantee that she would continue to grant Reverie her light.

No, Aurora would not allow that.

She knew the stories of the mountain well, had grown up with them and fallen asleep to them and taken comfort in them. They had been her constant companions all her life, and if the

Sun could not recall her own story, then Aurora would tell it back to her until she did.

A plan began to form in her mind, slowly at first and then so fast that Aurora struggled to keep up with her own thoughts. By the time she had let go of the light and journeyed back to the castle, she knew exactly what she was going to do.

Helping the Sun remember wouldn't bring Caspian back or undo Aurora's failures, but it would ensure the safety of her home, ensure that there would be many more love stories to come.

Caspian had once told her that she would find meaning and purpose in lasting things. As the snow deer came to a stop and Aurora stepped from the sleigh, she thought to herself that this was a very good place to start.

After all, there was nothing that lasted quite like a story.

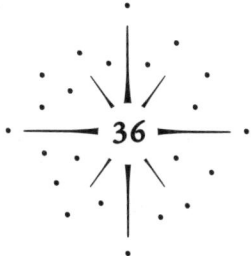

Standing at the Top of the World

The next evening, long after Aurora had let go of the light, she stood in the entrance hall of the castle, staring up at the statue of the Sun and the Starmaker. It really was beautiful, and the more the statue had cried over the past few weeks, the more lifelike it had become. Aurora would not pretend to understand how the magic that had gone awry worked, but she hoped that after tonight, the statue might find some peace.

"That's the last of them, Your Radiance," Ina said as two members of the staff carried a large mirror into the room. They leaned it up against the wall among dozens of others; Aurora had requested that every mirror in the castle—except for the ones that pointed at her cottage—be taken down and arranged around the statue, and as the castle was quite large, she had ended up with far more mirrors than she had intended.

"Thank you, Ina," she said with a smile. Ina looked around the room, eyeing all the mirrors, and Aurora could tell her mind was spinning, trying to figure out what it meant, worrying that she was about to lose the Starmaker to another bout of grief. Aurora walked to where she stood and gently placed a hand on her shoulder. "I am well, Ina, and I promise you that you will see the light come morning."

Ina looked embarrassed. "I apologize—I did not mean to make you feel as if I do not trust you."

"Trust is earned, and if you do not trust me at present, I understand why. Please do not apologize."

"Thank you, Your Radiance," Ina said.

"I still much prefer Aurora, if you don't mind."

"Aurora," Ina repeated, then nodded and left to see to the rest of Aurora's requests.

Aurora had hardly slept the night before, her mind spinning wildly as she formed her plan. It was elaborate and probably the most outrageous thing she would ever do in her life, but it also felt *right*, and she was excited to get started. She had taken Elsie home that morning, which was probably for the best; she doubted her sister would care for her plan, and more than likely she would try to talk her out of it. But Aurora's mind was made up.

Aurora would have preferred more time to perfect the logistics, but Caspian's burial was tomorrow at high noon, and it felt important to her to reach out to the Sun before then. By the time he was placed in the earth, she wanted to be sure that the Sun would continue to protect the mountain in which he lay.

THE SUN AND THE STARMAKER

Aurora had spent hours testing locations and drawing diagrams and figuring out the exact angle at which each mirror needed to be tilted to make her plan work. She had thought about Tilly's looking glass and how sometimes what one needed most was to see oneself, to be reminded that even in pain and grief, life continued on. Not exactly as it had before, but in a way that honored every loss and remembered every love. In a way that made space for both happiness and heartbreak.

Tilly had needed that, and so had Aurora. Perhaps the Sun did, too.

It had been centuries since the Sun had seen herself as a human, and while Aurora knew the Sun hadn't truly forgotten the first Starmaker, she wondered if being disconnected from that part of herself for so long had turned her protection of Reverie into a chore as opposed to something she did out of love. That was why Aurora wanted the Sun to see the statue so badly. It had been the Sun's parting gift to the Starmaker, a physical, tangible representation of the love they had shared. Aurora hoped that if she could reflect its image into the heavens where the Sun could see it, the Sun would remember what it had been like to be human. What it had been like to *feel*.

Once Aurora had perfected her measurements as best she could, she walked around the room and inspected every mirror until she found two that fit her specifications. Ina returned, and Aurora handed her the finished diagram, showing her the exact location and angle at which the first mirror needed to be placed and where to set the candles to ensure that the statue was properly lit. The second mirror would be handled by Aurora.

Assuming she had gotten the angles correct, the placement of the second mirror was the most likely failure point of the entire plan. It was also the most dangerous part, for Aurora needed to set the mirror atop the highest peak so that the reflection would clear the mountain and launch into the sky, where the Sun could see it. And while Aurora understood that she was immortal for now, at least in theory, she wasn't exactly keen to test the limits of it.

"The sled is ready, Your Radiance," Frederick said as he entered the castle. "It is rather... unruly."

"That is fine. Thank you, Frederick."

"Your Radiance," he began, clearly uncomfortable, "I don't believe it is wise for you to ride that sled. If you will allow it, I would very much like to place the second mirror myself."

Aurora was deeply moved by his words, by the way he had always looked out for her. "I will not even consider it, though I greatly appreciate the offer."

Frederick nodded. "Then I will be holding my breath until you return."

"As will I," Ina agreed.

"I will be as swift as I can," Aurora promised. "Thank you both for your help. It means more to me than you know."

Once Aurora was dressed in her warmest wool and thickest cloak, she walked outside to the sled and immediately understood why Caspian had banished it to the room upstairs full of magic gone awry. Even though it was connected to the wolves by a harness, it was pulling toward the side of the castle, trying to scale the

THE SUN AND THE STARMAKER

wall. The wolves growled at it, baring their teeth, but the sled paid them no mind.

For a moment, Aurora's resolve wavered, and she began to rethink her plan. But then she took a steadying breath and walked forward.

The sled was made of white oak, long with a curved front and flat bottom, and the mirror was already attached to it, wrapped in blankets so that Aurora could sit on top without breaking it. Ina and Frederick joined her outside, and she readily sat down, as she didn't want them to worry, but the truth was that she was scared. The sled calmed slightly once she was seated, but it was very insistent, and Aurora could only hope that the wolves pulling it forward combined with her weight and that of the mirror would be enough to force the sled to move horizontally until it was time for the final climb.

Ina and Frederick came over and strapped her in, wrapping rope around her shoulders, abdomen, and legs, securing her to the sled with many knots to ensure she didn't fall. They were both frowning, and Aurora tried her best to look at ease.

"I am sure this will do," she said, though she wasn't sure at all.

"Good luck," Ina said, and then the wolves began to pull.

It was a dark, clear night with little wind and no snow, and if Aurora did make it to the top of the peak, she would certainly be rewarded with an unmatched view of the stars. The wolves were fast, and Aurora wasn't used to being so low to the ground. She closed her eyes as snow flew up from the rails and splattered on her face.

The sled jumped beneath her—left, then right—but there was nothing to climb, and as the wolves raced toward the woods, the sled seemed to give up for the moment. Still, Aurora clung to the front with all her might. The trail pitched steeply upward as the wolves pulled her farther into the trees, closer to the peaks of Reverie. The wolves slowed, panting louder, but they persisted, digging their claws into the snow and pulling as hard as they could.

Aurora thought she would feel frightened venturing so far into the woods, but something about it felt like home to her. She had been raised outside of the light, and the Frost did not scare her, not with the magic of the Sun in her veins and the strength of her family in her bones.

If Caspian could see her now, she took comfort in knowing that he would, at the very least, not be surprised. He had never tried to dull her, to mold her into something she wasn't. From that very first meeting in the woods, he had accepted her exactly as she was. He had perhaps done it begrudgingly at times, but he had always given her as much space as she needed. And in so doing, he had enabled her to fully come into herself.

Grief was a very odd thing. One moment she was content, her entire body warm with the memory of him, overflowing with gratitude for the time they'd had together. But she knew she could just as quickly become overwhelmed with despair, a crushing wave she was certain would drown her. But for now, on this cloudless night in this very unruly sled, Aurora found herself able to laugh at how aggravated Caspian would undoubtedly be by her insistence on this outing.

After what felt like hours, the sled finally slowed as one of Reverie's giant peaks loomed over them, blocking out the stars with a sheet of total darkness. Aurora looked up, trying to see the top, but at that close distance she could not find it. The trees around her were so covered in ice that they cracked and popped, and when Aurora reached forward and freed the wolves from the sled, they began to whine.

"Go," she said, knowing the Frost would come for them if they didn't leave. "Back to the castle."

Their whining got louder, but they reluctantly did as she said, and Aurora was relieved when they were out of her sight and on their way to the palace. The sled seemed to realize then that it was no longer attached to the wolves, and it started jumping beneath her in excitement. Aurora checked her knots to ensure they hadn't come loose, then readjusted her grip on the front rails, trying to remain calm.

A sled that could only move vertically. Caspian had said it put anything it carried at risk of falling, and she hoped that the ropes were strong enough to hold her.

The sled launched itself toward the peak, and to Aurora's great horror, it began climbing with terrifying speed. They slid upward over the stone as easily as if they were on a steep downhill slope in fresh snow, and Aurora forced her eyes shut. Her back pressed hard against her ropes, and she strained to keep her hold on the front, her entire body aching. She was fully perpendicular to the ground, and as the sled climbed higher and higher, Aurora began to feel light-headed.

"No," she said out loud, not wanting to consider what would happen to her if she lost consciousness. She needed to be present, force herself to stay awake, and so she recited the wedding vows she had made to Caspian as the rails of the sled scraped against the stone, the sound too sharp. The mirror shifted beneath her, and Aurora gasped, fighting the urge to look behind her, trying her best to trust the ropes, the only thing between her and an unthinkable fall.

"I will carry you with the strength of the mountain and keep your soul tucked close to mine." She whispered it over and over again, voice shaking, palms sweating. The ropes dug into her back, pulling tighter around her until one of them snapped entirely. Aurora screamed, jolting backward, but the rest of the ropes held, and she wrapped her forearms around the front of the sled, terrified.

The sled slowed as they got higher, and Aurora kept her eyes shut, not wanting to see if they began to drop, if the climb had become too much for the sled. The scraping against the rock face sounded like screaming, and Aurora's breaths were too shallow, the air so much thinner. Her fear so much stronger.

Then finally, *finally*, the sled had nowhere else to climb, and it clambered onto the top of the peak with an uncaeremonious thud as if it was exhausted from the journey.

"That's good," Aurora said, forcing the words out between inhales. "You take a nap while I work."

After some struggling, Aurora freed herself from the ropes, then tied the sled around a large rock just in case it tried to escape.

Then, with all her strength, she pushed the mirror off of the wood, unwrapped it, and heaved it onto its side against the boulder.

She bent over at the waist, trying to catch her breath. She felt dizzy so high up, her head aching, her inhales sharp and strained. When she felt as though she could stand upright without fainting, she took in her surroundings.

The darkness seemed to go on forever, stretching beyond the confines of her imagination. Aurora had never beheld such beauty, and she suspected that she never would again. She turned in a circle, taking in the vast night sky, the millions of stars. It was the smallest she had ever felt, and also the biggest, and her chest ached with the majesty of it. As she stood on the top of the world, looking out into the infinite space surrounding her, she was at peace. She watched a falling star as it slid across the dark, so close she thought she might catch it, and she reached her hand into the sky. But it continued on, and Aurora laughed, so overwhelmed by it all.

No one in Reverie had ever seen beyond their mountain, and now she was standing at the very top, marveling at the absolute miracle of life and her incredible fortune to be living it.

Aurora walked along the edge of the peak, looking down toward the castle, waiting for Ina to place her mirror. She rubbed her hands together for warmth and tried to keep moving, and when she finally saw a faint glimmer below, she breathed out in relief.

The light got brighter and brighter until Aurora was certain it was the mirror at the castle, and she went to her own mirror and started to lug it into place. She began to sweat as the mirror sank into the snow, but she pulled as hard as she could, and when she finally made it to the right spot, she anchored the base between heavy stones so that the mirror stood tall over Reverie, adjusting the angle until a perfect reflection of the statue sat in the center of the glass. It wasn't as big as she'd hoped, given the distance between the mirrors, but it was clear and undeniably the Sun and her Starmaker.

Aurora stepped aside, and the reflection went out into the endless night, over the peaks, where the Sun would soon be able to see it. Aurora inhaled shakily, amazed she had actually done it. The Sun could not see into Reverie, but now she did not have to. Aurora had brought the image to her, an exact replica of the Sun in her human form with the man she had loved.

Aurora could feel a healing taking place inside of her, a deep understanding that helping the Sun to remember wasn't solely for the survival of her home. It was also a tribute to Caspian and the first Starmaker and Aurora's parents and every other love story that the mountain had ever held.

She sat down on the sled and wrapped her cloak around her torso as tight as it would go, then piled the blankets on top of her lap. She pulled up her hood, and the endless night began to fade to a hazy blue—the Sun was back on this side of the world. Under a veil of a million stars, Aurora spoke to her.

"I want to tell you a story," she said, her voice carrying out into the emptiness of space. The distance between them was so vast, but somehow, the Sun ensured that they had a connection through it all, and Aurora was grateful.

THE SUN AND THE STARMAKER

She was so grateful.

"There once was a village so far north that most considered it the top of the world," she began, and as she looked off into infinity, she recounted the tale of how the Sun and the Starmaker had fallen in love.

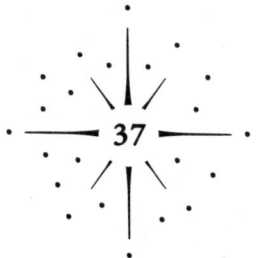

Asleep in a Haze of Lavender

After Aurora had finished telling the Sun her story, she'd had a very harrowing return to the castle during which she'd decided that sleds that could only move vertically were not for her. She was now fast asleep in her bed, enjoying an hour of rest before she had to pull in the light, when a flash of vibrant purple danced across the sky. It was so bright that she woke with a start. She jumped from her bed and rushed to the balcony, throwing open the doors and training her gaze on the darkness above. She gripped the railing as she watched, hope swelling in her chest.

She stayed outside for several minutes, feeling more defeated with each second that passed until she finally admitted to herself that she must have dreamt it. She walked back inside and burrowed into her blankets, drifting off once more.

THE SUN AND THE STARMAKER

When the next burst of color came, Aurora did not see it behind her closed eyes and heavy quilt, neither of which would have blocked her view had she truly been dreaming. She continued to sleep as the northern lights shone brilliantly beyond her window, casting her dark room in a lavender glow.

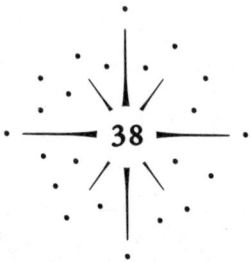

The Most Brilliant Thing

Aurora hurried back to the castle as soon as she had pulled the light over Reverie. Today was Caspian's burial, and she wanted some time alone with him before the observance began. A light snow was falling, and she petted Fate and the other deer before walking around the palace and into the gardens.

She picked up some shears and found the rosebush she had planted with Caspian, then cut several full blooms from the plant and tied them together with a piece of gold ribbon. The icy-white petals glittered in the light, and Aurora held them close to her chest as she made her way toward the small sanctuary where Caspian's casket was waiting.

Her boots left prints in the fresh snow, and she thought for a moment how nice it might be if they stayed there forever, her final path to her great love. But they would be gone by morning, just as Caspian's casket would be.

A small wooden door carved with planets and stars led into the sanctuary, and Aurora gently opened it to let in the light. She knew logically that Caspian would not perceive it, but it made her feel better, being able to give him a few more hours of warmth before he was placed in the earth.

Aurora stepped inside the small room. Sitting in the center was Caspian's casket, beautifully constructed of white marble and complemented with gold hardware and crystals inlaid in the handles. It sat on a platform covered in dozens of roses, and she ran her hand over the smooth surface before resting her forehead against it.

"Hi, Caspian," she whispered, placing the sparkling roses atop the marble. She sat down beside the casket and leaned against it, tilting her head back and closing her eyes. "I can't believe the day is finally here."

Aurora knew that Caspian had worried there would be no rest for him, that even in death he would continue to serve the mountain at the expense of his own peace. She hoped with everything in her that he had been wrong and that he had found the tranquility he so deserved.

"I worry that the Sun has forgotten," she whispered, recounting the previous night to him, the way she had taken the sled up the face of the mountain and stood atop the highest peak, the way she had seen into eternity. She told him of her mirrors and the statue's reflection and the story she had told the Sun, and even though it had just happened, in so many ways it felt like a dream.

Aurora was glad she had done it, and though she was scared that it hadn't worked and the Sun had not heard her, it was of great solace to her that she had done everything she could think of to help the Sun remember.

Upon Aurora's arrival home, Ina had asked if she should take down the mirror outside the palace entrance, but Aurora had said no. She knew that one day, a storm or time or snow would render the mirror on top of the world useless. But unless Aurora was certain it was no longer in place, she would continue to keep the doors to the castle open and reflect the image of the statue into the heavens. The palace would be cold, but then again, Aurora suspected it had ways to keep itself warm.

The grief that sat heavy on Aurora's chest made her feel connected to Caspian, and she hoped that even if she lived a thousand years, she would continue to feel it, continue to carry the painful reminder of how deeply she had loved. Mama had said that grief was love's reflection, and Aurora found that an incredible comfort.

She thought back to what Caspian had said in her room after he had brought her home from the cave. He'd told her that the last thing she needed was to care for another person, but he had been wrong. Caring for him—loving him—was exactly what she had needed, then and now. She knew it as well as the peaks of this mountain, as well as the stories she had grown up with, and it had become a source of strength.

Just then, the sunlight outside seemed to dim, and Aurora

stood. Perhaps a storm was moving in. She hoped that wasn't the case, not on the day of Caspian's burial. She stepped outside and looked up, but everything was as it had been when she had arrived at the sanctuary, and Aurora shook her head.

She had just ducked back into the stone building when the voice of the Sun surrounded her, laced with discernable sorrow, the sound heartbreakingly beautiful. It invaded Aurora's senses like the scent of the freshly cut roses that filled the castle's halls, heady and sweet. *I see it now*, she said.

Aurora ran outside, tears burning in her eyes. They were the words from the story her mother had told her so many times, the same story Aurora had told the Sun last night.

"You remember?" The words were barely a whisper, and Aurora swallowed hard, trying not to lose herself to the rush of relief washing over her.

It is a myth that time erases pain, the Sun said. *I no longer wanted to feel it, so I chose to release it into space, let it scatter like the dust from a dying star.*

Aurora felt a pang of guilt, forcing the Sun to remember something she had chosen to forget. She didn't want the Sun to be in pain; she only wanted her to remember. But Aurora understood then that there was no disentangling the two.

But it was not worth it, the Sun said, her voice so anguished that it hurt to hear it. *The love left along with the pain, and I have been trying to get it back ever since.*

"Why couldn't you?"

I was trying to fill an emptiness, but I had no recollection of what had caused it because I had let go of the very thing—the only thing—that could satisfy it. You gave it back to me, and for that I thank you.

Aurora's tears fell freely now. The Sun remembered, and Caspian would be buried in a mountain that would retain her protection. It was everything Aurora had hoped for, and she nodded because she could not speak.

Immortality is a fickle thing, the Sun said, and Aurora took a shaky breath. It was the same thing Caspian had written in his letter, the same thing Aurora had deduced from all her reading. *I once loved a human so deeply that I gave him my magic so that he could live.*

"I am thankful you did," Aurora said, uncertainty in her voice. She didn't know why the Sun was saying this, and a knot was forming inside her, pulling tighter and tighter.

There was a long, heavy silence, so drawn out that Aurora wondered if the conversation was over. Then the Sun spoke again.

You have given me back my love, and I would like to do the same for you.

All the air left Aurora's lungs, and she couldn't speak. She wanted to plead, to scream into the heavens, but she was stunned into silence. She must not have understood, must have misinterpreted the Sun's words.

My magic is in your veins, Aurora Finch. I could split your immortality with Caspian, if not for the problem of the mountain.

It took Aurora several seconds to find her voice. "The mountain?" she asked, no louder than a whisper.

THE SUN AND THE STARMAKER

The mountain needs a body. The Sun's voice was sad, and Aurora nodded, because yes, the mountain needed a body. It was the same understanding Caspian had come to when they had last patrolled the woods together, and it felt as if her heart dropped through her diaphragm and all the way to the snowy ground below, her hopes dashed.

Then she remembered the phlox, the flowers that had turned from gray to pink before her very eyes.

"My blood," she said, almost disbelieving. "I can give the mountain my blood."

The Sun was quiet for several moments, and Aurora could hardly stand it, her throat aching and her palms sweating. She held her breath for so long that her chest began to burn.

Yes, the Sun finally said, a hint of pride in her lovely voice. *I believe that will work. But before you make your decision, you must understand that if you choose to do this, I will take some of your years and give them to Caspian. Your life will be shortened.*

"Yes," Aurora breathed out in a rush. She didn't have to think about it, didn't even hesitate. "Yes," she said again, louder this time.

You both must give the earth your blood until you are buried. Without it, the Frost will advance.

"I understand." Aurora's voice shook and her body trembled, so overwhelmed by the Sun's offer. Not entirely trusting it.

Then you are decided?

"I am."

You must bring Caspian's body out in the open, where I can reach it. Then we will begin.

Aurora ran into the sanctuary, forcing herself to breathe, then stood behind the casket and pushed as hard as she could. The platform upon which it rested began to roll, and Aurora didn't let up until it left the stone floor of the sanctuary and met the soft snow. The snow built up in front of the platform, and when Aurora could not push it any farther, she walked to the side of the casket and readied herself to open it.

Caspian had told her that the remnants of magic within him would sustain his body, but Aurora still hesitated. She looked around to make sure she was alone, silently counted to three, then squeezed her eyes shut and pushed the top of the casket open. Slowly, she lifted her eyelids and blinked several times before focusing her gaze.

Caspian had been right, and relief moved through her. He was still beautiful, still himself, the magic in his body preserving him perfectly. He almost looked like he was in a deep sleep, and the image tugged at her chest, thinking he would rather enjoy that.

"I'm sorry," she whispered, smoothing down his hair.

Then she climbed into the casket.

She moved quickly, terrified someone would find her, and she grabbed hold of Caspian's wrists, pulling him toward her. He was heavy, though, and it took several attempts before his head and shoulders finally came up. Once he was bent at the waist, Aurora paused a moment to catch her breath, wiping her forehead with her cloak. Then she moved behind him and hooked her arms under his, grunting as she heaved his body up to the edge of the casket.

Then she pushed.

It wasn't graceful or respectful. In fact, it was outright blasphemous, and as Caspian's body rolled over the side of the casket and dropped into the snow with a heavy thud, Aurora hoped with everything in her that this would remain a secret between her and the Sun, one that no one else would ever hear of.

She tried not to imagine the look that would cross Caspian's face if he could see her right now, and the thought made her want to laugh and cry in equal measure. He would be absolutely horrified, and Aurora would probably laugh because she wouldn't know what else to do, and it would only make things worse.

When Aurora had pulled him away from the casket and out into the open, she looked up at the sky, waiting. She could not imagine how she would ever explain this if the Sun changed her mind, and when she could no longer take the silence, she said, "It is done."

Aurora's entire body was full of hope, overflowing with it, so much that she thought she might lift off the ground and float away. For another beat of her heart, there was nothing but quiet, and Aurora started to worry that she had misunderstood, somehow made it all up to ease her pain.

Then the Sun spoke again.

I sit at the center of the universe, and the most brilliant thing I have ever been witness to is love, she said. *Treasure it, protect it, and above all else, enjoy it.*

With that, the sunlight vanished, and a vast darkness settled over Reverie. Aurora began to shiver, and she heard the wolves howl in the distance. Then, in a sudden rush, the mountain began to shake, violent and strong, and Aurora dropped to the ground to cover Caspian. A radiant light reached between the peaks and illuminated the earth where they lay, Aurora squinting against the intensity of it.

Keep your hand tightly around his, the Sun said. *Do not let go no matter what.*

Aurora grabbed Caspian's hand in hers, and before she could reply, the Sun began speaking. Aurora could not make out the words, though she could hear the power in them. The force of them.

The love.

And she knew the Sun wasn't thinking about Aurora's love for Caspian but rather her own love for the first Starmaker.

An excruciating pain began in Aurora's right arm, rolling down the length of it and out through her hand that held Caspian's. At first she thought the Frost was coming for her, but it was an entirely different kind of pain, a hollowing out. Aurora screamed in agony, and she had an unbearable urge to pull away and bury her skin in the snow, anything to stop the hurt. She didn't know how she managed it, how she kept her hand around Caspian's, but even as her body shook and her insides felt as if they were being scraped out, she held on tightly.

All at once, Aurora understood what was happening. Her life was being shortened, the thread of her very existence pulling apart as year after year was sucked out of her and given to Caspian. Tears streamed down her face from the pain or the grief or the awe of what was happening, and in a rush she could see all

THE SUN AND THE STARMAKER

the years she was giving up as if they were memories playing out in her mind. Years of laughter and sunlight and warmth. Years of longing and sleepless nights and incurable aches deep inside her. All of them beautiful. All of them hers.

And perhaps the most stunning thing of all was that in each year she saw, Aurora was content. She had found a way to build a life for herself around all the grief, because the loving had been worth it. Loving her sister and her family and her nieces and nephews who hadn't even been born yet. Loving her animals and her roses and her mountain.

Loving.

Aurora mourned each year she lost, but as they were torn from her body in an excruciating stream, her grasp on Caspian's hand was strong, never once faltering. She saw what she was giving up, and still she held on, knowing she would treasure and carry those years as she embarked on a different path with Caspian by her side.

Aurora loved Caspian, not in a way that stitched her world together but in a way that broke it apart entirely, and she wanted to pick up every piece and every shard and create a new world that was big enough to hold them both.

Aurora looked up to the sky, her breath catching as the darkness came to life with the northern lights. Streaks of purples and greens, pinks and yellows, reds and blues glided across the sky like a perfectly choreographed dance. The Sun was crying along with her, and it was a moment so dreamlike, so mesmerizing, that Aurora was sure she would look back on it and question whether it had been real.

Then, almost as suddenly as the colors had arrived, they vanished. Aurora watched as a star fell through the darkness, falling and falling and falling until it landed directly on Caspian's chest.

The mountain stopped shaking, and sunlight once again claimed the day. An incredible silence followed, the wolves no longer howling, the voice of the Sun gone. Aurora's breathing was the only sound that remained, and she scrambled to her knees and propped Caspian's head in her lap, searching his face for any sign of life.

But there was nothing. Aurora stared at him, not understanding why he wasn't moving. Why he wasn't breathing.

"Come back to me," she whispered, pleading with him. "Please come back."

The mountain was still, as if the trees and the rabbits and the flowers were all spectators, waiting to see what would happen. Aurora held her breath.

"Come back to me," she said again, this time more forcefully. She brushed his hair out of his face and smoothed her hand down his neck, coming to rest over his heart. "Come back."

She would stay there, holding him, until she had to let go of the light, and after she had fulfilled her duty to the mountain, she would return to him and stay through the long night, letting no one near him until the Sun herself told her it had all been a dream, a vivid, wild dream to cope with the sadness of his burial.

She would stay because even though he wasn't moving, even though his heart did not beat and his lungs did not breathe, she could feel the years she'd given to him moving beneath his skin like a gently rolling river.

They were there, and she would stay until they woke.

Then Caspian's chest rose. She couldn't be sure, but it felt as if her hand had moved, rising with his rib cage. She watched him but saw nothing. She kept her palm firmly on his chest and her eyes fixed on his abdomen, but after several minutes of stillness, she realized she'd imagined it.

"Please," she whispered.

Then Caspian gasped, his eyes flying open and his chest expanding with a huge intake of air. He looked around, taking in the sanctuary and his open casket and the falling snow before he found her eyes. He stared at her, bewildered, and he blinked several times, as if trying to prove that what he saw was real. Then his breathing slowed, and Aurora watched as understanding settled on his face.

He thought Aurora had brought him back, just as she had said she would. And while it was the Sun who had done it, perhaps it was Aurora after all, telling the Sun a story she had desperately needed to hear.

His mouth opened slightly, and he shook his head in disbelief. He pushed himself up so he was sitting directly in front of Aurora. Slowly, he slid both hands up her arms, over her neck, settling on either side of her face. He rested his forehead against hers.

Then finally, he spoke. "My god, you're a stubborn thing."

Aurora laughed, big and loud, and with tears streaming down her cheeks, she flung her arms around Caspian's neck and kissed him.

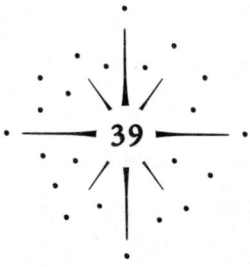

She Lives

I *would like to tell you a story. It begins, as so many stories do, with a ~~stubborn~~ spirited girl.*

Aurora set down her pen. She could not understand how she could pull literal sunlight over a mountain and yet beginning her first column for *Eternal Reverie* felt like an entirely insurmountable task that was surely taking years from her life.

When Aurora had told Caspian that she wanted to extend an invitation to Farren to visit her at the castle, he had simply scowled in response, which Aurora had taken as somewhat displeased agreement.

Farren had been deeply apologetic about what had happened at the cave, but Aurora hadn't had any desire to speak about that. It felt like a lifetime ago, and when Farren had arrived at the castle, Aurora had found she held no ill will toward him.

She had wanted to write—she had *always* wanted to write—and she had wanted a place to do it. She'd wanted to connect with the people she was protecting, to be a person to them instead of just a role. And *Eternal Reverie* had been the best place to do that. It had been a gift for herself, certainly not for Farren or his family's business, but he had been grateful all the same.

Now that she actually had to write the thing, though, she was tearing her hair out over how to begin. She crumpled yet another piece of paper and leaned back in her chair, groaning.

"You're quite captivating when you're frustrated," Caspian said, coming up behind her and trailing his fingers down her neck.

"And it's a good thing, too, given your propensity for bringing it out in me." Aurora turned to face him.

"Careful," he said, bending down to her ear, kissing her softly. "That bears a striking resemblance to something I would say."

"I'm being serious." Aurora stood from her chair and stepped back from Caspian with great effort. "You're distracting me. Farren wanted this weeks ago."

"I could not care less what Farren wants." He took a step toward her, running his hands up her arms, caressing her collarbones. "Perhaps a distraction is exactly what you need."

Aurora could feel her resolve wavering, fading away like the mist at dawn. She leaned into his touch, closing her eyes. He could touch her a thousand times in a thousand ways and she would still want more.

"You're incorrigible," she said, and Caspian laughed.

"I should hope so." He kissed her eyes, her cheek, her mouth, and Aurora wrapped her arms around his neck and pressed into him, reveling in the way her body fit perfectly against his, in the way he pulled her closer. He was here, right in front of her, and Aurora didn't know how long they would have together, but she would treasure every single moment.

Having Caspian back would not save her from unspeakable loss—that much she was sure of. There was immense grief waiting for her on the horizon of her life, but after everything that had happened, she believed deep in her soul that the only way to live was to love and that the eventual pain would keep her connected to the people and things she cherished most. And so she would love her family and her animals and her mountain with absolute abandon, because that was the only way she knew how.

Reluctantly, she pulled away from Caspian.

"I need my energy; it is my day to water the phlox."

It was how they referred to giving their blood to the mountain. It worked better than Aurora could have hoped, and the phlox were all back to their vibrant pinks after only one month. She and Caspian traded off, and for now, they only needed to water once a week; even though it was just a few drops of blood, it left them both feeling weak and depleted. Aurora didn't understand why it had that effect, but Caspian had said simply that magic has a cost. It was worth it to see the Frost retreating, though, to see her family's crops healthy and the woods coming back to life.

"You need not expend any energy, my love. I am more than

happy to take the lead." He had a mischievous glint in his eye as he took Aurora's hand and led her to the bed. A fire ignited deep in her belly, and she lay down, watching him.

"This will not help me get my column written any sooner," Aurora said, but there was no fight in her voice. She wanted him as much as she always had.

"Once upon a time," Caspian said, trailing his lips down her throat and onto her sternum, "there was a stubborn girl with magic in her blood who lived beyond the reach of the light." He kissed her ribs and rested his head on her chest, Aurora's hands in his hair.

"I decided that *spirited* was a better term," Aurora murmured.

"If you are going to write, you ought to write what is true."

Aurora was about to argue with him, but then he brought his mouth to hers, kissing her with the same reverence he always had, and all thoughts left her mind entirely. It was that way with him. He made her mind race and her thoughts quiet, a beautiful contradiction that Aurora couldn't get enough of.

"What happens to the girl?" Aurora asked, pulling away just slightly.

Caspian ran his hand through her hair, down her neck, settling directly over her heart.

"She lives," he said simply.

The truth of it made her eyes burn with tears, because if there was one thing Aurora was certain of, it was that the greatest wonder of all was not the Sun or the Starmaker or the magic or the mountain. It was life, in all of its imperfect splendor.

Caspian pressed his mouth to hers, and Aurora smiled beneath his kiss.

What an extraordinary thing it was, to live.

✚

Caspian

She lives, he had said, and Caspian thought they were the two best words he had ever spoken.

Epilogue

Double Star

Deep in the mountains of the Lost Range, in a small village on the tallest peak, a young girl was listening to a bedtime story. It was a story she had heard many times before, and yet when her father tucked her in, it was always the tale of the double star that the girl wished to hear.

"There is a double star that can only be viewed from Reverie on the clearest of nights," her father began. "Normally, the two stars are so close together that they appear as a single point of light, but when the sky is cloudless and the moon is new, both stars are visible."

"I want to see them!" the girl exclaimed.

"Then I will show you one day," her father said. "The fifth Starmaker had always thought it romantic: two stars gravitationally bound together, held in each other's orbit."

"Aurora?" the girl asked, her voice full of wonder.

"That's right. When you're older, we can read everything she published during her reign."

"Promise?"

"I promise. Shall I continue with the story?"

The girl nodded eagerly, and her father smiled. "The world is full of love stories, from the Earth to the sky and beyond, each one different from the last, each one beautiful. The fourth and fifth Starmakers had one such story."

The girl tugged her blanket closer to her chin, her eyes lighting up the way they always did when her father told this story.

"They came to be known as the Double Star, a name that the fourth Starmaker scorned and the fifth Starmaker adored. They fell in love with each other so deeply that they could not bear to be parted, the Sun changing the very rules of the mountain so that one's beginning was not the other's end."

The girl's father recounted their remarkable reign, speaking of the record warmth and minimal Frost, the new species of roses they had created. He told of their devotion to the mountain and to each other, and as he did, the girl's eyes remained wide open, not a hint of sleepiness making her eyelids heavy.

"When their reign was over, they were buried together, their magic feeding the mountain they had given not only their lives to, but also their deaths. And though we can never be certain what awaits us in the endless after, Aurora herself wrote that she believed they would find rest.

"Many stories just like this one tell of their love and affection,

THE SUN AND THE STARMAKER

their fierce passion and their undying loyalty. Sonnets and poems proclaim how fortunate Reverie is to have had them, how they have always belonged to the mountain.

"But while we are indeed fortunate to have had them for a time, the fourth and fifth Starmakers—the Double Star—did not belong to the mountain. They belonged to each other, and Reverie simply borrowed them."

A small tear rolled down the girl's cheek, and her father wiped it away. "The end," he said, kissing his daughter on the forehead before softly closing her door.

The girl fell into a deep sleep, and as she slept, the story wove its way into her mind, its roots growing deeper and deeper until it had become a part of her. Only time would tell what it would bloom into, but as was the way with stories, it could be anything.

Perhaps, then, the end was not an end at all, but rather, a beginning.

Author's Note

The Author and the Brain Injury

I was more than halfway through my first draft of this book when I fell playing tennis. It was a hard, sudden fall; I had no time to brace myself, and when I hit the ground, a severe pain began in my head.

I have played sports for most of my life and have fallen many times, so I should have recognized that this fall was different. When I was able to stand back up, I was completely disoriented, and tears were streaming down my face. I didn't understand at the time why I couldn't get hold of my emotions, and I kept apologizing for crying.

Over the next several days, I developed a persistent headache, dizziness, nausea, light and noise sensitivity, balance issues, difficulty sleeping, speech problems, memory problems, lightheadedness, irritability, and heightened emotions, and because I remained in a state of confusion, it never occurred to me to visit my doctor. It wasn't until my sister saw me three days after my fall that she insisted I go in.

I was immediately diagnosed with a concussion.

I had never had a concussion before, and I assumed that I would rest for a day or two and then be back to normal. I was wrong.

For the first six weeks, I could not write, read, or look at a screen. When I tried to email my publishing team to let them know about my injury, I got two sentences in before I became physically ill and had to step away from my computer.

I was terrified I would never write another book.

A brain injury is an incredibly lonely, vulnerable injury. I have never felt so far away from myself as I did after I fell, and I have been trying very hard to get back to myself ever since.

As the weeks turned to months, I talked with other people who had experience with traumatic brain injuries, and I also did research of my own. It became clear that the old advice to sit in a dark room and rest was outdated and, more importantly, unhelpful in aiding recovery. The brain needed to be reminded of what it had been capable of before the injury, and so I tried to get back to the things that made me *me*.

That is where this book comes in. If I had loved this story less, I know I would not have gotten back to work on it, because the truth is that every word, every sentence of this book was drafted or revised while I was in pain. It would have been easy for me not to work at all, but I missed this story, missed spending time in it, and I desperately wanted to get back to it.

THE SUN AND THE STARMAKER

Writing makes me feel like myself. It is such an innate part of who I am that returning to it was my top priority. My first day back, I wrote fifty-one words before my symptoms flared so aggressively that I had to stop. Eighty-six words the next day. Seventy-four the day after that. It went on like that for a while, until one day I wrote one hundred words. Then two hundred. Then four hundred.

Creativity is always a vulnerable thing, but trying to create in the midst of a brain injury has been something else entirely. I don't fully trust myself, and yet I am publishing a book that was written entirely during this hazy phase of not feeling like myself and not trusting my brain. It is strange.

Tilly, my snow angel, ended up inheriting some of my struggles, and she needed to see herself just as she was before she could heal. This book became my own sort of looking glass, and slowly, *so* slowly, after days and weeks and months of sitting down at my desk, this book pulled me out of my intense grief over losing who I was before my injury and gave me back my hope.

At the time of this writing, I am ten months out from my fall and still in the process of healing. I've had a persistent headache every day since; I have yet to wake up without it, and it has been an extremely difficult adjustment, learning to live with daily relentless pain. My balance remains impaired, I struggle to remember things, light and noise are still tough for me, and I'm not sleeping through the night, but I can also see areas of vast improvement: my speech has returned to normal, I am back to reading and screens, and while I am much, much slower than I used to be, I can write for several hours at a time.

This book has kept me company and helped me cope with the absolute worst season of my life, and I will be forever grateful to it for that. It was a much-needed distraction from my constant worry and fear over how or if I was progressing, and it has undoubtedly helped me recover.

I still have a long way to go, but this book has shown me that I am stronger than I realized. I believe that one day I will look back on my concussion as a blip in the overall story of my life, and I'm not sure I would have that optimism had it not been for *The Sun and the Starmaker* (and, of course, my phenomenal medical team).

I am immeasurably proud of this book. I love it with my whole heart, and I am thankful to you for reading it.

If you or someone you love has had or currently has a brain injury, I see you. You are not alone.

Acknowledgments

This book was extremely difficult for me to write. The entire process was touched by my brain injury, from first draft to finished product, and there were many setbacks along the way. If not for the following people, I don't think this book would have made it past the halfway point of the first draft—the point it was at on the day that I fell. I am so thankful my injury wasn't the end of this story.

First, to my incredible agent, Pete Knapp. You have never once made me feel bad about my delays or the many adjustments to my schedule and instead, constantly encouraged me to take the time I need. I should have known you would be just as fierce of an advocate for me as you are for my stories—thank you.

To my editor, Annie Berger. You were happy to wait for this book and gave me the time to get it right, and your belief in it (and me) from the very beginning made all the difference. Thank you for the extra reads, the reassurance when I needed it, and for making this book better. How lucky I am to have worked on four books with you.

To the healthcare professionals who have worked by my side to help me recover. Thank you to Dr. Christopher Pepin; Heidi McGill, PT; and the entire team at the UPMC Sports Medicine Concussion Program: Dr. Raymond Pan; Anne Mucha, PT; Sarah Ostop, PT; and especially Dr. Michael Collins. Thank you for the incredible work you do. You gave me my life back, and I am forever grateful.

To the entire Sourcebooks Fire team, working with you is an absolute joy. Karen Masnica, Rebecca Atkinson, Lia Ferrone, and Delaney Heisterkamp, thank you for your tireless work getting me and my stories out in the world. Gabbi Calabrese, thank you for your thoughtful notes and for making this such a seamless process. Thea Voutiritsas and Alison Cherry, thank you for readying this book for publication and making it shine (especially since this one probably needed a bit more work!). And finally, to Hannah DiPietro and Erin Fitzsimmons for the impeccable cover design, and to Viv Tanner for bringing it to life more beautifully than I ever could have imagined. Thank you for the cover of my dreams!

I am so fortunate to work with the brilliant people at Park, Fine & Brower. Thank you to Stuti Telidevara, Danielle Barthel, and Olivia Valcarce for your amazing insights and for freeing up my brain to focus on the writing. Kat Toolan, Abigail Koons, and

Ben Kaslow-Zieve, thank you for bringing my books to readers all over the world—it is such a dream. Emily Sweet and Andrea Mai, I'm thankful for the ways you help me think through strategy and branding.

To Anissa and the entire FairyLoot team, thank you for getting this book into the hands of so many readers. Working with you is a dream come true.

Rebecca Mix, you gave me my first glimmer of hope when I felt hopeless, and I'm very thankful for all of your encouragement and support. I'm so glad we finally connected, even if the circumstances were less than ideal.

To Stephanie Garber and Adalyn Grace, who broke this story with me at thirty-five thousand feet on our way to Spain. You helped me find my inspiration when I desperately needed it, and I'm so thankful for your wisdom and friendship.

Adalyn, your notes helped me make this book exactly what I wanted it to be, and you're also just one of the best things this industry has given me. Please can we set utterly absurd word count goals and have some soup together soon?

To my friends who have listened to me cry and encouraged me that this injury is not the end of anything. Your FaceTimes, hugs, and messages help more than you know.

To Dopps, thank you for finishing out this book with me and for all the joy and love. I miss you so much. Chip, you somehow make everything better. It turns out you are an even more spectacular neighbor than I thought you would be (and my expectations were pretty high). I love seeing you all the time.

Mom and Dad, your love and support mean the world to me, and I feel so very lucky that you are such a constant presence in my life. Thank you for making me a reader, thank you for always encouraging me, and thank you for all the dinner dates. I love you.

Mir, you constantly remind me there is light at the end of the tunnel, but you also sit with me in the dark when I just can't see it. You hold me while I cry, bring me food, pick up my slack, and make me laugh—honestly, you deserve some kind of medal. There aren't words to express how much I love you, and walking side by side through every season (and just being walking distance in general) is my favorite thing.

Ty, you let me take each day as it comes, giving me the space to write or not write, to feel hopeful or hopeless, to cry or scream, to lie down or challenge myself. You have been with me every step of the way, on my good days and on the absolute worst, and you have loved me through it all. You are my epic love, in sickness and in health, and our story is my favorite. I love you so much.

And finally, to Jesus. Thank you for this extraordinary life.

About the Author

Rachel Griffin is the *New York Times* bestselling author of *The Nature of Witches*, *Wild Is the Witch*, and *Bring Me Your Midnight*. When she isn't writing, you can find her wandering the Pacific Northwest, reading by the fire, or drinking copious amounts of coffee and tea. She lives in the Seattle area with her husband and growing collection of houseplants. Visit her online at rachelgriffinbooks.com or say hi on Instagram @TimesNewRachel

Home of the hottest trends in YA!

Visit us online and
sign up for our newsletter at
FIREreads.com

....

Follow
@sourcebooksfire
online